"Don't forget your toothbrushes," Butterfly said.

Even Crystal had to laugh.

"Okay," I said, "let's study the map we're going to use."

Crystal looked at Raven and Butterfly to see if they were still all for this, and then she put one of the maps on her desk. We gathered around. . . . We estimated where we might be the first day and the second, all of us talking at once. It felt wonderful; it felt like hope.

Later, it was almost impossible to fall asleep. Minutes after the lights were out in our room, Raven called to me. "You're not going to change your mind, are you, Brooke?"

"Absolutely not."

"Brooke? I was just thinking . . . this is our last night here."

I thought for a moment. She was right. Good-bye and good riddance to these four walls, I thought. Good riddance to feeling like nobody, nameless and alone. Tomorrow, tomorrow we'll be on the road to our future. . . .

V.C. Andrews® Books

Flowers in the Attic
Petals on the Wind
If There Be Thorns
My Sweet Audrina
Seeds of Yesterday
Heaven
Dark Angel
Garden of Shadows
Fallen Hearts
Gates of Paradise
Web of Dreams
Dawn
Secrets of the Morning
Twilight's Child
Midnight Whispers

Darkest Hour
Ruby
Pearl in the Mist
All That Glitters
Hidden Jewel
Tarnished Gold
Melody
Heart Song
Unfinished Symphony
Music in the Night
Butterfly
Crystal
Brooke
Raven
Runaways

Published by POCKET BOOKS

V.C. ANDREWS®

Runaways

POCKET STAR BOOKS

New York   London   Toronto   Sydney   Tokyo   Singapore

An *Original* Publication of POCKET BOOKS

 A Pocket Star Book published by
POCKET BOOKS, a division of Simon & Schuster Inc.
1230 Avenue of the Americas, New York, NY 10020

ISBN: 1-56865-913-X

V.C. ANDREWS and VIRGINIA ANDREWS are registered
trademarks of the Vanda General Partnership.

POCKET STAR BOOKS and colophon are registered
trademarks of Simon & Schuster Inc.

Jacket design by Jim Lebbad, back illustration by Lisa Falkenstern

Printed in the U.S.A.

Runaways

Prologue
✿

*M*y eyes snapped open to the muffled sound of whimpering coming through the walls. These rooms shrunk to closets when you squeezed in our desks and chairs along with a dresser and two beds with a nightstand between them. To get the most space possible, the beds were smack against the walls. My ear was practically part of the wallpaper when I slept.

Two of the new kids we called The Unborn were in the adjoining room. They sounded like puppies. We nicknamed them The Unborn because coming here, living in a foster home, was like being born again, only this time to live in limbo. They had been delivered here yesterday and had spent their first night at the Lakewood House, the foster home Crystal, Butterfly, my roommate Raven and I had christened Hell House.

Information about any new wards of the state, as we were known, spread faster than jam on a fresh roll around here. When it came to learning about one of The Unborns, everyone was suddenly an attentive student, and if you overheard something, you almost felt obligated to be a gossip.

According to Potsy Philips, one of the orphans who made a habit of picking on each and every new kid who came to our home, these Unborns had no father. They were alone with their dead mother for days before anyone noticed.

So what's new about that? I thought. We've been here for years and no one's really noticed—or cared. Actually, that's not entirely true. We care about each other. Not all of the kids get along, but I'm lucky to have found true friends here, my sisters, Raven, Crystal, and Janet, who

1

we call Butterfly because she is so fragile. We all arrived at the house within weeks of each other and became fast friends. When we feel like crying, or our hopes get so low we can't imagine them ever being high again, or when we have happy news to share we know we can count on each other. And that means more than anything.

I lay in bed wondering if the new orphans would be as lucky, then realized that it was almost time to rise and shine. Louise Tooey, our foster mom, whose sickening smile reminded me of the Joker in *Batman*, would come knocking on doors in ten minutes, and if we weren't up and dressed in time, her husband, Gordon, might follow soon after, his boots falling like sledge hammers on the stairs and wooden floors as he approached the rooms. If we were still in bed, he was capable of ripping the blanket off and glaring down at us like some giant buzzard, his eyes wide, his thick lips curled, baring his teeth.

"What do you think this is, a hotel? Are you waiting for breakfast in bed? I have to interrupt my work to come up here? That's ten demerits!" he would bellow, his tan face turning dark red, the muscles and veins in his neck looking like thick rubber bands about to snap.

Your name would go up on the Big Board, a large cork bulletin board in the dining room. When you reached twenty demerits, it was room restriction, a day for every five points over twenty.

Just looking around at the rooms would explain why it was a punishment to be restricted to one. We weren't permitted to put anything on our walls—no posters, no pictures. Supposedly, that was to protect the wallpaper, which looked like it was ready to peel itself off and roll itself into the garbage anyway. No radios or CD players were permitted because the walls were too thin and you couldn't possibly play your music low enough not to disturb someone, especially Gordon and Louise. If you were lucky enough to be brought here with a tape deck or radio, it had to be stored in the utility room and you could have it only during recreation time. You actually had to sign out for your own things!

All the rooms had two windows. The older residents, like the four of us, had the rooms with a view of the lake. We had no curtains, just faded window blinds, most of which had something wrong with them so you had to put a pencil in the roller to keep the blinds down. We were told they were once a buttercup yellow, and the wallpaper was the color of fresh milk with circles as vibrant as newly bloomed violets. Now the walls were the bruised gray of two-week-old hard-boiled eggs, and the circles looked more like dead violets, faded and dried and stuck in someone's book of memories.

Just to make us appreciate where we were lucky enough to be, Louise liked to describe the Lakewood House as it had once been when her parents and grandparents ran it as a resort. She would stop to check on everyone in the recreation room and then gaze around and sigh, her eyes glazed with tears as she drank in the worn oak floors, the tired walls and peeling paint on the ceiling.

"In its day, children, this was the most desirable tourist house in upstate New York, nestled between two mountains with a lake fed by spring water that was once crystal clear."

Some of the younger children might smile. It did sound nice. Now, however, the lake was brackish, full of weeds, oily on the bottom and off limits to all of us. No fishing was permitted. The old dock was rickety and rotten and there were two damaged rowboats nearly completely submerged beside it. If Gordon caught you within ten feet of that lake, you received a full twenty-five demerits and one day's restriction immediately. No one knew what the punishment might be for a second violation. Gordon left it to our imaginations. Maybe he would put you in the barrel.

There was a story going around that Louise and Gordon kept old pickle barrels in the rear of the house and if you were very bad, they put you into a barrel and closed the top with just tiny holes for air. You were left cramped up in there for days and had to pee and do your business in your underpants. When your sentence was over, the barrel was turned on its side and you were rolled hundreds of feet before you were taken out, shaken and dizzy. Most of the younger Unborns nearly wet themselves just hearing about it. When they then saw Gordon come lumbering down the hallway, his jaw slack, his rust brown eyes panning the room and the children for signs of misbehavior, they shook in their shoes and held their breath.

Gordon was enough to give any kid nightmares for life. The fact that he and Louise became qualified as foster parents is, as Crystal says, testimony enough that foster children are on the lowest rung of the social totem pole. That's the way Crystal talks. You'd think she was already a college professor or something.

I ground the sleep out of my eyes, ran my fingers through my hair and sat up. Raven was still dead asleep, her right leg out and over the blanket, her long dark hair fanned out over the pillow.

Raven is by far the prettiest of the four of us. Her face is as beautiful as a model's, and everyone is jealous of her shoulder-length ebony hair.

All she has to do is shower and shampoo and her hair gleams as if a fairy godmother touched it with her magic wand.

"Hey, sleeping beauty," I called. She didn't move. "Raven, it's time to wake up," I sang out. Nothing, not even a twitch was visible in her body.

I reached down and scooped my socks out of my tennis sneakers, rolled them into a ball and then flung them across the room, bouncing them off the back of Raven's lovely head. That got her attention.

"Wha . . ." She turned, looked at me, and smirked, sinking back into her pillow as if it were made of marshmallow.

"Rise and shine, Miss San Juan, before you-know-who comes around and does you-know-what," I said and rose to open the dresser drawer to pluck out a fresh pair of panties. We had to share the one dresser, a reject from a thrift shop, that was here when the first tourist arrived from New York City, back when the trains were running and the Lakewood House was listed in a resort magazine called *Summer Homes.*

"My grandparents began this as a small farm, couldn't make a living at it, and started to take in boarders," Louise told us for the four hundredth time yesterday. "From that they developed a well-known tourist home. My parents were very successful, but the economy changed so Gordon and I decided why waste all this? Why not do a good deed and become foster parents? You lucky kids are the beneficiaries."

You lucky kids? Do a good deed? Louise and Gordon care about someone else besides themselves? Crystal, who is smart enough to become President someday, if women could ever become President, told us how Louise and Gordon receive money for each child and how that money grows as the child gets older, and then how that money is tax free!

"It's Saturday. Why can't we sleep later on Saturday?" Raven moaned.

"Bring it up at the next meeting of the directors," I quipped. "You better move your rump, Raven, before the rug rats take up both bathrooms."

On our floor we had to share the bathroom with six other orphans. Gordon was always lecturing us about running the hot water too long. We were convinced he was the inventor of the two-minute cold shower. The Lakewood House had its own well, and he threatened us with the horrible possibility of our running out of water and having to bring it up in pails from the lake.

"I hate this," Raven grumbled. For a moment I stared at her as if she had said something unexpected.

Yes, I hate it too, I thought, but neither of us has had any prospective parents nibbling around us. And chances were, we never would. Crystal, who was a junior computer whiz, spent the most time of anyone on the home's one donated computer. She often presented us with wonderful facts, especially about foster children. On any given day, she claimed, there were nearly 50,000 foster children who no longer lived with their mother or father and have been declared by the courts as free to be adopted, but who usually remained in state-run, state-funded substitute care. Good luck to all of them. Crystal told us the population of foster children is growing 33 times faster than the U.S. population in general. Maybe we'll take over the world, I joked, but no one laughed.

I slipped into my panties and reached for my jeans just as Crystal burst into our room, her face flushed. She was still in pajamas, which for Crystal was very unusual. She was Miss Punctuality.

"What?"

"She's doing it again! She worse. She's like . . . petrified wood!"

I looked at Raven, who then leaped out of bed, threw on her robe and followed Crystal and me to Crystal and Butterfly's room. There was Butterfly with her legs pulled up and in, her hands clenched into fists, her eyes shut so tight the lids looked sewn together. Her lips were pursed stiffly, her nostrils quivering with her heavy breaths. We looked at each other. Butterfly went into these catatonic trances more and more lately. It didn't exactly take a rocket scientist to figure out the reason. She was lonely, fragile, afraid of rejection. For her, going into this trance was like crawling into a cocoon. Crystal, our resident child psychologist, said Butterfly was trying to return to the womb. Raven thought she was nuts, but I understood. I never said anything, but I sometimes wished I could go back as well.

I shook Butterfly's upper arm and her whole body moved as if it were one frozen piece.

"Butterfly, come on. We're all here. Stop this, now. You know what's going to happen. Gordon or Louise is going to come in here and see you and call for the paramedics or something and then you'll end up in some looney ward."

I shook her again, but there was no response.

Crystal stepped up beside me.

"We need to join," she said.

I looked back at the door.

"Shut it, Raven."

She did so and the three of us surrounded the bed, Raven and I on one side, Crystal on the other. We looked at each other and then as if we were all going under water, took deep breaths and leaned over so that all our heads touched. Linked this way, we began our chant. It was our secret ceremony.

"We're sisters. We will always be sisters. One for all and all for one. When one is sad, we're all sad. We all must be happy for one to be happy. We're sisters. We will always be sisters."

Butterfly's eyelids fluttered.

"We're sisters," Crystal continued, and we joined in once more. "We will always be sisters."

Butterfly's eyes opened and her mouth moved softly until she was into the chant with us. Then we stopped and stood back. Butterfly looked from Raven and me to Crystal.

"What happened?" she asked.

"You're all right now," I reassured her. "Let's get dressed and get down to breakfast. I'm starving."

It had been Crystal who had come up with the joining and the chant and all because of Butterfly. It was really Butterfly who had brought the four of us together in the first place. No one was more vulnerable here. Crystal was her first protector because she was rooming with her and then Raven and I came in to keep the older girls from taking advantage of both of them. Crystal used her sharp wit and tongue to put down anyone who ridiculed Janet for her size and shyness. Eventually, the three of us circled her like three protective sisters and inevitably became closer to each other because of it.

Crystal labeled us the Four Ophanteers instead of the Four Musketeers. We were always saying, "All for one and one for all." For now and maybe forever, we were the only family we had.

Crystal said the ritual and the chanting would defeat our sense of isolation and loneliness. She really was like a schoolteacher. "Man is a gregarious animal," she lectured. "Religious and meditation groups favor group recitations. There's security in hearing other voices saying the same things or making similar sounds. Touch is intimate and a commitment," she explained. I didn't know what it all meant, but I knew it made sense because it usually worked.

Once again, it had worked this morning, but I feared the day when it wouldn't.

1

A Glimmer of Hope

As I got ready to go downstairs for breakfast, I couldn't help but worry about Butterfly, and wonder how my other sisters and I were spared the same fate: each of us had tragic stories, some, I was beginning to realize, more tragic than others.

I was almost adopted when I was nearly thirteen by Pamela and Peter Thompson, a young couple who had never had a child of their own. Pamela was the most beautiful woman I had ever seen and, though I thought it was strange that she wanted me to call her Pamela instead of Mommy or even Mother, I did what she asked. Orphans learn at a very young age to do anything, well, almost anything, to please prospective parents.

Pamela had been a beauty queen and chose me because she thought I looked like a younger version of her. No one had ever told me I was beautiful before, or had the potential to grow up to be beautiful, so when Pamela and Peter chose me for that very reason I was completely surprised, but happy, and for the first time in my life I thought that maybe I was special. That I wasn't just a little girl no one wanted.

I soon realized, though, that Pamela didn't think I was special because of who I really was, but because of who she thought she could make me into. All the pretty clothes and fancy lessons that at first made me feel like a charmed princess, soon became suffocating to me. I wasn't allowed to excel at the sports I played so well or to even be myself. I was getting all mixed up inside—I wanted to please Pamela, she *was* my new mother, but I also knew that pleasing her meant losing myself.

Peter tried to help, and explained to Pamela that I could do well in sports and be a beauty queen, but Pamela just got nastier and nastier. Finally, when it seemed that she just wouldn't ever listen to the dreams that were in my heart, I did the only thing I knew how to make her understand. I cut off my beautiful long hair—the hair that she so loved to brush and wash, the hair that would help me win her precious beauty pageants.

Pamela went into such a rage when she saw me that she started to hyperventilate, gasping for breath, declaring she was on the verge of a heart attack. She said I would be an enormous embarrassment to her and was no good as a beauty pageant contestant, or even as a daughter. Peter didn't know how to deal with Pamela's fury and so he sent me back to the Child Protection Services like a defective toy. And, years later, I am still here at Hell House.

Butterfly's experiences must have been much worse than mine, since she can barely talk about them. We've learned a bit over the years, but mostly when she tries to speak about it, or something reminds her of that time, she goes into one of her trances. Her foster mother, Celine Delorice, was a woman in her early thirties who had once had a promising career as a ballet dancer. She married a well-to-do businessman, Sanford Delorice, who supported her attempts to become a prima ballerina. However, shortly after their marriage, Celine was in a serious car accident and had to spend the rest of her life in a wheelchair. She talked Sanford into adopting a foster child and Celine chose Butterfly because she was so dainty and supposedly had perfect feet. She believed Butterfly would become the dancer she had expected she would be, and she had her start training almost the same day they brought her home from the orphanage.

Butterfly was a good dancer, but not a great dancer. She didn't progress as quickly as Celine had hoped and began to freeze under the pressure and the possibility of failure. Celine Delorice actually suffered a nervous breakdown from it. At least, that's what Butterfly told us, and soon after Sanford returned her to the system, claiming his wife's handicap made it impossible for them to bring up a child properly. Crystal thought there had to be something more, but she never pressured Butterfly, who could turn to stone if you forced her to talk about her past.

Despite her reserved façade, Raven wasn't all that different from the rest of us. She had lived with her real family, her mother's brother, for a while after her mother had been arrested for a drug related crime and put into rehabilitation. We didn't know the nitty-gritty details, but something happened and Raven was brought here. All she would tell us was her uncle and aunt were not fit parents, especially her uncle. She did tell me that whatever had happened at her uncle and aunt's home involved her cousin, Jennifer. I wanted Raven to trust me enough to explain what had happened, but it seemed like Raven had trouble trusting anyone, even Crystal, Butterfly and me.

Raven's situation was really a lot more complicated than ours because Raven had a natural blood parent out there, somewhere, and the state made it almost impossible to adopt a child if there was even the slightest possibility she or he could be returned to that parent.

Crystal was the only one who really had a good experience with foster parents. She didn't speak about them very much, but when she did talk about them, she described Thelma's obsession with her soap operas and Karl's obsession with being efficient and organized. She told us he was an accountant and saw life as a balance between assets and liabilities. He often lectured her about being sensible. She said her adoptive parents were pleasant enough people, but from the way she spoke of them, I think she believed they were both living in a fantasy world. When they were both killed in an automobile accident, none of the relatives wanted to take her in, which resulted in her being returned to the system.

So here we were, the four of us, the Orphanteers, so different from each other, and yet, drawn to each other, feeling safer in our own little group, each of us adding something that we all needed, each of us willing to risk pain and unhappiness to protect the other or the group. Just looking at us, no one would think we had anything special to hold us together.

I usually wore dungarees and a tee shirt or old sweat shirt. I had sneakers and one pair of dressy shoes, but I favored my clodhoppers, as Raven called them, with sweat socks. I always wore the pink ribbon my real mother had tied in my hair before I had been given over to foster care. Of course, it was quite faded by now. I just tied it on my wrist. I hardly ever wore lipstick or makeup and used a stick deodorant rather than a cologne, when I even cared. Raven always wore a skirt or a dress.

Crystal wore simple one-piece dresses, and kept her dark brown hair either in a bun or sometimes in a ponytail. She would wear lipstick rarely, much less any makeup. She could walk around with an ink stain on her chin all day because she rarely looked at herself in the mirror.

Butterfly had much of the clothing she had when she lived with the Delorices, dainty little dresses, multicolored sneakers, a nice pink leather jacket. It was as if her growth had been stunted by her unhappiness. She hadn't grown out of much. She kept her golden hair in curls and only wore lipstick when Raven helped her with makeup.

Despite our four individual personalities, we did have something special, something we knew the other girls coveted. Maybe it was just the "Joining." Maybe there was some spiritual tie. At least we had something to believe in: each other.

Despite the episode with Butterfly, we were dressed and on our way down to the dining room in plenty of time. The Lakewood House was physically a perfect dormitory for two dozen or so foster children. Very little had been changed since its resort days. There was still a large sitting or recreational room where there once were card tables used for board games, dominos, card games or a game none of us had ever heard of before, something called mah-jongg. Louise said it had been the most popular game the tourist women played. She showed us the pieces, all with Asian writing on them, but warned us never to touch them. She explained that she and Gordon were just waiting for the right time to sell them as valuable antiques.

Most of the house was antique, or just plain old. The stairway we took down to the dining room shook and squeaked. The pipes groaned like arthritic old people, windows froze in their grooves, even in the summer, and very often, electrical fixtures didn't work. Gordon hated doing any maintenance, and usually waited until it was absolutely necessary. He didn't replace a step that had cracked badly on the stairway, for instance, even though it was dangerous, until he knew someone was coming from the state to inspect the premises. If something broke in our rooms, or if there were plumbing problems, he blamed it on one of us and let it remain broken for as long as he could.

Early on we noticed Louise was almost as afraid of Gordon as we were. If she ever contradicted him in front of us, he would just glare at her, his face crimson, his eyes glowing like embers in a fireplace, his neck muscles straining so hard, the arteries and veins would pop out, and his two large hands tightened into mallets. He was unusually strong. When he felt like showing off, he would permit the children to watch him chop down a tree. He did it with an ax, never pausing from the beginning until the tree actually began to topple. Chunks would fly around him like pale yellow moths; the tree seemed like it was made of paper. These demonstrations of power were indelibly pressed into the minds of the children. Woe to those who were the target of Gordon's fury.

And yet, whenever there were guests or state officials at the house, Gordon metamorphosed into a soft, smiling, gentle giant of a man who could walk around with a seven-year-old on his shoulders, loving, caring, protective. To see someone with such obvious physical power behave so gently was heartwarming to the visitors. Once, he caught me staring with disgust at him while he was putting on one of these Academy Award performances. He glanced my way and then he turned back to me, fixing his gaze on me with such a cold, bone-chilling look, I had to walk away quickly, my chest vibrating with the hammerlike thumping of my heart. I avoided him for days after that and finally he seemed to forget about me.

None of the wards seemed of any real interest to him. He knew our names and he knew which children to use when he wanted to demonstrate his concern and care in front of state people, but he usually left the real parenting work to Louise. She was the true administrator of the Lakewood House; he was more like a work boss.

However, Gordon was always after her to keep some distance between herself and the wards. He would complain about it, out loud, right in front of us.

"You're getting too involved with that one, Louise. I warned you."

Afterward, she explained that she and Gordon had been specifically instructed not to get too close with or form any sort of bond with a foster child. The logic was we were here only temporarily and soon were going back to our real parents or off to new adoptive families, and no one wanted any of us to feel sad about leaving or resent our new homes. What a joke. Who would resent leaving this? For my part, I was happy Gordon kept some distance and happy he was always after her to do the same.

Sometimes, she looked at us as if we really all were her children. Childless, she regretted losing any one of us. A real mother couldn't be more possessive at times, but warm affection around here was like contraband. She had to look for Gordon first and be sure he wasn't around before she planted a kiss on a child's forehead or held someone close to her ample bosom.

Louise wasn't the only one who tried to make us feel like a family here. A sweet elderly lady who insisted we all call her Grandma Kelly prepared our meals each day and always had kind words or a smile for us. Grandma Kelly lived in the nearby village of Mountaindale and had actually worked for the Tooey family when the Lakewood House was still a tourist retreat. She was only about five feet three with a round face that always had scarlet tinted cheeks, especially when she worked over a hot stove. She had soft eyes as blue as blue jay feathers. Her hair was the color of pewter and even more curly than Butterfly's, but she always wore a cap when she was in the kitchen. She told us she hadn't been brought to America until she was nearly twelve. To this day she still had an Irish brogue. Crystal said she reminded her of a leprechaun.

"It would be great if Grandma Kelly really was a leprechaun and led us to treasure so we could get out of here," I said.

Of course, Crystal didn't believe in such fairy tales, but we all liked to think that there was a pot of gold out there for us.

We joked about what Grandma Kelly would have made for breakfast that morning as we walked down to the dining room and while we stood in line waiting for our meals Crystal told us she planned on spending the day at the library, using their computer.

Crystal's dream was to become a doctor, and she told us she'd been researching information on getting college scholarships. She claimed that anything we wanted to learn about could be found on the Internet.

"What about my future?" I asked.

"As I told you before, there are statistics about foster children. Every year about fifteen thousand graduate from foster care by turning eighteen with no permanent family, and forty percent of all foster children leaving the system end up on welfare."

"Thanks for the encouragement," I muttered. "Miss Good News."

"You could get married," Raven said. "That's what I'm going to do as soon as I find someone rich enough."

"Why should he marry you?" I asked.

"Because I'm the prettiest girl he'll know," she replied, turning her shoulder and fluttering those long, black eyelashes. "And I'm the next Selena who will make one hit song after another, that's why." Butterfly laughed and Raven hugged her. "Someone loves me," she said. "Butterfly will be a famous dancer too, Crystal, so put that into your stupid statistics."

"I hate to disappoint or discourage you, but it's pretty hard to make it in the entertainment industry," Crystal joked back. "And look what happened to Selena!"

Raven stuck out her tongue as she turned to take Butterfly's hand. "C'mon Butterfly, let's get our food and let Crystal be grumpy by herself. She just doesn't know how to believe. We can be anything, as long as we believe." Raven's words sounded brave, but I knew that they were mostly for Butterfly's benefit; she was still shaking from this morning's episode.

As we waited in line for our food we surveyed the dining room.

Along the walls were the old photographs of the Lakewood House's bygone days, group pictures of guests gathered at the lake or around

the lawn chairs. In most of the pictures, the people were dressed for-
mally, men in jackets and ties, women in ankle-length dresses with high
collars and frilly sleeves, all with pale faces, and all looking years and
years older than they really were. There were many photos of families
because the Lakewood House catered to families. The foster children
now living here looked at these pictures closely, usually with soft,
dreamy smiles on their faces, imagining themselves as part of one of
those families, hugging their mother, holding their father's hand, standing close to their brothers and sisters, having a name.

It did look like the Lakewood House was a pretty, happy place once,
full of laughter and music. According to Grandma Kelly, the guests sat
on the big wraparound porch and talked into the wee hours while the
crickets chirped and the owls peered through the moonlit night, curious
about the murmur of voices, the sound of screen doors, the cry of a
child. Sometimes, although I would never say it, even to one of the
Orphanteers, I thought I heard the ghostly laughter and even the quick
steps of happy children running through the house, out the screen door
and down the steps to play on the carpeted green lawns, safe, happy
and full of hope.

Maybe someday we would run out of this house to a place full of
safety, happiness and hope.

The din of conversation, clanking dishes and silverware, laughter and
screeching that greeted us this morning was a hundred decibels louder
than on weekdays. School-age children knew they had two days off and
except for the final afternoon hours of Sunday, could put school work
aside. On nice days, we could play softball or go down to the dilapi-
dated, cracked and crumbling tennis court and volley or play doubles
after our chores. Raven and I were the house champions and I was
always the captain of the softball team. Louise permitted the older kids
to have a picnic lunch if they took a few of the younger ones with them
and watched over them. She trusted the four of us with more children
than any of the other older children.

Often Gordon would find work for us, however. We painted the
house, cut grass, collected leaves or washed windows. Inside, we
washed floors, helped with dishes, dusted and vacuumed. We were told
this was our home so we had to take care of it ourselves.

"You'll appreciate our home more," Louise explained to soften the
blow of Gordon's assignments.

"You don't have to justify anything I tell them to do. They should
work for what they get," Gordon blasted at her before turning to us,

his eyes fixed like two laser beams. "I don't ever want to hear complaints."

Chores were rotated. None of us four had to do kitchen work this weekend. We stepped into the dining room, a long, wide room with the biggest windows and the only windows that had new blinds because this was where the state people were entertained when they came. We saw Meg Callaway running the food line. A few long tables were placed together at the other end of the room and all of us walked by, filling our plates. Meg was fifteen, tall and gangly, with braces that looked like car bumpers on her teeth. Crystal said she could be the daughter of Ichabod Crane from Sleepy Hollow. She read the description of him that said he had a neck so long and a nose so long, he looked like someone had perched a weather vane on his shoulders.

Meg was always trying to get in with us, be one of us, but whatever chemistry existed among us didn't exist in her. She was sneaky and conniving and full of so much jealousy and envy that Raven said her eyes had to be green no matter what. She was always whispering and trying to turn one of us against the other. She spread rumors like fertilizer in a garden hoping to grow conflicts and make herself look like everyone's hero. No one really liked her, but many were afraid if they didn't pretend to be friendly, they would be the object of some mischief. Twice last week, I had caught her taking stuff from younger kids.

"Here comes Goldilocks and the three bears," she quipped as we approached the food table. She studied Butterfly a moment and then her lips thinned and hinged at the corners to form her icy smile. "Why was Goldilocks crying now? Someone pour glue into her dancing shoes?"

"Come outside after breakfast and I'll show you why she was crying," I said. Her smile quickly evaporated. She turned to one of the ten-year-olds assisting her.

"Get more toast, I told you," she said and avoided looking at me.

We took our food to our table.

"Why is it these rolls are so hard?" I muttered. Crystal finished her orange juice and signaled with her eyes so the four of us drew closer.

"I overheard a conversation between Grandma Kelly and Gordon yesterday when I was working on the computer. Grandma was complaining that he was buying two-day-old bread because it's cheaper. She said she knew he was not buying the best grades of meat too. He denied it and told her to mind her own business. She said the food was her business and he said maybe she should think about retirement."

"The creep," Raven said, her eyes fiery.

"I don't want Grandma Kelly to retire," Butterfly said mournfully. She almost always looked down quickly after she spoke as if she were afraid of what reactions her words would create in listeners. Her foster mother had to have been a tyrant.

"Don't worry, she's not," I told her. "Doesn't anyone check on him, check on how he uses the money that's supposed to be spent for us?" I asked Crystal.

She shrugged and thought a moment.

"Bills are doctored, I suppose, or deals are made under the table with suppliers."

"We oughta turn him in," I said. The four of us were still crouched over our trays, whispering. It felt like a conspiracy.

"If we didn't put our names on the complaints, he would accuse Grandma of doing it now that she has complained to him," Crystal pointed out. "And I don't think any of us want to sign anything against Gordon Tooey."

As if on cue, Gordon entered the dining room. Almost immediately, the din diminished. He panned the room as if he were looking for an intruder, his dark eyes just narrow slits, his big hands on his hips. He wore a white long-sleeve shirt with the sleeves rolled up past his bulging forearms. On his right arm was a tattoo of a shark, something he had gotten when he had been in the navy.

"I don't expect to see no lollygaggin' about today. Right after breakfast, everyone get to his or her assignments pronto. We got an inspection in a week and I want this place looking tip-top."

I wanted to shout out "Then burn it down and start over," but I just looked at my food. Louise came bustling in behind him, full of smiles. She was somewhere in her fifties, a five-foot-ten brunette with shoulder-length hair. I thought her best feature was her startling cerulean blue eyes. She had a way of looking at you, but clicking on and off you as she spoke so that you never felt you had her full attention. It was as if she really was afraid of what Gordon told her, afraid that if she looked too hard or long at one of the state's wards, she might form a deeper relationship and suffer if and when the ward was adopted.

"Good morning, everyone," she cried, looking more at the ceiling than at us. She turned toward the windows. "Isn't it a glorious day? Let's all do our work quickly and efficiently so we can have time to enjoy the fresh air and sunshine. You know, children, years ago, people came to these mountains to recuperate from lung ailments like tuberculosis and that's because we have the best fresh air. You're all lucky

15

to be living here," she declared, slapping her hands together before she went to a table to help some of the younger kids.

"She has syrup in her veins instead of blood," I murmured. "I can't imagine them making love. They look like oil and water. She probably keeps her eyes closed the whole time and holds her breath until it's over."

Raven laughed so loud she drew Gordon's gaze for a moment. All of us dropped our eyes to our plates. When we looked up again, he was marching out. There was a collective sigh of relief.

"Welcome to another joyful weekend of slave labor at Hell House," I said, loud enough for the kids at the next table to hear. Some laughed, others checked the doorway to be sure Gordon was gone.

"I don't want to whitewash that fence again," Raven declared. "He better not have put that down for me. The fumes from the paint make me cough for days."

"That's because it's bad for your lungs," Crystal explained.

"Come on," I said, wanting to change the subject. "Let's eat this mush and get outside, even to work."

The assignment list was posted. I was given the task of cutting grass—I didn't like that chore but at least it got me outside. Crystal and Raven were told to rake up and Butterfly was assigned dusting and polishing in the recreation room.

"Is she all right enough to be by herself this morning?" I asked Crystal before we left to go outside.

"She'll be fine," she said. "Won't you, Butterfly?"

"I'm okay," she said. She gave me her Sweet Pea smile. "Really, I am."

"If anyone bothers you, especially that Megan Callaway, come outside," I told her.

"I don't like being a tattletale."

"You're not a tattletale if someone is bigger than you and picks on you, Butterfly," I assured her.

"Everyone's bigger than me," she moaned. I looked at Crystal. I always looked to Crystal when I needed another answer or a better one.

"Everyone's bigger than Grandma Kelly, too, but that doesn't make her less of a person and certainly not less of a cook, does it?" Crystal said. "When you think of what she accomplishes with what she's given . . ."

"That's right. Good things come in small packages," I said.

Butterfly beamed again.

"Picnic lunch today," I announced. "Near the tennis court."

Grandma Kelly wrapped sandwiches for us on weekends. We could choose from ham and cheese, just cheese, peanut butter and jelly or chopped egg, take a container of milk or juice, a small wrapped cake or cookie and spread a blanket on the grass. We almost felt like real people on beautiful weekend days. Raven hated when I said that.

"We are real people. It's not our fault no one's noticed lately," she would declare angrily.

Weekends were almost like auditions for us. Prospective adoptive parents were brought to the home to look at and talk to any child they might want to adopt. Having us working like little elves on the property was thought only to enhance our prospects, for potential mothers and fathers would see that we were productive and far from spoiled by our lives as wards of the state. Today was no different. Just after we had spread our blanket and sprawled out to enjoy our picnic, Louise came looking for Butterfly.

"There you are, Janet," she said walking over to us and gazing down at Butterfly. "They've seen your pictures and come to meet you," she declared in that official voice of hers. Whenever she took on that tone, I felt my heart flutter.

"Who?" Butterfly asked.

"Their names are Mr. and Mrs. Lockhart," Louise replied. "Come along, Janet. Brush down your dress, please," she ordered. She stepped up to her and played with her curls. "I hate when they just come by like this without a full day's warning."

"Don't they often come by on Saturdays or Sundays?" I asked.

"You know what I mean," she replied. I shook my head. "Honestly, Brooke, you can be so . . . uncooperative sometimes. Why don't you model your behavior on Crystal? She knows when to speak and when to be silent," she added.

"I speak when I have something to say and when I know it will do some good," Crystal said.

"See?" Louise followed, missing Crystal's sarcasm by a mile. "Janet, please stand up straight and don't squint so much. Come now, Mr. and Mrs. Lockhart are waiting."

Butterfly looked back at us nervously. I held my thumb up.

"Good luck," Raven called.

"I can't understand why she hasn't been grabbed up before now anyway," I said as they walked toward the house. "She's adorable, sweet, bright."

Crystal put down her book and looked at both of us.

17

"Each of us has something special, if anyone would ever take the time to notice. People shop for children these days almost the way they shop for everything else. They don't see us as people, just as another kind of possession. This home is like a department store. I'm tired of waiting, tired of feeling like a piece of merchandise," she added with uncharacteristic emotion. I raised my eyebrows.

"That's exactly how I feel," Raven said. "I just hate being looked over like an animal in the pet store."

"You better get used to being stared at, Raven," I joked. "You're beautiful . . . everyone looks at you."

Raven suddenly became subdued. "It's not like I ask for the attention; and besides, that kind of attention I don't need. You know I'm always trying to get people to see the real me, the singer, the one with dreams."

"I was only kidding, Raven, we know you don't go looking for boys to follow you around like puppies. They just do." I felt bad now; Raven was really upset.

"It's all right. I know you guys understand me. It's just that I get sad sometimes. I don't think I'll ever find anyone who likes me for me, not just for how good they think I'll make them look."

Crystal and I looked at each other sadly. We knew what it was like to feel like we'd never be loved.

Butterfly didn't come out again until we had finished lunch. We were just folding our blanket when she appeared, head down, walking slowly. Crystal was right about us all feeling like some item in a department store, I thought as I looked at Butterfly. How do you audition for life, for a family? Do you try to speak correctly? Do you smile as much as you can so they will think you're generally a happy person? Sometimes, they look at you closer than a doctor. You wonder if you should have washed behind your ears. Do you have bad breath? Shouldn't you be wearing the best thing you had? What were the right answers to their stupid questions? "How would you like living with us?"

How would we like it? What do you think? We'd hate it. We'd rather stay here and be nobody.

"What were they like?" Raven asked Butterfly immediately.

"They were nice," she said.

"Old or young?" Crystal asked.

"Not old. She's very pretty. She has nice eyes my color and my color hair. She said I looked like I could be their child."

"Wow!" Raven said. "Good-bye, Butterfly."

She looked at us, her face suddenly full of fear.

"If they want you, Butterfly, they'll make a warm, loving home for you," I said. "You will be happier."

She nodded.

"Where do they live?" Crystal asked.

"Near Albany."

"That's nice," Crystal said. "I bet they'll put you in a good school too."

"We're not going to be here forever, Butterfly," I said when I saw her sadness at the thought of leaving us. "Raven, Crystal and I would love to have the chance you're getting. We're happy for you."

She nodded, her eyes filling with understanding.

"Let's play Ping-Pong," Raven said, taking her hand. There was a table behind the house.

"I'll meet you all in a while," Crystal said. "I'm going to run down to the library."

Butterfly looked at me.

"I'll see you guys later. I want to get the softball equipment and hit a few."

We all separated and I went to the supply closet off Louise's office where the sports equipment and our CD players and radios were kept.

As I went into the closet, I saw the Lockharts, the couple who had met with Butterfly. They did look like a nice, young couple, happy, well-dressed, the sort of parents who would love and cherish someone as sweet as Butterfly. The walls were so thin in this house, it was easy to put my ear to the one between the closet and Louise's office and listen to their conversation. I was hoping I would hear the good news and bring it to everyone first.

"Yes, I know how you feel," Louise said. "She's adorable. However," she continued, "I must give you some more detail about her so you won't have any unpleasant surprises," she added.

"Unpleasant?" the young woman asked warily.

"Well, difficult is a better word, I suppose. She's been seeing the psychotherapist more lately. I'll read you a bit. 'Janet suffers from a deeply entrenched sense of inferiority. Her catatonic seizures are a direct result of this. She withdraws to a state of immobility, shutting down her senses, as a defense against the fear of rejection.' "

"Catatonic? That little girl?"

"Oh yes. I've had to call the paramedics a few times," Louise said.

My mouth dropped. She hadn't. Not once.

"Oh dear."

I heard the deep note of resignation. Their retreat had begun.

Furious, I marched out of the supply closet and pounded up the stairs to Crystal's room, hoping to catch her before she left for the library. She took one look at me and dropped her book bag.

"What?" she asked.

"Louise is sabotaging Butterfly. I heard her telling the prospective parents about Butterfly's psychological condition. She made Butterfly sound like some lunatic who falls into catatonic states all the time and needs constant medical attention."

Crystal just nodded.

"Why would she do that, Crystal?"

"Simple," Crystal replied. "I told you before. Foster parents receive more money as the children under their care get older. So the longer the system fails to find permanent homes for kids like us, the more money flows in. We're a little money machine for the Tooeys."

"That's horrible! How can Louise use us like that?" I asked angrily.

"Well, in Louise's case, I think it's more complicated. She really hates to give any of us up. Gordon wants the money, but Louise really cares in her own way. She thinks of us as her own children."

"What use is having someone care for you if they just end up holding you back, trying to turn you into their idea of the perfect child?" I'd been through that before—I couldn't believe that it was going to happen again.

"Do you have an alternative?" Crystal questioned. I stared at her a moment.

"Yes."

"What?"

"Let's just run away," I said finally.

She didn't laugh, as I'd expected; instead she looked at me intently and then shook her head.

"I better stay here today. Butterfly might need me," she said with a sigh. "Let's not tell Butterfly what Louise is doing. It would make her too sad to think she may never leave here. And I wouldn't mention the running away thing either."

"But I'm serious, Crystal."

She turned her back to me and stared out the window.

I was serious. I really was. I just had to make everyone else believe me.

2
ℬ
A Close Call

After Raven and Butterfly played Ping-Pong they came down to the ball field and I pulled Raven aside and told her what Louise had done. She wanted us to barge into her office and confront her.

"We'll turn that place upside down and then rip out her hair," she threatened.

"I'd like to, but we can't. I don't want her to know I was eavesdropping," I explained, "and second, do you want to face Gordon afterward?"

Raven simmered down. The image of Gordon Tooey enraged was enough to calm even her Latin temper. In the winter when it was very cold and Gordon's breath could be seen at his nostrils, I thought it looked more like smoke from a dragon.

"Well, it's not fair. We should be able to tell someone," she moaned.

"Like they'll listen to us," I said. "The only hope we have is to run away and make our own lives."

"Run away?" She stared at me with wide eyes. "That's an idea," she said and looked disappointed for not thinking of it herself. "Yes, that's a good idea."

"Let's wait to talk about it," I said. "I want to come up with a plan first."

"You're serious?" She smiled. "Well, Brooke, I think you're definitely on to something." She then told us she was going up to her room to get ready to go to the movies with Gary Davis, a boy our age who was really more of a friend than anything else.

We were permitted to go out on dates once we reached sixteen, but we had to be back before eleven P.M. The curfew was strictly enforced. Violate one of the rules and you couldn't go out on a date for a month, maybe two. Crystal and I had been out on a few dates, but Butterfly got nervous every time a boy even tried to talk to her.

Raven was always trying to fix us up on double dates though I never really understood why until Crystal told me that she thought Raven didn't really like to be alone with the boys she dated. I asked Crystal why Raven agreed to dates then and Crystal just said that Raven was an optimist, always looking for the good in people.

Since Raven had had the most dates, she was always willing to give advice to us about boys, how to find out if they were sincere, or if they were just out for cheap thrills. She also had lots of ways to get rid of the ones who tried to go too far. Apparently she had a lot of experience fending off unwanted advances. She said that half of the boys she dated could go by the nickname "Octopus."

When I had a crush on a boy on my tennis team, Bobby Sanders, I asked Raven why he never looked twice at me. She said it was probably because I never let him win when we played against each other.

"Boys don't like girls to be better than them at sports. You hurt their egos," she explained.

"I just tried to make the game fun," I claimed.

"No, you didn't. You tried to win. You always play to win," she accused with a smile. I couldn't deny it. She was right. It wasn't in me to deliberately lose at anything. Would that make it impossible for me to ever find someone to love and to love me?

I hated asking Crystal's opinion about such matters. She would take off her glasses, wipe her lenses, think a moment and then start describing the mating habits of whales or something.

"Don't tell me about animals," I would complain. "People are different."

"Not really," she would say and then go on to discuss evolution and how people are really a lot more like animals than they think.

Spare me, I would think and find some excuse to get away before she gave me a test.

It was easier living vicariously through Raven, easier to lie in bed and wait for her to return from her date, and then, as she got undressed, listen to her describe the night, watching the images form behind my eyes. She usually enjoyed telling me about her dates as much as I liked to listen, but when she returned from her date with Gary I could tell that something was wrong.

"I don't know what got into Gary tonight," she said angrily. "I guess he's just like all the others. His hands were everywhere. When I finally kicked him to get him off of me he laughed." She paused for a shaky breath. "He said everyone knew what girls like me were good for. He said he'd heard stories about me!"

"What kind of stories? Have boys been spreading lies about you?" I was suddenly so angry I wished I had been in that car to tell Gary what I thought about him and his slimy friends.

Raven took a few deep breaths and then began. "When I was younger and I lived with my mother, I swore I would never be like her, Brooke. Every time she brought another man into our home, I hated her more, not for what she was doing to me as much as what she was doing to herself. I never could understand why she was like that.

"Afterward, when I came here and started to go to school, I hated that we were all thought of as being 'Those orphans, those foster care girls,' like we were so inferior. Then, I saw how boys were attracted to me and how easy it was to feel like someone when I walked down those corridors looking a little sexier than most girls. Sure, I guess I tease a lot, but I felt good, almost powerful sometimes. I wasn't just one of those 'orphans.' Maybe my mother did what she did so she wouldn't feel like nothing. I know it doesn't make sense to you, but maybe she was trying to be noticed, too, and she just got caught up in it all, the drinking, the drugs . . .

"That's not going to happen to me, Brooke, but I'm not ashamed of having boys look at me and want me. I guess I don't hate my mother as much. I've changed a little, but we all change, don't we, Brooke?"

"This place makes you change," I said, unable to hide my bitterness. "I don't really blame you for flaunting yourself, Raven, but just remember it's dangerous."

"I know. Gary said that a lot of the boys I've gone out with said we'd gone all the way. That's not true, I swear. That's going to always be the big difference between me and my mother, Brooke. I really have to care for a man before I'll be that way with him. Those creeps make things up. It's so . . . frustrating. I want to be liked, but I don't want the bad reputation."

"That doesn't matter, Raven. You know who you are. People who care about us, people who really matter, will understand," I said.

"Will they? We're orphans, Brooke. We don't have anyone to defend us. Who we are doesn't matter as much as who people think we are.

"It's all like a curse, some curse we can't quite throw off," she muttered. "And we did nothing to deserve it," she whispered and turned her back to me.

As I drifted off to sleep, I wondered if she was right. I sincerely hoped not.

Butterfly had no word about the Lockharts all the next week. Finally, one morning at breakfast, Louise stopped by our table to tell Butterfly that the Lockharts wouldn't be able to take her.

"They're not ready for children yet," she said. "But don't you worry, darlin'. Someday soon, some nice couple is going to come by and scoop you up. All of you," she added, looking at Crystal, Raven and me.

"We won't hold our breath, Louise," I said.

"That's not a good attitude, Brooke. Be positive," she lectured.

"Oh, I'm positive," I said. Raven swung her gaze back to me and smiled.

Louise pulled herself up and marched to another table to instruct someone how to use his silverware properly. Butterfly looked like she was wilting. Her head went down and she toyed with her food, pushing her eggs from one side of the plate to the other.

We all looked at each other and then Crystal went to work.

"Don't be sad about it, Butterfly," she said. "If they don't want you, they weren't going to be good parents for you anyway. You don't want to be with the wrong people again, do you?"

Butterfly looked up and shook her head, her eyes glazed with tears. It was as though all four of us had been rejected once again.

"When the right people come along, you'll know. There'll be a sort of chemistry between you, a good feeling. It will be like you had known them all your life," Crystal continued. She was going to make a great doctor, I thought. She knew just how to make someone feel better.

"They liked me," Butterfly said, "and I liked them, too. They were nice."

"If they changed their mind, they weren't good for you," I chimed in. "You heard what Crystal said. She's right."

We didn't want to tell her how Louise had sabotaged her chances. Without hope, she could become even more withdrawn than she was. I knew that much because I felt that way myself.

"Besides," I said, winking at Raven, "I have another idea I'm going to bring up soon."

"Don't," Crystal warned.

"Don't worry. I won't talk about it until I have a good plan."

"To do what?" Butterfly asked, now intrigued.

"To . . ."

"Brooke." Crystal widened her eyes and raised her eyebrows like she did when she was angry.

"Just be patient," I told Butterfly. "It's a surprise."

Crystal shook her head.

"False promises can hurt more, Brooke," she warned.

"This won't be false. You'll see," I said.

"I'm with you," Raven declared, turning her black onyx eyes on Crystal.

"Why is it that I'm not surprised to hear that?" Crystal said with a shake of her head.

We went back to finishing our breakfast.

This was the last week of classes. Most of the time now was being spent in review for final exams. There was the usual excitement in the air anticipating the summer break. The older kids at the foster home could apply and get jobs. Companies, retail stores, even professional offices that needed summer help would send a notice over to the house and Louise would post it on the general bulletin board. Those who were interested filled out applications that Louise then forwarded to the businesses. It was part of the state agency structure to appeal for cooperation from area enterprises. To us it sometimes seemed more like charity. The company usually bragged that they were employing foster children. Crystal, Raven and I had worked last summer and still had a little money in our savings accounts. I had plans for that, but it was going to take something more dramatic to convince Crystal and I knew without her, it would be impossible to include Butterfly. Besides, despite her pessimistic attitude and her lectures, I really loved Crystal. I loved all of them and they all loved me.

That Friday night, the last weekend before finals, Louise came up to our rooms before dinner and barged in on Crystal and Butterfly. Raven and I had just started studying when we heard Louise's shouts.

"You know the rules about cigarettes in this house!" Louise was saying to Crystal and Butterfly. "Gordon gets very upset. This building could go up in flames in minutes."

"We don't have any cigarettes," Crystal said. "Neither of us ever smoke. I know what smoking can do to you."

"Of course she doesn't smoke," I said, practically laughing as I stepped up beside Louise. "She would be the last one to have a cigarette in her room. She's always bawling out everyone else. If you really looked at us and saw us for who we are, you'd know that," I said defensively.

"Mind your own business, Brooke, or I'll give you ten demerits." She turned back to Crystal and Butterfly, who was cowering in her chair. I could see she was beginning to hyperventilate. "This is just as unpleasant for me as it is for you," she continued. "I wish you girls hadn't put me in this position, but I am a parent."

"Why are you doing this, Louise? Who told you Crystal and Butterfly were smoking?" I demanded.

"Never mind," she said. "Just go back to your room. Both of you."

Raven started toward her and I grabbed her arm and shook my head.

"Just wait," I said. "She'll realize how wrong she is in a minute."

Suddenly Louise crossed the room, went to Crystal's makeshift bookcase and began pulling the books off the shelf, finally revealing a pack of cigarettes. She held it up with her thumb and forefinger as if it were diseased.

"And what is this, might I ask?"

Crystal shook her head, her eyes wide.

"I don't know how that got there, Louise."

"Maybe it walked in," Louise said. She glared at Butterfly, who was crimson with fear. "This will be twenty demerits. The two of you are confined to your room for the weekend."

"But I have to go to the library tomorrow to use the computer," Crystal wailed.

"Not tomorrow you don't. You two get your meals and come back here. Your names will be posted and your room is off-limits to everyone else," she emphasized, glaring at Raven and me.

"You know that someone else put those there, Louise. Crystal wouldn't have anything to do with cigarettes, and you can't possibly think Butterfly did," I said.

"Did you put them here, Brooke?" she asked, her eyes small, as if she could see right through us to the truth.

"Of course not. None of us smoke, Louise, you've got to believe us."

"I'd advise you and Raven to turn around and return to your room before I give you twenty demerits, too."

I was about to respond when we all heard Gordon come up the stairs.

"What's going on?" he demanded.

"Nothing. It's under control," Louise said quickly. She seemed terrified of him. He glared at Raven and me and then looked at Louise and saw the cigarettes. "Whose are those?"

"I have it under control, Gordon," she said a little softer. "The guilty parties have been given their punishment."

"Lucky for them it was you and not me," he muttered, the muscles in his jaw straining. All sorts of rage erupted inside Gordon Tooey, I thought. One day he was just going to blow apart. He was, as Crystal often said, combustible. He marched past us, his boots pounding the wooden floor down the corridor toward their private quarters. Everyone, even Louise, released a trapped breath.

"This isn't fair," I said. I was going to say more, but I saw Crystal shake her head and practically beg me to remain silent. "Ridiculous," I mumbled, turned myself and Raven around and retreated.

After we heard Louise leave, we snuck back to Crystal and Butterfly's room. They both looked stunned, Crystal slamming her books and grumbling to herself.

"I just have to get to the library to use the computer. There are some things I need to finish my papers," Crystal complained.

"Just write out what I have to get and I'll go to the library for you, Crystal," I offered. She sank in her seat.

"Who did this to us?" she asked, bewildered by the speed of the events.

"I don't think I have to take too many guesses," I said. She looked up. "Sweet Megan Callaway. She's been plotting to get back at us for days, especially after I embarrassed her in the dining room."

"Then why didn't she put the cigarettes in your room?"

"She probably thought it would hurt you and Butterfly more to be confined than it would me and Raven," I said. "And she knew that what happens to you, happens to all of us."

"I hate this place," Crystal moaned. She wasn't one to say it so vehemently. "It turns us all into . . . monsters."

"I'll take care of Megan," I said.

"It won't do me any good now," Crystal wailed.

"I don't like staying in the room all day," Butterfly whimpered. "Especially when it's nice out. Little flowers need sunshine," she added, mouthing something she often recited, something her stepmother had told her.

"Give some more thought to my suggestion, Crystal," I said, fixing my eyes on her. She stared at me for a moment, glanced at Butterfly and then turned back to her books.

Some of the other kids had come out of their rooms to see what had caused the commotion. Megan and her roommate were at the far end of the hall and I could see the look of satisfaction on Megan's face when everyone passed the news down the corridor.

"I'm just going to go down there and let her know we're on to her," I told Raven. I turned to walk toward Megan, but Raven held me back.

"I have another idea," she whispered. "Come on."

Confused, but intrigued, I followed her down the stairs. We went to the supply room and Raven snapped on the lights. She nodded at Patty Orsini's Polaroid camera.

"It has film in it too. She's saving the last three pictures for a special occasion. She told me yesterday," she said.

"So?"

"I have the special occasion in mind," she continued with a sly smirk, taking the camera off the shelf.

"You can get fifty demerits for this," I warned her.

"We'll just borrow it. Don't worry." She stuffed the camera under her blouse and we quickly retreated, returning to our room where she outlined her idea.

"Raven, you little devil," I said excitedly. "Why didn't I think of that?"

She lingered at the door, which we kept slightly open while we waited. The girls were taking turns getting ready for bed. Megan Callaway, as usual, came out of her room with her towel. She wore her robe and went to the bathroom to shower. As soon as she closed the door, Raven nodded and the two of us slipped out and made our way to the bathroom. We listened at the door. When we heard the shower going, Raven opened the door by wedging her plastic library card between the tooth of the lock and the jamb. I had the camera in hand. Raven moved slowly, quietly and then we entered. Raven pulled back the shower curtain and I snapped the picture before Megan knew what was happening. It was a great shot, all frontal. She screamed and we were gone.

Hysterical with excitement, we returned to our room, shut the door and waited for the Polaroid to develop. The image emerged, clear and perfect. Revenge was at our fingertips. We put the camera back and then showed our prize to Crystal.

"What if it wasn't Megan who planted the cigarettes?" she wondered.

"I'm sure it was and even if it wasn't, she was somehow behind it, Crystal."

"We're all going to get into more trouble, you know," she said.

"At this point, I really don't care," I said, but Crystal looked toward Butterfly. "Don't worry, we won't involve her or you. Leave it to Raven and me."

Megan Callaway had no idea what we were going to do, but we anticipated her going to Louise so we hid the picture under a bulge in our wallpaper, confident that a thorough search of our room would reveal nothing. For whatever reason, Megan didn't tell Louise anything.

The next day I put our plan into action. When we entered the dining room, I slipped into a seat beside Megan.

"That wasn't funny last night," she said.

"It wasn't meant to be," I said and then I opened my hand and she saw the picture. She turned pale as a ghost before a wave of red swept through her face. "There isn't a boy in this place who won't get to see this and don't think you can tell Louise because she'll never find it on us," I said.

She was near tears.

"You get up from here and go to Louise and tell her you planted the cigarettes to get back at Crystal or Butterfly. If you do, I'll give you the picture and no one will see it. If you don't . . ."

I looked toward Billy Edwards. Then I rose and deliberately headed in his direction. She watched in horror as I sat beside him and began a conversation, my eyes on her. I saw her take a long hard swallow and then stand up, her head down, as she made her way out of the dining room.

Quickly, to be sure she didn't turn me in with the picture, I gave it to Raven who left the dining room and hid it in the storage room. We were nearly finished with breakfast before Crystal and Butterfly appeared. Crystal wore a look that told us she and Butterfly had been excused from restrictions.

"What did you do?" she asked before sitting.

"Not much. Showed her the photo we had, told her we were going to make sure every single boy here saw it, and then promised to give it to her if she confessed."

"She did," Crystal said. "She's confined for the weekend."

"Raven gets the credit. It was all her idea," I said.

"I know how to deal with that sort of trash," she bragged.

"I'm going to the library," Crystal said. She stared at us a moment. "Thanks for helping us, but I wish . . ."

"It had never happened?" I suggested.

She nodded.

"I told you what I think we should do."

"Let me think about it," she said.

"About what?" Butterfly asked.

I looked at Crystal and she nodded.

"About running away," I said.

"Running away!"

Raven practically leaped out of her seat to put her hand over Butterfly's mouth and told her to keep her voice down. Some of the others were looking our way and Gordon was talking to Grandma Kelly about a stove she said was malfunctioning.

"Run away?" Butterfly asked again in a lower voice when Raven took her hand from her mouth.

"Yes," Raven said. "Why not? I'm tired of doing chores, working for Gordon and Louise and pretending we're growing character and earning our keep. They're exploiting us. Crystal found out about the food, didn't she?"

"But . . . no one will ever be able to adopt us again if we run away," Butterfly moaned. "And even if they could, they wouldn't want to adopt runaways."

"No one's going to be adopted from here, Butterfly, at least not one of us."

"Why not? I was almost adopted this week, wasn't I? It could happen. You said it could. You said I should want it to happen. You . . ."

"Louise stopped it from happening," I blurted. She stared at me with her big, beautiful sad eyes.

"What do you mean?" she asked, and I told her what I had heard and what had happened. Her face softened, her lips trembling. "They think I'm crazy?"

"No. They know you're not crazy," Crystal said, "but they use whatever they can to keep us here for one reason or another, but especially for the money. It's all tax exempt, too. I'm afraid Brooke's right."

"It's getting too late for us, Butterfly," Raven said. "Teenagers are too much trouble. Parents want their children to be five forever."

"Raven's right," I said. "I even heard Gordon say it. Little children, little problems, big children, bigger problems. Anyway," I said, sitting back, "I don't know if I even want to be adopted anymore. I've been on my own so long, it just feels right, like an old shoe or something."

"Me too," Raven said.

"Then we should do it," I followed quickly, turning to Crystal. "We should finally take control of our lives."

"Where will we go?" Butterfly asked.

"West," I said, "to California."

"That's across the whole country," Butterfly said in a low whisper.

"We'll stop wherever we want and wherever we decide we're wanted," I replied. "But my guess is we'll go all the way."

Everyone was quiet, pensive, full of imagination and dreams.

"You can become a dancer much easier out there, Butterfly," I told her. "And you can become a doctor, Crystal. And you can become a singer or an actress, Raven. You can go to auditions all day, all week until you become a star."

"What about you, Brooke?" Crystal asked.

I thought.

"I could be me," I said.

Raven didn't want to do it, but I gave Megan the photograph as we had promised.

"A deal is a deal," I explained.

"You don't make deals with people like that," Raven said. "Believe me, Brooke. I know."

There was a lot she did know about mean, manipulative people, but I didn't want to turn into someone I hated. I slipped the photograph under Megan's door and forgot about it.

All that following week, I devoted as much time to planning how we would run away and where we would go as I did to studying for my finals. I asked Crystal to go on the computer and see if she could find a travel route from New York to California.

"How would we travel?" she asked. "The four of us can't just hitch-hike our way."

"Leave that part to me. I'm working on it," I said.

"Working on what? Trains, planes? I mean, how am I supposed to plan out a route if I don't know what you're thinking?" she asked.

I was afraid to say it, afraid that if she heard what I really had in mind, she would back out before we even began.

"For now, plan it by car," I said.

"A car? And just where are you going to get a car? You don't have a license; you don't have enough money for a car. Even if we pooled all our money, what sort of a car could we get? And then we would have no travel money. Really, Brooke, I . . ."

31

"Can't you just do that one thing for me? Please?" I asked, knowing she liked a challenge and loved to show off her ability on the computer.

"Fine. I'll just go to the Web and get into the Automobile Club. They provide routes and maps. Where are we going in California?" she asked, taking out her pen and notepad.

"Let's think about Los Angeles, first."

"Okay." She thought a moment. "It's almost summer. We can take a middle route or even a northern route. I'll get a few and we'll think about the pros and cons of each."

"That's exactly what I'd like to do, think about the pros and cons," I said. She gazed at me and smirked.

"I'm not going to do this if you make fun of me, Brooke."

"I'm not," I swore, but I couldn't help smiling at her. Finally, I just hugged her. "Do it. I'll take care of all the rest," I said.

"This still sounds like a pipe dream, Brooke. I'm doing it more as an intellectual exercise than anything else. I don't see how it will be possible," she said, as she gathered up her book bag and headed for the library.

I knew I still had a lot of convincing to do when it came to Crystal. She would have a hundred good and logical reasons why my plan was full of holes, but neither of us could know that just that very evening, Gordon would push her so far over the edge that I could have come up with a plan to ride a magic carpet, and she would have gone along.

Just before ten o'clock, Crystal went into the bathroom to take a bath and relax. Besides researching our travel route, she had been studying all day. Tomorrow was her last final and she was determined to get all A's.

About fifteen minutes after Crystal had gone to take her bath, Raven slammed her book closed, swearing never to look at another notebook or textbook again.

"I don't care if I fail everything," she declared. Raven was a good student, but we'd all had our fill of studying by now.

I was about to agree when we heard Crystal's scream. It was so loud it came right through the closed bathroom door and our closed bedroom door as well. I charged out and saw Gordon lumbering away, a tool box in his hand. He gazed back guiltily and then headed down the stairs. Raven looked at me and then at the bathroom door, her eyes full of wonder and fear. Butterfly came to her doorway.

"What is going on?" she asked.

"I'm not sure," I said, slowly approaching the bathroom. "Crystal?" I heard a sob and then we all entered the bathroom.

Crystal was sitting on the edge of the tub, a towel wrapped around her body, her arms around herself, shuddering. She was still soaked, the soap dripping from her hair.

"What happened?" I asked. Raven closed the door behind us.

"He . . . he . . . just came in here and . . ."

"Gordon? While you were bathing?" Raven asked quickly.

Crystal gazed up at us, her eyes filled with tears. She nodded.

"I didn't hear him open the door. I was practically asleep in the tub."

"Didn't you lock it?" Raven asked.

"Yes, of course. He must have unlocked it," she said. "He didn't knock or anything. Next thing I knew, he was standing right here, looking down at me. I had my head back and my eyes closed. I was resting and suddenly, I felt his presence and looked up. His face . . . it was . . . so red and he had this mad grin. For a moment I couldn't speak."

"What did he do?" I asked, my own breathing quickened.

"He started to touch me," she said.

"I knew it," Raven muttered.

"He touched you?" I asked.

"He reached down and said . . ."

"What?" Butterfly asked.

" 'Let's see how ripe those apples are.' That's when I screamed and he pulled his hand away. 'I'm just here to fix a leak in the sink,' he claimed. 'Don't get yourself in an uproar.' I screamed again and he turned and left."

"Leak in the sink? No one said there's any leak in that sink," I declared, inspecting the pipes quickly. "He didn't come in to fix any leak."

"We should tell Louise," Butterfly said.

"What good would that do? He'd claim Crystal left the door unlocked and how was he to know she was in the tub," I said.

"Brooke's right," Raven said.

"But what about the things he said to her. They were nasty things," Butterfly declared. "He didn't really mean apples."

"He'll deny saying it, Butterfly," I said. "Please. Let me just think a minute."

We all looked at Crystal again. She was still shaking. Raven went to the tub and sat beside her, putting her arm around her.

"Easy."

"I was so . . . scared."

"Let's join," Butterfly said.

"Now?" I asked.

Raven nodded.

We moved closer to them and we all touched our heads.

"We're sisters. We're together. Nothing bad can happen to one of us as long as we're together," we chanted, Crystal finally joining in. Color returned to her face.

"It was awful," Crystal whimpered.

"I know how it can be," Raven said. She looked from one of us to the other. "I've caught him looking in on me sometimes, too."

"You never told me that," I said.

She shrugged.

"He didn't ever touch you, did he?" I couldn't believe that Gordon was so evil.

"No. Never. I didn't tell anyone because I didn't want to get everyone any more scared of him," she said. "But if he ever tried to touch my apples, I'd raise his voice a few octaves."

"What does that mean?" Butterfly asked.

"Never mind," I said. "Are you all right?" I asked Crystal.

"I'm fine now. I'll just dry myself off and go to bed. Thanks, everyone."

"Let's all get to bed," I decided. We started for the door.

"Brooke."

I turned.

"What?"

"I want to hear your plan, every detail. After tomorrow's tests," Crystal said.

I nodded, sad that this was the way Crystal had come to believe in me and my plans.

"You really have a plan, I hope," she said, swallowing down her sobs.

"Oh yes," I answered. "I have a good plan. Did you get the maps?"

She nodded.

"Tomorrow," I said and gazed from Butterfly to Raven and then to Crystal. "Tomorrow we get together and put the finishing touches on it."

I was so angry about what Gordon had done to Crystal and anxious about leaving at the same time that I couldn't get my mind to stop racing. I had to get some rest for my exams, but it was as if my mind had turned into a pinball machine with the idea of our escape bouncing from one exciting possibility to another, lighting up the darkness, ringing bells and rattling chimes.

Finally, I got up and went to the bathroom. When I returned, I paused because I saw a light sweep across the front of the Lakewood House. Raven was fast asleep and hadn't noticed anything. Curious, I went to the window and gazed down at two silhouetted figures walking toward the driveway. One was definitely Gordon. I couldn't mistake that hulking figure no matter how dark it was outside. The other man was considerably shorter. For a moment I thought they were arguing. Gordon raised his arms and then lowered them quickly to put one around the other man's shoulders. They disappeared around the corner and then reappeared near Gordon's station wagon. I knew a door was opened because it lit up inside the car, but no one got in. Then the shorter man departed and Gordon closed the door, watched the other man as he walked away, got into his car and drove off.

Gordon stood there a moment longer and then turned and looked up as if he sensed me in the window. My heart fell into my stomach. I backed away and waited. When I looked out again, he was gone and the darkness seemed thicker than before.

3
❧

Like Thieves
in the Night

I wanted to get started on plans for our trip as soon as we were finished with school the next day. It was difficult to concentrate on anything else. There were things I wanted us to have on the journey and I thought we could stop by the department store on the way home from school. But I had forgotten that Raven, Crystal and I had dining room duty at the house. Crystal reminded me when we met at the lockers and I told her what I wanted to do.

"We can't. We've got to get right back and help Grandma Kelly get things ready for supper. If we're late, Gordon will come after us," she said. After what he had done to her in the bathroom the night before, she was absolutely terrified of the thought.

"Stop worrying. We won't be late," I assured her. "It only takes us twenty minutes to walk home."

"We'll get whatever we need tomorrow. We have all afternoon, don't we?" she said, her face twisted with fear.

Crystal didn't look like she believed we were going to run away. It was as if she were still humoring me. Raven gave me a look of warning and I nodded my understanding.

"All right. Let's go," I said reluctantly.

So we took the bus back instead of preparing for our trip. We didn't even talk about it on the bus. Instead, along with the other students, we babbled about the exams we had just completed. I began to feel like maybe Crystal was right, maybe it was just a pipe dream, a fantasy.

Remarkably, I hadn't found my final exams as difficult as I had anticipated. Most of what I had been studying stuck or could be easily

36

retrieved from the shelves and boxes in my memory. It was as if my brain had been electrified by the excitement and every thought had a neon sign announcing where it was stored.

Crystal remained pensive. She simply said she had done well, but uncharacteristically, refused to elaborate. Usually, she gave us a critique of her tests, whether we wanted it or not, rating the teacher on how well he or she covered the important things. I knew what Gordon had done to her the night before lay like a lump of lead on her mind. She was terrified of setting eyes on him or him setting eyes on her, but she was just as nervous and afraid of what I had proposed we do.

When we arrived at the Lakewood House, she rushed into the building and up to her room to change, hoping to avoid seeing him.

"She's a mess," I told Raven. "Getting her out of here is the best thing we could do for her."

"Best thing we can do for all of us," Raven responded. "I hope you really do have a good plan, Brooke."

"I do," I promised.

Butterfly, who trailed along like an anxious puppy, listened and widened her eyes with worry. She wasn't on the roster with us, but she came along to work in the kitchen anyway. With the knowledge of just what kind of evil Gordon was capable of, she was too nervous to stay anywhere by herself.

I wanted to go over our plans in detail as soon as possible, but with Grandma Kelly hovering over us, it was difficult to talk in the kitchen. I was so frustrated, I thought I would burst like an overly filled balloon. Raven and I looked at each other expectantly, but worked efficiently and quietly beside Crystal and Butterfly, stacking dishes, organizing silverware and preparing the serving trays.

"We'll meet in your room right after we clean up," I whispered to Crystal soon after we had gotten started in the kitchen, "and I'll explain everything."

She nodded, her eyes darting from the doorway to our work periodically. It wasn't difficult to see that she was terrified.

Gordon did appear at one point and stood in the doorway of the kitchen gaping at the four of us. Raven, the most defiant, flashed her black eyes at him and then turned her back on him. I saw his lip twitch in the right upper corner. Crystal, practically shaking in her shoes, kept her eyes down, her fingers fumbling around the hot plates carelessly until she burned the tip of her thumb. Gordon's smile widened and then he left us.

Raven muttered a curse under her breath.

"What's that, dear?" Grandma Kelly asked.

"Nothing," I said quickly. "We're just hungry and wish it was time to serve and eat," I added.

That started her on a story about the Lakewood House in its prime, describing how the guests appreciated the food and gorged themselves to the point of bursting.

"They usually had to take long walks after each meal. I would drive home and see the line of them along the road. Afterward, many of the guests would fall asleep in the big wooden chairs or hammocks in the shade. Everyone wanted to be sure he got his money's worth," she added with a laugh. Then she sighed deeply and shook her head as she gazed around the kitchen. "It was so different when Louise's mother and father ran things. I wish you girls were here then."

She looked down at Butterfly, who listened to her stories as if they were fairy tales.

"Look at this sweet little face," she said and hugged her. "If I were twenty years younger, I'd adopt you myself. I'd adopt all of you," she told us before continuing her cooking.

We would miss her, I thought sadly. She was practically the only person we would miss. I wanted to walk up to her and hug her, too, and then say, "Good-bye, Grandma Kelly. This is the last time we'll be in the kitchen helping you. Thanks for liking us, for caring about us, for treating us as you would treat your very own grandchildren. Now take my advice and get out of here right after we go."

Of course, I said nothing. We couldn't give anything away and we didn't want to burden her with any of our secrets. We served the meal, ate and cleaned up as quickly as we could. Megan noticed how hard we were working and remained behind to tease us.

"Boy, you're all working like little eager beavers tonight. What are you trying to do, get on Gordon's good side?" she taunted.

"He doesn't have a good side," Raven quipped.

"How would you like me to tell him you said that?" Megan replied. Crystal glanced at me fearfully.

"Just leave us alone, Megan," I warned.

She stared a moment, deciding whether or not to challenge me. She was still smarting from what we had done and from suffering room restriction for an entire weekend.

"I'm watching you all," she said. "I'll get my chance. You can bet on that."

She turned and left us.

"If she ever figured out what we were planning . . ." Crystal said.

"She won't. We'll be long gone before she does," I promised.

We said good night to Grandma Kelly and just as she had a hundred times before, she thanked us for being good helpers. We quietly made our way up to our rooms along with the others who had to study for the final day of exams. The young children went to the recreation room to watch television. After we settled in, Raven and I joined Crystal and Butterfly in their room. I closed the door softly behind me. Finally, we were getting down to it. The air was so thick, I felt like I was moving through a room filled with cobwebs.

"Where are the maps?" I asked, my voice barely above a whisper.

Crystal turned and produced them side by side at her desk.

"This is the northern and this is mid-country," she said. "There is also a southern route. I found out that it could still snow and be nasty in the Rockies," she continued, "so we might want to avoid that. We take 17 East to the Jersey Turnpike for starters," she said.

"How long does it take to get all the way to California?" Butterfly asked.

"It depends on the route we eventually follow, but if someone traveled all day, every day and didn't sightsee, probably four days," Crystal replied. Then she turned to me.

"All right, Brooke, I did what you asked. Now, tell me just how you intend to get us all across the United States of America," she said and sat back with her arms folded across her chest.

"I'm driving us," I said, shrugging as if it were the most obvious thing.

"You don't have a license," she quickly pointed out. "You never went for your test."

"You need a license to be legal, not to drive. Don't forget, I took drivers' education."

"Okay, but you need something to drive," she countered. It was as if we were playing chess with words.

"We have it."

"We have it?" She looked at Raven, who shrugged, and then at Butterfly, whose eyes widened with surprise. "Where is it?"

"Right out there," I said, grinning and nodding at the window, "waiting for us."

Crystal started to smile, thinking I was joking, and then stopped as she realized what I meant. She rose and went to the window. Butterfly and Raven joined her and they all looked down at Gordon's station wagon.

"You want to take his car?" Raven asked first.

"Why not? He takes from us, doesn't he?"

They were all quiet, staring at me as if I had gone completely bonkers. Then Crystal gathered her wits and put on her teacher's face.

"If you take his car, he'll call the police and they'll come after us," she said.

"Not for a while, and anyway, all we need is to get far enough away to find other means of transportation, maybe buses or a train. We can study those maps and try to stay off the most traveled highways. We don't have to cross the country in four days or five or even ten. We can take our time," I said.

"It takes money to take your time, Brooke. Traveling is expensive," Crystal said.

"I know. Tomorrow, we'll all go to the bank and take out our savings. Unless you all spent some that I don't know about, I calculate that together we have nearly fourteen hundred dollars," I said.

"It's not a lot of money when you consider what we want to do. We'd probably use it up the first few days. There's gas and food and tolls," Crystal replied. "Not to mention motel rooms and unforeseen problems with the vehicle."

"So? We'll find work along the way. You, Raven and I have all held jobs before and Butterfly . . ." I smiled at her. ". . . Butterfly can probably get people to give her money easily. She'll dance on a street corner or something."

"This is a pipe dream," Crystal said, wagging her head. "I knew it."

"Stop saying that," I cried. "It's not a pipe dream to me. I have it all planned out. I know where Gordon keeps his car keys. He keeps them in that beat-up leather jacket that he leaves hung on the inside of his bedroom door. I've seen him put them there."

"You're going to sneak into Gordon's bedroom and steal his keys?" Butterfly asked.

"I am. It won't be hard. Louise doesn't lock their door at night."

Butterfly stared at me, amazed at my courage.

"He might not call the police," Raven said suddenly, her eyes dark with thought. "He might just come after us himself in his truck."

That made even me quiet for a moment, contemplating a maddened Gordon Tooey racing over the highway, his mouth contorted, his nostrils flared, his eyes bulging as he pressed down on the accelerator in pursuit. If he caught up with us, there was no telling what he would do. We'd be luckier to be caught by the police.

Crystal gazed down at her maps.

"We could send him on a wild goose chase," she muttered, still looking at the documents.

"How?" I asked.

"We'll leave the route we don't choose behind. Maybe . . . pretend to drop it. He'll find it and think he has an easy way to find us and go off in the wrong direction," she said.

"That's brilliant, Crystal. That's really brilliant," I said, encouraged that she offered a helpful suggestion.

"It's still a huge long shot, Brooke. I don't know," she said, taking off her glasses to wipe the lenses as she shook her head.

"It's better than just sitting here and waiting to turn eighteen," I said, "or until Gordon tries to touch one of us again. There's no telling who he'll go for next."

I turned toward Butterfly and gazed at her. I was determined to use anything and everything to get Crystal to see.

"She's right, Crystal," Butterfly said. "I'm willing to try if you are."

"We don't have to spend money on motel rooms if we use the station wagon," I continued. "It's big enough to sleep the four of us when I put the back seat down. Tomorrow night, after everyone's asleep, Raven and Crystal will go to the kitchen and pack up as much food as you can. That will save us money, too. Between now and then, everyone choose only enough clothing to fill a pillowcase. We can't take much and we can use the stuffed pillowcases as pillows."

"You've really been thinking about this awhile, haven't you?" Crystal asked me.

"Longer than you can imagine," I said.

"Don't forget your toothbrushes," Butterfly said. Even Crystal had to laugh.

"Okay," I said, "let's study the map we're going to use."

Crystal looked at Raven and Butterfly to see if they were still all for this, and then she put one of the maps on her desk. We gathered around.

"We'll leave this route for Gordon to find," Crystal said, "to Pennsylvania, Virginia, Florida, Texas. Maybe he'll get as far as Florida before he realizes he's on a wild goose chase. By that time, we'll be long gone."

Butterfly laughed. We estimated where we might be the first day and the second, all of us talking at once. It felt wonderful; it felt like hope.

Later, it was almost impossible to fall asleep. Minutes after the lights were out in our room, Raven called to me.

"What?"

"You're not going to change your mind, are you, Brooke?" Raven's voice shook slightly.

"Absolutely not. You don't think we're doing the wrong thing, do you?" Suddenly I too was scared.

"Don't worry Brooke, no matter what happens to us on the road it won't be half as bad as what could happen if we stayed."

"Good night," I said quietly.

"Brooke?"

"Yes?"

"I was just thinking . . . this is our last night here," she whispered.

I thought for a moment. Of course, she was right. Good-bye and good riddance to these four walls, I thought. Good riddance to feeling like nobody, nameless and alone. Tomorrow, tomorrow we'll be on the road to our future.

"I couldn't be more happy about it," I said. "I don't care how hard it's going to be for us after we leave. I'm glad we're doing it. I'm glad we're finally taking charge of our lives."

"Me too. Good night."

"Good night," I said and turned over into my dream.

Now that the last week of school was under way, students didn't have to go unless they had a test to take, and if they didn't have an afternoon exam, they could go home. We were all finished with our exams in the morning, but neither Louise nor Gordon knew. After our morning tests, instead of going home, we went to the bank to get our money. The teller seemed very suspicious. Crystal was afraid she would call Louise, but she didn't. We spent the rest of the day picking up little things we might need on the trip.

When we returned to the Lakewood House, we found our chores were posted as usual. Gordon wasn't going to make today any exception, regardless of final exams. We all went to work, hoping to hide our excitement and anxiety. For all of us, it felt strange to move around the property and in the building knowing that tonight we were going to leave forever. While we ate dinner that evening, we gazed at each other with conspiratorial looks. Butterfly was so nervous she hardly ate. I made her try because I didn't want any of us to do the slightest thing to draw suspicion or curiosity about our behavior.

With what felt like butterflies floating in our stomachs, we went up to our rooms to wait for the passage of time, the darkness and silence that followed when everyone went to sleep. Louise stopped by each of our rooms to ask how we did on our exams.

"I hope everyone got A's," she said. "I've always been very proud of my children when it comes to their school work. Next year Crystal will be the class valedictorian. Imagine that, one of Louise Tooey's children, a class valedictorian."

No one said much since we hoped to move her along by not responding, but she lingered to talk about the upcoming summer, the prospect for jobs and improvements she hoped to make on the property. Finally, she said good night and left us to go downstairs to her office.

"I thought she'd never leave," I said with relief. "Let's get to bed and act as normal about everything as we always do. Just keep your clothes on under your blanket so you're ready," I advised.

My gang looked frozen with anticipation, all holding their breath.

It grew late. I heard Louise and Gordon come up and go to their bedroom. From the sound of his voice, I thought Gordon might have been drinking. I hoped he had because he would fall asleep faster. I had seen him do that before. When he drank, he could sleep anywhere, even in one of those old, awkward wooden chairs, his arms and legs dangling like the appendages of some giant, dead insect.

A little after midnight, I rose, my heart pounding. Raven sat up. She had obviously been lying there with her eyes wide open, watching me.

"Is it time?" she asked.

"Yes. You go get Crystal and go down to the kitchen. The coast should be clear. Be real quiet and careful about it and remember, don't take too much. I'll go get the car keys," I said as if there was nothing more to it than fetching them from the Tooeys' bedroom.

"You're the one who has to be careful, Brooke," she warned. "If there's any chance he'll catch you, don't do it."

"There's no chance," I assured her, building my own courage.

"Maybe we should join heads first and chant."

"I'm all right, Raven. Don't worry. I can do this," I said. I was anxious to get those keys into my hands. Then I knew it was really going to happen.

Before I got out of bed, I tapped lightly on the wall between our room and Crystal and Butterfly's. One of them tapped back.

"Let's do it," I said.

I left my shoes off so I could move more quietly down the corridor. I stepped out. Crystal and Butterfly were in their doorway.

"I'm fine," I said before Crystal could ask. "You and Raven go get the food. Butterfly, just be a lookout."

The two of them hurried away and I turned to gaze down the hallway toward Louise and Gordon's bedroom. The hallway was lit by three rather weak ceiling fixtures. A pale yellow light spilled down the tired walls. The door to Gordon and Louise's bedroom looked farther away than ever. Every step I took caused a creak in the wood floor and to me, those creaks were loud. I hesitated, listened for the sound of anyone waking. It would be hard to explain why I was wandering about down here barefoot if I were discovered. I was afraid one of the other kids would see me and make a commotion, too.

The thumping under my breast grew so hard and fast, I feared I might lose my breath, get dizzy and fall. What made me think I had the strength and ability to do this? I wondered now that I was actually out here doing it. Crystal was right. This is a pipe dream. I can't open that bedroom door and reach around to find his jacket. What if the jacket falls and the keys jingle? What if he's not asleep?

I was beginning to panic. My heart was skipping beats now. Raven was right. We should have joined and chanted. I was too confident. I looked back. Butterfly stood in the doorway, waiting with bated breath. The sight of her, small and anxious, but hopeful too, restored my strength. I had to get her out of here. I had to.

I waved and then nodded to assure her I was all right, even though I was far from it.

I looked at Louise and Gordon's bedroom door again and started toward it, sliding along the wall. Finally, I was there. I closed my eyes, took a deep breath and tried the handle. It turned and the door moved with just the slightest creak.

I had been in their bedroom a half dozen times for one reason or another, sometimes bringing something up for Louise. I knew that the door opened to a little entryway. Around the corner to the left was their bedroom with two large windows that faced the lake. There was a large closet left of that. On the right were their dressers and in the corner, the entrance to their bathroom.

I continued to open the door until I had enough room to slip between it and the jamb. I did so quickly, closing the door behind me so there would be a minimum of light spilling in from the hallway. There I was, standing in the darkness in their bedroom entryway, holding my breath. I had done it. It was too late to turn back now.

Moving in tiny increments, taking what seemed like an hour just to turn my body, I found the jacket just where it always was and slipped my fingers into the first pocket. The tips of my thumb and forefinger touched the set of keys, but just as they did so, a night light snapped on. I froze.

"What is it?" I heard Gordon moan.

"I've got to go to the bathroom," Louise said.

"Can't you go without turning on that damn light and waking me up, for crissakes."

"I didn't want to stumble on anything," she explained.

He groaned, a muffled sound into his pillow. I didn't move a muscle, didn't release a breath. I heard her go into the bathroom and close the door. I remained as still as I could and waited. I heard the toilet flush, saw the light when she opened the door, and then heard her get back into bed and snap off the night lamp.

"Sorry," she muttered. He didn't respond. I waited, the sweat now dampening the back of my neck. I wanted to be sure they had fallen back asleep. My whole body was numb and cold and suddenly, my legs felt as if they were melting. I would soon just fold up on the floor in a heap, I thought. I better do what I came to do.

I reached in again, found the keys and started to inch them up and out of the pocket. The back of my hand touched something else and I paused, realizing what it could be. If it was what I thought it was, it would be great, I thought. I drew out the keys and then felt around and brought out the gas credit card. What luck, I thought, a real bonus.

Now I had to slip out as quietly and as quickly as I had slipped in. I pried the door open, again inches at a time, keeping the creak as low as possible, until I had enough room to squeeze through. I did it on all fours and then I closed the door as softly as I could behind me. For a moment I just squatted there, listening, waiting for the terrifying sound of Gordon's growl as he came after me, but all remained quiet. Way up the hallway, I saw Crystal, Raven and Butterfly in the doorway watching me. Raven and Crystal had returned from the kitchen, a sack of groceries in hand. I lifted my hand, thumb up, and then I rose and tiptoed my way back.

We all gathered in my and Raven's room, whispering.

"You were in there so long, we thought he caught you for sure," Raven said.

I quickly told them what had happened and then showed them the credit card.

"Gordon's not only lending us his car, but money for gas," I said.

"You sure neither of them heard you?" Crystal asked.

"If they had, Gordon would be here by now," I said. "How did you do?"

She showed me what they had in the sack, mostly canned goods and nonperishables.

"Good choices," I commented. "We're all set. Nothing can stop us now."

"I'm afraid," Butterfly whimpered. The realization that we had everything we needed to go frightened her.

"Let's join," Raven suggested, looking from Butterfly to Crystal and then to me. "I need it, too," she confessed. I looked at Crystal. She nodded.

The four of us joined hands and chanted under our breath, building our courage, filling ourselves with strength. Then we separated, swallowed hard, and gathered our things. We moved like four ghosts along the wall toward the stairs, but just as we got there, Megan Callaway came out of her room to go to the bathroom.

Everyone froze.

"What are you idiots doing?" she asked, sauntering over.

"Keep your voice down," I whispered, looking frantically toward Gordon and Louise's bedroom door.

She looked at our pillowcases and the sack of groceries.

"What is this?"

"We're running away," I said matter-of-factly.

She looked at each of us and then at me.

"Serious?"

"That's right. If you make a sound, I swear I'll take so many pictures of you we'll be able to wallpaper the dining room."

I kept my eyes fixed on hers and she saw I meant it. She wilted.

"What do I care if you run away. Good. Good riddance to you all," she said. "Have a nice life."

I nodded at Raven and she started toward the stairs again. Megan remained behind us, watching. Crystal grabbed my arm and I looked at her. She moved her eyes and then pulled the phony map out of her pocket. I understood and smiled.

Just before we descended, she dropped the map as if by accident and we moved quickly down the stairs, trying to become light as air as our footsteps made the old steps creak and moan.

"She won't be able to contain herself," Crystal said, referring to Megan. "As soon as we're gone, she'll give the map to Gordon."

"Crystal, you know you are brilliant," I said, "and even a bit evil."

"I know," she said with a small smile.

We continued through the house. Butterfly was practically on her toes all the way to the back door.

I opened it slowly and looked back at my sisters, each with her eyes full of anticipation and fear.

"It's a piece of cake," I said, trying to sound braver than I felt. Raven smiled nervously. Butterfly still looked like she was about to cry. I decided to move quickly before she could think about turning back.

We hurried out of the house and to the station wagon. On summer nights like this one, Gordon left it outside of the garage. He even left the vehicle unlocked. Quietly, carefully, I opened the door and got in behind the wheel. The others rushed around, Raven getting in front, Butterfly and Crystal in the back. All the doors were closed with a soft kiss of metal on metal. I inserted the key into the ignition, my fingers trembling just a bit.

"It smells like a musty cellar in here," Raven said, holding her nose. "Ugh."

"Here's one reason," Crystal said, showing us a bottle of cheap wine that had probably spilled on the floor.

"We'll have to clean it up before we sleep in here," Butterfly said.

"Are you really sure you can drive this thing?" Raven asked.

"You know I can," I said with a confident smile. "I did really well in drivers' education class. Didn't I get the highest mark on the exam?"

"That's an exam. This is really doing it and without an instructor at your side all the time."

"Stop worrying, worrywart," I told Crystal. "Ready, girls?"

They all mumbled yes and I turned the key. The wagon started immediately with a rumble that shook the whole vehicle.

"The fuel tank's full," I announced. "Good old Gordon," I said, "keeps his vehicle tuned up and ready." I gazed back at the large, dark house. "Thanks, Gordon."

I put the car into drive and accelerated just a bit too fast. The tires spun some gravel, but I held the wheel firmly and drove down the long driveway to the street. I didn't want the others to know, but I was amazed at myself.

We continued down the highway, now spread before us like the road to Oz, a streak of silver pointing to the unknown. Everyone was quiet. It was so late it felt like darkness had turned to stone.

"I wish I was there to see his face in the morning," Raven said.

"Not me," Crystal mumbled.

"He'll blame Louise," I said. "He's always accusing her of being too soft with us."

"I feel sorry for her," Raven said. "I don't know why she ever married him."

"She'll be wondering the same thing tomorrow morning," I said. Suddenly, I broke into a loud laugh.

"What?" Raven said.

"I was just thinking about Megan. She'll give him the phony map in the morning so she can be his little hero and then he'll go off in the wrong direction."

"So?" Raven said. "That's what you wanted to happen, right?"

I looked at Crystal and she smiled. She turned to Raven.

"He'll think she did it on purpose, that she was part of our plan."

"Oh. Oh, that is funny. Maybe not," she said after a moment. "He'll kill her."

We were all silent again, contemplating Gordon's rage.

"Maybe we should go back," Butterfly said a few minutes into the silence.

"Back? Back to what? There is no back. There is only forward," I said. "Don't worry, Butterfly. We're all together, all with you."

No one spoke. No one could disagree.

"We did it," Crystal said, amazed. She kept her eyes forward on the road ahead. "We really did it."

"I always knew we could," I said. Above us, the sky blazed with stars.

"Turn on the radio," Raven said.

I leaned over and did so. We found a rock station and Raven turned up the volume and began to sing along, filling the car with her melodious voice.

I grew more confident behind the wheel and accelerated.

Our journey had truly begun.

4
ஐ

The Road Less Traveled

*H*igh on excitement, none of us noticed how tired we really were. The tension was enough to exhaust any of us, and the late hour just made it more difficult to stay awake. Driving at this time of night had one big advantage: there wasn't much traffic. I knew the roads that would take us to the main highway, but after that I had to rely on Crystal and her maps. Once we were on the main highway and I saw a sign that read, NEW YORK CITY 90 MILES, my heart fluttered. The realization that we were actually doing this, that we were on the highway putting miles and miles between ourselves and the only lives we had known for years settled in and for a few moments made us all quiet, made us all look deeper into ourselves.

All our lives we had been watched over and protected either by adoptive parents for a while or by the system. It was always difficult to make someone who had lived with their parents all their lives understand what it was like to be one of us. Without family, we felt without history, felt as if we had just been plopped down someplace and told to eat, sleep, play and grow like normal children. It was hard to live as a ward of some giant entity called The State. When we were afraid or lonely, when nightmares trickled into our dreams, when failures and disappointments rained down on our lives, we couldn't run home to Mommy or Daddy. We could talk it over with a counselor when our time came, of course. We could be analyzed and given some textbook prescriptions to cure our common sense of meaninglessness, but they hardly ever made us feel better about ourselves.

Once, when someone at school made me angry, I accused her of being spoiled and not knowing what it was like to live without a real family. She just smirked until I leaned into her, our faces only inches apart, and said, ''Just imagine sitting in front of the television set every night and seeing these commercials about children with their parents going to Disneyland or sitting around a breakfast table. Just imagine looking at it and thinking as far as you were concerned, it was science fiction.''

Her smirk evaporated and everyone around us looked down, ashamed because they had been born luckier than me.

I never really felt like anybody special. Except for the time I spent with Pamela and Peter. But if being special meant I couldn't be me then I didn't want it. I'd rather be lonely old me than someone's special project, poked and prodded into the mold they'd made for me.

Now, driving this car, rushing with my best friends in all the world through the night, I felt a sense of freedom. It was as if we had all thrown off the chains of who we were and what people tried to make us into and had finally become free. As recently as a few hours ago, we were better known by the numbers on our files. We were, as Crystal often said, ''in the system,'' labeled and described by some official, our little histories summarized in a few pages that included biological facts about our blood type, our eye color, our inoculations.

None of that mattered to us now. We were launched, sailing into space, searching for a new planet, a new place to call home. We would soon make our own histories, fill our own files. For the first time, I felt like I was in control of my destiny.

''Watch your speed,'' Crystal said. ''Even at this hour, there could be a radar trap, and we can't get pulled over, Brooke.''

''I know,'' I said and glanced down at the speedometer. The truth was I hadn't been watching it. I had been daydreaming and I was going too fast. Good old Crystal, I thought, always thinking.

I glanced in the rearview mirror. Butterfly had slumped down in her seat, her head to one side, her eyes closed. She looked like a rag doll, so vulnerable, so dependent. I think all three of us saw something of ourselves in Butterfly and that was why we were so protective of her.

The radio droned on. Miles and miles of highway rolled out before us and then disappeared into the darkness behind us. Occasionally, another vehicle drew closer and then passed us. I held the wheel steady. We were making good time. I felt like the pilot of a space ship, launched and moving closer and closer toward that point when we would break out of the earth's gravity. Soon, the past's strong grip on us would be broken and we wouldn't look back.

"Maybe we ought to check your map now, Crystal," I suggested as we left more familiar places.

Crystal unfolded the map and found the switch for the light in the rear, but it didn't work. She leaned forward to catch some of the illumination from the front.

"We could either get onto the New York Thruway or take Route Six to the Palisades Parkway and find the exit for I-95," she explained.

"Which is better?" I asked.

"The fewer people who see us and can trace us, the better off we are," she concluded. "Avoid toll booths. Take route six. The exit should be coming up shortly."

We watched for it and when we saw the signs, I slowed down, made the turns and followed the highway.

"You're really doing very good," Raven said, impressed. "I should have taken drivers' education, too."

It would have been a great help to have another driver, I thought.

Crystal sat back and yawned.

"If Megan didn't wake anyone, they still don't know we're gone," she said after a long moment.

I glanced at the clock on the dash. It was nearly three-thirty in the morning. Gordon, his brain soaked in whiskey, lay dumb in his bed. Everyone else slept quietly. In a few hours, they would all be surprised.

Raven rested her head against the window. The exhaustion we had staved off with our excitement was settling in our limbs, in our eyes.

"Are we going to drive all night?" Crystal asked me.

"It's probably a good idea to make as much distance as possible, don't you think?"

"Of course, but are you all right? You don't want to fall asleep at the wheel."

"I'm fine," I said even though my eyelids wanted to slide closed like elevator doors. I concentrated on keeping them wide open. The radio station had become all talk. "Find some music again, Raven," I asked. "Something lively, okay?"

She turned the dial until she found some upbeat sounds and sat back again.

We drove on. I should have kept up the conversation. Butterfly was in a deep sleep by now and Crystal, despite her efforts, permitted her eyes to close one time too many and drifted off as well. Raven, emotionally and physically exhausted, stopped talking and let her head lay back. I suddenly realized I was the only one awake. I started to count, to sing to myself, to move with the music, anything to keep myself alert, but I went into a daydream at the wrong time and suddenly blinked and saw a sign that said: GEORGE WASHINGTON BRIDGE.

"Crystal? Crystal!" I cried.

"What? Oh, I'm sorry. I must have fallen asleep. Where are we?"

"Are we supposed to go over the George Washington Bridge?" I asked. The toll booth was directly in front of me. There was no way to avoid it.

"*No, No!*" she cried. "Oh Brooke, you missed the exit."

"What should I do?" I asked in a panic.

"What's wrong?" Raven asked. Butterfly groaned and sat up, rubbing the sleep from her eyes.

"Just cross the bridge," Crystal said quickly. "Don't act lost. Act natural. Act as if you've done this before. I'll figure something out afterward," she said, unfolding her maps.

I slowed down, read the toll cost and reached into my pocket for the money. An African-American woman who looked like she was about forty took the bill and gave me change without even looking at me.

"She couldn't care less who we were. That has to be one boring job," I muttered and then looked ahead at the George Washington Bridge all lit up. What a daunting sight, I thought as I started us across it, my heart thumping like a parade drum again. New York City came into view against the night sky.

"Look at that," Raven said, her voice full of amazement. The three of them put their faces to the window and gaped at the Empire State Building and the Twin Towers, all the buildings twinkling. Commercial jet planes seemed close enough to crash into them. It was breathtaking.

"I bet Broadway is lit up like a carnival," Crystal said excitedly.

"Broadway! Can we see Broadway?" Raven asked, jumping up and down in her seat.

"Yes, can we?" Butterfly chimed in.

"We've got to get back on track," I said. I wasn't sure I'd be able to drive in the city traffic.

"Oh, please. Let's just see it. It can't be far, right, Crystal?" Raven pleaded. "We're already here. We might as well make the best of the mistake."

"What do I do?" I asked as we approached the Manhattan side of the bridge.

"Stay on your right. We'll take the Henry Hudson Parkway and go downtown. Then, we'll let Raven and Butterfly see Broadway before we go through the tunnel and I get us back on the route. Stay alert now, everyone," Crystal ordered.

This late at night, there thankfully were no traffic jams. Following Crystal's instructions, I got off at 42nd Street and drove very slowly through the city streets until we suddenly burst out on Times Square. The lights and the signs were so overwhelming, I had to pull over. All of us just gaped at the big screens, the number of people walking the streets despite the time, and the traffic.

"Everything's so gigantic," Butterfly said, sticking her head out and looking straight up at a towering building. "It's beautiful," she cried.

"Someday, Butterfly, your name's going to be up there in lights," I said. "And Raven will sing on a stage here."

"And what about you?" Crystal asked.

"I'll own one of the theaters," I said. Everyone laughed, and then jumped when we heard a loud rap on the side of the station wagon.

A tall policeman stepped up to the car.

"And what do you think you're doing?" he asked. He leaned down, looked in at all of us and then stood up and squinted at me.

Oh no, I thought. If he asks for my license and registration, it's all over. All we would have accomplished was a ride to New York City.

"We just wanted to see the city at night, officer," Crystal interjected. "We just came in to visit my aunt."

"Well you can't park here. See? It says 'No Parking or Standing.' " He pointed to the sign in front of the station wagon.

"I'm sorry," I said.

He took a closer look at all of us.

"You should all be asleep now anyway," he continued. "Your aunt know you're out here?"

"We've just arrived. We're on our way to her apartment," Crystal said.

"You know how to get there?" he asked.

"Yes sir, we have good directions," Crystal replied.

"Move on, then," he said.

"Thank you," Crystal said. "Go, go, go," she muttered behind my ear.

I put the car in gear and pulled away, again a little too fast. Everyone held her breath. Crystal looked back.

"It's all right. He's not chasing us."

"You did great, Crystal," I said. "Fast thinking." Were we all just naturally good liars? I wondered. Had our lives made us that way?

"Just stay alert. Turn here," she commanded. "We're looking for the Lincoln Tunnel." She glanced down at her map. "Make a left ahead and keep going."

Despite the hour and our fatigue now, it was impossible not to be wide awake. I followed Crystal's directions precisely. When we entered the tunnel, Butterfly was afraid we would never get out. It did seem to go on forever, but suddenly we burst out and then carefully, now with all eyes on the signs and directions, found our way to the route west.

I gazed at the clock again. In a few hours, Gordon Tooey would wake, get dressed, have his coffee, complain about something, step out of the Lakewood House and see his car was missing.

And then, it would begin.

We drove into the dawn, seeing and feeling the sun come up. When it became very bright, we saw a clear, blue sky ahead with just a puff of a cloud here and there against the horizon.

"Why don't we stop for some coffee?" Raven said. "I need some caffeine, and I need to use the bathroom."

"Me too," Butterfly chimed in.

I was glad they asked. I hadn't wanted to be the first to say it, but I was getting to feel like a balloon filling with water. I saw a sign advertising a rest stop in ten miles.

"We'll stop there," I said nodding.

Just a little more than ten minutes later, we pulled into the parking lot and stepped out of the car, all of us stretching. Probably from the tension, my lower back ached and my legs felt as if I had been squeezed into Gordon and Louise's famous pickle barrel.

"It feels great to move around," Raven said.

"If you're complaining already, can you imagine what you'll be like by the time we reach the Midwest," I said. I had to keep them all strong and determined, which meant I had to be even stronger.

"Who's complaining? Was I complaining, Crystal?"

"Let's not argue about it out here," she said. "Come on." She took Butterfly's hand and the two of them started for the restaurant.

There were three motorcycles parked in front of the restaurant, and through the window I could see three young men in leather jackets gaping at us. Actually, they were all staring at Raven.

"Uh oh. Here we go again." I warned.

"What?" Raven had been fiddling with her purse and hadn't noticed the motorcyclists.

"Brooke's just pointing out that you seem to have a fan club inside," Crystal said in her matter-of-fact way.

"Ugh. They look like the guys my mother used to date. Trouble. With a capital T." Raven shuddered a little as she wrapped her arms around herself.

"Don't worry, Raven, we won't let them bother you." Butterfly was always eager to protect Raven. She knew what it was like to be lavished with unwanted attention.

"Come on, let's just go in and sit down. They'll leave us alone if we ignore them." I said, opening the door to the diner.

After we'd ordered I got up to use the bathroom and when I returned to the table I saw that one of the motorcyclists had sat down in my vacant chair. I cleared my throat and he started to get up. Crystal, Raven and Butterfly all looked up at me gratefully, as if I'd saved them from some sort of torture. When I heard the motorcyclist speak, I knew I had.

"Well, if you girls need anything you just holler for Paulio. I'll be right over there," he said, pointing to the table where his greasy friends sat.

Thankfully the waitress came then with our order and we settled in to fill our grumbling tummies. As we finished the last of our food Crystal asked if we'd need gas soon.

"I'll get gas here before we leave," I said. "The wagon's a guzzler. Lucky we have Gordon's credit card."

"Don't you have to sign his name?" Butterfly asked fearfully.

"We'll use those tanks where you just stick the card in," I said. "When we drove up, I saw they had them here."

Crystal took out the map and we started to discuss the trip, where we thought we would be after another day's travel, and how far we would get by tomorrow.

Suddenly, all our hearts fell. A police patrol car pulled up and parked right under our window. The officers got out and gazed toward Gordon's station wagon.

"It's too soon for there to be a description," I said and looked to Crystal for confirmation.

"Unless Megan went right to him after we left and he got on the phone with the police," she replied.

Butterfly looked ready to cry.

"They'll put us in jail," she whispered.

"Everyone take it easy. Don't act suspicious," Crystal said.

The waitress brought us the coffee and juice as the policemen entered. "What are they doing?" I asked Crystal. She glanced up. "They're going to the counter. They're not even looking our way." I blew the air out of my lungs and sat back.

"You know," I said mournfully, "we're going to have this sort of reaction every time we see policemen."

"That's why we want to get off the main highways as soon as we can," Crystal said. She went back to her map. The waitress served our toast and muffins and we all started to eat.

"So where are you all going?" I turned to see one of the motorcyclists standing by our table.

"To visit relatives, like I said," Crystal replied.

"Early start on your summer vacation, huh?"

"Something like that," I said quickly and gave him my best look that said "Buzz off." But he ignored me and turned to Raven again.

"Where do these relatives live?" he pursued. His dirty, dark brown hair, although tied back, had strands popping up like broken piano wires. He had a thin nose and deep-set dark eyes. If he had shaved recently, he had done a poor job. Patches of stubble were on his chin and cheeks. His sideburns looked coated with motor oil.

Raven looked at Crystal for help.

"We're going to a little town outside of Philadelphia," she said and pointed to it on her map.

"Oh, you got a map, huh?" He leaned over. Then he looked back at his two buddies who were paying their bill. "Be right along," he called. "I know that town," he told Crystal. "What you want to do is get off at the next left down here," he said pointing through the window and up the highway, "and follow that road for ten miles to I-78. You can cut in here," he said tracing his long, bony finger on Crystal's map, "and you'll save about fifty miles."

"Really?" Crystal studied the map intently.

"Yeah, really. We're from here so we know the shortcuts and stuff. Well, have a good trip," he said with a smile and joined his friends.

"Thank God he's gone," Raven said in a rush, and it was obvious she'd been holding her breath.

"Maybe he wasn't as bad as we thought. And, if he's right," Crystal said, "that would cut miles off our trip and also give us a way to avoid heavy traffic. It looks like it makes sense."

We gazed out the window as the three mounted their cycles, all of them looking back at us. The one with the ponytail waved and then they roared out of the parking lot. We finished our coffee, toast and muffins, paid the bill and left as quietly as we could. One of the policemen at the counter gazed at us, but quickly went back to his eggs.

"My stomach was doing flip-flops when that cop looked at us," Raven said after we all got into the station wagon. "Brooke's right. We're going to be in a sweat every time we see a police car or a policeman."

Crystal paused and studied her map again.

"Let's try the shortcut he gave us. It looks like a very quiet way and maybe we won't see any policemen for a while."

"Good idea," I said. We got in and I drove up to the gas pumps, filled the tank, paid with Gordon's credit card simply by slipping it into the slot on the pump, and then drove away without looking back.

"This is it," Crystal said, pointing to a road on our left. It looked poorly maintained.

"This? Are you sure?"

"It's what he told us," she said. "First left turn after the restaurant."

"Okay," I said, turning. The road was chipped and cracked and after only what seemed like a mile or two, was nothing but potholes. I had to slow down considerably. "This can't be right," I said. "No wonder it's quiet, it's unused."

"I'm sure this is the road he pointed out," Crystal said. "It's what he told us," she repeated and then, as if they could hear her, the three motorcyclists appeared, two crisscrossing right in front of us, the other, with the ponytail, riding alongside. I had to stop. The two cyclists in front of us stopped, parked their motorcycles right at the front bumper, and got off.

"What's going on?" I demanded, my voice quaking.

"I see you took my advice on your shortcut," Paulio said. "You girls must be in a big hurry."

"So?" I said. I hoped he couldn't hear my voice shake.

"So you're on a toll road," he said with a grin.

"What?" I started to smile, but one of the other two opened the door on Raven's side and leaned in.

"Hello again," he said. He was short and stocky with light brown hair and blue eyes, a thin mouth and a round jaw with pock-marked cheeks and a bulbous nose. "Nice hair," he said, reaching in and touching Raven's ebony strands. She pulled away from him.

"Don't touch me," she cried and we could see the fear in her eyes.

"I'm just giving you a compliment. Don't get so uppity, Maria."

"My name's not Maria," Raven mumbled under her breath, not wanting to talk to him any more than she had to.

Paulio reached into his pocket and pulled out a switchblade.

"We could cut some of that off and tie it to our bikes, Duke, huh?"

"Good idea," the one practically on Raven's lap said. The stench of whiskey was so strong on his breath, it filled the car and turned my stomach.

In the rearview mirror, I could see the look of terror on Butterfly's face and the anger on Crystal's. We were out in the middle of nowhere, no houses, no other people and certainly no other traffic. They had tricked us, just hoping we would take their advice.

"How much money you got?" the one called Duke asked me.

"We've got tons of money. That's why we're driving such a nice car," I said with defiance. Instinctively, I knew that if I showed any fear, we would be even worse off.

"Oh, you're a wise guy, huh?" he said. "Maybe we'll cut off your hair, too. Not that you have much."

"What about her ear? You could wear that on your belt, Tony."

The third man put his foot on the front bumper and laughed.

"The toll is fifty dollars," Duke said, "but in five minutes, it goes up to seventy-five."

"That's two minutes, Duke," Paulio said. Duke laughed.

"He's right. Two minutes. Well?"

"I think we'll take another route," I said.

"Too late. You're on this one," Duke insisted. He reached for Raven's hair again and she pushed his hand away.

"We'll tell the police about this if you don't leave us alone," Crystal threatened.

"You know," Duke said, twisting his mouth until it curled in the right corner, "somehow, I don't think you will. Am I right, four-eyes?"

"No, you're all dead wrong about everything," I said and dropped my foot on the accelerator.

The wagon shot forward, the opened door swinging back on Duke and jarring him so that he fell to the side. The one in front just got his foot off the bumper in time, but that threw him off balance and he fell. The wagon slammed into the bikes parked in front of us, one flying to the left, the other to the right. I felt the tires go over it.

The cyclists shouted curses at us. Raven shut the door and I backed up. Paulio turned his bike toward us, but I put the wagon in drive and headed for him and he had to speed up to get out of my way. He practically flew off the road and into the ditch, somersaulting head over heels in midair. I didn't wait to see what happened. We bounced over the bumps and potholes so hard, our heads nearly hit the car roof. As soon as I saw the highway, I sped up. In minutes the side road was behind us.

"Don't go too fast, Brooke," Crystal warned. I slowed down quickly.

Butterfly was crying. Raven looked stunned. I kept my eyes on the road, numbed by our escape. Crystal was watching out the rear window.

"No sign of them. I think you totaled their bikes," she said with a smile.

"Just keep going," Raven gasped. "Don't slow down too much," she begged.

I didn't. We drove on, no one speaking, only the sounds of Butterfly's sobs and our heavy breathing filling the air.

"Butterfly, it's okay, we're fine," Crystal said as she put her arm around Butterfly and started to comfort her.

"You better watch the map and the road, Crystal. We can't afford mistakes now," I said.

"This exit," she said. "It's about twenty-five miles to I-287. Watch for that."

When it came up, I made the right turns and we were heading southwest. Crystal directed us to another highway and then we were going west toward Pennsylvania. There was no sign of the bikers. I was confident enough to sit back and relax, but Crystal was worried about Butterfly. I could see it in her face when I looked in the rearview mirror. Instinctively, I pulled off the road at the next rest stop and we all took a deep breath. Butterfly looked like she could go catatonic on us at any moment.

"We need it," Crystal said. I looked at Raven and she nodded. The two of us got into the back seat alongside them and we put our heads together.

"We're sisters. We'll always be sisters . . ." We chanted and held each other and after a few moments, it was as if the tension rose out of our bodies and floated away.

Then we sat back.

"Did you see the look on that Duke's face when Brooke put her foot down on the gas pedal?" Raven said and laughed.

"The door whacked him hard," Crystal said.

"I wonder if he lost any of his own hair."

"I felt the wheels crunch on one of the bikes," I said.

"They can't exactly go complaining to the police either, can they?" Raven asked.

"Your ponytail guy sprouted wings," I added.

We laughed again and then grew quiet for a moment.

"I think we make a pretty good team," I said. "We're the super Orphanteers, aren't we, Butterfly?"

She nodded, smiling.

"Let's get back on the road," I said and got behind the wheel. "How about a song, Raven?"

She thought a moment and began. Soon we were all joining her in the chorus. We're all right, I thought. We're going to be all right.

We traveled for nearly three hours before stopping for lunch and the bathroom again, this time in a noisy restaurant. It was a little more expensive than I had thought and I could see that Crystal was right about how fast we'd spend our money. Despite using Gordon's credit card for gas, traveling was still going to be very expensive, especially on our budget. Thinking about ways to economize, I suggested fast food chicken for dinner and that was just what we had.

By this time, because we had traveled all night and most of the day, we were all feeling and looking drained. Night was some ways off, but I didn't think I could drive much longer.

"I think we're just going to have to turn in early tonight," I said.

"Good idea," Crystal said. "Find what looks like a dead end road," she suggested.

We had to go almost another twenty miles before something looked promising to all of us. We nearly missed it because the entrance was hidden by lush maple trees, their branches forming a natural arch of rich green leaves and branches. The road had once been blacktopped, but now it was mostly gravel.

"Perfect," Crystal remarked.

"Aren't there bears in there?" Butterfly asked worriedly.

"Bears are not normally aggressive unless they're threatened or a mother bear's cubs are in danger," Crystal replied.

"Normally?" Raven said raising her eyebrows.

"We'll probably frighten most of the wildlife away anyhow," Crystal concluded.

I turned in and drove very slowly until we found a place that looked safe beside the road.

"Now what?" Raven asked.

"Now, we can clean up the car and make it as comfortable as possible,'' Crystal said. ''I think we're all tired enough to sleep on the roof.''

She was right about that. It took a while to get the back seat down. The latches were rusted and jammed. Under the seats we not only found candy wrappers, hamburger trays and empty bottles of beer and wine, but a tray that once had some Chinese food, now hardened and moldy.

''Let's sleep with the windows wide open,'' Raven said.

''The bugs might get in,'' I said. Crystal nodded.

We worked it out where she, Raven and Butterfly could spread out fairly comfortably in the back and I stretched out on the front seat. I didn't expect more than ten minutes to pass before we were all asleep.

The sun had just gone down behind the birch, maple and hickory trees that surrounded us. Darkness felt like a warm blanket. It was very quiet. The birds had gone to sleep, too.

''I wonder what Gordon's doing now,'' Raven said.

''Thinking of us, that's for sure,'' I replied.

Raven laughed.

''I don't want to think of him,'' Butterfly said.

We all grunted.

''Good night,'' I told them and they all said good night.

I didn't wake again until the car was filled with light. It lit up my eyelids and washed out my dreams. My lids flickered and I realized it wasn't bright because of the morning sun.

''Oh no,'' I thought and sat up. A car was right behind us, right on top of us.

Before I could warn the girls, there was a tap at my window and the face of an elderly man. He was peering in with his hand over his eyes. My heart did flip-flops. The window on my side had been rolled completely closed. Slowly, I lowered it. As I did so, the others began to stir.

''Well, I'll be darned,'' the old man said, ''a bunch of lambs who have lost their way. What'cha doin' sleepin' in a car, for goodness sakes, when there's plenty of room in the house? Go on,'' he said, pointing ahead. ''Follow the road. Go on. Nana will be happy to see you all. Go on.''

I looked back at Crystal.

''You better do as he says,'' she whispered. ''After all, we can't very well run a little old man off the road.''

I started the engine and drove slowly ahead. He got into his car and followed right on my bumper.

There was nothing else we could do.

5
∞

A Glimpse of Heaven

*T*he two-story house that appeared before us looked lost in time. There was a small patch of lawn, the grass in desperate need of cutting and weeding. Trees near the house, and especially three very large weeping willows, had been permitted to grow wild. Their untrimmed branches actually touched the roof in places. I imagined that in the daytime, the leaves blocked a great deal of the sunlight, and when the wind blew, the inhabitants probably imagined giant fingers scratching overhead.

The house had a fieldstone foundation and a rough, grainy stucco exterior. There was an arch on the right that opened to a small patio and garden. When the car headlights illuminated it, I saw what looked like a broken fountain shaped like a large saucer with a cherub rising out of the middle.

The windows had black shutters, and some of the windows on the bottom floor had lights in them. To the right of the house was a field filled with tall weeds. It ran on for some distance until it reached a dark wooded area. The separate garage was on the left. The old man pulled around us, jabbing his finger at a spot where he wanted me to park and then pulled his car into the driveway, which was pitted and cracked. He got out of his car as I turned off the engine.

"Maybe we should just back up and get away while we've got the chance," Raven suggested.

"He could call the police and have them after us in minutes," Crystal said. "He's seen us and the car and the police surely have Gordon's description by now."

"Let's see what he wants," I said.

"Don't just sit in there. Get out, get out," he cried as he drew closer, rubbing his hands together. "Nana's in there listening to music, knitting something for Gerry's kids."

"Who's Gerry?" I asked. No one moved.

"My boy. He's the only one left living around here. Helen got married and moved to Akron. Burt's down in Atlanta. I don't expect Burt will ever get married. Come on," he urged. "We'll all have some hot chocolate."

I glanced back at Crystal. She nodded and the four of us stepped out of the wagon.

"Well, lookie here," he said fixing his eyes on Butterfly. "Aren't you a pretty little thing? Gerry's got a daughter with Goldilocks hair just like yours. What's your name?"

"Janet," Butterfly said shyly.

"Janet, Janet," he repeated, scratching his scalp as if he was trying to find her in his memory. He had small clumps of thin white hair around his bald crown and very bushy, Santa Claus eyebrows. His face was round and jolly, too. It was too dark to make out much more about him except that he was just an inch or so taller than Raven, who was the tallest of the four of us. He had long arms with thick forearms and big hands. He was stooped over, his shoulders rising close to the back of his wide neck. Despite his apparent age, there was still something powerful about him, something that reminded me of an old tree stump, aged, pale, but stubborn and strong.

"Come on," he urged and headed down a slate walkway, some of the stones cracked and some rising up from years of freezing and thawing.

The front door had a small multicolored window at the center. He just turned the knob. It wasn't locked.

"Nana, we got guests," he called and stepped back to let us enter as he held the door open for us.

As soon as we stepped into the house, I smelled the aromas left from the evening's dinner. It smelled like pot roast and home-baked bread. The house had the warmth of an old blanket, comfortable, broken in, cozy. Family photographs filled the walls on both sides of the small entryway. There was a wooden hat-and-coat stand on our right and an old cast iron radiator on the left. A knitted light pink cover had been placed over it and some unopened mail lay on top of that.

We could hear music coming from one of the rooms off the entryway.

"Debussy," Crystal whispered. She said it so fast I thought about that game, Name that Tune. Crystal can name that tune in two notes.

Raven closed the door quietly behind us as a thin, elderly lady, her white hair loosely pinned over her ears and around the back of her head, appeared. She wore a light blue cotton dress with a large cameo pin at the neck. The hem of the dress went down to her ankles. It had three-quarter length sleeves and we could see the glitter of her gold, jeweled bracelet on her right wrist and her expensive looking watch on the left.

She had large, hazel eyes and nearly perfect lips that formed a gentle, friendly smile. Her skin looked remarkably soft with just deep crow's feet at her temples and some age spots on her forehead and cheeks. She wore no lipstick or makeup. I didn't think she needed it. She must have been a very pretty woman when she was younger, I thought.

"Who's this, Norman?" she asked in a soft, friendly voice.

"Four lost chicks, Nana. I found them sleeping in their car in our driveway."

"Oh dear," she said.

"We didn't mean to trespass," I said quickly. "We thought it was an unused driveway."

"Yes, it does look like we never use it. I told you, Norman. You should have Gerry get Billy Powers up here to fix that."

"Gerry says it'll cost an arm and a leg and you know how he feels about this place," the old man said. He turned to us. "My son don't want us living here anymore. He says it's too much upkeep—especially for prime candidates for the rest home like us."

"Oh stop that, Norman Stevens," Nana chastised. "He never said nothing of the kind."

Norman smiled at us.

"He don't have to say it. I know what he's thinking. He's my boy. I should know, eh? Well," he continued, "tell Nana your names. Go on."

She smiled at us with her hands folded against her stomach and waited. I wished I had asked Crystal if she thought we should use our real names, but there hadn't been time.

"I'm Brooke," I said and each of us introduced ourselves. When Butterfly spoke, Nana's eyes softened even more and a wider, deeper smile settled on her face.

"Oh look at her. She's so precious," she said. "Imagine, sleeping in your car. I want to know all about you girls and why you're sleeping in a car when I have all these bedrooms available," she added as if we had known her all our lives.

"I was thinking I'd make us all some hot chocolate," Norman said.

"You do that without dirtying up my kitchen, Norman Stevens," she told him with a kindly twinkle in her eyes.

"She's always after me," he said with a chuckle. "For nearly sixty years, too."

"You all come right in here," Nana indicated and led us into their living room.

Cluttered was the word that came immediately to mind, but not dirty or messy. Every table top, every shelf, every available space was covered with antiques, vases, picture frames or figurines. There were lots of brass and rich woods, soft cushioned chairs and two sofas, all worn but not ragged. Some vain attempts had been made to polish and redo the arms of chairs and the tables. On the right wall was a bookcase filled with what looked like first editions, leather and cloth bindings. I saw Crystal's eyes get magnetized immediately. She was sweeping the book spines, absorbing the titles and authors like some literary explorer who had just stumbled on a real discovery.

"Just find a place to sit anywhere," Nana urged. "It will take Norman a while to locate a pot and measure out six cups of hot chocolate. His eyes aren't what they used to be. Gerry doesn't want him driving anymore, but Norman's not one to admit to age or weakness of any kind. Never was."

"You've really been married sixty years?" Raven asked, lowering herself to a chair slowly. Nana sat in the rocking chair.

"Sixty-two years this coming November fifth," she said proudly.

To Raven this was like meeting someone on the pages of *Ripley's Believe It or Not*. She stared, amazed.

"Seems like yesterday to me," Nana continued. "I can see him coming around to my parents' house down in Denton, his hat in hand, under his arm a small box of chocolates for my mother and a bottle of his mother's homemade blackberry brandy for my father. He had a bunch of baby yellow roses for me. Very expensive in those days. 'I come to ask for your daughter's hand in marriage,' he declared. You could tell he had been rehearsing the line all the way over. Daddy pondered just to make it seem like it was a whole new idea, when everyone who knew us and knew how long we had been courting expected it.

" 'Do you think you can make her a good life?' Daddy asked him.

'Yes sir, I do. It's a farmer's life,' Norman said, 'but it will be a good and honest one.' " She laughed. "We've been here ever since."

"You mean you've lived all these years in one house, in one place?" Raven asked.

"Why, yes honey. Norman wouldn't move off this property no matter what. He plans to die here and so do I, if the good Lord sees fit. That's why Gerry's just barking up the wrong tree with all his talk of rest homes and the like. He might as well howl at the moon. Now you girls tell me about yourselves," she said looking from Crystal to Butterfly and then me. "How do you come by sleeping in a car? Where are you from? Where are you going?"

I looked at Crystal. It was time for her to reach back into that imagination and provide some sort of cover story for all of us.

"We're good friends who attend an all girls' school back east," she began. "We hung out together because we're the poorer girls, all there on scholarships. I invited everyone to my home for part of the summer vacation and we were heading there and trying to economize on the trip, so we came up with the idea of sleeping in the car to save on motel money. We thought it would be safe and it was fun, like camping out."

I sat amazed at the way Crystal could spin a tale. All those books she read really gave her a wild imagination.

"But won't your mommies and daddies be worried if you don't call them and let them know where you are?" Nana asked.

"Oh we did, just before we pulled in for the night. They know we're taking our time, seeing some sights," Crystal replied.

Nana shook her head and rocked.

"Ain't you kids something nowadays. When I was your age, I was afraid to go fifty miles by myself and here you are going all over the country. Of course, you can't be too careful now," she warned.

"Oh we're careful," Crystal assured her. Nana looked at Butterfly.

"I bet you're not much older than my granddaughter Lindsey. How old are you, sweetheart?"

"I'm nearly seventeen," Butterfly said quietly, her voice barely above a whisper.

"Really? I thought you were closer to twelve. I'm sure your mother misses you and those golden curls something awful," she said.

Butterfly pressed her lips together and glanced quickly at Crystal.

"Her mother's passed away," Crystal said. "She lives with her father and he travels on business a lot."

"Ooooh," Nana said sympathetically. "I'm sorry about that."

"Butterfly's talented. She's going to become a famous dancer someday," Raven said.

"Butterfly?"

"That's her nickname," I said quickly.

"You do remind me of a beautiful butterfly. What sort of dancing do you do, sweetheart?"

"Ballet," Crystal said. "She can dance to this," she added indicating the music playing on the ancient record player.

"Oh, how wonderful. I'd love to see that," Nana cried clapping her hands together.

Crystal looked at Butterfly, who went from a look of terror to a look of pride. Maybe she wasn't good enough to make some big dancing school, but she sure could get lost in her dancing when she started.

"Show her a little," Crystal urged.

"Yeah," Raven said. "Show her."

Butterfly looked at Nana, who smiled with expectation and then she stood. She took a position and we all sat back just as Norman appeared with the hot chocolate.

"Here it comes," he cried.

"Just be quiet and sit down," Nana ordered. "We're being entertained."

"What's that?" He looked at Butterfly. "Oh. Sorry," he said setting the tray down and taking a seat quickly.

Butterfly began. She didn't dance long or do anything very special. We had seen her practice the movements often, but to Nana and Norman, it was as if some prima ballerina had wandered into their home. Nana clapped hard when Butterfly finished.

"Well, I'll be, I'll be," Norman said. "That's very good. Are you in shows?"

"No," Butterfly said, her face crimson.

"Well, you certainly should be," he remarked.

"She will," Raven said.

"Raven's a singer," Butterfly said, trying to shift the old couple's attention.

"Really?" Norman said, impressed.

"She can do show tunes. Do that one from *The Phantom of the Opera*, Raven," Butterfly urged. "I love that one."

"Well . . . okay," she said hesitantly. She got up and walked to the fireplace. Norman served everyone the hot chocolate as quietly as he could while Butterfly settled down near Nana, who leaned over to stroke her hair and smile.

Raven began, her voice as melodious as I had ever heard it. Everyone was impressed, even us.

Nana clapped hard again and Norman sat back shaking his head with amazement.

"Are you girls from some sort of artistic school?" Nana asked.

"There is an emphasis on the arts, yes," Crystal said in that teacher's voice she could put on as easily as I put on a tee shirt.

"Crystal's going to be a doctor," Raven said, wanting Crystal to feel included. "But she writes poetry sometimes, too."

"You do? Well, let's hear something," Norman asked and sipped his hot chocolate.

Crystal thought a moment, gazed around the room, and then stood by her chair.

"I wrote this for my own grandparents a long time ago," she said. My eyebrows rose as if they were going to fly off my face. How did she come up with this stuff so fast?

"I do not know my past, except through you," she began, her eyes focused on the ceiling. "I do not know my name, except through you. When I wonder about my own voice, my own face, why I laugh and cry at different things, I stop and think of you, the roots of my being, my grandpa and grandma, who shared their own love and dreams with me whenever they could. Even now, I think of them whenever I think of myself."

She paused, looked down and then took her seat again.

"Oh, that's beautiful, honey," Nana said. "Norman?"

"I'm overwhelmed," he said. "I think I understood it, too," he added and we all laughed.

"Go on with you," Nana said and then turned to look at me expectantly.

"I don't sing or dance or write poems," I said quietly.

"Brooke is our star athlete—she's good enough to compete in the Olympics," Butterfly happily piped up.

"That so?" Norman said, nodding at me. "I was an athlete myself, back in my day. Never was one for being cooped up indoors—can't keep me out of the fresh outdoors. Not that you could tell by the state of things around here," he added with a sad chuckle.

"Well, the lawn does look like it could use a good mowing," I agreed slowly.

"Can't deny that. I was getting around to it."

"You should be ashamed of yourself, Norman Stevens," Nana scolded kindly.

"The place is getting away from me some," Norman confessed with a smile.

"Oh, it's hard work to keep up a yard," Crystal broke in. "We should know, yardwork was our assigned chore at school."

"Maybe you girls would like to help Norman clean up a bit out there in the morning," Nana said after a moment. She put her cup and saucer down and nodded firmly.

"In the morning?" I looked at Crystal, who started to shake her head.

"Yes, of course. You don't think I'm going to let you girls go back out there and sleep in a car when I have two perfectly fine bedrooms, each with a pair of beds in them, do you? There's fresh linen on them, too. Always is because I like to be ready for my family, should they come," she said, and from the sad tone of her voice it was obvious that they didn't come very often.

"That's very kind of you, but . . . ." Crystal began.

Nana stood, cutting her off.

"In the morning we'll have an old-fashioned country breakfast. I haven't been able to make one for some time now, being there is only Norman and me. I eat like a bird and he's happy with a bowl of oatmeal these days."

"And prune juice," he said, smiling.

"Let's not get into that. You girls are probably exhausted, being woken up and all. Let me show you the rooms. No argument now," she finished as Crystal raised her eyes. "This way, sweetheart," she told Butterfly, putting her arm around her. It was amazing how even strangers could pick up on Butterfly's special need for love and acceptance.

Butterfly beamed a smile at her. Raven looked at me. I shrugged and the three of us followed Nana and Butterfly up the stairs.

Each of the bedrooms had beds with fluffy comforters and plush pillows. There was pretty light blue wallpaper on the walls of both rooms, each with dark blue curtains on the windows. The beds were separated by nightstands which held brass lamps with frilly shades. There were oil paintings of sweet country scenes hanging on the walls; one had a man and a woman looking out at a herd of cows and the other had two girls with pails coming up from a pond.

Each room had two dressers with pictures in pewter frames on top.

Nana explained which ones were her children and her grandchildren. She told us how much she missed them and how happy she was whenever they did come to stay with her.

"Nothing's as happy as a house full of family," she said sadly.

The four of us gazed at each other. If she only knew how much we wanted that, too, I thought. I felt bad lying to her, and saw that Crystal was uncomfortable about it, as well.

"The bathroom's right across the way," she explained. "Does anyone need something to sleep in? I have some pretty things to share with you girls."

"I could use something," Raven said, happy to change out of her rumpled clothes.

"I'm okay," I said, thinking I would sleep in my tee shirt.

"Me, too," Crystal added, pulling out a nightshirt from her backpack that she'd brought into the house.

Butterfly had left her things in the car and told Nana she'd like to borrow something if she could.

"I have just the nightie for you, dear," Nana said, looking at Butterfly. She went to one of the dressers and opened a drawer to produce a pink and blue nightgown with a bow at the collar. "Just the right size, I bet," she said.

Butterfly took it and looked at it as if it were gold.

"Well, now, you girls decide how you want to pair up," Nana said.

"We'll pair up as we do at the school," Crystal explained.

"Anyone need anything else?" Nana asked. We shook our heads. I was really feeling tired now, as was everyone else. "I'll get you that pretty nightgown, dear," she told Raven and left to get it.

"Look how nice this is," Butterfly said, sitting on one of the beds. "I used to sleep in a room like this when I lived with Celine and Sanford."

"I'm so tired, I could sleep on a park bench," I moaned. "See you guys in the morning."

"Is this really okay?" Crystal wondered aloud.

I shrugged.

"Okay by me," I said. "It's better than the front seat of the car for sure."

"I wish this was really our home," Butterfly said, "and they were really our grandparents."

Everyone was silent, each of us agreeing in her own thoughts.

Nana returned with Raven's nightgown.

"It was mine when I was younger," she told her. "I hope you like it."

Raven's eyes were full of pleasure when she saw it and held it against herself.

"Thank you," she said, rubbing the fine white linen against her cheek, running her fingers over the tiny embroidered flowers along the collar.

Seeing Raven in the beautiful antique gown made me wish I'd asked to borrow one too. I imagined I would feel like a princess in such a gown, but I'd had enough of pretty things and pretending. I wouldn't let myself hope for things I'd never have, never be. It was much better to be satisfied with my life as it was, that way I knew I couldn't be disappointed.

The moment my head hit the soft, fluffy pillow, my nostrils filling with the sweet scent of flowers, I fell asleep. It was the best night's sleep I'd had in a long time, and apparently, from what everyone said the next morning, it was; the best each of them had, too.

The aroma of fresh bread, coffee, eggs and bacon was better than any alarm clock. As soon as my nose filled with the scent, my eyes snapped open and Raven's weren't far behind. In seconds my stomach was churning.

It was a beautiful morning, too. Birds were chirping outside our window. Sunshine poured through the curtains, brightening all the colors in our room. What a difference waking up here, I thought, and seeing beautiful things as opposed to waking up in that dreary room we called home for so long back at the Lakewood House.

When I poked my head out into the hallway I was surprised to see Butterfly and Crystal already heading downstairs. Raven was just emerging from the bathroom and from the look on her face I could tell that she, too, was happy to be in a nice, safe home.

"Hurry up, Sleepy," she called to me as I headed into the bathroom. "I'm so hungry I just might eat all of your breakfast, too, if you don't get downstairs soon."

I chuckled softly to myself. It was nice to have the old Raven back.

As soon as I sat down to breakfast Norman came in through the back door, huffing and puffing up a storm.

"Land sakes, Norman, what's got into you?" Nana asked.

"Oh, it's that darned old lawnmower. It's acting up again." He sat down with a groan.

"Did you check the gas?" I asked.

"Hmm . . . I forgot to check that," Norman admitted and got up.

I followed him outside. He went straight to the lawnmower and unscrewed the gas cap. He gave an embarrassed chuckle. "Well, I'll be," he said, scratching his head.

"Do you have any gas around here?" I asked, hoping he wasn't too embarrassed.

"Oh, I've got a bit in the shed, I believe."

"Let me get it for you," I said as I started walking toward the tool shed.

After I brought Norman the gas I went back inside. Everyone was waiting, Nana standing by the window with a sly smile on her face.

"You helped old Norman out there a bit, didn't you?" she asked.

"Oh, not much really," I answered quickly. I wasn't sure how much she'd seen.

After breakfast Raven, Crystal and Butterfly helped Nana clear the table, and I went out to help Norman rake up the grass after he'd mowed it. I was glad to see Raven, Crystal and Butterfly come out to help us shortly after we'd started out in the yard. There really was a lot to be done.

We each took turns keeping Nana company as she sat on the porch and knitted, talking into the lazy afternoon. She brought out fresh lemonade for us and then suggested we have lunch behind the house on their picnic table.

"We haven't done that in years," Norman said. The two of them looked as happy about it as we did.

A number of times during lunch, Butterfly, and even Raven, almost gave away the truth about us. References to the Lakewood House, to Gordon and Louise brought questions to Nana's lips. Crystal always came up with some logical explanation, but it put some strain on us.

"We should get back on the road," I suggested as lunch came to an end.

"Oh, why don't you all stay another night. I'm roasting a turkey and planning on making my special mashed potatoes."

"She's famous for her mashed potatoes," Norman said. "No pie, Nana?"

"That was going to be a surprise, Norman." She turned to us. "I do an apple that's won some compliments."

"And prizes at fairs," Norman added.

"I love apple pie," Butterfly said. She looked at me hopefully and I looked at Crystal and Raven.

"Another day off the main highway might not be so bad," Crystal said. Raven nodded.

"Why is that?" Nana asked. "Why off the main highway?"

"Oh, I just meant, another day not fighting traffic," Crystal said quickly.

Nana's eyes shifted from Butterfly to me and then to Raven before she nodded with a soft smile. The longer we remained here, I thought, the thinner our story was going to get.

"Maybe we'll leave after dinner," I said.

"You'll do no such thing. I'll tell Norman to block the driveway if you try," she said. "It's better to travel in daylight. You girls earned your keep, helping Norman with the lawn. The grounds almost look the way they used to when Norman was young enough to take care of them regular."

"Okay, Nana," I said, giving in. "We'll stay."

Butterfly beamed.

"Maybe Janet will do some dancing for us again and Raven will sing a song. I bet if we leave Crystal alone out here, she'll write a nice new poem," Nana added. "I got some groceries for you to pick up at the corner store, Norman. Maybe Brooke will ride along and help you."

"Sure," I said.

"That'd be fine," Norman said. He looked at all of us and smiled. "Some grandparents somewhere are sure lucky folks," he said.

If we could, we would have all burst out with the truth, just to keep the tears from clouding our eyes.

I was happy to ride along with Norman and I enjoyed hearing him talk about his farming days, his family and growing up in the area, how he met and fell in love with Nana and how much he loved his grand-children. He wished he could see them more, for Nana's sake as much as his own, he said, and I wondered why they weren't brought around more often. I gathered from what Norman said that his daughter-in-law wasn't fond of visiting the old homestead, as he called it.

He started to ask me questions about my own family and I found myself backed into a corner once or twice. I wasn't as good at making up stories as Crystal. Usually, it was better to let her come up with everything. I know I contradicted myself a few times and made state-ments that made little or no sense.

I could only imagine what my family would be like. I told him I had no brothers or sisters and used my memories of Pamela for a reference.

"She sounds a lot like Gerry's wife," he muttered.

I went around the aisles in the grocery store, locating the things Nana had put on her list. He said I cut his shopping time in half because I could find things easier.

"I oughta adopt you," he quipped on our way out and I almost lost my breath. I looked down quickly so he wouldn't see the expression on my face. I was never as good as Crystal or especially Raven when it came to hiding my feelings and thoughts. Raven always said I might as well have two tiny television screens for eyes because my thoughts get played on them as clearly as any show on TV.

Dinner was wonderful. None of us could recall anything like it, even when we had lived with foster parents. Butterfly declared it felt like Thanksgiving, which made us all laugh. It was hard to describe the feeling of warmth we all experienced, but it was as if Norman and Nana were truly our grandparents, the family we had never known, and one night, just by accident, we had stumbled upon them. We felt as if we had known them all our lives. Our laughter came naturally, our smiles and concern for each other just seemed to flow.

After dinner Butterfly danced again, only this time she danced longer, truly performing better than ever before. Raven sang two songs. She would have sung a third if she were asked. Crystal had written a short poem about nature, about the way it embraces us and makes us feel alive and spiritual.

I kept my eyes on Nana. I couldn't help but be drawn to her. She was so gentle and so beautiful in her way. There was a sincerity of feeling we all had missed most of our lives. When she watched Butterfly, heard Raven and Crystal, her eyes filled with tears of joy. It brought tears to my own.

Norman thanked us all again for helping him out in the yard.

"I oughta hire you all on for the summer," he said with a chuckle.

"I wish you would," Nana said. "I'd love to have you all stay."

"So would I," Butterfly piped up, her longing for home and family so strong she couldn't contain herself.

"But we have to get to my house," Crystal said, her eyes narrowing as she looked at Butterfly, who looked down quickly.

"Of course, you do, dear. Your families will be worried enough as it is and I'm sure your mama and papa are looking forward to seeing you," Nana said. "Well now, I'm a bit tired," she revealed. "You girls can go into the den and watch television, if you like," she added, rising. "We missed all the shows we would watch."

"Oh, I'm sorry," Crystal said.

"No, no, this was better than anything we could have seen on television, wasn't it, Norman?"

"About a million times better," he said, nodding.

"I'll have breakfast on for you girls in the morning," Nana said starting for the door. She did look tired and suddenly, very old.

"No need for that, Nana," I said. "We'll be getting an early start."

"We get up early," she declared. "You don't leave this house without something hot in your stomach, you hear?"

"Yes, ma'am," I said quickly and she smiled.

"Good night, girls. Sleep well."

"Good night, Nana," we all chorused.

Norman remained behind a moment.

"I want to thank you for visiting with us," he said. "It's been a joy. Really has," he added and stood up with a groan. He felt his lower back and shook his head, smiling at me. "You got me working harder than I have all month, girls. Could be you're dangerous to have around," he said with a laugh. I smiled at him. " 'Night, girls."

"Good night," we said.

We heard them both go up the stairs and then we sat back, letting the silence envelop us for a moment. Crystal was the first to speak.

"Maybe we should just leave now, Brooke," she said.

"No," Butterfly moaned.

"It's better to travel at night and it's going to be hard to say goodbye, Butterfly," she pointed out.

"I don't care. It's not a nice thing to do to them, sneak away like that," Butterfly insisted. She looked at me for support.

"Crystal's right about the traveling, but Butterfly's right about what's nice and what isn't," I said.

"I'm just evaluating the situation and giving you my conclusion," Crystal replied.

"Raven?" Butterfly asked, hoping Raven would break the tie.

"I don't feel like riding in that car all night with that soft bed up there waiting for me," Raven concluded. "I'd like to watch some television, too, maybe some MTV and see what's been happening in music. What harm can it do to stay one more night?" she asked.

No one replied because no one could anticipate just what harm daylight could bring.

* * *

We watched television, Raven the last to turn it off and come upstairs to bed. I drifted in and out of sleep, tossing and turning with guilt because we had accepted their hospitality under such a cloud of lies. Finally, after Raven crawled into bed, I settled down and fell asleep, too.

We were all awakened by the sound of a gruff voice coming from downstairs. Raven looked at me and I sat up. Crystal came to our room and opened the door quietly.

"Get dressed quickly," she said. "I went to the stairway and listened. It's their son Gerry and he's mad at them for taking us in, four strangers. He's ranting and raving that this proves they need supervision and shouldn't be living on their own here anymore. Nana was crying. I heard her."

"That creep," I said, thinking he sounded just like Gordon.

"Just get dressed. Butterfly's ready. We'll make as fast an exit as we can."

"Right."

Raven and I were out of bed in a flash. We threw on our clothes and washed our faces. In minutes, the four of us were descending the stairway.

Nana and Norman's son Gerry was a big man, probably six feet four and two hundred and twenty pounds. He looked more like Norman, but had Nana's eyes. His light brown hair was trimmed short, making his ears look larger. He was wearing a dark brown sports jacket, a white shirt opened at the collar and a pair of slacks. When we entered the kitchen, he was leaning against the counter, his arms folded across his chest. Norman was at the table, his head lowered. Nana was keeping busy at the stove, but looked very disturbed.

"Who are you?" Gerry demanded before we could say good morning or be introduced.

"We're just on our way to my house," Crystal said. "I'm Crystal. This is Brooke. This is . . ."

"I don't mean your names," he followed. "What the hell you doing sleeping in our driveway?"

"I told you why," Nana said. "Just sit down girls. Everything's ready."

"Maybe we should just be on our way," I said.

"Maybe you should," Gerry declared, his eyes full of distrust and anger as he shifted them from one of us to the other.

"You have to have something in your stomachs," Nana moaned. She looked on the verge of tears. "Let them eat, Gerry. Please."

"This isn't a hotel," he muttered, but he looked away.

"Sit at the table, girls," Nana said. Norman looked up and smiled.

"Sure, come on," he urged.

Butterfly was the first to take a seat. Raven followed, her eyes on Gerry, and then Crystal and I sat. Nana began to serve us scrambled eggs.

"I don't like my mother being someone's maid," Gerry said.

"I'm not being anyone's maid, Gerry. The girls have helped us a great deal. Didn't Dad tell you how he got the lawn all cut and raked?"

"Um," Gerry grunted. He watched us eat. It was very uncomfortable, all of us keeping our eyes down, trying to be friendly, trying to make Norman and Nana feel comfortable too.

"Wait a minute," Gerry said suddenly, "where's your bracelet and watch, Mom?"

"What's that?" Nana looked at her wrists. "Oh. I guess I must have left them upstairs."

"Where upstairs?" he demanded, looking at us.

"On the dresser where I always leave them, Gerry. Really, I wish . . ."

He didn't hesitate. He left the kitchen quickly and went to the stairs.

"Don't mind him none," Nana said. "He's always suspicious of strangers, always was, even as a little boy, right Norman?"

"Yes, he was."

"And he's worrying about us all the time," she added with a forced smile.

"I would too," I admitted.

We ate a little faster, despite the effort Norman and Nana made to make us feel comfortable again. Moments later, we heard Gerry's heavy footsteps on the stairs and then saw him fill the doorway. He had a wry smile on his face.

"None of it's there, Mom. I checked your jewelry box, too."

"It's not?" She looked puzzled. "I'm sure I put them there," she said.

He scanned us.

"No one's leaving this house until that watch and bracelet are returned," he announced.

"We didn't take anything," I cried.

"Of course we didn't," Crystal said. "Why are you accusing us?"

"Please, Gerry, these girls . . ."

"You don't know anything about them. There are girls on the loose everywhere these days, running away from home, from jails, becoming little prostitutes."

"That's not who we are," Crystal cried defensively.

"You don't look exactly like Mary Poppins." His face grew stern again. "I want that jewelry."

"We didn't take it," I insisted. "We don't steal."

He nodded. "Sure you don't."

"Wait a minute," Norman said. "Seems to me I remember you taking them off before you started cooking last night, Nana."

"Yes," she said her eyes growing sharper. "Yes." She turned and then she went to a drawer in the cabinet by the sink and produced the watch and bracelet. "Here they are. I just forgot," she said.

Everyone was silent a moment.

"I think we're owed an apology," Crystal declared, her eyes fixed on Gerry.

"I think you got enough from my parents as it is."

"I wasn't referring to them," Crystal said.

"You should apologize, Gerry," Nana said.

"Aaa. I don't like it," he said. "I'm leaving for work, Dad. I'll talk to you later." He glared at us. "I expect you'll be gone when I return."

"We will for sure," I said angrily.

"Good."

He turned and left the house. As soon as the door closed, Nana apologized for him again.

"We've got to get going," Crystal said. "It's all right. I'm glad you found everything."

"It's easy to forget things these days," Nana said mournfully.

"Shouldn't we stay and help with the dishes?" Butterfly asked.

"No, you don't have to do that," Nana said. "I don't have much to do with myself as it is."

They followed us out of the house, once again apologizing for Gerry.

"Maybe on your way back, you can stop in again," Norman said.

I smiled.

Nana hugged Raven and Crystal and then gave Butterfly an especially long hug before hugging me, too. I got into the car and started the engine. Everyone got in afterward and I turned it around and headed toward the driveway entrance. The two of them stood side by side watching us, waving, looking smaller than ever.

"I wish we could have stayed," Butterfly said sadly.

No one spoke.

"I only hope that son of theirs doesn't report us to the police," Crystal remarked.

It was a worry we carried with us for nearly two hours before we felt more comfortable.

It had been a great stopover, I thought, but then when I looked at everyone and saw the sadness in their faces, I thought again. Maybe it would have been better if we'd never met Nana and Norman.

Our time with them seemed to confirm what we'd always feared: we'd never have a chance to be loved, to be part of a family. Being orphans had tainted us forever.

6
∽

A Ray of Sunshine

Crystal returned to her maps to find us the safest routes because she was still worrying about Nana and Norman's son Gerry and Gordon's inevitable report to the police.

"Even if Louise talked him out of it for the time being, hoping we would come back, thinking we might have just gone off on a joy ride, he would be furious by now, especially if he followed that false map," she explained. "Let's continue to stay away from heavily traveled highways where policemen patrol more frequently. Turn here," she instructed. "Yes," she said reading her map, "just follow this until I tell you to turn again."

"Can we have a picnic today?" Butterfly asked once we'd been on the road for a while. "It was fun eating in the backyard with Nana and Norman yesterday."

"It looks like it might rain," Raven said, sounding a note of discouragement.

The dark clouds crawling toward us seemed to have already seeped into the car. Raven didn't even notice that I hadn't turned on the radio. She sat staring out the window, watching the scenery go by, looking like someone hypnotized. When I gazed at Crystal and Butterfly in the rearview mirror, I saw they were both pensive, Butterfly looking sadder than ever.

"You want to sing or play riddles?" I asked. No one responded. "Great. You're all a lot of fun. I might as well have stolen a hearse to drive," I said.

"What's that up there?" Raven suddenly said, sitting up.

Maybe a half mile ahead of us, at the side of the road someone was sitting on a suitcase. I slowed as we drew closer.

"It's a hitchhiker," Raven declared. "A girl. Pick her up, Brooke."

"No," Crystal said.

"Why not? She's probably all alone, like us. Who else is going to pick her up? Besides, she might get caught in a rainstorm," Raven fired back at her.

"We can't take chances," Crystal said.

"Some chance, helping someone. Stop for her, Brooke," she pleaded. "We could use the change in company," she added, throwing a look back at Crystal.

"I don't mind," Butterfly said. "It could be fun."

As we drew closer, we could see that the hitchhiker was a young woman, maybe seventeen, eighteen years old. She wore a short skirt the color of light tea, shoe boots with no socks and a tie-dyed tank top. A lime green and white bandanna was wrapped around her peach and blue colored hair and her forehead. The faded brown suitcase upon which she had been sitting looked like it had been tossed out of a speeding train. It was cracked and battered so badly, some of her clothing was actually leaking out. She had tied a rope around it to keep it shut.

"All right. She does look pretty pathetic," I said and stopped.

She wore only one earring that looked like a thin string of leather with a blue marble on the end. Her small framed, dark blue sunglasses hid her eyes. She wore no makeup, but it looked like she had a patch of tiny, blue dots on her left cheek.

The tank top was snug and revealed she was braless, despite her full bosom. She had lean arms with a tattoo of what looked like a sunflower bursting open on her left forearm. Her right hand was covered with metal rings, none looking very expensive. Despite the tattoo, the dots, the strange clothes and appearance, she was a pretty girl. Her nose was perfect and her lips were full and straight with just a tiny dip in the left corner. When she spoke, a dimple flashed on and off in her right cheek.

"Thanks for stopping," she said breathlessly. "I didn't expect to see anyone on this road for days. Where should I throw this?" she asked, indicating her suitcase.

For a long moment, the four of us just gaped at her.

"Well, are you giving me a ride or not?"

"Oh, I'll open the back door for it," I said and got out. I flipped open the rear door and she put the suitcase in quickly.

"You can sit up front," Raven called out the window and she went

81

around and got in when Raven moved over. I started the engine and drove on.

"Thanks guys," she said, smiling back at Crystal and Butterfly, who continued to stare at her as if she were an extraterrestrial.

"Where are you going?" I asked.

"Anywhere but here. How about you?"

I glanced at Crystal in the rearview mirror. She shook her head slightly.

"To my friend's house in Ohio," I said.

"Great. I'll go to Ohio," she said. The way she said it, I thought she would agree to go to Alaska if we said we were heading that way.

"What's your name?" Raven asked. She was the most taken with her.

"Sunshine. What's yours?"

"Sunshine?" Raven hesitated as if her own name wouldn't match up in value. "Um, I'm Raven. This is Brooke," she said nodding at me. "Crystal and Butterfly," Raven said nodding at each.

"Butterfly? Great name. I had a friend who named her daughter Beetle Bug because she was born with these dark eyes so close together she looked like a little bug in the blanket."

"Butterfly is just a nickname," I said. "Her real name is Janet. What's your real name?"

"I told you, Sunshine. I have no other name," she insisted.

"How come you were hitchhiking?" Raven asked.

"Because my darling boyfriend, Sky, left me out there. We broke up."

"Sky?" I said with a smile.

"In his case he had another name, Ormand Boreman. It was on his driver's license. It should be Ormand Boring instead."

"He just left you there?" Crystal asked. Sunshine turned and smiled at her.

"Well actually, I opened the door and said if you don't stop and let me out, I'll jump. So he stopped and I got out there. He drove away with the door still open."

"What kind of boyfriend is that?" Butterfly asked.

"The worst kind," Sunshine said. "Good riddance, huh? Men make me sick anyway. They always think just cuz you're pretty or funny you're up for grabs."

"I know exactly what you mean," Raven said. Sunshine looked at her, a small smile on her lips. It was obvious that they were kindred souls.

"Who are you guys? Where are you all from?"

"Back east in upstate New York," Crystal said quickly, "except for me. I come from Ohio. How about you?"

"I was born in California, but I haven't been back there since . . ."

"Since when?" Crystal asked.

"Since good old Mom and Dad split," she answered.

"Oh, sorry," Crystal said quickly.

"It's all right. There's nothing to be sorry about," she remarked.

"Do you have any brothers or sisters?" Raven asked.

"Probably," Sunshine replied.

"Probably? What do you mean by that?" I asked.

"I mean probably. Knowing my father, I'm sure I do somewhere." She looked at me. "Maybe one of you is related to me. I don't know."

"Where are your parents now?" Butterfly asked. Sunshine's appearance was definitely getting her out of her funk.

"Last I heard, Mom went to Rosarita Beach in Mexico and Dad went to Oregon," she replied.

"You haven't seen or heard from them since?" Butterfly pursued.

"Nope. Far as I'm concerned, I'm an orphan," she said, "and I don't mind."

"That's because you really aren't one," Crystal muttered.

"What?"

"Nothing," she said.

"How old were you when you left home?" I asked.

"Sixteen. Well, maybe just fifteen. It seems so long ago now, I can't remember."

"How old are you now?" Butterfly asked. "Seventeen?"

Sunshine laughed.

"I'm twenty," she said.

"Twenty!"

"Yeah, I'm an old lady." She dug into the pouch she had swinging on her neck and came out with a sad-looking cigarette, the paper barely holding the tobacco together. "Anybody want a drag?" she asked as she lit it.

"We don't smoke," Crystal said sharply.

"Me neither," Sunshine said.

"That isn't a cigarette," Raven said, suddenly suspicious.

"No. It's a joint," Sunshine replied with a smile. She offered it to

Crystal, who shook her head and then to Butterfly, who stared with big, frightened eyes.

"She doesn't want any." Crystal spoke for Butterfly.

"None of us do," Raven said. "That stuff is nothing but trouble."

"With a capital T!" Crystal and I chimed in, laughing nervously.

"It's all right. One puff can't hurt," Sunshine said, taking a long drag. "It never hurts, that's the point." She leaned to me and I shook my head. The sweet smell filled the car. Crystal coughed.

"Throw it out," she demanded.

Sunshine looked at me.

"Please," I said. I didn't want to have to stop the car and kick her out, but I knew we'd have to if she kept this up.

"What a waste," she muttered, took another long drag and then threw the joint out the window.

"You could start a fire in a field," Crystal complained looking back.

"Who are you, the national leader of the Girl Scouts?" Sunshine asked.

Raven gave her a dirty look and Sunshine changed the subject.

"So what were you all doing back east?" Sunshine asked.

"Going to school, a private school," Crystal said quickly, maybe a little too quickly.

Sunshine looked at Raven and then back at Crystal. She raised her eyebrows and slowly took off her sunglasses and gazed at Butterfly, who quickly looked down.

"Something tells me you're not telling the truth. Am I right?" she followed. No one spoke. "What, are you all running away or something?"

"No," I said. "We're going to Crystal's home in Ohio. We've been invited."

"Really?" She looked back and then smiled. "Pack light, do you? All I see are some pillowcases. I know this isn't some kind of pajama party. You guys are on the run. You don't have to tell me. I know enough about people on the run."

"I told you not to pick her up," Crystal complained.

"Relax," Sunshine said. "I'm the last person you have to worry about. I've been running away for years."

She sat back with a laugh.

Despite Crystal's reluctance to let Sunshine continue on with us, we couldn't help but be interested and intrigued with our new acquaintance. She described her travels, the places she had been in America, hitchhiking, developing relationships with men who took her along on their own journeys and then either deserted her or did something to cause her to want to desert them.

"I was nearly murdered in Texas," she said. None of us even breathed for fear of interrupting her. "I met this trucker at a rest stop . . . best places to pick up rides," she inserted. "Even the ones who have *No Riders Permitted* stickers on their windows take you along if you ask them nicely, know what I mean?"

"No," Crystal said with her eyes narrow and her lips tight. "What do you mean?"

"Well, Pollyanna, it's like this," she said infuriating Crystal more.

"My name is *not* Pollyanna."

"Whatever. You show them some skin, flirt, fill their mind with fantasies," she explained.

"Then what happens?" I asked.

"Depends. If you really like the guy, you pay up. If not, there are ways to worm your way out. Only this time in Texas, Roy was not taking no for an answer. He put a knife this long to my throat," she said, holding her hands apart. Raven gasped.

"What happened?" Butterfly asked. Sunshine glanced at her.

"You really want to know?"

"No," Crystal answered for her.

"I didn't think you did, Pollyanna."

"I want to know," Raven said. "We should hear this and learn," she added.

"Why? Do you plan on asking for rides at truck stops?" Crystal shot back at her.

"You never know," Raven said.

"That's the way to think," Sunshine said, grinning at Raven.

"There wasn't anything I could do but let him have his way, or start to," she said. "You get to know when men are at their . . . let's say weakest moment. I waited for my chance, kneed him where it hurts right down to his birthday and got away. I lost some of my stuff. That's why I only have that bag, but I wasn't about to go back and ask him for my things," she said.

No one spoke for a moment, all of us lost in our own imaginings, each of us seeing the terrifying moments from our own prospective.

"Why do you do this?" Crystal finally asked.

"Do what?"

"Hitchhike everywhere, pick up rides from strangers, go off with strange men, live like this?'' she elaborated, raising her voice a few octaves.

''I'm not exactly enrolled in some private school back east,'' Sunshine replied. ''I'm on my own.''

''So just get a job, learn something, get a life like everyone else,'' Crystal continued. ''A lot of people are on their own but don't end up nearly raped and murdered in some truck cab.''

Sunshine stared at her and then blew some air through her lips.

''Everyone in this country thinks she knows what's good for everyone else. When you're on your own for a while, come see me. I'll make some time in my busy schedule,'' she added.

''We've been on our own all our lives,'' Crystal said, ''mostly.''

''Is that right?'' Sunshine looked at her and then at the rest of us. The skepticism was replaced with new interest. ''What do you mean? Who are you?''

''We're real orphans,'' Crystal said. ''We come from a foster home. Ever hear of them?''

''You're kidding? Really?'' she said, smiling as if our stock went up tenfold in her eyes.

''How come you never ended up in one?'' Raven asked.

''I almost did once. I was picked up for vagrancy in some small town in Oklahoma and the police were going to turn me over to the state, but I managed to fake my way out. I had this friend in Phoenix who pretended to be my aunt and wired the money for my bus ticket. The police bought it. I actually left on a bus and got off the first stop. They weren't really interested in me. They just wanted to get me out of their hair. As I said, Pollyanna, you've got to learn how to live on the road.''

''Stop calling me Pollyanna,'' Crystal snapped.

''Sensitive, isn't she? First rule on the road is not to be sensitive. You've got to get a shell like those turtles you see crawling along. I turned one upside down once just outside of El Paso.''

''Wow, you really have been everywhere,'' Raven said with awe. She'd never been west of New York State.

''Not New York,'' she said. ''I've stayed away from New York City. You can get eaten alive there.''

''We were just there,'' Butterfly bragged. ''It's beautiful.''

''Really? How long were you there?''

''Only for a few minutes,'' I explained. ''I made a wrong turn and ended up on Broadway.''

''A lot of people are trying to end up on Broadway,'' Sunshine said with a laugh. She nudged Raven and Raven laughed with her. "I like you guys. You have any money?"

"Our savings. We got paid for work around the foster home and summer jobs," I explained.

"How much do you have?"

"Almost fifteen hundred," I said.

"Fourteen hundred and twenty now," Crystal reminded me.

"She's right. She's the banker," I agreed.

"Oh." She glanced at Crystal again. "Well, it looks like your money's in safe hands. I don't think Pollyanna is the type who wastes a penny."

"If you call me that one more time . . ."

Sunshine laughed.

"Please, don't tease her," I begged.

"Okay." She turned to Crystal. "I even like you . . . what's your name again . . ."

"Crystal. It's Crystal!"

"Well, that's like Pollyanna anyway, but okay, Crystal. I like you, too. Anyway, how did four orphans get a car like this? Not that it's any great-looking automobile or anything."

No one said anything.

"Oh, I see. Crystal's not as lily white as she pretends to be, huh?"

"It wasn't very nice where we were," I explained, "and we didn't see any future for any of us there."

"It was called the Lakewood House and the owner's name is Gordon. He's a monster," Butterfly said. Crystal poked her to stop her from saying too much more.

"Yeah, he's a delight to be with," I said. "Anyway, we borrowed his vehicle to get away."

"I've done that," she said with a shrug.

"Done what?" Raven asked.

"Borrowed things. It's the way you survive on the road. There was this guy I knew in Vegas. That's a fun city, Vegas. Anyway, he borrowed a car, but he changed license plates on the way out of the city. Did you do that?"

"Change plates?" I shook my head.

"The police are looking for the license number. You switch plates with another car and you have a better chance. Most people don't even notice their plates have been switched."

"That's a good idea," Raven said.

"No," Crystal said. "We're not doing anything else that could get us into any more trouble."

"If the police catch you in this car, Pollyanna, you'll be in enough trouble anyway. Switching plates won't add much to it," Sunshine said.

"I don't know, Sunshine," Raven began.

"I'll help you," Sunshine broke in. "It's easy."

When my eyes shifted to the rearview mirror, I saw Crystal flash me a very worried look.

"We'll see," I said. "Let's take it a day at a time."

"Exactly," Sunshine says. "That's what I do. See," she said, turning to Crystal, "you're starting to live like me already. We're all going to get along great. We'll be like . . . sisters, sisters on the road."

We stopped for lunch at a restaurant that also had gas pumps in front of it. Despite its size and where it was located, it did a brisk business and filled up soon after we arrived. Crystal wanted us to be thrifty and order carefully from the menu, but Sunshine kept interrupting, telling us to order this and that.

"It's one of the cheapest stops on the road," she said. "Take advantage."

"I'm hungry anyway," Raven grumbled.

"We had a big breakfast," Crystal reminded her.

"I'm still hungry. I want a shake, too. And Sunshine says the fries are good here."

"I stopped here once before," Sunshine explained. "Maybe twice."

She ordered a double burger, fries, a shake and a scoop of chocolate ice cream for dessert.

"You pay the bill," she told Crystal afterward, "and I'll straighten up with you later."

Crystal gave me one of her looks, but I didn't want to make a scene at the table so I just nodded. Reluctantly, Crystal paid the bill. We left a tip and started out.

"I'll just be a minute," Sunshine said and went in to the bathroom.

"Let's drive away and leave her in there," Crystal said the moment we were back in the wagon. "We're never going to get the money for her lunch. She's only going to be trouble, Brooke."

"We can't do that," Raven said. "Her suitcase is in the car."

"Leave it in the parking space," Crystal suggested.

"Someone might steal it," Butterfly said.

"Steal that? I doubt it. The road department might take it to prevent disease, but no one's going to steal it, Butterfly. Let's do it, Brooke."

"I can't, Crystal, she's as bad off as we are. We'll take her along a little farther and then tell her we're going someplace else."

"She won't care. She'll stay with us as long as she can," Crystal warned. "You'll see."

"Here she comes," Raven said.

Sunshine walked quickly from the restaurant and got in.

"Drive on," she ordered and we pulled away. As we did, she turned to hand Crystal some money.

"Here's for my lunch," she said with a smirk.

Crystal took it, surprised, glancing at me before she rubbed the bills a moment as if she thought they might all be counterfeit. Then she looked up with more surprise, even shock.

"Where did you get this five-dollar bill?"

"What do you mean, where did I get it? I had it on me. That's all," Sunshine said.

"No, you didn't. This was the five I left with the tip. I know it is because it had this ink spot on Abraham Lincoln's face," Crystal said.

"Jesus, what do you do, memorize the way your money looks?" Sunshine asked.

No one spoke.

"I remember because I thought it was odd that there was an ink spot on it," Crystal said slowly. "You took the waitress's tip."

"What of it? She'll get tips from people who can afford it better," Sunshine said.

"That's awful," Crystal insisted.

"Oh, and I suppose stealing someone's car will get you the Nobel Prize," Sunshine retorted.

Crystal turned all shades of pink before biting down on her tongue and sitting back.

"It's just not right," she muttered.

"Money is money, especially when you're on the road. You girls will learn. Hang around me a bit, you'll learn real well," Sunshine said.

"That's just what I'm afraid of," Crystal grumbled.

Sunshine laughed.

"Let me tell you about this time in Kansas," she said instead of continuing the argument. "Talk about being desperate. I had about twenty cents to my name."

She went from story to story, telling us about places and people and events, stringing the tale of her road trips crisscrossing America, describing her instant love affairs without the slightest embarrassment or regret. It became apparent to us that men were there to be used in her eyes and sex was just a good way to a meal ticket, a bus ticket, or a way not to spend another lonely night someplace in the heart of nowhere.

However, for me and my sisters, it was more than entertainment as we traveled along. It was a description of what could possibly be our own fate if we weren't careful. The problem was how do you be careful when you're in Sunshine's world, where we were now? It made me wonder if we should just turn back and be grateful for what we already had.

We didn't pull off the road again until we all had to go to the bathroom. Crystal returned to her role as navigator and guided us on roads paralleling the main highways for as long as she could. We drove on, holding our breath every time we saw a police car.

"Don't worry so much," Sunshine told us. "There are so many vehicles stolen in this country every day, the police couldn't possibly keep up or care. You've got to develop the mask, anyway," she continued, behaving as if she were our tutor, teaching us how to scrounge and claw out an existence with barely nothing to our name.

"A mask?" Butterfly asked her. She didn't seem as alarmed as we all were by Sunshine's actions and that was beginning to worry me.

"The look," she replied. "See?" she said turning, batting her eyelashes and looking as sweet as could be. "You have to appear innocent and never give anyone the feeling that you're worried they'll discover something bad about you. Just relax, be casual."

"How?" Butterfly pursued.

"Tell yourself everyone else is wearing a mask, too, and you can do it. Everyone is, you know. Everyone's taking something from someone else. Some do it legally because they have the government behind them or because they know how to bend laws and take advantage of people. I've seen plenty of it. You ever hear that old expression, whoever didn't sin can throw stones?"

"Let he who is without sin cast the first stone," Crystal said dryly. "It's in the Bible. Jesus said it."

"I knew it was from the Bible," Sunshine replied sharply. "Anyway, that's the way to think and you can get the mask. No one can throw any stones, sweetie pie. Believe me."

"I'm surprised you call yourself Sunshine with all that dreary, dark thinking," Crystal commented.

Sunshine turned to her and smiled.

"That's the mask, Pollyanna. Now you're getting it. See, she's smarter than you all thought."

Even I had to laugh at that. Crystal sat back sulking. Soon, Raven began telling her more and more about us. I saw how it made Crystal nervous, but I couldn't see why it mattered. What was Sunshine going to do to hurt us? She was truly an experienced runaway. We were only freshmen. She talked as if she had graduated from the college of hard knocks years ago.

As night began to fall, we thought about dinner and sleeping. Things were more complicated now that Sunshine was riding with us.

"Where did you guys sleep last night?" she asked and Raven told her what had happened.

"Well, we're in luck tonight too," she declared and pulled a credit card out of her pocketbook. "We'll be able to get a motel room."

"Whose card is that?" Crystal asked suspiciously.

"Mine," she said.

"I don't believe it," Crystal said.

Sunshine shrugged. She did have a hard shell. Nothing Crystal said could get to her.

"When it gets us the room, you'll believe it, Pollyanna."

"We should just sleep in the car," Crystal insisted.

"I don't know, Sunshine, we could get caught if you're using a stolen credit card," Raven said, and I could tell she was already worried about the few times I used Gordon's gas card.

"Well, I'm getting a room. If you all want to sleep in the car, go ahead," Sunshine said with a shrug. "You know, it's not exactly safe sleeping in a car," she added, looking back at Butterfly. "Someone could come along and steal the car with you in it!"

Butterfly's eyes nearly popped.

"That's ridiculous," Crystal said.

"So it's ridiculous. Learn the hard way if you want," Sunshine replied.

We drove on in silence, the sky darkening as storm clouds continued to drift over us. Finally, a motel came into view.

"This is a good enough place, not too busy. They'll be happy to see us. Let's get a room and get some pizza delivered," Sunshine said.

"I guess it will be okay," Raven said reluctantly. She looked at me. I glanced at Crystal, who was fuming, her arms folded across her chest, her face turned to the window.

"This is a democracy," I declared. "We'll vote. All in favor of stopping here for the night, say aye.'' Everyone but Crystal did. ''The aye's have it.''

''Since when does she vote for us?'' Crystal asked.

''She gets a vote. She's paying,'' Raven insisted.

''Do what you want,'' Crystal moaned.

I pulled into the motel entrance driveway and Sunshine stepped out. ''This won't take long,'' she said. We watched her go into the office.

''How can she have a credit card, Brooke? She has no permanent address. She stole it for sure and we're letting her use it,'' Crystal pointed out.

''She's signing everything, not us,'' Raven said.

''You're letting her take over. We're going to get into more and more trouble,'' Crystal predicted.

''We're on the road. We have to survive. I don't want to go back, do you?'' Raven challenged. ''Do you, Brooke?''

''Of course not,'' I said.

''Me neither,'' Butterfly said.

''Let her do something for us in return for picking her up,'' Raven concluded. It was obvious that Raven didn't want us to jump to conclusions about Sunshine—she believed everyone deserved a chance to prove themselves.

We watched the office door. After another five minutes, Sunshine emerged, smiling, holding up a room key. She got into the car.

''Drive over to 32,'' she said. ''Straight ahead.''

''There wasn't any problem?'' I asked.

''No. Why should there be?''

''You had identification?'' Crystal asked skeptically.

''Sure. I have lots of identification,'' Sunshine said with a laugh. She opened her bag and produced a few licenses, other credit cards and even a college I.D. The college I.D. had her picture on it.

''Where did you get all that?'' Raven asked.

''I.D.'s R Us. Where do you think?'' she replied with a laugh. ''Some of this friends got me. Some I got myself. If you're all nice, I'll tell you how to do it. And guess what, the clerk said there's a great pizza delivery place nearby. I can't wait to take a hot shower. Oh, the manager is willing to bring over a foldout cot. I guess you guys are used to sleeping together, so I'll use the cot.''

No one objected. Just as Sunshine had told us, the manager, a young, balding man followed, rolling a cot into the room. He handed Sunshine the extra bed linen.

"Thank you," she told him with a seductive smile. He smiled back. "See you later," she added.

"What's happening later?" I asked when he left.

"Nothing. I just promised him I'd meet him after work to have a drink in a nearby bar. Maybe I will," she said.

"But you said you promised," Butterfly reminded her.

She laughed.

"It won't be the first promise I broke or the last. Let's order the pizza. I'm starving."

We ordered two pies and some soft drinks. While we waited, we took turns showering. The pizza arrived and Crystal dug into our bank to pay. We had our feast, everyone talking at once, except Crystal, who was still upset. Afterward, we watched some television and then, just a little after eleven, Sunshine said she had decided to meet the manager as promised.

"I won't be long," she said. "Can I borrow the car keys, Brooke? I want to get my suitcase and put on something else."

Crystal looked at me with worry, so I followed Sunshine out and opened the car myself. She got the suitcase, brought it in and changed her skirt and tank top to a pair of jeans and a blue sweatshirt.

"I hope I'm not overdressed for this place," she said with a laugh. "Sleep tight, guys. I won't wake you when I come back," Sunshine promised and left.

"Good riddance," Crystal mumbled.

"Will you just let it go, Crystal. So far she's only given us good advice and helped us," Raven said.

The rain that had threatened to fall all day began, the drops tapping on the window and the roof, falling so hard it sounded more like hail.

"I hope she doesn't get caught in the storm," Raven said.

"It serves her right," Crystal answered.

"I'm exhausted," I said before they could get into another argument. I glanced at Butterfly, who was already asleep. "Don't wake Butterfly," I whispered.

Crystal turned off the lights.

"I like Sunshine," Raven whispered. "She's a little nuts, but she's fun, isn't she, Brooke?"

"Yes, but Crystal's right, too. We can't take her with us forever, Raven. I'm worried about how we're going to get rid of her down the road," I said.

As it turned out, we didn't have to worry about finding a way to part company with her.

We all fell asleep soon after we closed our eyes. When we opened them again, the first light of morning revealed Sunshine had never used her cot. The linen was still folded beside it. Raven was the first to notice when she sat up in bed.

"Look," she pointed, "Sunshine never came back last night!"

Crystal moaned and rose slowly. Butterfly sat up and I followed. Everyone stared at the unused cot for a moment.

"Wait a minute," Crystal said. "Her suitcase . . . wasn't it right there by the door?" she asked.

"Yes," I said.

"She came and took it and left us?" Raven said. "Why?"

Crystal shook her head.

"I don't know, but I'm happy and . . ."

Something else caught her eye. She gasped.

"What?" I cried.

Crystal moved so slowly across the room, I felt I was still dreaming. She lifted her blouse from the floor beside the chair where she had placed it and her skirt. Her purse was gone.

"Our money!" she cried and turned to me. "Brooke, all our money is gone!"

7

Just in the Nick of Time

*"I*t's all your fault!" Crystal screamed at Raven. "I told you we shouldn't pick her up, but you insisted. Now look," she shouted, pointing at the chair where her purse had been.

Raven's lips began to tremble and her eyes teared. She turned to me and then looked at Butterfly, who was sobbing hard, her arms wrapped around her body as if she were freezing. Her eyelids fluttered and then her sobbing stopped so suddenly I thought her vocal cords had snapped.

"Butterfly?" Raven said.

Butterfly fell back to the pillow, her eyes wide open, staring up at the ceiling, her mouth open too. She looked so scary. Her face was turning whiter every moment.

"Crystal! Something's happening to her," I cried and hopped off the bed.

"It's all right, Butterfly," I said, taking her hand. It felt so cold. "Crystal."

"Don't panic," she said in a controlled, deep voice. "If she hears your panic, she'll get even worse."

Raven stood behind us, waiting, her head down. Crystal turned to her.

"Get a cold washcloth," she ordered and Raven went to the bathroom. When she brought it back, Crystal put it on Butterfly's forehead. She patted her hand. "Come on, Butterfly. Don't drift off now. We need each other."

Raven bit down on her lower lip, embracing herself as if she were freezing too. We were all falling apart and fast. I moved quickly to put my arm around Butterfly and then carefully lifted her into a sitting position. Her eyes looked like they were rolling back in her head. Crystal came around the other side.

"What's wrong with her?" I asked Crystal.

"It's just another anxiety attack, a little more severe. Stay calm," she coaxed. She was really going to make one great doctor, I thought. "Quickly," she said to Raven who crawled up on the bed. She put her head down and met Crystal's and mine. We brought Butterfly closer until she touched gently and then Crystal started, "We're sisters. We'll always be sisters. What happens to one, happens to all."

Raven chanted along with me and soon our voices melded into one voice, one hope, one prayer. I felt Butterfly's taut body soften. Her skin became warmer. Soon, we heard her voice along with ours.

"We'll always be sisters. When one is sad, we'll all be sad. When one is happy, we'll all be happy."

The four of us separated and Butterfly blinked her eyes rapidly, looking from one face to another.

"What's going to happen to us?" she asked as if time had stopped, as if the attack had never happened.

"You scared us to death," Raven said shakily.

"I did?"

"Forget about it, Raven," Crystal advised, giving her those big eyes.

Raven, still smarting from Crystal's accusations, was quick to listen. Butterfly looked from one of us to the other, confused.

"What will we do, Brooke?" she asked me. I had no answers and neither did Raven nor Crystal. Then Crystal went to her clothes.

"We're going to have to go back," she said.

"No!" Raven cried. "I won't go back."

"I don't want to go back either," Butterfly said.

I didn't say anything. Crystal was probably right, I thought. We couldn't live off a gas credit card and soon, Gordon would get his bill and put a stop to that anyway.

"You think I want to go back? Remember what Gordon did to me," Crystal said, "but I don't see as we have much choice now. At least with that money, we had something of a budget. Now, we have nothing."

"I've got two dollars," Raven said.

"I think I have a few dollars, too," Butterfly said.

"We all have a few dollars. Pool it and what do you get, ten dollars? How far is that going to get us?" She sounded defeated.

"Crystal's right. All we have now is some clothing in pillowcases.

It's ridiculous to think we could drive across the whole country with that.''

"We can't go back," Raven pleaded.

No one spoke for a while. We all got dressed, used the bathroom and then left the room. Raven stood on the sidewalk, holding her pillowcase of clothing, looking miserable as the three of us got into the vehicle.

"Raven, don't be ridiculous," I said. "We'll go back and we'll think of something else."

"No, we won't. If we go back, Gordon will make our lives a living hell—that is, if the state doesn't separate us and make us live somewhere worse than the Lakewood House." She started to sniffle. "It's all my fault. I thought Sunshine was just like us; that she deserved a chance."

"She took our money, Raven. No one's blaming you. We all bear some responsibility. I let her in the car, too. Just get into the car, please."

"Get in, Raven," Butterfly begged. "We can't leave without you."

"I'm sorry I yelled at you, Raven," Crystal said. "I can't blame you for wanting to help someone out."

Raven gazed at Crystal and then softened. She looked down the row of motel rooms and then back at us.

"You know Gordon will probably have us arrested," she said as she reluctantly got into the station wagon. "We should drive awhile to see if we can find Sunshine. I'll make her give us our money back."

"We won't find her," Crystal said. "Now that she has our money, she won't be hitchhiking, I'm sure."

"How could she do this to us? She knew we were just like her!" Raven cried as I drove out of the motel parking lot.

"We're not just like her. We're better off than she is, Raven. She's alone. We've got each other. How do you think she's going to end up? She'll probably die in some dark alley somewhere," Crystal predicted.

"Which way?" I asked when I got to the road.

Crystal referred to her maps.

"It looks like we should continue west for about twenty miles. We'll pick up the entrance to one of the main highways and take our chances. Now that we're going back, it won't matter if we get stopped anyway," she decided.

The funereal atmosphere I had felt earlier yesterday was like a happy celebration compared to the mood we were all in today. Compounding it was the heavy overcast sky. It began to sprinkle and then rain harder.

It rained so hard at one point, I had to stop and pull over to the side of the road.

"I hope she did try to hitch a ride and she's out there caught in this," Raven mumbled. Then she sighed and slumped in her seat as the water gushed over the windshield and down the sides of the station wagon.

"I'm hungry," Butterfly said. "Won't we stop to get some breakfast somewhere?"

"I don't have any money," Crystal said. "Brooke, how much do you have exactly?"

"Just some change. Maybe ninety cents. You had everything in your purse."

"We could share something," Butterfly suggested.

"And then what do we do about lunch and supper? We have to travel a few days to get back," Crystal said. "Maybe we should turn ourselves in to the police."

No one spoke. Every moment that ticked away seemed to be bringing us closer and closer to a disaster even worse than we had imagined. Finally, the rain slowed down until it was just a fine sprinkle, but it was still windy.

"I feel like such a fool," I said. "Why didn't I realize what she was like?"

"Don't," Crystal commanded.

I looked at her in the mirror. Her face was firm. She was right, of course. I hated self-pity and despised it in other people. It made me feel that much worse to hear myself moan and groan.

Raven suddenly sat up.

"Listen. I have an idea. Once when I was with Dede and we were with Charlie Weiner, we didn't have enough money for cold drinks and Charlie thought about pulling up the back seat to look for loose change. Maybe we'll find some now," she said.

"What good is some more loose change?" Crystal asked.

"At least it will get us some breakfast. I'm hungry, too, Crystal," she said. "And we'll have some time to think," she added, turning to me.

I shrugged.

"So we'll pull up the back seat," I said.

She and I got out and opened the doors. Crystal and Butterfly stepped out and Raven and I dug our fingers into the rear of the seat and pulled up. It came out easily and there we saw a few dollars worth of change, but we also saw something else.

"What's that?" I asked. I didn't touch it. Raven reached down slowly as Crystal looked over her shoulder and Butterfly looked over mine.

It was a heavy clear plastic bag filled with what looked like white flour. Raven opened the bag slowly and put her finger in. She looked at me as she scooped up the powder and brought some to her lips. Her eyes widened.

"It's cocaine!" she declared, holding up the bag. "And a lot of it."

"Cocaine?" Crystal said. "Are you sure?"

"I'm sure. I've seen it before," Raven said. "My mother and her boyfriends used to leave some around our apartment. This is worth a lot of money."

"Gordon must have been selling it," I said. It started to rain harder again, but none of us seemed to care. "Now I understand what he was doing when I saw him with someone at the station wagon late at night. I bet that was his supplier or a customer."

"You did?" Butterfly asked.

"Yes, a few times. I thought he saw me watching him from the window last night and I got scared," I said. "Wow, cocaine." My mind reeled. "And we've been driving around with it stashed right under us."

"Yes, and across state lines, too. Let's get rid of it right away," Crystal said.

Raven started to heave it.

"Wait," Crystal said. Raven hesitated.

"You want to keep it?"

"No. Give it to me," she said. Raven handed it to her. Crystal opened the bag. "We can't just throw it on the side of the road like this. Someone else might find it and sell it, even to kids, and we'd be responsible." She walked away from the car.

"What are you doing?" Raven cried.

Crystal shook the bag into the wind. The powder flowed out and began to spread on the ground. The rain started to dissolve it quickly.

"Hurry up before someone comes and sees this," I cried.

Crystal shook harder. A small white cloud appeared and then thinned out and was gone in the wind along with most of the powder. Crystal walked a few feet deeper off the road and put the bag under a rock.

"Let's go," she called as a car appeared coming toward us.

We fixed the rear seat and everyone got back into the wagon. I started driving away as the approaching vehicle slowed. A man and woman gazed at us. They looked about fifty or so. They didn't stop, however. I watched them in my rearview mirror.

"I hope we're never sorry we did that," Raven whined.

"We'll be sorry about a great many things we've done," Crystal assured her, "but never about that."

"Wait a minute," I said as we continued to drive on. "We can't go back now."

"Why not?" Crystal asked.

"Gordon might not kill us for taking his car, but dumping his drugs . . ."

"Brooke's right, Crystal. There's no telling what he might do to us," Raven said.

Crystal was silent.

"We could go to the police," she said.

"They're going to ask why we didn't come to them when we had the drugs in our hands," Raven said.

"We should have," Crystal said mournfully. She looked back through the rearview window as if there were some way we could return to the spot and put the cocaine back into the plastic bag. "We're really in deep water," she said. "We just better keep running until we think of something else to do."

Together with the change we had found under the seat, we had a little more than eleven dollars. My stomach was growling, too, so when we saw a sign advertising the Crossroads Restaurant, I turned off the highway.

"I just hope it's not an expensive place," Crystal said.

When we set eyes on it, we didn't think it would be. It wasn't run-down, but it looked unpretentious: a restaurant in a building that might have once been someone's home. There was a parking lot in front, two gas pumps, and the road sign advertising, CROSSROADS RESTAURANT, EAT HERE AND GET GAS.

"I hope that isn't a comment on the food," Raven quipped. Crystal and I laughed.

We saw a large trailer home to the right of the restaurant with a sick patch of lawn and a run-down mower in front. Behind the restaurant there was a small cottage, the front windows boarded up, a drainpipe dangling from the right side of the roof. There were a half dozen other cars and three pickup trucks in the parking lot when we pulled up. The screen door was open and we could hear the sound of country music being played inside.

"What do you think?" I asked.

"Beggars can't be choosers," Crystal answered cheerily. I could tell she was trying to make everyone feel better.

We all got out and entered the restaurant. It wasn't as small inside as we thought. There were tables on the right and left but no booths. Directly in front of us was a counter with very worn-looking black vinyl–covered stainless-steel stools, and behind it was the kitchen, wide open to view. A short, thin black man with two patches of stark white hair on the sides of his head was cooking over a grill. He gazed up with some interest and then went back to his griddle cakes, eggs and bacon, and muffins, all of which filled the air with delicious aromas. My stomach did flip-flops in anticipation and from the looks on the faces of Crystal, Butterfly and Raven, theirs did, too.

A tall woman with drab-looking dark brown hair that had dull gray strands woven through worked the counter and apparently was the only waitress. Her eyes looked watery, bloodshot, and tired, which fit her ashen complexion. She wasn't stout, but she had large upper arms. Her full bosom strained the tight white blouse, which had the top two buttons undone, divulging a deep cleavage. I could see it was a sight not missed by her customers, all males. Her black skirt was tight, so tight that her hipbone was embossed on both sides. She paused, put her hands on her waist and gazed at us.

"If you're here to eat something, find a seat yourselves," she ordered.

The customers, all looking our way, smiled. One man stuffed his face with an egg-soaked piece of bread as he watched us go to a table.

"Looks like you should go wake Danny, Patsy. This is a real morning rush, huh?" he said.

"You go wake him. Might as well try to wake the dead," she muttered. Everyone laughed.

"I can wake him for you," a tall, well-built man of about forty claimed. He was sitting at a table. It was apparent that the place was small enough and the customers familiar enough with each other to participate in everyone's conversations.

"If you were the one to wake him, Gordy, I know he wouldn't be any good to me ever," she replied.

"That's not much of a loss. He's not any good to you now," Gordy responded and everyone smiled or laughed again.

"Don't remind me," she said, turning to take a plate of hot cakes from the cook and then slap it down in front of a customer at the counter. She wiped her hands on a dishtowel and came around the corner to us. She had no menus in her hands, but seemed to know immediately what I was thinking. "Breakfast menu's on the wall," she said, nodding to a blackboard on the left.

Everything was cheap enough, but if the four of us ordered something each, we wouldn't have enough money. Crystal studied the board.

"What are you girls doing out this way?" she asked, looking from me to Butterfly and then to Raven and Crystal.

"We're traveling," I said, "and saw your sign."

"Told you it pays to advertise," the man called Gordy shouted. Some of the customers at the counter laughed.

"Shut your face," she told him. "I have real business here."

He laughed harder. She turned back to us.

"Can we get one order of pancakes, two eggs, two large orange juices and two coffees?" Crystal asked.

"For all of you?"

"Yes, ma'am," she said.

The woman stared.

"How much money do you have?" she asked sharply.

"Enough for that," Crystal replied.

"That's not what I asked," she snapped. Crystal held her gaze for a moment and then looked at our money.

"We have eleven dollars and forty-three cents," she told her.

"Total?"

"Yes, ma'am," Crystal said.

"How far are you going?" she asked. Raven started to squirm in her seat. Butterfly looked more terrified.

"We're supposed to get to California eventually," I said, "but we were robbed last night and that's all we have."

"No kidding?" she asked, scratching her head. "How were you robbed?"

"Someone we trusted took our money while we were sleeping," I said.

"Damn," she said. "And so you have only eleven dollars left, huh?"

"And forty-three cents," Crystal corrected.

"Right, forty-three cents." She sighed deeply and shook her head. "Just call me Mrs. Soft Touch," she declared, turning toward the cook. "Charlie, four pancake specials." The cook nodded.

"But we can't afford that," Crystal said anxiously.

"No one leaves Patsy's place hungry," she replied. "It's a rule of the house."

She returned to the counter. We watched her pour four glasses of juice for us.

"That's very nice of her," Raven said warily. Raven wasn't about to trust a stranger again so quickly.

Two more customers arrived and before we got our food, three more customers followed. Patsy was very busy. I saw the cook put our plates up.

"I'm going to help her," I said, getting up from the table.

"What?" Raven said.

Patsy was taking an order but saw me move behind the counter. She didn't complain as I picked up the plates and began bringing them back to our table. I had worked as a waitress before and knew how to carry four plates. I served the girls and sat.

"This is good," Raven said between bites.

"Very good," Butterfly said. "The eggs are just like I like them, too."

Patsy had to take orders, work the counter and bus the tables. Her restaurant obviously had a good reputation with the local people despite the slow service because more customers arrived and all seemed to know her. Everyone looked patient, but eager. I ate quickly and then rose again before the girls had finished.

"What are you doing?" Crystal asked.

"Helping her," I said. I began to clear the dishes off the tables where customers had left. I found the tray for dirty glasses and dishes behind the counter and beside it, a clean wet rag with which to wipe down the tables. As soon as Raven was finished, she rose and began to do the same.

Patsy stood by smiling at us and shaking her head.

"Got new hired help?" someone asked.

"Looks like it," she replied with a half-smile.

When we had cleared the empty tables, we began to set the tables with clean silverware. A young man with red-gold hair complimented Raven on her waitressing abilities and I could tell from her shy smile and quiet "Thank you" that she was flattered.

"Thanks for jumping in," Patsy said as she hurried by me with an order.

"Should I see if anyone wants seconds on coffee?" I asked her after she shouted another order at the cook. She stared at me a moment.

"You work restaurants before?"

"Yes, ma'am, summers," I told her.

"Okay," she said. "Thanks." She went to deliver another order and I followed, offering coffee. Crystal sat astounded and Butterfly looked at us with a beaming smile.

"We could use more help," I told Crystal. "Raven seems occupied." The young man had asked for more coffee and was lavishing praise on Raven. She looked a little uncomfortable but kind of interested at the same time.

Finally, the place began to empty and Patsy was able to catch up on her work. The breakfast rush was over. She gave a man coffee at the counter and then walked over to Crystal and me.

"How come you girls are on the road by yourselves?" Patsy asked.

"We were heading out to California to visit my aunt for two weeks," Crystal said. "We all go to the same school back in New York and our parents gave us money for the trip. It was supposed to be a summer adventure. Now, we have to turn back," she said sadly.

"When were you supposed to be in California?" Patsy asked.

"It didn't matter. We could take our time. We had the whole summer," I added, embellishing Crystal's imaginative concoction. It was funny how I always thought of Crystal as telling creative stories rather than lies. I guess it was because I knew she had no meanness in her, no real deceit. She always looked as if she enjoyed making up the lies as much as she would enjoy making up a story for English class.

"We made the mistake of picking up a girl hitchhiker yesterday and she robbed us," Crystal continued, mixing the truth with fantasy.

"I see," Patsy said, shaking her head.

She looked at two of the tables where customers had left tips.

"Some of that money is yours, girls," she said.

"Oh no. You gave us food. We can't take that," I said.

She laughed and thought a moment as we watched Raven say goodbye to the young man she had been talking to all this time.

"Well, if your aunt can wait a few more weeks for you, I could use some help here and you can earn enough money to get to California," she said. "I have a cottage behind the restaurant you four can use. It's not much. You'll have to fix it up some, but I can give you fresh towels and linen. It was once used for travelers," she added. "Back when my husband was alive."

"What happened to him?" Crystal asked.

"He was killed in a car crash, drunk driver. You heard mention of my son Danny. He's not much help here, I'm afraid. He's been a handful ever since Eddie was killed. Charlie there has been our cook for over ten years.''

"That's right," Charlie said, smiling. "You girls were really good out there. Real professional.''

"This was once a pretty busy little place before they built the new highway. In those days we could afford a full staff of waiters and waitresses. I had a counterman, too. I can't pay you much, but you can make some good tips and have free room and board. This is a busy time of the year for me, the busiest," she added.

"We can do that, can't we, Crystal?''

Raven joined us.

"Do what?''

"Stay here and work a few weeks to earn back the money we lost last night," I said and hoped Raven wouldn't say anything to contradict our story.

"Really? Oh, that would be great," she said, looking dreamily out the window. Suddenly she caught herself staring and shook her head. "I don't know what's wrong with me. I think I'll go splash some cold water on my face. I'm feeling hot all of a sudden. This waitressing stuff is harder than I remembered.''

"What's that all about?" Crystal wondered aloud.

Butterfly, who was looking out the window, turned to us. "Who is that man, Patsy?" she asked.

"Taylor Cummings," Patsy answered with a scowl. "He doesn't miss a pretty face. Tell Raven to be careful—that boy's a wild one," Patsy advised.

"You don't have to worry about Raven. She looks like a knockout, but she knows enough when someone is giving her a line," Crystal replied. Usually I would have agreed with her, but suddenly, I wasn't so sure.

"Yeah, but Raven acted different with this guy . . .'' I murmured, more to myself than anyone else.

"Well, then, let's go see how bad the cottage is," Patsy said. "Charlie, keep an eye on things. I'll be right back.''

"Yes, ma'am," he replied and came around from the kitchen.

When we walked out of the restaurant, Raven came hurrying over. We watched her new male friend pull away in his truck.

"Are we staying for sure?" she asked. That was definitely hope I heard in her voice.

"We'll see," I said, gazing at her closely. "We're going to look at the cottage and then we're going to get ready to do some work," I added.

Although the cottage was small, it had a bedroom with two single beds and a pull-out sofa that would sleep two. There wasn't much of a kitchen, just a nook with a sink and a small stove. The refrigerator looked broken, the door dangling open. Since we wouldn't be cooking anything anyway, that didn't matter. The bathroom was tiny, too, but it had a small tub and a shower head on a hose that connected to the faucet. There were rust stains around all the drains and rings around the sink and the tub. The whole place had a musty odor. There were cobwebs in almost every corner and dust coated everything.

"Looks a little worse than I thought," Patsy muttered.

"It's not so bad," Raven said quickly. "We can stay here, can't we, Brooke? We'll roll up our sleeves and make it look like a palace in no time."

"We'll manage," I agreed. "Crystal?"

"Let's talk about it," she said.

"Oh, I understand, honey," Patsy said. "You girls discuss it and come back to the restaurant when you've decided one way or another."

As soon as she left us, Raven turned on Crystal.

"Why did you say that? This is a chance to stay free," she cried.

"If we look too anxious, she'll get suspicious," Crystal said softly. "Why would four girls from homes that could afford to send them to California on a summer trip put up with this?" she asked, her arms out.

"We were just robbed. That's why!" Raven replied.

"Well-to-do people could wire the money to get us home or even to California, Raven. Don't push it." She studied the scene and thought while Raven waited anxiously.

"I think we could sleep here all right," Butterfly said.

"Of course we could," Raven said, eying Crystal. "Didn't we almost sleep in the car the other night?"

"Okay," Crystal said. "We'll do it. We'll make it seem as if this is all part of an adventure for us, but don't say anything to her that might make her suspicious about us, Raven."

"I won't say a word," she promised, her right hand raised.

Crystal nodded and then looked at me.

"Maybe this will work out for us. Maybe our luck is changing," she said. "Let's decide who takes the pull-out."

"Butterfly and me," Raven said quickly.

"Raven snores," Butterfly complained.

"I do not."

"I'll sleep on the pull-out with Raven," I said, eying her. I was determined to get to the bottom of Raven's strange new mood.

The four of us returned to the restaurant to tell Patsy we had decided to take up her offer. When we entered, there was a long-haired boy of about nineteen slumped over a steaming cup of coffee at the counter. He wore a Grateful Dead sweatshirt that looked as if it had died and been resurrected because it was so shredded and faded, and a pair of jeans and dirty sneakers with no socks.

"Here they are," Patsy said and he turned.

"We'd like to stay, Patsy," I said.

"Good. This is my son Danny," she said, her smile stiffening into a look of disapproval.

He squinted, squeezing his hazel eyes into slits, and then smirking rather than smiling at us, as if he was disappointed in either what he saw or what he had heard. He had a soft mouth with a lower lip that appeared swollen, and a small cut on his chin. He had Patsy's nose, a little broader at the bridge, but his ears were larger and came more to a point at the tops.

Danny wasn't fat or physically impressive, but he did have the beginnings of a beer belly. There was no question he wouldn't win any contests, unless it was a contest to choose the least hygienic looking man under twenty-five.

"You could say hello, Danny," Patsy urged.

"Hello," he muttered and turned back to his coffee. "What the hell are they going to do?" he asked her.

"Mostly what you should be doing," she replied. "Come along, girls, and I'll get you some linen and things to use to clean up the place. Danny, could you pull the boards off the cottage windows, please?"

He grunted.

She shook her head sadly and we followed her to the trailer. The moment she opened the door, she began a string of apologies. Danny had his clothes strewn about, empty beer cans, cigarette butts, and dirty dishes on the kitchen table. She made an attempt to pick up some of it.

"I begged him to clean up before he came out today. He had some of his friends over last night. Late," she added. She groaned and put her hand on her lower back as she straightened up after getting a beer can off the floor. "Be right back," she said, going farther into the trailer.

Crystal looked at me and shook her head.

"Why is he so mean to his mother?" Butterfly asked.

"What he needs is a good kick in the rear end," I mumbled.

Patsy brought us sheets, towels and a pail with cleaning liquids. She gave Raven the mop and some sponges.

"Let me know what else you need. About four, we'll get ready for the dinner crowd. We've been getting a pretty good one lately," she said. "Well," she added, "welcome to the Crossroads, girls."

We were at a crossroad, I thought—a place to catch our breath and decide if we were just fooling ourselves with our dreams or if we were really halfway toward finding a real home.

8

In Sickness
and in Health

*S*ince both Raven and I had experience working as waitresses, we decided that for the first day or so at least, Crystal and Butterfly would be in charge of cleaning up the cottage. Danny had grudgingly removed the boards from the windows and we realized immediately that we'd need curtains or shades. I improvised using towels so we would have some privacy and keep the sunshine from waking us too early in the morning, although getting ready for the breakfast crowd meant we'd usually be up before the sun anyway.

Raven was the first to grumble about the early hour, though we all wanted to crawl back under our sheets and warm blankets. "It's turning out that we're worse off being free!" she exclaimed.

Crystal started to laugh and then stopped, put on her schoolteacher face, and told Raven that real freedom meant responsibility, not only for yourself, but often for someone else.

"I know, I know, I just wish we could sleep in a little longer," she said with a yawn.

Crystal looked at me as if to say, "I tried," then dropped the subject. Whether we liked it or not, we would be up very early every morning for as long as we stayed.

Charlie was always there before daylight, making fresh pancake batter, grits, oatmeal and coffee. He could make some wonderful omelettes, too; and from what we quickly learned, his reputation as a cook was, along with the attractive prices, what kept Patsy's following consistent and loyal.

"You girls are a breath of fresh air," he told us. "I ain't seen Patsy

109

this bright and cheery for a long time. Lately," he added, "she ain't had all that much to make her bright and cheery."

Hanging around Charlie, you would never know there was any doom and gloom about the place. No matter how busy we got or how flustered one of us became, Charlie was always cheerful and lighthearted. He was easy to work with, patient and friendly. He never lost his temper when one or the other of us would mix up an order, but I did see his eyes grow darker and the smile leave his face whenever Danny appeared. Danny didn't speak to him with any respect either. He always made demands rather than requests and he never thanked Charlie, or anyone for that matter.

That first night we all ate dinner early. I asked Patsy where Danny was. She didn't know and I was sorry I had asked. It brought darkness to her eyes. By the time we were ready to greet our dinner customers, Danny appeared. He wasn't exactly cleaned up, but he had changed his shirt to a newer, fresher-looking tee shirt with the words *Lions 5, Christians 0* on the front, and a pair of less faded and grubby-looking jeans. He wore the same grungy sneakers and no socks. Some attempt had been made to brush his hair back and he had shaved.

Not only had he avoided all the dinner preparations, but it was quickly apparent that he wasn't there to work.

"It doesn't look like you'll need me here tonight, Ma. I'm going out with Terry and Mark," he announced. Before Patsy could respond, he added, "I need ten bucks."

He marched right to the register, took out a ten, glared my way, and then closed it.

Okay?" he said to Patsy.

She wiped a dish and looked down.

"Where are you going, Danny?"

"I said out," he replied. "Out's out. Right?" he said, challenging me.

"Well, there's far out, there's out of the way and there's out of your mind," I responded.

Raven laughed.

"Very funny," he said. "Remind me to laugh."

"Is your memory that gone?" I countered.

He glared and then marched out of the restaurant. When I looked back at Charlie, I saw a wide smile on his face, but Patsy looked despondent.

"We'll be all right, Patsy," I told her. "If it gets too busy, I'll send for Crystal."

"I'm not worried," she said. "I've often had to do it all. Just me and Charlie manning the old fort, right, Charlie?"

"Yes, ma'am," he said, "and we ain't had no one leave unsatisfied. That's the truth," Charlie told us.

The customers began to stream in. Charlie's meat loaf was the favorite choice. Patsy had it up as the night's special, but from what we heard that was always the night's special and rightly so. It was delicious. To our amazement, the restaurant filled up within the first half hour. Crystal and Butterfly saw what was happening and came rushing over. I told Patsy Crystal could work the register if she liked. She thought that was fine. Butterfly pitched in busing tables, and soon we had things well under control.

However, Raven quickly found herself the object of attention and began to feed off it, stopping at tables to flirt and talk. Taylor Cummings, who had attracted her attention earlier in the day and asked her for a date, reappeared. Now that I looked at him more closely, I saw he was a good-looking man of about twenty-five with long, reddish-blond hair and impish blue eyes. I had to admit that his smile could melt ice.

Patsy stepped beside me to whisper.

"They call him The Love Dozer because he's crushed so many young hearts. Tell Raven to be very careful," she warned.

I couldn't think of a more futile thing than trying to advise Raven when it came to love and romance. Every time I passed by her, I commented on how busy it was and how we sure could use some help.

"Be right there," she kept saying, but it was as if Taylor Cummings held her in orbit. Even when she left his table, she was drawn back to him repeatedly.

"He's coming back for me in an hour," she told me when he finally paid his check and left the restaurant. "We're going dancing," she declared.

"You don't know him. How can you go out on a date with a complete stranger?" I turned to Crystal for help, but she simply shook her head. "Raven?"

"I'll be all right," she assured me. "I've been out with strangers before, Brooke."

"But we're on the road, Raven. We're . . . helpless."

"Maybe you're helpless," she said with a cold, arrogant smile, "but when it comes to men, I'm not, not ever."

There really wasn't anything else to do. I put it out of my mind.

By the end of the evening, Patsy was getting tons of compliments on how smoothly and quickly the dinner hours had gone. Looking at the receipts, she said because they were able to turn over more tables, they had made more money that evening than they had in a very long time.

"You girls are a blessing from heaven!" she declared.

After the last customer left and we were alone, we all sat at a table, resting and having some of Charlie's apple pie. Patsy felt the need to apologize for Danny's behavior earlier.

"I'm really at my wit's end about what to do about him. I know he's headed for serious trouble."

"Danny's suffering from a low self-image," Crystal began. Patsy looked up at her and I thought, uh oh, here we go. "I don't know what his relationship with his father was like, but you told us that he became more of a problem after your husband's death. He probably felt inadequate, unable to fill your husband's shoes and be half the man he was. Rather than struggle with the anxiety, he gave up and went completely in the opposite direction, giving in to his weaknesses in order to live with them, so to speak," Crystal lectured. "It's a classic psychological defense mechanism, especially in teenagers."

Patsy stared at her with her mouth agape.

"How do you know so much?" she asked.

"Crystal's a genius," Butterfly declared with pride.

"She was first in her class and probably would have been class valedictorian," Raven added.

"What do you mean, probably would have been?" Patsy asked quickly. If she didn't catch the way we shifted our eyes, she had the perception of a stone, I thought.

"She means probably will be," Crystal corrected. "Don't you, Raven?"

"Oh, yes." Raven offered, laughing nervously. "I always make mistakes with grammar. If it wasn't for Crystal's help, I would fail English every year."

Patsy, however, still studied the four of us with a little more suspicion.

"Did you call your folks and let them know where you'll be for a while?"

"Yes," Crystal said, jumping into the role of spokesman. "We didn't exactly tell them we had been robbed though," she added. Hearing Crystal confess to a little deception appeared to go a long way at easing Patsy's doubts about us. She smiled the smile of understanding.

"Well, I expect you girls will make back that money pretty quickly here. How'd you all do?"

"I made forty-one dollars," I said.

"I made thirty-three," Raven said. I saw she was wondering why I had made more.

"Just do less talking and more working," I joked. Raven smiled sheepishly.

"Well now, that's good, and with the wages I'm paying you two," she said to Crystal and Butterfly, "you won't have to wait too long to be on your way again. I can see I'll miss you, so maybe I should hope for slow days."

We laughed along with her, but deep inside ourselves, it wasn't funny; it wasn't cute. If she only knew how much we needed to be wanted like this, she'd understand why it wasn't something we took lightly.

Suddenly, we heard a horn beeping outside. Raven jumped to her feet.

"That must be Taylor!" she cried, throwing off her apron as she went to the door. "It is him! You guys won't really worry if I go, will you? I'll be fine. Honest." She was so happy none of us wanted to burst her bubble.

When I saw the look of grave concern on Patsy's face, though, I knew I had to warn Raven, even if it meant she'd be angry with me. I ran outside and called out to her before she reached Taylor's truck.

"What's wrong?" she asked.

"You better be extra careful, Raven. Patsy says that Taylor is a ladies' man."

Disappointment darkened her face. "No, I don't believe it. He's been so nice, nicer than other boys I've dated."

"But he's not a boy, he's a man, Raven, and Patsy wouldn't lie."

She thought about that for a minute. "You're right, she wouldn't. But I have to give myself the chance to find out. Why is it so hard for everyone to believe that someone could actually be interested in *me,* not just in my looks?" Her voice caught in her throat and she turned to run the rest of the way to the truck.

Late that night Raven returned to our little cottage, where all of us were up and waiting anxiously. We all let out a collective breath when we saw the tiny smile on Raven's face as she came through the door.

"Hey, what are all you worrywarts doing up? I thought we left curfew behind at Lakewood House," she joked.

"We just wanted to make sure you were okay, that Taylor hadn't been a jerk or anything," Crystal spoke up for us all.

"Well you can all go to sleep now, because Taylor was a perfect gentleman, just like I knew he would be. He likes me. For real. And I really like him too." Humming softly, Raven walked into the bathroom and began to wash up for bed.

Crystal, Butterfly and I all looked at each other and shrugged our shoulders. As it turned out, Taylor Cummings wasn't a problem. Yet.

Early the next morning, even before the sun lit up the makeshift curtains I had improvised, I heard Butterfly's moaning. Crystal was in a deep sleep and apparently hadn't heard. I knew Raven could have a fire truck roar past her bed and she wouldn't even flutter her eyelashes, especially after coming in so late. I listened again and heard the moan repeated, only deeper and longer. I rose and walked over to the bed.

"Butterfly?"

She coughed.

"My eyes ache," she told me.

Crystal stirred. I turned on the lamp. As soon as my eyes grew accustomed to the light, I gasped.

"Crystal!"

"What?" She sat up quickly and looked down at Butterfly. Her nose was running, she was grimacing with pain, but her cheeks were blotched red. Crystal put her palm on Butterfly's forehead. "She's burning up," she told me.

"Wha . . . what's happening?" Raven called. "It can't be time to get up. It just can't be."

"Butterfly's sick," I shouted and turned to Crystal. "What's wrong with her?"

Butterfly coughed again and sniffed. Without replying, Crystal went to the bathroom and wet down a washcloth. She brought it back and put it on Butterfly's forehead.

"Where does it hurt, Butterfly?" she asked quietly.

Raven appeared in the doorway, finally realizing what was happening around her.

"What is it? What's wrong with her?"

"My eyes hurt," Butterfly said. "Here," she added indicating where they ached.

Crystal opened Butterfly's shirt and looked at her chest and stomach.

"Do you know what's wrong with her?" I asked.

114

"I think so," Crystal said.

"What?" Raven demanded impatiently.

Crystal looked at us. "I think she's got the measles."

"The measles! Oh no," Raven said. And then her eyes filled with fear. "Will we all get it?"

"I won't. I had it."

"So did I," I said. "Raven?"

"I'm not sure. I can't remember if it was the measles or the chicken pox," she said in a panic.

"If you get it, you get it," Crystal said stoically. "You're better off getting it over with," she added.

"But isn't it a kid's disease?"

"No," Crystal said. "Adults can get measles if they never had them as children."

Butterfly moaned again.

"I don't feel good," she cried.

"What do we do, Crystal?" I asked.

"There isn't much to do. Keep her comfortable, get some acetaminophen . . ."

"What's that?" Raven asked.

"It's just Tylenol."

"Well, why don't you just say what it is then?" she said.

"That's what it is," Crystal replied coolly.

"Stop arguing about it. We don't have any, do we?" I asked.

"Maybe Patsy does," Crystal said. "She should be up in about an hour."

"Do you think she'll make us leave?" Raven asked. "Do we have to tell her?"

"I don't think she would do that," I said. "What do you think, Crystal?"

She considered while Butterfly squirmed with her discomfort, coughed and sniveled before moaning.

"She might want us to take her to a doctor and that could create problems," Crystal said. "Maybe Raven's right. Maybe we shouldn't tell Patsy anything just yet, Brooke. We'll just say she's got a headache and a little cold. If she comes in here and sees Butterfly like this she's liable to figure out it's the measles."

I nodded.

"Being a mother herself, she probably went through this with Danny boy," I said. "But do you think it could be something else, Crystal?" I asked. "Something more serious?"

"We'll have to watch and see. If it is . . . that's it," she added. "Once we take her to a hospital emergency room or a doctor, we have to have a guardian or parent."

"Oh no," Raven spoke for us all.

"We'll need a thermometer so we can watch her fever," Crystal continued. "If it goes up too high . . ."

"Why don't I get dressed and look for a drugstore," I offered.

"It's too early, but sometimes gas stations with convenience stores sell Tylenol," Crystal said.

"I'll go looking around," I said, happy to be able to do something to help Butterfly.

After I washed my face and dressed, I left and went looking for an open store. The sun was coming up now. It was really the best part of the day. I imagined the earth itself opening its eyes, greeting the warm kiss of light, shedding the blanket of shadows, drinking in the radiance. The small village nearby was still waking up; all I saw in the streets were a few wandering dogs, sniffing around for breakfast. On the other side of the village, however, there was a self-service gas station and inside the little office area were coin operated machines that contained aspirin and Tylenol as well as stomach antacids.

Good old Crystal, I thought. She predicted it. She was really a very smart person and it gave me confidence and a sense of security to have someone with her thinking power in our little family. I had faith in her diagnosis of Butterfly, too. She wanted to be a doctor more than anything and spent most of her leisure hours studying as if she were already in medical school. Her appetite for knowledge never ended.

By the time I returned, Patsy and Charlie had started working in the restaurant. Crystal had gotten Raven to go over there first, so Patsy wouldn't think anything was amiss. One thing about Crystal, she was always anticipating potential trouble. The tragedy of Sunshine was the best example I would ever have, I thought. I wouldn't ignore her warnings again.

I brought in the Tylenol and she gave Butterfly two tablets.

"She isn't going to be all that hungry, but we'll bring her juice and fluids to drink all morning," she said. "For now, let's get to the restaurant. You go and I'll follow. I want to make Butterfly as comfortable as I can before I leave. I want to sponge her down and see if I can help reduce her fever, too."

"Right, Doc," I said and Crystal smiled and then looked very serious. "This could be it, Brooke."

"I know, but Butterfly's health is the most important thing."

Patsy was curious about Butterfly, of course, but when Crystal arrived, she did a good job of making Butterfly's problems sound insignificant.

"She's been fighting a cold for days. I told her bed rest, lots of liquids and some hot oatmeal would help," Crystal said as if she had already acquired the medical degree she dreamed of having.

Patsy nodded, looking from her to me and Raven.

"It's very nice the way you girls look after each other. It's almost as if you've been together for years and years," she remarked. "You're more like sisters than friends."

I nearly gave it away when she said that. I had to look down quickly.

Crystal didn't want to ask her for a thermometer. She was afraid that might stir up her concern, so as soon as the breakfast rush was over, I went back to town, stopped at a drugstore and bought one.

When we took her temperature, we found Butterfly had a fever of a hundred and one. By the late afternoon, it went to a hundred and two.

"And that's with Tylenol," Crystal reminded us. "She's having a hard time."

Crystal and I continued to sponge Butterfly down. Raven was terrified of getting too close to her and continued to shiver with the thought that she would soon be following in Butterfly's footsteps. She racked her brain trying to remember if she'd had measles, but she just couldn't remember.

"You should probably stay away just in case, Raven," Crystal warned her. "We can't afford to have both of you get sick."

Suddenly, we heard a knock on the door. Everyone froze.

"It's Patsy!" I said peering through the improvised curtains.

Crystal told Butterfly to turn over on her side and pretend to be in a deep sleep. Then she opened the door.

"How's she doing?" Patsy asked.

"She's sleeping comfortably," Crystal said.

"Poor little dear. Let me know if there's anything you need. If you want to take her to a doctor, I'll call my physician and get you an appointment. He's very nice and . . ."

"Oh, I think she'll be fine," Crystal said.

"Any fever?"

"No," she said quickly.

Too quickly, I thought. Patsy's eyes filled with that gleam of suspicion again as she looked from Raven to me and back to Crystal.

"How do you know?"

"We have a thermometer," Crystal said. "We took along a small first-aid kit when we left on our trip," she added.

"You mean Brooke didn't just buy one?" she asked with a smile. "I heard you drive off," she said to me.

"No, I just sent her for some Tylenol," Crystal replied.

"I have that. You should have asked. In fact, we have some in the restaurant under the counter." She stood there a moment longer. I thought she was going to ask to examine Butterfly, but she just said, "Okay, girls. Rest up. Tonight's a big night. Call me if you need me," she added.

I flashed a smile and Crystal thanked her. We watched her walk toward the trailer and then Crystal closed the door softly.

"I hate lying," she said. "Making up our past is fun, like storytelling, but sometimes I hate being deceitful."

"You had to do it, Crystal," I comforted.

"I just hope she doesn't get suspicious," Raven said, shaking her head.

"I'm sorry I'm sick," Butterfly cried. We all returned to her bedside.

"Don't be silly, Butterfly. You couldn't help it," Crystal said.

"I'm going to get it. I just know I'm going to get it," Raven worried. "What'll we do if I can't work? It will take us forever to earn our money back!"

"Let's not worry about things until we have to," Crystal advised. "We've got enough problems right now without thinking up more."

And that was the truth.

We had a very busy dinner that night and could have used Butterfly's help. Danny popped in almost an hour after the rush had begun. He started to bus some tables and then disappeared in the back when two friends of his arrived. Raven said she thought they were smoking dope. She had gone to the stockroom for Charlie and observed them through the partially opened rear door.

"Don't tell Patsy," I said. "Not now."

Whenever we had a lull in activity, Crystal left to check on Butterfly. The second time, she returned to tell me her fever was nearly 103.

"If it doesn't break in an hour or so, Brooke, I think we ought to take her to the hospital. I'm afraid I might not be right. Maybe she's having a reaction to some virus, or something she ate.''

Raven and I looked at each other. Disaster was looming. The hands of the clock ticked us closer to it every minute. Working hard was the only way not to dwell on it. Finally, business slowed and the last few customers began to think about leaving. That was when Danny reappeared.

"Where were you? You saw how busy we were, Danny. Why did you leave the restaurant?" Patsy called after him.

"I hate the restaurant," he screamed back at her.

Her shoulders sank as she raised her head to hold back her tears. No one said anything. We all went back to work, helping Charlie clean up. Before we were finished, Taylor showed up for Raven. He'd asked her out for a second day in a row.

"Maybe you shouldn't go with him tonight, Raven," I said. She wore a pained expression.

"Brooke, I can take care of myself. Besides," her eyes got that dreamy look again, "no one has ever been as nice to me as Taylor's been. He really likes me, I know he does."

"I'm sure you're right, Raven. We just don't want to see you get hurt." From the look on her face, it was clear that Raven didn't hear anything I had to say.

Crystal tried to break through Raven's love-induced haze. "C'mon Raven, why don't you stick around tonight. Butterfly could use some cheering up."

"Would you guys please stop worrying. I'll be fine. Besides, even you said yourself, Crystal, I shouldn't get too close to Butterfly in case I never had the measles." And with that she grabbed her sweater from behind the counter and headed for Taylor's table.

Crystal and I just shrugged at each other in defeat and wished the lovebirds a good time as we made our way out of the diner and over to our cottage.

When I awoke the next morning I found Crystal sitting at the tiny kitchen table counting our tips. I groggily made my way to the table and asked where everyone was.

"Raven's helping Butterfly wash up—she must have had a good date last night. She's got a smile permanently attached to her face." Crystal's tone was wary and from the way she shook her head I could tell she was just as concerned as I was about Taylor's intentions.

"Do you think Patsy could be wrong about Taylor?" I asked. "Raven wouldn't fall for a jerk."

Before Crystal could answer, the bathroom door flew open and Butterfly and Raven appeared before us. Butterfly was still flushed, but at least she was giggling, a sign that maybe she was back to her old self. Raven on the other hand looked suspicious.

"What are you two crows talking about so quietly?" she asked.

Crystal, always the quick thinker, had a ready answer. "We were just discussing the fact that we should have enough money in a week or two to get back on the road."

Raven paled and we knew she was thinking of Taylor. "I wish we didn't have to leave . . . at least not so soon."

"This guy has really gotten to you, hasn't he, Raven?" I wanted to understand what had come over Raven in the past few days. I'd never been in love and couldn't imagine what it could feel like.

"I know you guys are worried," Raven began, "but Taylor really is special. And there's something . . . something almost magical about Taylor and me. I've always dreamt I would meet the perfect boy and I think maybe I finally have."

Finally Butterfly spoke up. "I hope my heart leads me to Prince Charming one day too." A huge coughing attack hit her and Crystal escorted her back to bed.

Up until now Patsy had accepted our excuses for Butterfly staying in the cottage, but by the next morning she was beginning to get a little suspicious. Thankfully Butterfly's fever had broken during the night and she was feeling well enough to join us for the lunch shift.

Just when we thought we were safe, Patsy made an announcement that made our blood run cold.

"Payday tomorrow," she declared cheerily. "I'll need everyone's social security number and addresses."

We looked to Crystal.

"Can't you pay us off the books, Patsy? We'll accept less money," Crystal proposed.

Patsy shook her head slowly and a curious expression came over her face. "You girls should be able to tell by now that that's not the way I run my business. I'm totally on the up and up." She shifted around to glance at each and every one of us, and it felt like she was waiting for one of us to crack.

I couldn't stand the silence any longer and finally spoke up. "We'll have to dig through our things for the social security cards. Is it okay if we bring them tomorrow?'' Crystal glared at me while Raven and Butterfly looked on wide-eyed.

Patsy let us go that evening without another question, but as soon as we got to the cottage Crystal let me have it.

"What were you thinking, Brooke? How are we supposed to come up with those cards?'' She was livid.

"I couldn't help it. Patsy was staring at us with those big eyes and I just thought we had to make up something!'' I knew I'd gotten us in bigger trouble, but as far as I could tell we were already in pretty deep.

"Well, I suppose we can tell her our social security cards were stolen ... and we'll have to just make up our addresses,'' Crystal conceded.

Raven finally spoke up. "What if Patsy checks up on us and finds out the addresses are fakes?''

"She won't,'' I answered, trying to sound confident.

Once again, I had the feeling that our lies were tangling up around us, trapping us in a web of deception that we'd never be able to flee.

9

Caught in the Act

That night Crystal worked out what everyone's home address would be. She did have her social security card with her and decided she would give hers to Patsy and explain how ours were stolen.

"I think we'll get by with this, but I don't know how much longer we should stay here under false pretenses," she said. "Lies are like bubbles. They eventually float to the surface."

"We'll stay until we get enough money, at least, won't we?" Raven asked. She was pacing by the cottage window. Taylor hadn't shown up as he usually did after the dinner rush and Raven was getting anxious.

"I can't make any promises, Raven," Crystal said in a careful, non-committal tone.

"Promises? Why does everyone all of a sudden think I'm looking for promises?" Raven cried. She went out, slamming the door behind her.

"Why is Raven so upset?" Butterfly asked.

"I think she and Taylor had a fight. At least he hasn't shown up yet tonight," I told her.

Crystal sat at the table working on some kind of revised budget for us based on the money we had already made and the money we could anticipate making. Butterfly wanted to go out and be with Raven, but Crystal told her it would be better to leave Raven alone for now.

"You can help me, instead," she told her and spread the map out on the small table before them. "Let's look at where we should go next and what we can see along the way."

I went to take my shower. When we had first moved into the cottage, the water had come out brown and it took a while to get it reasonably clear. It was running clear now, but there wasn't very much pressure. Taking a shower was more of a pain than a pleasure. For one thing, the shower head wasn't tall enough, so all of us but Butterfly had to crouch. There wasn't much room to move and adjusting the hot and cold took a laboratory technician, but we managed.

I went into the bathroom and began to undress. Naked, I played with the faucets and worked on getting the water not too hot and yet warm enough to enjoy. As I did so, I caught some movement in the corner of the small window above the tub and I froze. I waited and saw it again. It was definitely someone's head.

I didn't scream. Calmly, pretending to still be interested in my shower, I backed away until I was out of sight and slipped my shirt and pants on as quickly as I could. Then I crouched down, keeping below the sight line of the window, opened the door and crawled out.

Crystal turned, a look of confusion on her face when she saw me on all fours.

"What are you doing?"

I put my finger to my lips and both she and Butterfly became paralyzed with fear and curiosity. Then I rose and charged out the door and around the house to find Danny and his two friends squatting by the window. None of them had heard me and they all had their backs to me.

"Enjoying yourselves?" I asked, and they spun around. "I suppose this is how you get your kicks. Is it the best you can do?"

His two friends laughed nervously, but Danny showed no embarrassment or guilt. He sauntered toward me.

"We just wanted to see if you were a male or female," he quipped.

"How would you know the difference?" I shot back. His friends laughed at him, and in the dim glow of the light that flowed from the bathroom window, I could see him turn a dark crimson.

Raven, who had been waiting in the parking lot, started to hurry around the side of the building. Crystal and Butterfly were behind her.

"Usually, I do," he said. "But you're the exception. Maybe we'll find out now," he added, throwing a look at his buddies, who drew closer, their faces full of lusty smiles. He reached out to seize my wrist and pull me to him. "How about showing us what you're hiding under there?"

Once, in the ninth grade, I got into a fight with a boy. His name was Eddie Goodwin and he was always teasing me because I had gone out for the boys' basketball junior varsity team and almost made it. The girls had their own team, but the coach, maybe as a way of jolting his lackadaisical players, let me come to a tryout. Eddie telegraphed his every move, so I was able to steal the ball from him twice. He took a great deal of razzing from his friends about it and afterward came after me in the hall. I realized he wasn't just going to call me names and make fun of me. He was going to do something more, maybe even punch me. I didn't give him the chance. When he was close enough, I jammed my knee between his legs and he crumbled to the hall floor, squirming in pain.

Later, I had to go to the principal's office. Because I was the one who had been physical first, I got into the most trouble. I was suspended from school for two days. It didn't matter that I had felt threatened. I was punished at the foster home, too. I thought it was very unfair, but being treated unfairly in this world was not terribly unusual for me. Of course, beating up a boy like that didn't do my reputation much good. It simply reinforced the image of me most of my fellow students and even my teachers already had.

But I was tired of being put down for it, tired of being looked upon as some sort of freak just because I didn't fit some preconceived idea of what a girl had to be. We might as well be robots or mass produced in genetic laboratories, I thought, and I held onto my own self-image and self-respect, regardless of the cost, even if it meant I wouldn't ever be the object of some handsome boy's interest.

Danny's fingers squeezed down on my wrist. It stung. I felt my skin burn as he twisted my arm. He reached out to open my shirt with his other hand and I turned swiftly, bringing my right knee up and into his groin. The pained look in his face demonstrated his complete surprise. He let go of me, doubled up, and fell over, screaming and cursing.

His two friends gazed down at him writhing like a snake that had just been run over, and then they looked at me with rage.

"Get her," Danny ordered.

They started toward me. Out of the corner of my eye, I saw a broken wood crate and seized a piece of it that still had nails protruding. They stopped their advance when I raised it like a club.

"I'll use it," I said shakily.

Raven came up behind me.

"What happened?" she asked, looking down at Danny, who was now on all fours, taking deep breaths.

"He tried to pull off my shirt," I said. "I saw them in the bathroom window when I went to take a shower. He and his idiot friends were being Peeping Toms, getting their kick of the year.''

Danny's friends helped him to his feet.

"You bitch," he said. "You'll be sorry."

"Go soak yourself in tar," I spit back.

"Now you've gone and done it," Raven said. "What's Patsy going to do?"

"Probably give me a medal," I replied.

"Are you all right?" Crystal asked, coming up alongside us.

"Fine. Let's go back inside. I doubt he'll say anything to Patsy, Raven," I told her. "He'll have to explain why he was behind the cottage and at the window."

We saw the three make their way to a car in the lot. They lit cigarettes and glared our way.

"Let's go inside," Crystal said.

I told them the whole story, every gritty detail.

"I forgot to hang a towel over the window," I said. "He's probably been there before.''

"I'm sure it's the only way he'll ever see a girl undressed," Raven quipped. She kept her eyes toward the window, waiting, hoping for signs of Taylor.

Finally, I calmed down, but I never got up the nerve to take that shower. Crystal, Butterfly and I decided to go to bed, but Raven insisted on staying up, sitting in a chair, refusing to go to bed because Taylor might still come for her. She sat in the dark, staring out at the parking lot.

"He's not coming, Raven. Why torture yourself?" I said after a while.

"Something very unexpected must have happened," she muttered.

"Sure."

"You're glad, aren't you?" she fired at me.

"Don't be stupid, Raven. I'll admit I wasn't happy about your getting too involved with someone while we stopped over here, but I don't want you to be unhappy. I just worry about you," I said.

She simmered down and returned to feeling sorry for herself.

"I can never have a decent boyfriend. I'll never meet anyone but dorks," she whined.

I turned over in bed and closed my eyes. A little more than a half hour or so later, I heard her sigh deeply, get up and prepare for bed. She finally crawled under the covers.

"Brooke?"

"What?"

"Are you still awake?"

"No. I'm talking to you in my sleep," I said. "What?"

"I lied to you guys," Raven said. She was quiet. Damn it, I thought. I felt like a fish, hooked. Reluctantly, I turned over.

"Okay, I'm biting. What?"

"I'm not as experienced as I pretended to be. Actually . . ."

"What, Raven? Actually what?"

"Last night was the first time."

"Last night?" I started to sit up. "You were careful, right?"

"It was hard to be careful, Brooke. It's never happened to you, so you don't know what it's like. You just forget how far you're going. It feels so good and you keep telling yourself, there's time to stop. There's time to be careful, but . . ."

"But what?"

"There wasn't time."

"He wasn't wearing any protection?"

"No."

"Oh Raven. He's a creep to do this to you. Why wasn't he careful?"

"He's not a creep," we heard Crystal suddenly say from the bedroom. "He's stupid. He doesn't know you from a hole in the wall and he takes a chance being sexually active with you? That's stupid."

I smiled. Good old Crystal, pretending to be asleep and listening to everything.

"I did the same thing," Raven admitted. "I was stupid too."

Crystal came to the doorway and looked at us.

"Yes, you were. Let's hope you're lucky this time, Raven," Crystal told her.

I'm scared," she said after a pause. "Could I get pregnant?"

"Of course you could," I said. "Right, Crystal?"

"When is your period due, Raven?"

"About three days," she replied.

"You're probably all right. You've always been regular, haven't you?"

"Yes," she said in a small voice.

"I think you'll be all right, Raven," Crystal reassured her. "But I wouldn't go out with him again. He didn't care about you, that's for sure," she said.

Raven was silent. She turned and buried her face in the pillow. Then we heard her sob. I touched her shoulder.

"I'm sorry," she said. "I'm sorry I'm stupid. And I can't help being afraid."

Butterfly was still asleep in the bedroom and apparently had heard none of this. Crystal approached the bed and gazed down at Raven whose shoulders were shaking with her sobs. She looked at me and then she crawled onto our pullout bed. She and I brought our heads to Raven. We touched Raven's head.

"We're sisters," Crystal began. "We'll always be sisters."

We chanted and held each other and prayed that Raven would be lucky.

The following morning we all rose and got dressed without any more mention of Taylor Cummings. We didn't even talk about Danny and his creepy friends. It had been a restless night for Crystal, Raven and me, so we were moving like zombies. Finally, we walked over to the restaurant and threw ourselves into the work.

Patsy was very chatty, happier than ever, talking about when she would close the restaurant for her holiday and where she might go for a vacation.

"Maybe I'll go to California, too," she said. "I haven't ever been there. Have any of you?"

As always, we waited for Crystal to answer the question and I saw that this was beginning to sharpen Patsy's interest in us. She watched us as Crystal replied.

"No, this is going to be our first trip, too. That's why we were all so excited about it," she said.

"Mighty courageous of your parents letting the four of you travel across country like this," she said. The first customer had yet to arrive.

"Well, we don't exactly have the perfect home life we made out to have," Crystal continued. Raven and I polished silverware and straightened chairs while Butterfly folded napkins, but we were all listening. It was just as much new information to us as it was to Patsy.

"What's that supposed to mean?" she asked.

"Butterfly's mother died a few years ago. Her father travels a lot. My parents are divorced and so are Raven's. Brooke's adopted," she added. "And recently her adoptive mother had a serious operation. Her adoptive father thought it would be good for her to travel with us while he concentrated on her adoptive mother," she concluded.

Crystal was like a spider, weaving her cobweb of personal lives, events, tragedies and comedies to trap the unsuspecting listener. Patsy looked trapped. She turned and viewed each of us in a more sympathetic way.

"Oh," she simply said.

"But we're fine," Crystal jumped in quickly. "We were having a really great time until we ran into that unfortunate person, weren't we, Brooke?"

"Yes, and I've enjoyed working here. We all have," I said.

Butterfly nodded vigorously. Raven stepped up to her.

"The girls told me about your wanting to warn me about Taylor. I should have listened. He's a creep."

"Did he hurt you? Because if he did . . ."

"No, I don't want you to do anything. If and when he comes around here, I'll deal with him, Patsy. Thank you," she said.

"I bet you will," Patsy said, smiling.

The first customers arrived and we all began to work. Two young men who were friends of Taylor's were there, but Taylor didn't show. I saw Raven speaking to them and then I saw her go off to the side and wipe her eyes. I left my tables and hurried over.

"What's the matter?"

"They told me Taylor went back to his old girlfriend. He was out with her last night. He just used me, Brooke. I'm such a fool."

I hugged her quickly.

"It's his loss. He's the one that goofed up," I said. "Let's get back to work and take your mind off of the creep."

She wiped her eyes and nodded.

"Thanks," she said and we returned to the tables. It was another successful breakfast, every available table taken with people waiting to be seated. Butterfly ended up working the counter. Afterward, when she did her count, Patsy told us again how the receipts were up.

"If this continues, I'll be able to retire soon," she kidded. "I'm going over to the bank now to make my deposit from yesterday and this morning," she said. "Anybody need anything from the drugstore?"

"I don't think so," I said, looking at Raven.

"No, nothing," she said.

We remained in the restaurant, having coffee and talking to Charlie, who wanted to tell us about his travels when he was a much younger man. He did have great stories. He had been as far as China!

"There is a lot of world to see," he said, "a lot to learn, but what you learn for sure is a good friend is hard to find. You girls look like you all found each other. That's gold," he said. "You don't have to travel anymore if you're looking for something more valuable than that."

He made us all feel good, and even Raven was beginning to cheer up. But we both knew that it would be a while before her broken heart healed. We were about to leave and rest up in the cottage when Patsy came hurrying through the front door. She hadn't gone to the bank yet. One look at her face told us something terrible had happened.

"My money's gone," she announced, "my deposit. All of it."

She stood there before us, the corners of her mouth trembling.

Crystal was the first to say it.

"Is Danny gone too?" she asked.

"No," Patsy said, surprising us. "He was home, just getting up. He swore he didn't know anything about it."

"When did you see the money last?" I asked her.

"Last night."

She just stood there, gazing at us. It began to give me a creepy feeling. I glanced at Crystal, whose eyes were getting narrow.

"I've been ripping the place apart," Patsy continued. "I searched Danny's room better than a hound dog."

"What'cha think happened?" Charlie asked.

She paused.

"Danny said he thought I was in the house again this morning. He said he heard me return after the breakfast rush. I didn't return," she said, moving her gaze from Butterfly to Raven and then to Crystal and me.

The creepy feeling in my stomach turned into a shaft of ice that slithered up my spine. I sat up straighter.

"You can't believe that one of us . . . that we . . . took it?" I said softly, hoping she would shake her head vehemently.

"I don't want to believe anything bad about anyone," she said, nearly in tears now. "Danny claims he heard footsteps."

"He's lying," Raven said. "Did he tell you what happened last night?"

"No. What happened last night?"

"Raven," I warned.

"No," Raven insisted, "she should know, Brooke. He and his friends were peeping in our bathroom window. Brooke caught them when she went in to take a shower. They even tried to . . ."

129

"To what?"

"To attack her," Raven blurted.

"What?"

"It was nothing, Patsy," I said. "They went away when I confronted them."

She stared at us.

"Look," Crystal finally said. "The best thing to do is to go over to the cottage and search if you like."

"I don't want to do that, girls. I want to believe you wouldn't steal from me," she said.

"And we wouldn't," I emphasized.

She nodded and I expected that would be the end of it, but she sighed and looked back a moment.

"He says I never take his word. He says I'm always accusing him first. I know it's insulting, but if you girls and I just walked through the cottage . . ."

"Fine," Crystal said jumping to her feet. "Let's do that."

"Yes, and afterward, let's have a heart to heart talk with Danny boy," Raven fired as she stood up.

"These girls wouldn't steal from you, Patsy," Charlie said.

"I know," she said, forcing a smile. "Thank you, girls."

We followed her out. As we started around the restaurant, we heard a door slam and saw Danny come out of the trailer, pulling his tee shirt over his head. He sneered and started after us.

We entered the cottage. Crystal and Butterfly had made their beds before we left for work and I had put the sofa back together. The blanket and pillows were beside it where I had left them. Except for Raven's blouse draped over a chair, none of our things were scattered about. The bathroom was neat, too. We all stood in the center of the small living room.

"You're welcome to look anywhere you want, Patsy," I said. I couldn't hide the disappointment in my face and voice.

"Check those sacks, Ma," Danny said from behind us. He was referring to our pillowcases.

"Danny, they wouldn't do such a thing," she said, shaking her head.

"I'll do it," he cried and sauntered past us. He emptied each of our pillowcases onto the floor. Some of our clothing got mixed together, but there was nothing else in them.

"Satisfied?" I said.

He looked at his mother and shook his head.

"I ain't, no." He gazed around and then pounced on the small dresser, pulling out the drawers, feeling under the underclothing and socks.

"Didn't you learn your lesson last night?" I asked him when he held up Raven's bra.

He reddened.

"Danny, let's go," Patsy said. "The girls didn't take my money."

"Why don't you tell her where it is already?" Raven asked him.

He gritted his teeth and then he looked at the sofa as if a ghost had whispered in his ear. He fell to his knees and reached under the sofa frame. Everyone watched him. Raven started to laugh when suddenly, he backed up and held out a bank deposit bag.

"I knew it was here," he said with sick pleasure. He dumped the sack on the floor and Patsy's money flowed out.

"We didn't take that!" I protested. "You must have put it there."

"Right," he said. "I'm a magician." He looked up at Patsy. "Ma, call the police."

"No," Raven cried. "We didn't do it, Patsy. He's lying. He put it there!"

"If I put it here, why wouldn't I have gone right to it?" he asked, looking up at Patsy. "Why did I waste all that time looking everywhere else, huh, smart ass?" he said to Raven.

"Because you're putting on an act," she replied, backing away from him.

"You're the ones putting on the act," he spit back at her. "You knew my mother always left the trailer door open. I heard you in there this morning."

"It's not true, Patsy," I said, shaking my head. "I swear we didn't do that."

She pressed her lips together and looked seconds away from bursting into a storm of tears.

"Call the police, Ma. I bet they steal from everybody. I'll call," he said, standing.

"No," she said. "Just put the money back into the bag, Danny. Go on," she ordered.

"But . . ."

"Do as I say," she commanded firmly. "Put it back and give it to me."

"It's evidence, Ma. You've got to leave it right here for the cops to see," he argued.

"Danny! Please just put it back."

"You're making a mistake. You're taking their side even now," he added, his face twisting with rage. "You always believe everyone else but me!"

"I'm not believing anyone else, Danny. I . . ."

"Yes, you are. Damn you!" he screamed and charged past us and out the door, slamming it hard behind him. It was as if a tornado had just twirled through the small cottage. Crystal put her arm around Butterfly and pulled her closer. Raven looked at them and then at the floor. I knelt down to put the money back into the deposit bag.

"We didn't take this, Patsy," I said, handing it to her. "I don't know how it got under the sofa."

"I do," Raven said sharply.

Patsy nodded.

"I believe you girls. I really do, but I think it would be best for all of us if you all left now. I'll pay you what you're owed," she said sadly. "I need to deal with Danny, and I'm afraid I won't be able to get through to him with you girls here. He seems to blame you for his troubles. I'm sorry," she said. "I wish you luck. Come into the restaurant when you get yourselves packed up." She went to the door. All of us held our breath. When she opened it and turned, Butterfly stepped away from Crystal.

"We didn't take your money, Patsy," she said. "We wouldn't steal from you or anybody. Please don't make us leave."

Patsy's face crumpled.

"I'm sorry, dear." Tears finally broke free of her eyelids and began to streak down her cheeks. She took a deep breath and hurried out.

"That jerk, that piece of garbage, that poor excuse for a human being," Raven rattled off. 'Why is she giving him what he wants? He never liked us from day one."

"What else can she do? He's her son," Crystal replied. "And we're just strangers."

Frustrated, Raven stormed into the bathroom.

"Let's get our things together, Brooke," Crystal said. "The faster we're on the road, the better off we'll be."

It didn't take us long to get our things back into the station wagon. We were going to leave without getting our wages from Patsy, but she sent Charlie for us.

"I know that boy done that to you," he said. "He's not just an apple rotting the bunch. He's rotting the whole barrel too," he said. He was

132

as furious as we had ever seen him. "I'm going to let him know it, too," he promised.

"Patsy needs all the help and support she can get, Charlie," Crystal told him.

"I know. It's like swimming with a rock tied to your neck," he said.

We drove up to the restaurant and got out. Patsy was near the door, waiting with our envelopes.

"It's not much, but I hope it helps you along your way. Maybe you girls oughta turn back," she added, looking sharply at Crystal. "Save this trip for another time. Traveling can be very difficult, even for young people."

"Thank you, Patsy," Crystal said and took the envelopes for us. "We're sorry to leave you like this."

Butterfly looked like she was about to cry. Patsy hugged her and then hugged Raven, Crystal and me. Her eyes were little pools of tears. She bit down on her lower lip.

"Thank you for helping out. You're good girls," she whispered and turned away.

We stood there a moment, looked at the restaurant and at Charlie, who gazed at us glumly and then started his work. He looked like he hated good-byes as much as we did.

"Let's go," Crystal whispered.

We walked out in silence and I got behind the steering wheel. The heavy overcast sky that kept the morning dreary was beginning to break up. Clouds parted in the distance and rays of sunshine poured through.

"It's turning nice. At least we won't be driving in rain," I said. No one responded. I didn't think anyone else even noticed the weather.

I put the car in drive. When I gazed into my rear-view mirror, I saw Danny standing outside the trailer, his arms folded, looking very satisfied with himself.

I drove out, turned right on the highway and headed west. Still, no one had spoken.

"I guess you had better take out your map again, Crystal," I said.

She unfolded it without a word.

Raven had the right side of her face against the window. She watched the scenery flow by, took a few deep breaths and then closed her eyes.

"This must be some kind of record. Betrayed by two creepy guys in less than twenty-four hours," she said with a shaky laugh.

"I'm sure you'll find someone honest and true someday, Raven," I said. "We all will."

"I still can't believe that Danny." Raven wiped angry tears away.

Butterfly leaned forward and put her hand on Raven's shoulder. Raven turned, smiled at her and covered Butterfly's hand with her own.

"Why was he so mean to us, Raven?" Butterfly asked.

"Because he's mean to himself," Crystal replied for her. "He hates who he is so he hates everyone, even his own mother."

"I thought he was lucky having a mother," Butterfly said.

"He is," I said, "but he doesn't know it."

"Or care," Raven added.

We were all silent again and then Raven smiled.

"You know," she said, "I was just thinking. Maybe we're not so unlucky after all. Maybe we've got something better."

"What?" Butterfly asked her.

"Each other," she said. "We've got each other."

I drove on toward the emerging sun that, like us, was heading west again.

10

On the Road Again

It rained again. Driving had lost its excitement for me and became dreary and monotonous, especially on the longer Interstate highways where there was little to look at except other cars. Every time we saw a highway patrolman, we cringed a bit, but none appeared to take any real interest, some not even giving us a passing glance. I made sure to stay well within the speed limits. Our stops for gas, for lunch and finally for dinner were the only events that stirred any enthusiasm. Butterfly slept a lot. Crystal, who could read anywhere, had her nose in a book, and Raven, bored and upset, pouted, dozed, fidgeted and complained. Regret, like a determined snake, slithered into our thoughts, hissing at us periodically through small remarks, moans and sighs.

"Summers weren't all that bad back at Lakewood," Raven muttered just before we stopped for dinner. We had gone nearly an hour without anyone uttering a sound. The radio droned on, but I was no longer listening. "At least we got away from Gordon and Louise more when we worked."

"That's wonderful, Raven," I said. "I must have been on drugs because I wasn't aware you were in such a state of bliss back there. I was stupid enough to think you hated almost every minute of it. I guess I just imagined the continuous stream of complaints pouring out of your mouth."

"I didn't say I liked it," she snapped. "I just said it wasn't as hard in the summer. Maybe we should have waited until the fall to run off."

Crystal lowered her book.

"My hope is we'll find another place to live and finish school there.

135

If we first left in the fall, we would be way behind by the time we started a new school," she said.

"School? Who cares about school?" Raven cried.

"Don't you think Butterfly will have to go to school? And I still want to apply for scholarships," Crystal replied calmly. "If I knew you believed we would never return to school, I wouldn't have left."

Raven muttered something under her breath and stared angrily out the window.

"We shouldn't have let you throw away Gordon's cocaine," she said. "We should have just left it where it was. Now, we can't go back even if we wanted to," she griped.

Crystal returned to her reading. Raven closed her eyes. Butterfly moaned in her sleep and I stared at the long stretch of highway. I felt like I was sinking into a tub of cold mud. Freedom doesn't automatically make things better for you, I thought. You still have to deal with defeat and frustration and you have no one else to blame but yourself. Even I was beginning to have some serious second thoughts. Had I talked them all into a disaster?

We had our dinner in a fast-food restaurant and drove until we crossed into Indiana. Everyone was nervous about sleeping in the car, so we searched for a cheap motel. We found one that looked like it had been taken over by rodents, but the price of a room with two double beds was only seventeen dollars.

The room smelled moldy and stale. Raven said it smelled like something died in the walls. I tried to open one of the windows, but it was jammed shut.

"No one's opened this for some time. It won't budge," I explained.

"We should sleep with the door partly open," Raven suggested, but Crystal was afraid.

"We're out in the middle of nowhere and there doesn't seem to be anyone else staying here tonight."

"Let's just make the best of it," I said, trying to avoid another argument. We were all cranky and tired and getting on each other's nerves.

When we finally lay down on the beds, we found the mattresses were so worn, we nearly sank to the floor. All of us slept in our clothes with our own pillowcases instead of the soiled ones that were on the bed. Despite our horrible sleeping quarters, the driving and our emotional roller coaster ride made us tired enough to drift off, and none of us woke during the night.

The bright morning sunshine easily penetrated the thin window shades and gauze-like curtains, but instead of welcoming us to a warm, new day, it only spotlighted the decay, rot, rust and filth of the room we were in. We were even reluctant to use the toilet, but did what we had to do out of necessity. We couldn't leave quickly enough and when we found a place to have breakfast, we washed and freshened up in their bathroom.

None of us were particularly hungry. Crystal did an analysis of our small finances and concluded if we were extra frugal, and if Gordon didn't stop his gas credit card, we could still make it to California.

"Why hasn't he stopped it from being used?" I wondered aloud.

Crystal thought a moment.

"There is the possibility he is tracking our escape route by checking to see where we use it," she concluded.

It put a cloud of dread over us for a moment.

"Of course, he would always be a little behind us, but still . . . ," Crystal said and let her words hang like icicles dripping cold visions of horror.

"How much more thrifty can we be?" Raven asked, getting back to our present problem.

"I'm talking about real economizing," she said. "This is the last time we eat in a restaurant. From now on, we buy food and eat in the car. Everyone likes peanut butter. We'll eat that for lunch," Crystal said. "Every day."

"Great," Raven said. "We used to complain about the food in the Lakewood House and now that looks like a gourmet restaurant to us."

"If your heart is so set on going back, Raven, go back," I snapped at her.

"With what? Five dollars? And then what happens when I get there? Gordon uses me for target practice? Thanks," she said, her mouth sinking at the corners.

"Then stop talking about it," I pleaded. "You're not doing us any good reminding us we're in a difficult spot."

"Brooke's right, Raven. You've got to concentrate on the positive," Crystal began. "It's the only way to combat depression."

"I'm sorry, you guys, I don't mean to be so disagreeable. It's just that . . . that . . . oh I don't even know!" And with tears running down her cheeks she headed quickly for the bathroom.

"Why are we fighting so much?" Butterfly asked softly.

"Because we're afraid," Crystal analyzed, "and it's easier to take it out on each other. Raven will snap out of it, don't worry."

When Raven returned, however, she appeared to be even more despondent.

"I need a warm bath," Raven said, letting out a huge sigh. "I'd even put up with Gordon looking down at me in the tub." As soon as the words left her lips I could tell she regretted uttering them.

Crystal's head snapped up so hard and fast, I thought she would tear the skin on her neck.

"You think I was exaggerating about that? It was disgusting and terrifying the way his eyes drank me in. He brought his hand inches above my breasts. He was drooling. My insides were so twisted, I couldn't breathe. I'm sure my heart stopped for a moment. I was passing out and I kept telling myself, if I did, he would . . ."

"Oh Crystal, I'm sorry, you know I didn't mean it," Raven said.

"Let's just go. If we keep moving, we'll feel better," Crystal said as we left the restaurant.

The driving wasn't any more pleasant, except Raven tried extra hard to make the most of things. She played some games with Butterfly, sang silly songs, and got into a heated discussion with Crystal about feminism. For a while it felt like old times.

Just after we had crossed into Illinois, the station wagon began to overheat. I noticed the temperature gauge climbing and I slowed down and pulled to the side of the road as quickly as I could.

"What's going on?" Raven asked.

"I'm not sure. The temperature gauge just shot up."

"We've got to get off this highway, Brooke," Crystal said. Cars were whizzing by us. "We'll attract too much attention and maybe the highway police."

I flipped open the hood and studied the engine. I wasn't sure what I was looking for, but I knew that the water gushing out of one of the hoses wasn't a good sign.

"Do you know what the problem is?" Crystal asked.

"I think it's this hose. Look at it gush."

"What does that mean?" Raven asked.

"It means we have to get a new one," I snapped. I may have known how to drive the car, but I wasn't a mechanic.

"What are we going to do?" Butterfly cried.

I looked down the road and saw an old sign advertising a garage a mile away. The sign was faded and the bottom corner was cracked away.

"I'll walk down and see if that place is still open," I said. "If it is, I'll get someone to come up and help us."

"We can't afford this," Crystal said. "It might take all our money."

"Let's wait and see. Maybe they'll let us use the credit card," I said. "I'll come right back if there's no garage and we'll think of what to do then."

Crystal checked her map.

"There should be a small town around here. We'll figure out something."

"Okay." I got out. "Stay cool everyone," I added, fixing my eyes on Raven especially. "I'll be back as fast as I can."

I started away and then broke into a jog. There was only one house along the way, a small A-frame, but because of the overgrown lawn and the dark windows, I concluded no one lived in it now. I kept going and when I rounded a turn, I saw the garage ahead. From this distance it was difficult to know if it was still in business. I didn't see anyone or any cars at the pumps and it was an old building, the siding peeled and chipped.

As I drew closer, however, I heard the sound of power tools and sure enough, the door was open. I stopped and looked in, at first seeing no one and then a young man stood up. He had been squatting by a truck tire. He wore a pair of gray coveralls. I thought he was probably in his late teens, maybe twenty at most. He had thick, dark brown hair, and even from where I stood, I could see that his dark eyes were unusual, resembling two shiny black pearls. He had high cheekbones and a strong, nearly square jaw with a perfect mouth. He stared at me a moment as if I were an illusion.

"Where did you come from?" he asked. "I didn't hear you pull up."

"Our car broke down about a mile away, right before the exit," I explained.

He didn't move or show any interest at first. Then he put down his power wrench, wiped his hands on a rag, and came out of the garage. Despite his working indoors, he had a deep, even tan. He was at least six feet tall and had a firm, muscular build that refused to be disguised under the coveralls.

"I wasn't sure this garage was open," I said when he didn't speak. He just continued to stare at me, a small, tight smile on his lips.

"We just do some body work and some mechanical work now," he explained. "We gave up the gas pumps a little over a year ago. There's not much traffic going by these days. What kind of a car do you have?"

"It's a 1990 Buick station wagon."

"We don't have a tow truck anymore," he said. "Maybe you should just call the Automobile Club."

"We don't belong," I said quickly.

He stared at me again. When he took these long silent looks at me, he made me so self-conscious, I had to shift my eyes. I could feel my cheeks heating up as well.

He nodded and looked around, expecting to see someone else waiting.

"Where's your family? How come they sent you by yourself?" he asked.

"It's just me and three of my girlfriends. We're going to California," I explained.

"California?" He smiled as if I had said we were going to the moon.

"Yes, people go there," I joked. His smile only deepened.

"Someone must. It's the most populated state in the country. Well," he said putting his hands on his hips and looking in the direction of the exit, "what happened to your station wagon?"

"It started to overheat. There's water gushing out of one of the hoses," I said. He raised his eyebrows.

"Oh there is, is there?" he asked with a smirk. "So it sounds like you've diagnosed the problem, doctor."

"No, really, I'm not sure what's wrong, it's just that I could tell there's a leak—it gushed all over me." I held out my wet sneaker as proof.

"The hose probably rotted away. When was it serviced last?"

I took a deep breath and looked away.

"I don't know," I said.

"Whose car is it?"

"It's . . . mine, but I don't know when it was serviced last," I said.

"Seems to me that if I were going to California, I'd be sure my vehicle was serviced and checked," he said.

"We just decided at the last minute," I told him.

He smiled at me again, his eyes full of amusement as they fixed on my face. I tried to look away, but his look started a tingle in my spine that felt like a tiny bubble floating up and around to my heart.

"Where are you from?"

"New York, upstate," I said quickly.

"And you just decided at the last minute to drive across the whole country?" he followed, his voice filled with enough skepticism to weigh down the faith of a priest.

"Yes. That's the truth. Can you help us or not?" I questioned.

He didn't exactly stop smiling at me, but he did turn more serious.

"Well, I'll take my Chevy. I have a chain I can use to drag her back here, but just in case, I'll bring along some water," he said.

He nodded at an Impala that had its rear lowered and customized exhaust pipes installed. The driver's side door had been primed for a paint job.

"That's Betty Lou," he said. "Get in. I'll be right with you."

"Betty Lou?" I said, smiling.

"My sweetheart," he added, and went around the corner to fill a can with water.

I got into his car. The seats had been redone in a fifties' tuck and roll. The dashboard was spotless as were the floors. A pair of large cotton dice dangled from the rearview mirror.

He put the water can into the trunk, closed his garage door, and then got in and started the engine. It sounded a low growl.

"Pretty, ain't it?" he asked as though we were listening to a symphony orchestra. "Not as pretty as you, of course." This time it was his turn to look away shyly.

His compliment left me speechless, and we drove in silence until the wagon came into view. "That's you?" He nodded at our broken-down vehicle.

"Yes," I said and he made a U-turn and backed up. Then we got out.

"Don't get too close, girls," he said as he started fiddling with the hoses. "The water coming out of here is pretty hot. Uh oh. Looks like your water pump is shot, too."

I could tell by the look on his face that we were in serious car trouble.

"Can you fix it for us?" Raven asked. He glanced at her and then he turned to me. It was the first time I ever saw a boy take more interest in me than in Raven.

"I'll tow you back to my station. The nearest parts place is thirty miles to Grover," he explained.

"We don't have a lot of money," I said quietly. "You wouldn't take a credit card, would you?"

"We don't take credit cards anymore. It's just me and my dad and he's hardly at the station." He thought a moment and then said, "Let me ask around. I could probably get a deal for you."

"Great," I said, my eyes brightening.

He shut the hood and opened his trunk to get out a chain. Raven looked at me and through her sign language indicated she thought he was a hunk as he attached the chain underneath and then attached it to his own vehicle. I ignored her.

"Get behind the wheel and put it into neutral," he told me.

I got in and Raven quickly followed.

"Where's he taking us?" Crystal asked and I explained.

"He seems really nice, Brooke," Raven commented as he got into his car and started to tow us.

"He's nice enough," I said.

When Raven saw his garage, she moaned.

"Maybe we should go someplace else."

"Beggars can't be choosers," Crystal said. "Let's just see if he can fix it."

We all got out when he stopped.

"The junkyard's about fifteen miles away," he said. He looked at his garage. "I was thinking they may have the part."

He turned to me with a warm smile on his face. "Why don't you come with me? If you guys want, you can wait in the office," he suggested to the others. He unlocked the door and turned to us. "There's some cokes in the refrigerator, some cookies and stuff, too. There are a few magazines, but I don't think they'll interest you much," he added with a devilish little smile.

Raven tossed her hair over her shoulder and widened her eyes.

"Probably not," she said.

"Thank you," Crystal said. She and Butterfly headed for the office.

"Just answer the phone for me, will you?" he asked.

"Of course," she told him.

"How long is this going to take?" Raven asked.

"Could be a while," he said. "First we've got to find a pump that works and then we've got to install it. Matter of fact, you girls might have to stay over."

"Stay over? Where?" She glanced down the deserted road.

"I don't know the rates around here anymore, but there's a place called the Woodside, sort of a bed and breakfast, about two miles north of here," he indicated. "Nice old lady runs it, Mrs. Slater. Look it up in the phone book while we're away."

"Are you sure you should go with him?" Raven asked me as the mechanic walked back to his car.

"I'll be fine. He's gone out of his way to help us," I pointed out. "Besides, he seems really nice."

"Brooke, I of all people can warn you about 'nice boys.' Don't follow my mistake," Raven warned. I blushed and quickly walked over to the car.

"I'm Todd by the way," he said, "Todd Mayton."

"My name's Brooke," I said.

"Glad to know you," he said, nodding as he backed out. Raven stood there looking after us, her face a mask of worry.

Todd did most of the talking on our way to the junkyard. I found out that he was the youngest of three children, all boys, and his brothers were living and working for an uncle in Indianapolis. His mother had left his father four years ago and she and her new husband lived close to his brothers. It was obvious from the way he talked about her that he resented her for what she had done to his father.

"He was always a hard-working guy, my old man, and I guess our lives were never very glamorous. She claimed life with him made her ten years older than she was. She's a good-looking woman, my mother. When we had the pumps, men used to drive an extra ten, fifteen miles to get gas at our station because she was out there pumping gas, wearing these abbreviated shorts and a halter," he said with some bitterness. "I was just a kid, but I knew what their remarks meant and I hated the way they looked at her.

"Jeeze," he said after a moment's pause, "look at me running at the mouth like this. I never do that. You must be special, all right," he added with a smile.

I knew from the heat that traveled up my neck and into my cheeks that I was blushing like a full-blown red rose.

"So what about you?" he asked when I didn't reply.

"What about me?"

"How do four young girls come to be on America's highways by themselves, for starters?" he asked.

I hesitated. There was something about him, something about the way he had opened his own heart to me so willingly and without fear that made me resist lying.

"We're runaways," I said, taking a chance with the truth. The others would kill me.

He started to smile, looked at me and then stopped, his face suddenly serious.

"No kidding?"

"No kidding. We're foster children. We have no families. We've been living in a home for years, actually, and for a variety of reasons, we decided it was time to move on.''

His eyes narrowed as he studied me closer.

"This is a joke, right?"

"It's getting to be. We were robbed along the way, accused of stealing and now have car trouble. We can't go back so we're caught in a vise that keeps squeezing us tighter and tighter.''

He was silent.

"There's the junkyard,'' he indicated, nodding at the fenced-in yard directly ahead of us.

A man who looked close to seventy was piling some tires just inside the entrance. He wore a flannel shirt with the sleeves rolled to his elbows and a pair of jeans with a rather significant hole in the rear end that revealed his faded boxer shorts. The lines in his face looked etched by a scalpel. He had a complexion the color of burnt toast. When he smiled, he showed a mouth with a number of teeth gone.

"What are you doin' here so late?'' he asked as we pulled up. Todd had his window down.

"Breakdown. I need a water pump for a 90 Buick Wagon. Think you've got one, Lefty?'' he asked.

The old man turned, squeezed his grimy jaw between his left forefinger and thumb and thought a moment. I gazed at the pile of wrecks, the sea of metal, rubber and glass. To my eye there was no order or reason to why anything was where it was. I saw older wrecks mixed in with new vehicles, trucks with cars, a school bus turned on its side near a John Deere tractor and a recreational vehicle that looked like it had been on fire. In some of the wrecks, birds had made themselves homes.

"Take the freeway to the Golden Gate,'' Lefty instructed. "Seems I remember a Buick in there about that age. Johnny picked it up near Cranberry Lake a year or so ago.''

"Thanks.''

Todd drove in.

"The freeway to the Golden Gate?'' I asked. He laughed.

"Lefty's joke. He names the corridors and if you've been here enough times as I have, you know what he's talking about. This is the freeway. And this,'' he said turning right and slowing down to a crawl, "is the Golden Gate.'' We went over some sheets of metal that had been placed there to navigate over some deep ditches.

Cars were piled two and in some places three high on our right and left. We both looked and suddenly, I spotted it.

"There!" I said, pointing to my right, a few yards in from the corridor.

"Good work," he said, impressed.

The vehicle I had spotted had its roof bashed in, the windshield and side windows shattered and the driver's side door ripped off.

"Looks like it rolled," Todd said after stopping.

We got out and went to the wreck. He tried to open the hood, but it was jammed shut.

"Going to take some doing," he said.

"Will Lefty help?"

"Here it's find what you want and get it yourself. Then you go up to the gate and bargain with Lefty for a while. I have some tools in the trunk," he added and went back to the car. I studied the hood and saw where the latch had been jammed. While he walked around the car, I took out his rubber hammer and a chisel and began pounding the tooth of the latch. To my surprise it broke free and then I stood up, put my fingers under the hood and pulled. He stood by, smiling with amazement when it went up.

"Need a job?" he asked, half-jokingly.

"Actually, yes. We're pretty low on funds."

"I'll bet. Traveling isn't cheap."

"Especially when you get robbed," I said.

He shook his head, still not sure whether or not I was making it all up. Then he leaned over the engine, located the water pump and studied it for a moment.

"It looks good," he said.

I stood by and watched him remove the pump. As he worked, he talked a bit more about himself and the area, but occasionally, he snuck in a question about our lives in the foster home.

"So," he said just before pulling out the pump, "your foster parents aren't looking for you?"

"Oh yes. By now they surely are."

He nodded and then pulled out the pump. I helped him put back his tools and we started out of the yard, pausing at the gate to show Lefty what we had taken. He studied it a moment.

"Twenty dollars seems fair," he said.

"It seems fair," Todd replied, "but it's not. I got a ten that's fair." He showed the bill.

"You're robbin' me," Lefty grumbled.

"Wouldn't be the first time," Todd told him. Lefty laughed, just a silent chuckle.

"Your dad taught you well," he said, taking the ten. "I feel generous today."

"Thanks, Lefty. See you."

"Tell your dad hello," he called as we started away.

"Thanks for being such a good negotiator," I said. He laughed.

"It's just a game. Lefty always asks twice as much as he'll take. Everyone knows it. You were a great help," he added.

"Will your father be upset that you're spending so much time with us?" I asked him.

He shook his head and was silent for a while. Then he took a breath.

"My father doesn't do all that much with the station anymore. He's got a bad leg, diabetes," he explained. Then he turned to me and added, "He spends most of his time with a bottle."

"Oh. I'm sorry."

"I'll have to go home for a while," he said. "What I'll do is come back after dinner and work on this for you guys, but I think it's a good idea you all get a room for a night."

"Okay. Maybe Crystal called already. She's very efficient."

"Crystal?"

I told him a little about each of us. Talking to him was easy; it felt as though we'd known each other forever. He listened quietly and then turned to me and said, "You don't have to worry about me, Brooke. You all do what you think is best for you. I'm not going to call the police or anything."

"I know," I said. I truly did believe him. It put a soft smile on his lips. "I can come back and help you later if you tell me when," I joked.

"Sure. Like I said, if you want to stay and become my assistant . . ."

I laughed, just imagining.

"I'm the only one who drives. They'd all have to stay."

"Oops. That's too many girls for me," he said and we both laughed.

We were laughing when we pulled up. Raven was sitting on the step by the office, looking as if she was standing guard.

"It's about time," she cried the moment we stepped out of the car. "It's getting late. Crystal called the bed and breakfast and thinks we should sleep there."

"It's a good idea," Todd said. "You have to stay somewhere tonight."

Crystal came out and filled me in on the details.

"I took a chance, Brooke," she said, "hoping this wasn't going to cost more than twenty dollars. Is it?" she asked, her face full of worry. Todd overheard and stepped up to us.

"Don't worry about the car. The part cost just ten dollars," he said. "And I won't charge you for labor."

"Really? That's wonderful."

"I gotta go home for a while, so why don't I drive you all to the bed and breakfast," he suggested. "Oh, and Brooke, I could use some help later when I start working on the pump. Do you want to come help?"

"Uh . . . yeah, sure," I answered. The way my heart was beating you'd think I just got asked to the prom.

"I'm hungry," Butterfly said. "All we had were some candy bars in there."

Todd laughed.

"I know. I've got to start eating better. You'll get a good supper at the Woodside," Todd said.

We got into his car and he drove us to what looked like someone's private home. There was only a small sign to indicate that rooms were for rent.

"Tell Mrs. Slater hello for me," Todd said as we got out.

"I will," I said. "Two hours?"

"Two hours."

He drove off and Raven shook her head.

"I don't know, Brooke. I was worried about you going off alone with him, but if putting a water pump into a car engine is his idea of a date, I guess he's probably safe."

Everyone laughed as I turned beet red.

Maybe because I was very hungry too, I saw Mrs. Slater in terms of food. She wasn't more than two or three inches taller than Butterfly and as plump as a stuffed Thanksgiving turkey. Her jowls shook like Jell-O when she walked, or waddled along, I should say. Her hair was milk white with a hairpin the color of dark chocolate holding her bun tightly against the back of her head. Her eyes were almost mint green, bright and friendly, grandmother eyes, as Butterfly would say. She had arms that reminded me of large rye breads and fingers that looked like fresh dough, one of which trapped a marriage ring in the folds between her knuckle and hand forever.

The house, small but very pleasant and warm, was filled with the aroma of meat loaf and apple pie. She had one other guest, a salesman named Mr. Franklin.

"I'm sure glad Todd told you to come over here. As usual I made too much for supper," she said.

She showed us the room with two double beds. We had a bathroom to share with her other guest so she asked that we be considerate. Raven was happy because it meant she could get a hot shower and wash her hair, "before it falls out from the weight of the dirt. Maybe our breakdown was a lucky thing," she added.

"Which is why I tell you to concentrate on the positive," Crystal said cheerily.

"Mercy," Raven cried and hurried into the bathroom first.

Toward the end of our dinner, Raven leaned over and whispered, "Maybe I should come along with you to the garage to be a chaperone. It's pretty obvious that Todd likes you."

"No," I said, maybe too quickly. Her eyebrows lifted. "Todd and I don't have time to be friends. Our car has to be fixed tonight so we can leave early in the morning," I continued.

She didn't look convinced and just shook her head slowly. "Well, don't say I didn't warn you."

Crystal sensed the tension between us and came to the rescue. "I think we've all learned from your experience with Taylor, Raven. I'm sure Brooke will be careful." And with that she shot me a meaningful glare.

Butterfly reached over and grabbed my arm. "I think Todd's awfully handsome, Brooke. Would you let him kiss you if he asked?"

"Geez, will you all stop! I *am not* going on a date! I'm just going to help him fix our car," I cried, desperate to have them drop the subject. I couldn't hide the flames that lit up my cheeks and Crystal couldn't help but poke fun at me.

"Hmm . . ." she said. "Methinks the lady doth protest too much!"

As they sat there giggling at me I wondered, What if Raven was right? What if Todd really did like me? Would I let him kiss me as Butterfly had asked?

With all these thoughts and questions swarming in my head I barely heard Todd's car as he pulled into the driveway of the bed and breakfast. My legs were trembling as I went out to meet him and, when I turned back toward the house, I saw Crystal's, Raven's and Butterfly's faces pressed against the window.

They all looked so worried, as if they could see into my future. As if what they saw scared them.

11

Make New Friends

"So what's it like to be an orphan?" Todd asked as we drove to his dad's station.

"Well, I never knew who my father was and I have no idea if I have any brothers or sisters."

He nodded.

"How about your mother? Did you know her?"

"Not really. This ribbon," I said, showing him the ribbon tied around my wrist, "is the only thing I know came from her. She had tied it in my hair when she gave me up and someone had the sense to save it for me. It used to be bright red, but the color's badly faded," I added.

We pulled into the garage and got out. He unlocked the door and raised it. It rattled on its runners and stopped. Then he flipped a switch and the neon lights blinked a few times before illuminating the inside of the garage where Gordon's wagon was parked. The hood was up. Todd went to his workbench and studied the water pump for a few moments.

"How was your father?" I asked. He didn't look up to respond.

"He was sleeping when I got there and was still sleeping when I left," he said. He plugged in a light and brought it over to the engine. I held it for him and he studied our broken water pump again before choosing his tools almost the way a surgeon would choose a scalpel.

"I guess you've been working on cars all your life."

"From the moment I could hold a wrench," he replied. "I don't think I was more than fourteen before Dad started to leave me in charge of this place. He'd go off and do something for someone, which was

149

usually followed by a visit to the tavern. It was always supposed to be a quick cold beer, but it always turned out to be hours. The work would pile up. People would be furious about their cars not being done, and I had to make up stories.

"You know what?" he said pausing and turning to look at me.

"What?"

"You and I aren't that much different. I had a father and a mother, but it was as if I didn't most of the time. I cooked for myself, took care of my own clothes and cleaned the house after my mother left. I even wrote my own excuses for school when I was absent," he added with a smile. "Being here all the time, I learned to forge Dad's signature real good. Now, people think of this place more as mine than Dad's. He doesn't care." He thought a moment as if he were deciding whether to say something else, and then he returned to his work.

"I understand what you're saying," I told him, "but at least you didn't have to live in a state-run facility."

"I guess you girls had it real bad in that home, bad enough to run off like this without any money, huh?"

"We had some money," I said and told him about Sunshine. He listened and worked. Soon the broken water pump was out and he was fitting the used replacement into the engine.

"The road's no place for you, Brooke. There's lots of stuff like that going on. I hope you find what you're looking for soon and settle down," he said.

"Me too."

He wiped his hands on a rag.

"Want a cold drink? I've got some soda or even a beer, if you want that?"

"I'll take a soda," I said. He went to the office and returned with two Cokes. We sat on a bench and looked at the station wagon.

"So whose Buick is that?" he asked.

I was silent.

"It's not one of yours if you're all foster children, right?" he pursued with a gentle smile.

"It belongs to the creature who runs the house with his wife," I replied.

"Gordon Tooey?"

"Yes. How did you know that?"

"I looked at the registration in the glove compartment," he replied and drank from his Coke. "Serious business, stealing a car."

"Now you can appreciate just how desperate we were," I said.

"Yeah, but how's Gordon going to take it?" he asked with a wry smile.

"Not well," I said. "Crystal's afraid he might be coming after us."

"You guys really are on the run." He took another sip of his soda and looked at me. "You don't look like an outlaw," he kidded.

We stared at each other for a long moment. As I measured him, he was measuring me in just about the same way, I thought. I wondered if I reminded him of someone. Neither of us seemed intimidated or embarrassed by the other's long gaze. It made me feel warm and comfortable rather than self-conscious now. I liked the way his eyes softened and moved ever so slightly as he washed them over me with care that suggested he wanted to commit me to memory forever and ever.

He looked away, toward the door and the night sky.

"Beautiful night," he said. "It's actually my favorite time of the year. Late spring here is warm but not yet so warm it's uncomfortable or too humid. I tend to take more time just staring at the stars or watching birds. I like it, but I also hate it."

"Hate it? Why?" I asked quickly. "You sound almost poetic when you talk about it. Crystal would love to hear you."

He laughed.

"Poetic, huh? My old English teacher would topple over in hysterics if she heard you say that."

"Why did you say you hate it?"

"I don't know. I guess it's because I feel lonelier than I do other times of the year," he replied, putting his bottle down and returning to the car.

I sat there watching him replace the broken hose, feeling my own heart palpitate in ways and rhythms I had not felt before. I rose and stood beside him as he struggled with a rusted bolt.

"Don't you have a girlfriend?" I blurted out, and then quickly wished I could take the words back. It was one of those questions you don't want to ask because you dread the answer, but a question you know you have to ask.

"Did," he said. "We broke up about three months ago. She was rushing me into something I wasn't ready for," he added before I could ask why.

He sprayed the bolt and worked it out much easier, holding it up as if he had extracted a gold nugget.

"Ta-da!" he said. I smiled and he suddenly looked very serious.

"You've got the cutest nose I've ever seen," he said. It was a compliment that seemed to fall out of the darkness, completely unexpected, stealing my breath for a moment. "I guess you've heard that before," he added, turning back to the engine.

"No," I said softly. "Never."

He looked over at me like he didn't believe me and then went back to work. I watched, but my heart was pounding so hard, I didn't think I could hold the lamp steady enough. He didn't seem to notice how much my hand shook. Finally, the used part was installed.

"Time to test our work," he declared. "Go start the engine."

I did so and he watched it run.

"How's the gauge doing?"

"It's back to normal," I said. "We'll have to wait and see though."

"Why don't you let it run for a while," he suggested.

After a few more minutes, he asked me again and I told him it was fine.

"You girls lucked out," he concluded. "You can turn it off," he said and I did.

He began to clean up.

"So where do you think you'll end up?" he asked.

"We want to go to Los Angeles. We hope we'll find an inexpensive place to live and find work. Crystal wants to get back to school and we want to find a dancing school for Butterfly," I told him.

"Butterfly? The little one?" I nodded. "She seems so fragile, too fragile for this sort of thing."

"You're right, but she's got us to protect and watch over her."

"Is it enough?" he followed quickly. "Sorry," he said, "but I tend to be brutally realistic sometimes."

"It's all right." I took a deep breath. "I don't know all the answers, Todd," I said. "I know that we hated where we were and what was happening to us. We felt trapped. We felt as if we were merchandise left on a shelf, merchandise no one would want to take home with them. Maybe we were crazy. Maybe we were just a bunch of stupid girls, but we took charge of our lives, even if it's only for a little while, and that felt good. When I first drove out of there . . ."

"What?" he said, holding his smile.

"I don't know. I felt so free, so powerful. I just felt . . . alive. I guess I sound stupid."

"No," he said, shaking his head. "You sound pretty wonderful to me."

I felt my face warm. Why did I have to blush so much?

"I can understand how you felt." He walked to the doorway and I followed alongside. For a moment he just stared out at the road, the woods and the bushes. "This place sometimes puts me in a strange, sad mood, as if I've got to run fast to catch up with the best things in my life, things that are all slipping away from me. I feel the same sort of panic you felt. I feel trapped and alone."

He stepped out and we walked as he continued.

"Sometimes, I see a car with out-of-state plates go by and I think about just walking away from here, getting into my car and driving until I run out of gas. Wherever that is, I'll stay and make a life for myself," he said, looking out at the darkness.

There was a flatbed truck beside the garage. It looked like something from the sixties, rusting, missing a rear tire, the passenger side window shattered.

"Why don't you do just that?" I asked softly. His voice and mine were barely above a whisper now. He shrugged.

"Dad, I guess. I'm all he has, even though half the time, he doesn't even know I'm around. And then I think, what will I have out there? At least here I have something. It's not much, I know, but it's mine and I'm my own boss. Not many guys my age can say that," he added.

He boosted himself up onto the flatbed and sat, his hands on his lap, his head a bit bowed. I stepped on the bumper and jumped up beside him with such ease, he laughed.

"You're pretty nimble."

"I can stand on my head," I bragged, "but don't ask me to do it," I followed quickly.

The two of us looked at the dark street. It was still, quiet.

"Not much traffic goes by here this time of the night, does it?" I asked.

"No." He leaned back on his elbow, found a dried piece of grass on the flatbed and put it into his mouth. "What about you, Brooke? Did you leave a boyfriend back there?"

"No," I said quickly.

"C'mon, there must have been a few," he insisted.

"Well, no one important at least," I admitted finally.

"What do you mean? How can that be?" he kidded. "How could boys resist falling head over heels for you?" Something in his eyes turned serious, and I knew he was paying me another compliment.

"I used to ask myself that every day," I joked back, suddenly uncomfortable.

He laughed harder and then suddenly stopped and fixed his gaze on me. In the darkness, his beautiful ebony eyes glistened. When he turned, his body moved closer to me. We were only inches apart. I didn't turn away as his lips drew closer. We touched, almost as if by accident at first, tentative, soft, quick, and then he shifted his weight and kissed me harder, longer, his hand going to my shoulder to hold me to him.

"I like you, Brooke," he said. "I like you a lot."

"I like you, too."

"I'm glad your car's water pump broke," he whispered.

We kissed again and then we lay back. He had his arm outstretched so that my head rested on it and when I turned, I turned into his chest. Above us the stars blinked like candles in the dark. It made me dizzy to lie there, feeling his heartbeat as well as my own. His lips were on my forehead and then slowly traced the bridge of my nose, paused at the tip, kissed it and moved to my lips again. This kiss was long, softer, warmer. I felt the heat rising up my legs as if I had lowered myself into a warm bath.

I put my fingers into his hair and combed through it, moving down the back of his neck. I heard him moan and felt his excitement building. He moved closer, his right hand sliding down my arm and under to find my breast. I turned into him and buried my face against his chest. He kissed the top of my head and then nibbled gently on my ear. It sent a delightful chill down my spine.

He rose to his knees then and carefully, gracefully guided me back farther onto the flatbed until we were well hidden by the sides of the truck. There was a bale of hay at the rear. My head rested against it. He rose to his knees, lowered the straps of his coveralls and pulled off his shirt. His chest shimmered in the darkness, reflecting the starlight that was in my eyes as well.

"To me you're a breath of fresh air, Brooke," he whispered just before he lowered himself to kiss me again. His fingers moved under my sweatshirt. I lifted my back so the shirt would go smoothly up and over my head. He kissed my neck and reached behind to undo my bra. When I felt the snap unfasten, my heart stopped and then started like a parade drum. He didn't lift the bra from my breasts quickly. For a few moments, he continued to kiss around it, nudging my breasts. I had never before gone this far with a boy. I could barely breathe.

No voice within me told me to stop. I had no fears, no hesitation. I surprised myself with my eagerness, my desire to continue, to explore my own feelings.

Todd was so different than the other boys I'd dated. Every time he touched me, it was as though he asked first, as though he was careful to be sure it was what I wanted. He gave me the feeling he wanted me to enjoy him as much as he could enjoy me. It was lovemaking on that romantic level, that level of equality girls read about, dream about, but rarely have. I was having it and it flooded my heart with a warmth I never thought possible.

My nipples were so stiff so quickly, they ached. I couldn't help my moaning.

"Brooke," he whispered. "You're beautiful, as beautiful as any girl I've ever seen."

I quickly discovered that words could dazzle like jewels. They traveled through my ears and into my brain, but they kept going until they touched my deepest, most secret self. They nudged the woman in me and I longed for him in ways that had come to me only in my most private fantasies.

I felt his leg between my legs and I pressed myself against him eagerly. We writhed, kissed, drank at each other's lips. I was in such a daze, I vaguely felt his fingers undo my jeans. Before I could stop him, his hand was inside and found my most private place. I didn't turn away. His excitement grew rapidly now. His breathing came so fast, I felt my first tinge of fear.

"Todd," I said, "I've never done this before."

"I know," he said, "but I've never wanted it more with anyone."

His words were hypnotic. Finally, a tiny voice began to call out a warning. It called my name. I liked to think of that voice within me as my mother's voice, something I seized on when I was a baby, something I buried deep inside myself to resurrect only when I needed it the most.

He had undone his own pants and I felt his nakedness. He struggled with my panties and then, he stopped when I didn't move as cooperatively as I had before.

"I'm afraid," I cried. "I know we're going too fast, Todd. Please."

He slumped against me.

"You're right," he said, "we are, but you're running off tomorrow."

"I am, but I'm not going to forget you, if you don't want me to," I said.

His breathing slowed. He pressed his forehead against my shoulder and waited as if he had to endure some terrible agony for a moment.

"Are you all right?" I asked.

"Yes. Just give me a minute," he said. I let him lie there, his body against me. We listened to each other's hearts beating like jungle drums. Who knew the messages they were exchanging? Finally, he turned on his back, slipped his coveralls up, and took a deep breath.

I fixed my bra and put on my sweatshirt.

"I'm sorry," I whispered.

"There's nothing to apologize for, Brooke. You did something to me from the moment I first saw you and I couldn't help myself. Believe me. I'm not like this normally."

He sat up, pulling his knees in and embracing his legs with his head down. It was easier for him to open his heart to me that way.

"I have this fear that I'll be like my mother, wild, immoral. It's like it might be in my blood or something. I hated the way men treated her and I don't want to treat a woman, any woman that way.

"But it was different with you," he said, raising his head. "I just couldn't stop my feelings."

"I know. Neither could I," I said.

I could see his smile glisten in the starlight. "I guess your friends are going to wonder where you are."

"No, they have no idea how long fixing a car should take," I said. "It's all right."

"You can drive your own car back now," he said.

"I'm not in any rush." I lowered my head to his lap when he straightened his legs and looked up at him.

"I guess this is what they mean when they say love at first sight. Man, oh man, I don't know whether to feel foolish or happy."

"Be happy, Todd. I am."

"You really won't forget me?" he asked.

I laughed.

"You'll forget me first. I'm sure."

"I'll take that bet," he said. "As soon as you land somewhere, write or call and I'll make that my first vacation."

"Promise?"

"On every star in the sky. Every time you look up at night, you can think of me and my promise. Just remember I'm waiting back here and don't let me wait forever, okay?"

"Oh, Todd, I don't know where we're going to end up. I'm afraid now," I said. "And I'm the leader. I'm the one who got them all to go."

"You'll figure it out, Brooke. I can see you're someone who lands on her feet. My money's on you."

I laughed.

"Now you do sound like someone in love because when you're in love, you're blind to what's real."

"Who told you that?" he asked.

"No one. I came to that conclusion myself," I said.

"I told you I am too realistic. It won't apply to me."

"Oh sure," I said. "We've run away, stolen a car, been robbed, don't know where we're going or what we'll actually do when we get there, but I'll land on my feet. That's being realistic?"

"Yes," he insisted. "In your case, yes."

I reached up. He lowered his head so my hand could go around his neck, and then he let me pull his lips close enough for mine to meet them. It was our most delicious kiss because it was our seal, our promise, our kiss meant to last forever and ever.

Mrs. Slater didn't tell me that she locked the front door after eleven. It was embarrassing to have to ring the bell and then when no one came, to knock and knock. Finally, she was there. She wore a dark brown terry cloth robe at least two sizes too big and men's slippers.

"I'm sorry to wake you," I said.

"I didn't know you were still out, dear. It's always been my rule to lock my doors at eleven unless someone tells me otherwise. I thought you were all upstairs, snug in your beds. Where have you been?" she asked stepping back.

"Fixing our car," I said. "Thank you. Good night," I said before she asked another question. I hurried past her and up the stairs to my and Raven's room. She was awake, lying there with her hands behind her head, the small lamp on the nightstand lit.

"You don't have to tell me," she said as soon as I walked in, "I can see it on your face."

"What?"

She laughed and looked at the clock.

"Nearly four hours to fix the water pump?"

"It was difficult," I said. "The old pump was rusted and . . ."

"Pleeeze. I recognize that look on your face," she joked, but there was a bit of sadness behind her words. She, too, had felt this in love with Taylor, and his awful behavior still stung.

"Oh Raven," I cried in a voice that even I didn't recognize. The joking look dropped off her face.

"What?" she asked quickly, her eyes filled with more concern than curiosity.

"I think . . . I know I'm in love."

"What? In love? You hardly . . . now wait a minute, Brooke. You can't be serious," she declared, sitting up with her hands on her hips.

"Why not?"

"Why not? You just met him, Brooke. You know what can happen if you go too fast . . . you don't want what happened to me with Taylor to happen to you!" There was such grief in her face I wanted to listen, but my heart told me Todd and I were different.

"I know you mean well, Raven, and I'm sorry that Taylor broke your heart, but Todd is different, he's not like Taylor."

She looked at me closely and then sat back against her pillow.

"Tell me what happened, Brooke. I want to believe you're right about Todd."

"Well, I didn't go there expecting anything romantic to happen." Her eyes grew smaller. "Really, Raven, I didn't. We talked a little and I helped him as he worked," I continued.

She started to giggle and I shot her a mutinous look.

"I'm sorry. It's just a garage is probably the last place on earth I'd expect to have a romantic time." She pressed her lips together and pretended to zip her mouth shut.

"He's a very sensitive guy. I began to feel more sorry for him than I did for myself. His father's an alcoholic and his mother ran off with someone else years ago," I said.

"This is your Mr. Right?"

"You can't blame him for his parents, Raven. How would you like us to be blamed for ours?" I shot back at her. The devilish look in her eyes faded quickly.

"You're right," she said softly.

"He broke up with a girl recently. I guess she wasn't right for him and she wanted to get very serious."

"Uh huh, I see," Raven commented, raising her eyebrows and darkening her eyes.

"What's that supposed to mean? Raven?"

"Well, sometimes boys are more passionate or nicer when they're on the rebound, Brooke. They're suffering from broken hearts and along you come to help mend them," she explained.

"He wasn't suffering from a broken heart. If anything, the girl was," I insisted. She nodded, still skeptical. "We talked about that a little and then we went out to this flatbed."

"This what?"

"It's a kind of truck," I explained.

"Oh." She smothered a smile with the back of her hand.

"Are you just going to laugh at me or really listen?"

"All right. Sorry. What happened?"

"We kissed and . . ."

"And?"

"Kissed and kissed and stopped just before it was too late," I said. I looked down when she was silent. "I really didn't want to stop."

"Really? This *is* special." She was pensive a moment and then she leaned forward to touch my shoulder. "What are you going to do?"

"Nothing. What can I do? I promised I'd write him from wherever we land and he promised to come see me," I said.

She sat back, thought a moment and nodded with a small smile.

"You know, I think he just might visit. He really sounds like someone special. I'm sorry I was so suspicious—I just didn't want you to fall into the same trap I did."

I saw in her face that she meant it and I thanked her. We hugged and I went to brush my teeth and get ready for bed.

Later, in the dark, just before I turned over, Raven called to me.

"What?"

"It's nice, Brooke. It's nice to have someone to be in your dreams."

"What if it is never anything but dreams, Raven?"

She thought a moment.

"It will be more for you, Brooke. I just know it will."

"How do you know?"

"How do I know? I know because I'm jealous," she said with a voice filled with regret. I wondered how long it would take her to get over giving Taylor that very special part of her.

"Good night, Raven. Thanks."

"You don't need to thank me. You're my sister, Brooke."

"Forever and ever."

"The Orphanteers . . ."

We fell asleep, both of us drifting off to dreamland.

Raven didn't say anything about me to Crystal and Butterfly in the morning. They had fallen asleep rather quickly the night before and never knew when I had returned. As usual, Crystal woke us.

"Is the car fixed?" she asked as I ground the dreams out of my eyes.

"Yes. It's right outside."

"We get breakfast here," she said, "so you should hurry and dress."

I poked Raven, who groaned and mumbled to be left alone. Crystal poked her too, and she finally got up and practically sleep-walked her way through breakfast. It was a good breakfast, too, and Mrs. Slater was a very nice host, chatting about everything from the weather to the latest headlines in the newspaper left on her doorstep. She was curious about us, but not enough to really pry, and like everyone we met, she fell in love with Butterfly, who turned her winning smile and soft eyes on her like a searchlight for affection.

After breakfast, Crystal and I waited on the porch and went over the map, planning how far we expected to get and where we thought we would stop again.

"We have just a little more than a hundred dollars now, Brooke. I don't know what we'll do even if we get to Los Angeles in two days."

"Just go right out and look for work, waiting tables. Maybe," I thought aloud, "we could sell this car."

"Sell the car? How? It doesn't belong to us."

"There are people who won't care," I said.

"We wouldn't know how or where to find those sorts of people, Brooke, and I'm not going to sell something we've borrowed," she emphasized.

As long as we continued to tell ourselves we borrowed it, we wouldn't feel as guilty or think of ourselves as thieves. She was right.

"Something will come up for us, Crystal. You'll see," I said. I had promised to stop by Todd's before we left, but I was a little hesitant about it and considered just driving right by. I knew it would hurt him as much as it would hurt me, however.

"Ready," Raven sang and spun around in the doorway. "California, here we come!"

Butterfly came out with a care package Mrs. Slater had prepared for us.

"She said she couldn't let us go without lunch," Butterfly told us as we headed to the car. Once again, we'd found people who cared about us just when we had to leave.

We got into the station wagon and I started the engine. Mrs. Slater came to the door to wave good-bye as we drove off. When the garage came into view, I slowed.

"I'm just stopping to say good-bye," I said quickly.

"Oh?" Crystal said, looking up.

I pulled in and got out slowly. Todd was under a car in the rear of the garage. I heard him grunt and then he stopped what he was doing and pushed himself out to look up at me.

"We're leaving," I said quietly.

He got to his feet and looked out the door at our car. The girls were all staring. He nodded toward the far corner, which would be out of their view, and I went there. As soon as I turned, he kissed me.

"I want you to promise me that if you should get into some difficult situation along the way, you'll call me. Will you?" he asked.

"Yes."

"I had some business cards made up last year. I've got a drawer full of them." He dug into his coverall pocket and produced one which he slipped into my jeans pocket quickly. "Look at it once in a while so you don't forget me," he said.

"I won't forget you, Todd. That's silly. I'll be thinking about you all the time."

"Will you?" He smiled. "I hope so. You'll call as soon as you get where you're going, right?"

"Yes."

"You're like some sort of miracle that came sweeping into my life and rushed out."

"I'm not rushing out." We stared at each other. My heart felt empty, hollow. "I'd better get going," I said barely above a whisper. My eyes lowered. He touched my chin and I looked at him again.

"I'm memorizing your sweet little nose," he said. "I'm memorizing all of you."

We kissed once more and then I broke out of his embrace and hurried out to the car, trying desperately to swallow back the tears and sobs that wanted to escape.

"Everything all right?" Raven asked softly. I shook my head.

"What's wrong?" Crystal asked.

"Nothing," I said, starting the engine.

"Brooke likes him," Butterfly said. "Don't you, Brooke?"

I gazed at her in the rearview mirror and smiled.

"Yes, Butterfly. I do."

I started away.

Todd came to his door and raised his hand. I clicked the picture of him standing there and pressed it so hard and deeply into my memory, it would take a sledge hammer to get it out.

Someday, I'll see him again, I thought, and we'll be together forever. We'll marry and make a life because we not only loved each other, but needed each other. Or was this just a new pipe dream?

What sort of a wedding could I ever have? I asked myself. I have no father to give me away, no mother to help me chose my colors, my dress, my flowers and cake.

I have no one but myself.

12
&

Reality Check

We got a flat in the right rear tire just after we reached I-70. Fortunately for us, Gordon had a full-size spare in the rear and with Crystal and Raven's help I was able to change the tire. The lug nuts were so tight, it took all of us to turn the wrench and loosen them. Raven and I pulled while Crystal practically stood on the wrench until the nuts turned. I'm sure we were quite a sight. Many cars passed us, but no one stopped to help. Crystal thought we were better off because there would be less lying to people. Of course, we were terrified a highway patrolman would stop, but they must have all been having coffee. We didn't see a single one then or for the next fifty miles.

Just after lunch, Crystal directed us onto I-255, which took us into Missouri. We were in Missouri only a short time before we started west on I-44. Crystal said it would take us into Texas and from there we would go to New Mexico, Arizona and finally California.

California! It was beginning to feel like we were heading for the moon.

Every time we stopped for gas, we anticipated the gas charge card being denied, but every time it went through easily.

"He's right behind us," Raven predicted. "I can feel him in my bones."

No one contradicted her. We all had similar anxieties. It got so I actually gazed into the rear-view mirror from time to time in anticipation of seeing Gordon's pickup truck closing on us. His face would be up against that windshield, his teeth clenched between two whitened lips.

I drove on, forcing the images out of my mind.

Mrs. Slater's lunch was so filling, we weren't hungry until nearly seven. Crystal decided we should stop in one of the smaller supermarkets and buy ready-made salads. It was cheap and easy. Afterward, before we got back on the main highway, we decided to indulge ourselves and stopped for frozen custard. Finding a suitable place to sleep that wouldn't cost us a large portion of our remaining funds was our next challenge. Most of the motels were expensive and even the ones that looked seedy to us were more than we could afford.

"We'll have to try sleeping in the wagon again," Crystal said. "It won't kill us."

This time I found a truly unused side road. The macadam broke up and ended in a field. It was one of those roads that had been started and stopped, which was fortunate for us. The tall grass hid us from view. We locked our doors, set up our pillows, opened the windows a crack and went to sleep. Or at least, tried to fall asleep. Raven began saying what was on all of our minds.

"If we would have been able to work longer at Patsy's, we would have more money and wouldn't have to sleep in a field somewhere. We could eat like people. We could even buy some clothes. I've got to go to the bathroom. Now what am I supposed to do?"

"Pretend you're on one of the youth brigade camping trips the state used to organize for us," I said. "Go out into nature."

"I hated those trips. Anyway, there's mosquitos out there. There's snakes. There's . . ."

"Werewolves and vampires," Crystal chimed.

"Ghosts and goblins," Butterfly said and giggled.

"And serial killers. Don't forget the serial killers who have lost their way, too," I added.

"You're all very funny, but you're all going to have to go to the bathroom in a field, too," Raven reminded us.

"Our ancestors did," Crystal said. "You know, the concept of indoor plumbing is a relatively recent phenomenon."

"Oh, pleeeze, not a lecture on the history of the toilet," Raven begged.

I laughed so hard, I suddenly had to go.

"Come on," I said. "I'll stand guard for you and you can stand guard for me."

When we were finished, we got back into the wagon and tried again to sleep. After what seemed like close to an hour, but was probably only about fifteen minutes, I sighed deeply and loudly enough for everyone to hear.

"I can't fall asleep," Raven declared.

"Me neither," Crystal said. "I thought I was so tired, it would only take a minute."

"I'm awake, too," Butterfly said.

"Let's talk ourselves out," Crystal suggested.

"Talk about what?" Raven asked. "And don't say politics or science."

"I know," Crystal said, "everyone take a turn telling what's the most important thing she wants to find at the end of this rainbow. Who's first?"

"You go first," Raven said. "It was your idea."

"Okay. I want to find a good school in California so I can start applying for colleges."

"Boring," Raven sang.

Crystal continued, ignoring her.

"And then I want to go to the beach. And surf," she giggled.

"Don't you want to meet any movie stars?" Raven asked her.

"No, not really. I don't care if the actors are famous. I'd rather go to one of the UCLA medical conferences. Research is so important and those doctors are famous for their work in . . ."

"It's working, Crystal," Raven declared.

"What?"

"I'm falling asleep."

"Very funny," Crystal said. I subdued a giggle. "Let's hear from you then, Miss Songbird," Crystal challenged.

Uh oh, I thought, here comes Crystal's sharp wit. She's just setting her up.

"Okay," Raven chimed. "I want to get to Los Angeles, go to my first audition, and get picked to sign a record deal before I've sung my first note."

"That's not a goal, that's a dream. You ought to convert that story into a pill and sell it to insomniacs," Crystal advised.

"What is that supposed to mean? Can you understand anything she says, Brooke? I swear. Besides, what's wrong with having a dream?"

"I'd like to get an athletic scholarship to a great school," I said before they got into a real argument, "and after a few weeks, I'd write to Todd. He would come out and then we'd get married after I finished school and he could travel all over the world with me and my Olympic team.''

''Just think, you could have enough children to start your own softball team,'' Raven laughed.

''I don't think this game is helping us relax and sleep,'' I retorted.

''What about you, Butterfly?'' Raven asked her.

There was a long pause.

''I just want to find a new mother and father and maybe a grandmother and grandfather,'' she said in her tiny voice.

No one spoke.

''I am tired now,'' I said, closing my eyes and sinking deeper into the seat.

''Me too,'' Raven said, ''so everyone shut up.''

It was dark and very still, with barely a breeze coming through the openings in our windows. Somewhere far off, I heard what I thought was an owl. I closed my eyes. Butterfly's simple wish resonated like a powerful poem inside me.

Should I have told the girls what I really wished? I wished that at the end of my rainbow was my mother, who would come forward to claim me, to ask for my forgiveness, to tell me a story that justified and explained why she abandoned me. She would be filled with so much remorse, I would forgive her and she would hug me and kiss me and tell me that ever since that dreadful day when she had to deposit me in some state-run facility, she had dreamed of meeting me again.

We would pick up as if all the intervening years had been a bad dream. In minutes we would become like sisters, and she wouldn't be upset about my being more interested in sports than in beauty pageants. She would be intrigued and interested. We'd play tennis and swim and take long walks on those grand California beaches where the sand glimmers like tiny diamonds and the people are forever young.

How wonderful it would be finally to have someone I truly wanted to call Mommy.

Darkness wrapped itself around us, four lost and frightened souls safe for the moment, sleeping in the automobile owned by the man we had all come to hate, the demon in our nightmares, out there, chasing us, fueled by his rage, relentless, a reason never to forget to lock our doors.

As if she could read my thoughts even in her sleep, Butterfly had a terrible nightmare almost as soon as she fell asleep. She woke screaming and Crystal was immediately at her side, comforting her, assuring her she was safe.

"What was it?" Raven asked her. Butterfly couldn't talk, didn't want to tell.

"It's all right, Butterfly," Crystal said. "We're all here with you."

"She scared dinner out of me," Raven moaned. "My heart feels like a tiny fist pounding on the inside of my chest."

"Go back to sleep," Crystal advised.

"Go back to sleep?"

"Just go back to sleep," she said firmly.

Raven thought a moment, realized that Butterfly would remain calm if we did, and quieted down.

It was hard to go back to sleep. I felt so sorry for Butterfly. Maybe it was wrong to take her with us. Maybe Todd was right. She's too fragile. Even our love, our company, our joining and promising to be there forever for each other wasn't enough.

Who did we think we were anyway? I thought.

We're nobodies.

How did I ever come up with this idea?

The morning light woke us. It filled the car with so much sunshine that when I opened my eyes, I thought we were on fire and jerked myself up, a scream on my lips. After a moment I remembered where we were. It was just five-thirty in the morning. Raven wouldn't be a happy camper if I woke her, I thought as she moaned and turned, desperately trying to cling to sleep.

I got out, stretched and took deep breaths of the cool air. Crystal joined me. Butterfly was still asleep too.

"We've got to figure something out, Brooke, find a way to get money. We can't go on like this and what will we do if we should ever really reach California? We'll need an apartment. We might not get jobs right away and even if we did, we wouldn't get paid right away. How do we eat in the meantime? Who'll give us an apartment without putting up rent?

"I've been awake awhile," she confessed, "thinking about all this."

"What are you saying, Crystal?"

"Maybe it's time we stopped fooling ourselves. It's been an adventure, but that's about it. We can't expect anything more, realistically that is."

"You know we can't go back. You know what will happen," I reminded her.

"Not if we tell the police everything. They'll believe us, even if it means leading them back to the place where we left the cocaine. I put a rock over the bag. I'm sure it will still be there and there should be enough of a residue to convince them we were telling the truth. Gordon will be arrested.''

''What if he's not?''

''Even if he's not, they won't put us back with him. They'll know how bad that would be,'' she said.

''Would they?'' I kicked a rock and sighed, tears coming to my eyes. ''I think I'd rather take my chances starving.''

''Or becoming one of those girls Norman and Nana's son accused us of being . . . live on the streets?'' She shook her head. ''You don't want that, Brooke. We just have to . . .''

''What?''

''Be wards of the state awhile longer,'' she said. ''It's our particular miserable fate. I'm sorry.''

''Me too. Don't tell them yet,'' I said, gazing at the station wagon. ''Let's go as far as we can just for . . .''

''Fun? I don't think Raven and Butterfly see this as fun anymore,'' Crystal said.

''No, not fun, just to feel we really tried. Okay?''

''As long as you understand what the end will be,'' she said.

''I do.'' I swallowed down my sob and took a deep breath. She put her arm around me and hugged me to her.

Crystal could be very affectionate sometimes. She wasn't all brains. She was just good at keeping her feelings under an armor of words and logic and facts. I had no doubt that in her quiet, private moments, she cried as much as any of the rest of us did.

''Let's wake them,'' I said, ''and get back on the road.''

She nodded and looked at me with those perceptive intense eyes of hers.

''I almost wish we were stopped and caught. It would be easier than giving up,'' she said.

I nodded.

''Yes, I suppose we could live with ourselves much easier then.''

Butterfly was just rising when we opened the doors. Raven moaned and turned so she could bury her face in her pillow.

''Come on, Raven. We've got to put the back seat up and get going. I don't want anyone finding us here,'' I said, ''and arresting us for trespassing.''

She sat up, a look of exhaustion in her face.

"Slave driver," she said. "You should be working for the state prison system."

"We could all end up in it if we don't get moving," I replied.

She and Crystal fixed the back seat and then Raven got into the front and I started the engine. I backed out of the dead-end road and we were on our way again. When we saw a sign advertising an all-you-can-eat breakfast for one dollar, ninety-nine cents, Raven pleaded with Crystal.

"That's cheap enough so we don't have to brown bag it, isn't it, Crystal?"

Crystal relented and we stopped. It was cafeteria style and populated mostly by senior citizens.

"It's because they live on a strict fixed income," Crystal explained.

Many heads turned our way when we approached the line, got our trays and moved through.

"It almost feels like the Lakewood," Raven said. "I'm losing my appetite."

Nevertheless, she ate very well, going back for seconds on the scrambled eggs. We used the bathrooms, washed up, and got ready to get back on the road. In the parking lot, standing near our station wagon was an elderly lady wearing a coat that I thought was much too heavy for the time of year. She had at least a dozen brown and black bobby pins holding her wispy, gray hair up, strands falling loosely on the sides and back of her head. She wore no makeup, but her cheeks were rosy. Her dark eyes were small and her mouth, although full, slanted a bit in the right corner. When I mentioned that to Crystal, she said she thought the woman might have had a stroke. She stood straight enough in granny shoes with heavy, thick heels. However, they looked like they had seen their best days about ten years ago.

She held a shopping bag that was stuffed with garments, its sides bulging. As we approached, she stared at us cautiously and then smiled at Butterfly, who flashed one of her prizewinners back.

"What a sweet little girl you are. My granddaughter Donna has hair like you, although yours is a little more like spun gold. What's your name?" she asked quickly.

"Janet," Butterfly said.

"Janet, you're going to be a beautiful lady someday. Just like my Marion. She could have been a movie star. Are you girls all by yourselves?" she asked.

"Yes, ma'am," Crystal said. She looked cautiously at me and I started for the car door.

"I missed my ride," she said. "I got here too late and they left me behind."

I paused and raised my eyebrows. Crystal did the same.

"Who left you behind?" Raven asked.

"Friends of my dead husband," she said. "Once your husband dies, all his friends avoid you like the plague. Believe me," she said, "when he was alive, they were always around. Ain't that the truth? Ain't it though?"

"You were supposed to meet them in this parking lot and they left without you?" Crystal pursued like some lawyer cross-examining a witness.

"It's not the first time I've been left behind. When you're a widow, you have to fend for yourself more than you can imagine, girls. But you're all too young to worry about being widows. Old age isn't pleasant. Ain't that the truth? Ain't it though?"

Raven looked at me and then back at her.

"Where are you going?"

"Oh just down to Morrisville. Forty miles or so. I'll have to walk to the bus station, I suppose," she said.

"Where's that?" Crystal asked.

"I'm not sure. I think it's . . ." She turned and then turned back. "I'll have to ask inside."

"Just a minute," Crystal said. She pulled her map out and spread it on the hood of the wagon. "Morrisville. That's not out of our way, Brooke. We'll drop you off, ma'am," she said.

"Would you? Isn't that nice of you? That's so sweet. Most people are not so sweet to strangers anymore. Thank you, darling. Thank you."

"You can sit in the back with us," Butterfly told her and opened the door.

"Why thank you, Janet. See? I remembered your name. Janet. You remind me of my Donna. Did I tell you that?"

"Yes," Butterfly said, smiling at her sweetly.

The elderly lady got in and Butterfly followed.

Raven seized Crystal at the elbow and pulled her back.

"She better not rob us," she said sharply. Crystal smirked.

"I hardly think there's an analogy here, Raven."

"A what? Why don't you speak English?" Raven complained.

Crystal laughed.

"That is English." Crystal got in and Raven turned to me with a look of desperation.

"You have to carry a dictionary on you when you're with Crystal. I don't care what she says. It's like learning a new language."

I laughed too, and we got into the wagon. We started out of the parking lot.

"My name is Theresa James," the elderly lady said. "I've lived in Morrisville for nearly forty-one years. My husband Eugene was a shoe salesman. He used to say he peddled good soles and saved more than a minister." She laughed. "Ain't that the truth? Ain't it though?"

"How many children and grandchildren do you have?" Butterfly asked her.

"I have three children, a son Thomas Kincaid James, and two daughters, Marion and Jennie. Jennie's the most like me. She's a good cook. Marion doesn't cook. She has servants who do everything. She married well. Her husband builds boats, pleasure boats, and they live in a house that looks like a castle. It's near a lake, too. I spend a part of my summer there and I see my grandchildren. Oh, I have five grandchildren, three boys and two girls. Two boys are Thomas's. He has a daughter who just turned seven. Her name's Connie, but she has long dark hair, not curly gold hair like you, dear. She's a good speller. They're always sending me her spelling tests with A's on them and I put them all over the refrigerator. I have so many. I can hardly find the handle." She laughed. "Ain't that the truth? Ain't it though?"

I looked in the rearview mirror and saw Crystal grimacing. I raised my eyebrows and she indicated there was a strange odor. After a moment I smelled it too. It smelled like charred wood and it was coming from Theresa James.

"My husband was a very good salesman. He never lost a sale. He could talk the last dime out of Rockefeller. They wanted to make him a vice president and give him an office, but he said, no sir, no thank you, I would rather be on the road, out there with the people. He loved being with people, talking, pressing flesh as he called it."

"When did he die?" Butterfly asked.

"Oh. He died . . . let me see now. My goodness, it's almost ten years. It isn't easy being a widow. All my old friends look the other way when they see me."

"That's awful," Raven said.

"Oh, I'm getting used to it, dear. Sometimes, I just pretend they're not there either. It's like we're all ghosts, you know. When you get old, you become a ghost. Ain't that the truth? Ain't it though?"

"I wouldn't let you be a ghost if you were my grandmother," Butterfly said.

"Well isn't that sweet? I do believe you are the most adorable child I ever saw, even sweeter than my Donna who could bring a smile to the Grinch. Isn't that what he's called?" she followed quickly, "the Grinch?"

Butterfly laughed.

"When did you see her last?" she asked.

"Oh, let's see now. I think it was four months ago. No, I guess it was more like six or seven."

"Don't they call you every day?" Crystal asked.

"Oh yes. My phone never stops ringing. The neighbors think I'm a bookie. You know what a bookie is, sweet light?" she asked Butterfly, who shook her head. "It's a man you call to place a bet on a horse. If you win, he has to pay you, but if you lose, you have to pay him. I have a brother who used to be a bookie. Now he's in an old-age home. I never get to see him."

"Why not?" Raven asked. "Won't your son or daughters take you?"

"No, they don't like him. They never did. They don't want me to see him either. They say he's the black sheep of the family and he made my mother old before her time. Mothers can get old before their time if their children are bad. Ain't that the truth? Ain't it though?"

"Did you spend last Christmas with your grandchildren?" Butterfly asked.

"Oh sure. We all went to my daughter's big house and we had a very big tree with mountains of presents, and there was a turkey that could feed an army. I made a pumpkin pie and an apple pie and Jennie made a date and nut bread and some Yorkshire pudding. It was a big feast with music and the fireplace just roaring away like in those Christmas cards, the ones that play a little tune when you open them. Oh sure, I spend all the holidays with my children and my grandchildren, birthdays and . . . birthdays." She paused as if she had forgotten what she was saying, and then she found her way again.

"But for now I live alone in my little old house, paid for years ago by my husband who was the world's best shoe salesman. Did I tell you what he used to say? He said, I saved more good soles than a minister." She laughed.

"Ain't that the truth?" Butterfly said.

Everyone smiled.

Theresa James laughed and then said, "Ain't it though?"

She talked almost the whole way to Morrisville. Raven kept swinging her eyes at me as if I could stop it or as if I were to blame. Finally, she turned on the radio and then began to sing along with a song.

"You have a beautiful voice, dear," Theresa James said. "My Jennie has a nice voice, but not as nice as yours. You could sing on a street corner and collect money in a hat," she added.

Raven smiled proudly.

"I'm going to sing on a stage and be paid a lot of money for it someday," she declared.

"Oh, I'm sure you will. I'll come listen and I'll say I knew you when you were . . . when you were . . . I forgot what time I was supposed to be in the parking lot. Maybe I was early and not late," she suddenly said. "I'd feel just horrible if they waited and waited for me and I had already left. Maybe I should have stayed there and not gone off with you. Oh dear. I'm not sure."

No one said anything. I looked at Crystal in the mirror. She wound down her window to get some fresh air into the wagon and shook her head.

"Your children should take better care of you," Raven said suddenly.

"Oh, ain't that the truth? Everyone tells me that. They say, why is it one mother can take care of three children but three children can't take care of one mother? Maybe mothers are harder to take care of, huh?"

"No," Butterfly said. "They would be easy."

"You're so sweet. Your name is Janet. I almost named my Jennie, Janet. We were looking for a name that began with J. My husband said, maybe Joyce or Joan and I said, no, it just came to me we should call her Jennie after my grandmother on my mother's side. He agreed even though he never met her. If he had, he would have sold her a pair of shoes." She laughed and Butterfly joined her to say, "Ain't that the truth? Ain't it though?"

All of us were grateful when a sign indicated Morrisville was just a few more miles.

"Where do you live?" I asked Theresa. "We'll take you there."

"That's very kind of you. Look how nice strangers can be," she said to Butterfly. "Well now, I live in a very exclusive area. My husband thought it would always be a nice neighborhood and he said, let's invest in a home here. We'll never be sorry, and we never were. It's a lot of house for just a little old lady, you understand, but I am as used to those old walls as they are to me. I couldn't imagine living with my children. It's nice to visit, but remember what Ben Franklin said, 'Guests and fish smell in three days.' '' She laughed. This time Crystal joined. ''Ain't that the truth? Ain't it though?''

We were all chanting it by the time we entered Morrisville. The sky had darkened and there was a light drizzle falling. One of Gordon's windshield wipers was badly worn and only streaked the right side. I tried not using them.

''You go right down Main Street,'' Theresa directed, ''and then you turn on Fourth and I'll show you. Thank you, dear.'' She smiled at Butterfly. ''What a sweet child. You know, my mother said I was a pretty little girl. She said all the men would give me a penny and I would do a little dance. My father could whistle whole symphonies.

''He was a happy-go-lucky man,'' she said, ''but he never made a good living. Not like my husband, who sold good soles and saved . . . saved so many.'' She paused and wiped her face with her hand. ''I'm tired. I'm glad I decided to go along with you girls.''

I reached Fourth Street and turned right. It looked like a shabby neighborhood to me. The houses were old, worn, the small patches of lawn bald and messy, full of weeds and garbage. One even had some old tires on it. We didn't see many people. The rain started to fall a little harder.

''Looks like I should have remembered my umbrella. I don't think it was supposed to rain, though.''

With the dark clouds above, the drizzle falling, the neighborhood looked even more dismal. The gutters weren't very clean and in front of one house, four dogs had turned over a garbage can and were chomping through whatever food remains they could find.

''You don't live here, do you?'' Raven asked.

''Oh no. I live nearby,'' she said. ''When you come to the corner, turn left and I'll get out,'' she said. ''I can walk a little. You've been very nice, but I just can't ask you in. My house is a mess and I'm tired. I'm going right to bed. I'm sorry.''

''That's all right,'' Crystal said. ''We have a lot of traveling to do and have to make as much distance as we can before it gets dark.''

''Thank you, dears. Thank you, thank you,'' she said moving in her seat.

''Here?'' I said.

''Thank you, dears. Thank you.''

I stopped and Crystal opened the door. Theresa started to slide out. She paused and turned to look back at Butterfly.

"Don't you sell anyone any of your curls. And watch out for men who wink when they smile. Good-bye," she said with a wisp of a smile.

"Good-bye," Butterfly said sadly.

"Good-bye," Crystal told her. Raven said it too, and I followed. Crystal got back in the car and for a moment, we watched Theresa James waddle up the sidewalk. She paused near an open lot. I started the car.

"We better get back to Main Street," Crystal said. "We'll find our way to the main highway easier."

"Right."

I turned into a driveway and backed up. As we started down the street again, we saw Theresa off to the right of the vacant lot. She put her bag down by a large cardboard box. I slowed to a stop.

"What is she doing?" Raven wondered aloud. We all did.

A moment later, she got down on her knees and she crawled into the box. My heart did a flip-flop.

"Crystal?" I cried.

"She's homeless," Crystal said. "You know, I thought she might be. There was something about her and that odor of burnt wood. Everything she told us was either a dream or . . ."

"Or what?"

"Or she's the worse kind of orphan there is, Butterfly, a mother forgotten by all her children."

"How can we leave her sleeping in a box?" Butterfly cried as I continued.

"What can we do, Butterfly?" Raven said. "We can't even help ourselves."

The hard truth fell like cold rain around us. Silence was suddenly louder than thunder.

"Ain't that the truth?" Crystal muttered.

"Ain't it though?" I said.

We drove on.

13
❧

The Jig Is Up

After we had left Theresa James, I felt as if we were just drifting along, floating through space, aimlessly carried by the power of the station wagon's engine. Our destination had become so vague, our purpose lost and confused. I felt it wouldn't be much longer before Crystal's prediction came to be. We would give up, turn ourselves in, throw ourselves back on the mercy of that impersonal government agency that had served so long as our surrogate parents.

Reality had a way of making me numb. Theresa talked about old people, widows and widowers becoming invisible. In a strange way I believed that was exactly what had been happening and continued to happen to us. Without family to support us, we were truly invisible. We might as well have been assigned numbers. You never realize how big a role family plays in ordinary conversation until you had none. Around us our fellow students talked about their parents, their brothers and sisters, aunts and uncles and cousins. There was always someone who did something, looked like someone, said something brilliant or stupid.

The thing that interested my school friends the most was how much I knew or remembered about my real parents. I knew absolutely nothing about my father, which most seemed to accept or understand. There were a number of students whose parents had been divorced, and many who had little contact with their fathers. What intrigued them more were my vague references to the woman I called my mother.

Having lived with her for only a little more than a year, I had nothing I could specifically mention. I had my dreams and I had some details I picked up from administrators at the orphanage. I had learned that she was not quite twenty when she had me. She didn't come from a wealthy family and from what I could gather, was actually on her own at the time I was born. Maybe she had been disowned because of me. I don't know why I came to a conclusion about her whereabouts, but I believed there were hints or things said that led me to believe she had left for California herself.

In my secret putaway heart, I really hoped and prayed I could find her there. Of course, I knew how big the state was and how many people lived in it, and I knew how small my chances were, but nevertheless that was my dream. I couldn't tell Crystal or Raven or even Butterfly, despite their being my sisters. It was like being naked, exposed, taking off your armor. How could the bravest girl they knew be such a weak, sentimental fool?

"What's the matter?" Raven suddenly asked me. We had been driving for nearly two hours, the radio droning on and the rain going from showers to downpours to showers and drizzle. The clouds on the horizon looked charred, like burnt marshmallows. Occasionally, the wind whipped the rain into sheets that flashed and wiped across the highway. We had to travel slowly.

"Why?" I asked, turning to her.

She twisted a bit in her seat, throwing a look at Crystal.

"You're crying," she said. "There are tears on your cheeks."

I touched my face and felt the warm liquid drops. It surprised me more than it surprised Raven. I wiped my eyes quickly.

"I don't know. Something must have gotten into my eyes," I said.

"Both of them?"

"Yes, both of them," I snapped back at her. She spun around as if I had slapped her and stared out the window.

"We should splurge tonight and sleep in warm beds," I said, trying to make up for snapping at Raven. "With a television set and a hot shower. Then we'll all feel a lot better."

"If we do that, we'll have little left for food, not enough even for another day," Crystal commented.

"I don't care. I'll worry about food then. I'll go out and beg," Raven chimed in.

"Beg?" Crystal said. "Would you really stoop that low?"

"Maybe, maybe not." She smiled jokingly. "Just leave everything to me."

"That's the last thing we should do," Crystal said. She was tired of joking.

Raven nearly jumped around and over the seat.

"What's that supposed to mean? Why do you always have to be Miss Doom and Gloom?" Raven asked angrily.

"I'm not being gloomy. All I'm saying is begging for our meals isn't enough to keep us going," Crystal said calmly, which infuriated Raven more.

"And just what will be enough, Crystal? If you have all the answers why don't you share them with us?" Raven demanded.

"Will you two stop it!" I cried. "We're not acting like the Orphanteers."

"Orphanteers. What a stupid name," Raven mumbled.

"You used to think it was good," Butterfly reminded her.

"That was before I grew up."

"And when did this miraculous maturity occur?" Crystal asked sarcastically.

"Oh boy. Did you hear that, Brooke?"

"I asked you two to stop it," I said, slowing down even more. "If you don't, I'm pulling over and . . . what's that?" I asked instead.

Raven turned back around and peered out the windshield.

"It's a woman, waving. She looks hysterical," Raven said.

Off to the right, just before an exit, a woman who looked about forty was swinging her arms wildly. She wore no coat or jacket to protect her from the rain. Her light brown hair was already soaked, the strands stuck to her forehead and ears. She was so desperate she looked like she might leap into the path of cars if one didn't stop soon. Two passed us by, but didn't slow down to see what she wanted.

"Stop for her," Crystal said and I turned off and headed toward her. She came running.

Raven rolled down her window.

"Oh, thank God someone stopped," the woman cried. She wiped the rain from her face. "It's my husband," she said. "He was feeling dizzy and pulled off this exit. Almost as soon as we stopped, he slumped over the steering wheel. My two little girls are with him, but there's absolutely no traffic on that road. I thought if I came back to the main highway, I could flag someone down and get help, but you're the first to stop and I've been trying for a few minutes."

"Get in quickly and show us where he is," Crystal said in her take charge tone of voice. She opened the door.

The woman got in and I drove to the exit. We didn't have to go far after the turn. The recreational vehicle was parked awkwardly on the right side of the road, the right blinker light still going. A little girl was sitting in the grass on the shoulder of the road, crying.

"Denise, get up," the woman cried. She did so slowly. "I told you to stay with Daddy."

"He won't talk," she moaned.

Crystal was right behind the woman and stepped up into the recreational vehicle. We gathered at the door. A man in his mid-forties was slumped over the steering wheel. His forehead was against the top of the wheel and his face was turned toward us, his eyes closed, his mouth twisted. I thought he looked kind of blue, especially about the lips.

Their other little girl, only about five or six, was curled up on the sofa.

"George!" the woman cried. "Oh God, oh my God."

Crystal felt his wrist for a pulse and then turned to me.

"Brooke, get up here and help me get him prone," she ordered. I stepped up and the woman stepped back. She hugged her daughter Denise to her. It simply amazed me how efficient and competent Crystal could appear, even to complete strangers.

George was a rather big man, probably at least six feet one and easily more than two hundred pounds. We struggled and I looked to Raven, who came in quickly and helped. Among the three of us we were able to slide him off the seat and lay him gently on his back.

Crystal went to work immediately. Even Raven, Butterfly and I were surprised and impressed. I never knew she was capable of performing CPR. She knelt by his side and placed her right hand on his forehead and her left under his chin. I gazed at his face. He was a good-looking man with some gray at his temples. Crystal glanced up at me with concern and then she listened for his breathing. Without hesitation, she pinched his nose and brought her mouth to his. She gave two full breaths and I saw his chest rise.

Butterfly moved closer to Raven, who put her arm around her.

"Is he dead?" the woman whimpered.

Crystal put her fingertips on his Adam's apple and slid them into the groove next to his windpipe. She felt for a pulse.

"Is he? Oh my God, George!"

Crystal gazed up at me again, looking more sad than nervous now. I could see it in her eyes, which had become reflections of mine and of Raven's and of Butterfly's. We had all lost our fathers. None of us wanted to witness this.

"I think he's in cardiac arrest," Crystal said.

She opened his shirt and put her hands at the center of his chest, one hand on top of the other.

"We have to get him to a hospital emergency room, quickly."

"I can't drive this thing," the woman moaned.

"I don't want to move him," Crystal said to me. "Brooke?"

I looked at the dashboard and nodded. Then I went to the seat and started the engine.

Meanwhile, Crystal began pumping the man's chest, counting up to fifteen and then blowing in two more breaths before pumping again.

The older girl cried harder. Butterfly went to her and tried to console her while the woman went to her younger daughter, who looked like she was in shock. Raven joined her and they all watched Crystal work.

"I have no idea where I'm going," I muttered. I drove until I saw a convenience store on a corner and pulled up. "I'll find out where the closest hospital is," I told them and ran out. There was only one customer in the store and a short, gray-haired man with a dark mustache at the counter. "We need a hospital quickly," I cried.

"Hospital. Go down here two miles, make a left, go five and when you come to the light, make a right. About a mile in you'll start to see the signs. What's wrong?" he asked.

"Heart attack," I said and charged out and into the vehicle. It wasn't hard to drive, but I hadn't taken the time to adjust the seat and my feet barely reached the brakes. I tried fixing it as I drove off.

"How's he doing?" I asked.

"I think there's a pulse, but it's very weak," Crystal said. "Is it far?"

"No."

It was more difficult steering this vehicle than the station wagon, and I almost missed the turn because I was going too fast. The tires squealed. My heart pounded. I thought we would turn over or blow a tire.

"Sorry," I said. A compact vehicle was right ahead of me, crawling along. I pressed on the horn in hope the driver would just pull over, but she didn't react so I had to wait for a chance to pass. As soon as I thought it was safe I pulled out and around the compact car. I had no idea what sort of power the recreational vehicle had and its acceleration was slow. A car was approaching. Neither of us had anywhere to go. I mumbled a prayer, kept my foot down and then swung into the right lane just at the last moment. The other driver sounded his horn angrily.

"Sorry," I muttered.

I'm sure it was only minutes before we turned into the hospital driveway, but because of the tension, it seemed longer. I followed the signs that indicated EMERGENCY and we pulled up as closely as we could to the doors. Then I hopped out and ran inside.

Two nurses were chatting by a desk. On their right a man sat holding his arm. He looked like he was in great pain, but no one seemed to notice or care.

"I have a man having a heart attack!" I screamed.

The nurses stopped talking. An orderly stepped out of an examination room and the three of them headed for me.

"Where?"

"Outside in the recreational vehicle," I said. "Please, hurry. My friend has been giving him CPR but she doesn't know if it's working."

Another orderly appeared. They grabbed a stretcher and they all went out to the vehicle. Moments later, they were wheeling him into the hospital, with all of us trailing behind.

"Don't worry," Raven said to the woman. "He's going to be all right now."

"Oh dear," she said. Her two daughters remained under her arms, the younger one still in a daze, the older one wiping her bloodshot eyes.

"Who can identify him?" the older of the two nurses asked. She went behind the counter.

"I can," the woman said. "He's my husband, George, George Forbas. I'm Caroline Forbas."

The nurse smiled as if she were a hotel agent filling out a form for a hotel stay instead of a hospital emergency room.

"I need you to fill as much of this out as you can," she said.

Caroline looked frantically toward the room in which her husband George had been taken. A young doctor came running down the hallway and slipped in quickly. He was followed by another nurse and another orderly.

"I'll take care of Sophie," Raven said, referring to the younger daughter. "Come on, Sophie, let's sit over there and look at the magazines."

She took her hand and the little girl followed Raven to the seats. Butterfly trailed along.

"Go sit with Sophie, Denise," Caroline said. Reluctantly, Denise left her side. Crystal and I remained with Caroline. "Thank you, girls," she said gratefully. "Thank you, thank you."

"It's all right," Crystal said. "You don't have to thank us."

Caroline looked at the nurse.

"I can't think."

"Does she have to do this now?" I asked.

"She might as well let the doctor examine her husband and this is something to do in the meantime," she replied dryly. "You can take it over there," she said pointing to a chair with a desk beside it. "Take your time, Mrs. Forbas."

Caroline sat down with the paper work and I walked over to Crystal, who looked more scared than I'd ever seen her.

"What's wrong?" I asked quietly, not wanting to draw attention.

"I remember when my foster parents were killed," she said. "I was at a friend's house. We were studying for a math exam and someone called on the telephone. I don't remember who called, but my friend's mother came to the door of her room and said, 'Crystal, there's been a terrible accident. Do you know your Uncle Stuart's number in Albany?'

" 'I'm sure it's in my father's Rolodex,' I said. 'I'll go look it up.' We lived right next door," she explained. "I remember I ran out of that house not even thinking about the consequences. It never occurred to me that they were both dead, you see. I was young enough at the time still to think of death as something alien, reserved for the aged, but not something that strikes people close to you."

I nodded, listening as I watched Raven work miracles with Sophie while Butterfly sat by talking softly to Denise, keeping her from crying. It occurred to me that we were all as terrified as they were. Crystal hardly ever talked about her past like this and certainly not with such nervous energy. Every once in a while, Raven would stop and look over at Caroline and her lips would tremble. She would take a deep breath, too. Butterfly's eyes met mine a number of times, searching for the same reassurance.

We had lost enough parents. It was impossible to simply sit by and watch someone else approach the same sort of doorway to sorrow.

"I ran back to my friend's house with the telephone number and gave it to her mother," Crystal continued. "I saw the strange way she was looking at me, but I still didn't ask any questions. Instead, I stood by and listened as she called my father's brother.

" 'Stuart,' she said, 'This is Vera Raymond, Thelma's friend next door. Yes. Yes, I'm fine. Stuart, there's been a terrible accident. A car accident. Karl and Thelma . . . Both of them have been killed. I'm so sorry,' she said. 'Yes, it happened a few hours ago. A drunk driver in a pickup truck. I'm sorry,' she repeated," Crystal said. "I have it all committed to memory. I often relive it through horrible flashbacks.

Sometimes, it just takes the ringing of a phone and I see the whole episode," she explained.

"Anyway, that's when and how I first heard they were dead. For a moment it was like eavesdropping on someone else's life. I still didn't fully comprehend, Brooke. I listened attentively to every word. I heard her say, 'Yes, she's with us. What do you want to do?' She listened, nodded and then she turned and looked at me as if he was telling her something about me that she never knew. Of course, she knew I had been adopted, so that wasn't it," Crystal said quickly. "I don't know what he said, but she looked at me and nodded. 'I understand,' she said, 'but what do you want to do in the interim, Stuart? Really?' she followed. 'All right. I'll find out and take care of it,' she said. 'I'm sorry.'

"Then she hung up and explained that my parents had been killed and my uncle wasn't coming to take me to his home. He had told her to call the Child Protection Services. Later that afternoon, they came for me and I was back in the system," Crystal said.

"I attended the funeral," she told me, "but after that, I never saw any of those relatives again."

"I'm so sorry, Crystal."

She shrugged.

"I was lucky in a way. My life, as hard as it is to imagine, would probably have been worse if I had gone to live with people who really didn't want me."

Caroline rose and brought the papers back to the desk.

"Why is it taking so long?" she asked the nurse, who just took the papers and turned to file them and enter information into a computer.

Caroline looked to us and we went to her side. The doctor finally stepped out of the emergency examination room. The nurse behind the desk gave him Caroline's paper work. He looked at it, nodded and then turned to Caroline.

"You are Mrs. Forbas?"

"Yes, how is he? Is he alive?" she asked quickly.

"He's stable now, Mrs. Forbas. He's on his way up to the cardiac care unit. We'll wait for the specialist to examine him and give us a full diagnosis. Who performed the CPR?"

"She did," Caroline said, nodding at Crystal.

"You did real well, Miss," he said. "There's no doubt in my mind you saved his life. You should be very proud of yourself. Where did you learn it?"

"Health class," Crystal said.

He laughed at her matter-of-fact, modest tone.

"Well, you're proof of why students should pay attention. Tell your teacher."

We watched them wheel George out of the examination room, the oxygen mask over his face. Caroline rushed to his side. She turned back as they headed for the elevator.

"Can you stay with the girls a little longer?" she asked us.

"Yes, of course," I said.

We watched her disappear with her husband and the orderly in the elevator and then we sat with Raven and Butterfly and entertained Denise and little Sophie.

The rain began again. We didn't notice it until the wind started blowing it against the windows. The girls, tired from their emotional ordeal, had fallen asleep, Sophie, the little one, with her head in Raven's lap. We were all somewhat exhausted and groggy. Butterfly dozed on and off and Raven lay back with her eyes closed, her fingers clamped on her forehead. Only Crystal made productive use of the time catching up on past issues of *Time* magazine.

None of us took much note of the two policemen who stood by the nurse's desk talking softly, but when the elevator doors opened and Caroline appeared, the nurse nodded at her and the policemen approached her. They spoke for a moment and then they walked over to us.

"Thanks for waiting, girls, and taking care of Denise and Sophie. The nurse upstairs was kind enough to call the sheriff's department for me because I can't drive that R.V. and we have to get to a motel. Officer Donald will take you back to your car. I don't know how I can thank you. Can you give me your address," she asked Crystal, "so I can send you something later?"

"There's no need for that," Crystal replied quickly. "How is Mr. Forbas doing?"

"He's resting very comfortably. They think he'll be fine. Of course, his lifestyle is going to change. No more smoking for one thing."

"I told Daddy to stop smoking," Denise said. "We learned about it in school."

"Yes dear," she said stroking her daughter's face affectionately. "Well, now he's going to listen to you."

"I'll get you to the motel," one of the policemen said. "Dave?"

"Girls, come along with me," the taller policeman said.

Raven shot me a very nervous look, but Crystal never batted an eye-lash. We all said good-bye to the girls. Raven and Butterfly hugged Sophie, who was sad to see them go. Then, without any more comment, we followed the sheriff's deputy out of the emergency room to his patrol car.

"Three of you can get into the rear," he said. "Don't be nervous about sitting behind a cage and having no handles on the doors. We usually put suspects back there," he added with a smile.

Raven widened her eyes with anxiety. Crystal took Butterfly's hand and opened the door. I was the one left to sit in the front with the policeman.

"So you guys did a real good deed," he said, getting behind the wheel. "This is a nice thing to see. It restores my faith in young people. Most of the time, I have them in my car for a lot worse reasons." He laughed, started the engine, and pulled out of the hospital parking lot. "You the driver?" he asked, nodding at me.

"Yes sir," I said.

He made a turn and drove slowly.

"So you're all from New York?" he continued.

I turned and looked at Crystal. Had any of us said that? She pursed her lips and narrowed her eyes into slits of suspicion.

"Yes," I said cautiously.

"A long way from home, aren't you?" he asked.

"We're on our way to visit relatives," I answered.

"A huh," he said.

He made another turn and sped up. I couldn't be sure because I was so nervous and excited at the time, but it seemed to me he was going in a different direction from the direction in which we had come.

"When we got the call from the hospital, I was patrolling in the vicinity where you had left your vehicle. I saw your license plates," he added, leaning toward me and then making another turn. "That's how I know you're all from New York."

"Oh." I smiled and looked back at Crystal, but she didn't seem relieved. She stared ahead, her face full of anticipation.

He made another turn, taking us past a more populated area. Soon we saw stores, gas stations, shops, and then he drove down a hill, leaving the community behind.

"Is this a shortcut or something?" I asked. "I know I didn't come this way."

"Whenever we find a vehicle deserted on one of our highways, it's just procedure to run a make on the plates," he explained softly. He flashed another smile in my direction.

"Oh," Raven moaned. She sat back and stared out the window.

"You're not Gordon Tooey, are you?" he asked me after a moment.

"No," I said, swallowing down a lump in my throat.

"And I bet nobody back there is either, huh?" he followed talking to them through the rearview mirror.

"Hardly," Crystal replied.

I saw the sheriff's station directly ahead. He looked at me.

"We're going to stop by here," he said, "because there are some people who have a few questions for you girls. I bet you know what some of those questions are, huh?"

"Yes sir," I said, lowering my eyes.

He laughed.

"Well, no matter what, girls, I stand by what I said back there. It sure is nice to see young people do a good deed. Of course, it makes this whole thing as confusing as hell, but it sure is nice," he said and pulled into the station's parking lot.

"Are we under arrest?" I asked after he turned off his engine.

"We usually investigate, ask questions, gather evidence and then arrest people," he said. "All I have right now are four very suspicious looking people. Come on," he said, opening his door, "let's see if we can straighten all this out to where it makes some sense."

He opened the door for Crystal, Butterfly and Raven and the four of us walked with him toward the front of the building.

"It's all right," Crystal said. "It's just like we discussed."

Raven looked at her as if she had gone mad and then gazed at me as if I had betrayed her, betrayed them all.

They put us in a large conference room. There was a glass window across from us and I had seen enough television shows and movies to imagine that it was a one-way window with people observing us on the other side. A police receptionist came in first and offered us soft drinks. Crystal asked for some tea and the rest of us had Sprites.

"What's going to happen to us now?" Butterfly asked in a tiny voice as she sipped her drink.

"We could go to jail," Raven replied, fear raw in her voice.

Butterfly looked at Crystal and then at me.

"Let's not rush to any conclusions," Crystal said. "Let's see what they ask and say first."

Just then the door opened and a woman in her late forties entered, wearing a deputy policeman's uniform.

She didn't wear a pistol, but she had a pair of handcuffs dangling off her belt. She carried a clipboard and walked with a stiff, military posture.

"My name's Lieutenant Mathews," she said, pointing to a name tag that read MATHEWS above her left breast. She sat across from us and just studied our faces for a moment before looking down at her sheets. "Who's Brooke Okun?"

"I am," I said. She stared at me as if she wanted to memorize my face.

"Janet Taylor?"

"Me," Butterfly said. Again, a moment's hard look before she turned to read.

"Raven Flores?"

"Pleased to meet you," Raven said.

Lieutenant Mathews' eyes sharpened before she turned to Crystal.

"And that leaves Crystal Perry?"

"Yes," Crystal said.

"All right, girls," Lieutenant Mathews said, putting aside her clipboard. "I heard how you helped a family just now and what a wonderful thing you did, so I know I'm not dealing with delinquents, but unless I hear some reason why not, you're all suspects for grand auto theft. What's more, you've taken the car across state lines, and," she added gazing down at her sheet, "no one here has a legal driver's license. Are any of these facts untrue?"

"We didn't steal the car. We just borrowed it for a little while," Raven began.

Lieutenant Mathews did not smile, she just flipped some pages and folded them over.

"You are all legal wards of the state. I have sent for a representative of the Child Protection Services here and he's on his way."

"Well, why don't we wait until he arrives before we discuss our situation any further," Crystal concluded. She took her glasses off and wiped them clean. Her coolness did not win us any pity, nor did Raven's smug smile. Even Butterfly's face of abject terror won us no sympathy. I looked down, my heart thumping.

"The best thing you girls can do for yourselves now is tell the truth," Lieutenant Mathews said. "No one wants to make this any bigger than it already is. You did all the driving?" she asked me.

"We all drove," Raven said protectively. "Even Butterfly. We got her a pillow so she could see over the steering wheel."

"In a little while, Miss Flores, you won't find this to be so funny. I assure you," she added.

There was a knock on the door. She stared at us rather than answer it and there was another knock. Finally, she stood up and opened it. A tall, thin man who looked more terrified than we did gazed in at us. He wore a dark brown suit and tie and had a narrow face with a nose that looked like it could be a practice ski slope. His mouth curled down at the corners to frame his lower jaw, which was rounded, the bones sharp against his light complexion. He had light blue round eyes and shifted them from one of our faces to the other, the lines in his mouth deepening even more.

"Okay, Mr. Glashalter. They're yours for the moment. They need some real guidance, I'd say," Lieutenant Mathews told him. She looked back at us and then left.

He entered, carrying his briefcase and taking Lieutenant Mathews' seat.

"Hello girls. I'm Clarence Glashalter and I'm with the Child Protection Services here. I have some information about you, but I'll need you to answer a few questions. I do know you stole the automobile of the man who was your foster father, correct?" He didn't wait for us to reply. "And you've been driving west for days. Where were you headed?"

"We were trying to get to California," I said.

He nodded as if that were a legitimate purpose.

"Yes, and?"

"And get away from foster homes forever," Raven added.

"By stealing your foster parent's car, though?"

"He's not exactly Mr. Clean," Raven continued.

"Well," Clarence Glashalter said, gazing at his paper work, "apparently, he's Mr. Forgiveness. I was just told that he is willing to drop all charges against you if you will all return to the home. He's flying out here to pick up his automobile."

"Return? I'd rather go to jail," Raven said.

Glashalter looked at all of us and saw a similar desire. He shook his head.

"He claims his wife is very fond of you all and has been very upset, sick actually over this. They don't sound like monsters to me. Besides,

I don't think you want to go to jail for stealing a car,'' he added with a smile.

"Yes, we do. We'll survive," Raven insisted. "As long as we're together, we'll survive. We're sisters.''

"I understand that," Clarence Glashalter said. He shook his head. "But the four of you won't be going to the same place.''

Butterfly moaned and looked at me and then Raven with desperation.

"This isn't funny. It's not some game we're playing, girls.''

"What do we have to do?" Crystal asked quickly.

"You have to apologize and go back and behave yourselves. I might get you on probation then. It bodes well for you that you helped that family just now," he added.

"We don't want to go back. We can't go back," Raven cried. "He's a monster.''

"If you have any legitimate complaints about your foster parents, you should be telling your counselors back in New York, not stealing cars and driving across the country," Mr. Glashalter said. "Follow procedures. I'm sure you're familiar with them. You've all been in the system awhile and . . .''

"Oh, the system," Raven groaned. "I'll just run away again," Raven threatened.

Mr. Glashalter's lips lifted and stretched. His eyes narrowed as he stared at her.

"Then you'll just get into deeper trouble and you won't have an opportunity like this, believe me," he said. "I assure you, if you are not cooperative . . .''

"We'll cooperate," Crystal promised quickly. "Thank you for helping us.''

Mr. Glashalter returned to his plastic smile and directed himself at Crystal.

"Very wise decision, my dear. That's smart. That way I can do what I can to help you," he told her.

"What do we do now?" Crystal asked.

"For now, I want you all to sit tight. I'll explain things to the sheriff and speak with the assistant district attorney. It will take a while, but I think we can manage it all as long as you remain cooperative," he added with no veiled threat in his voice. He rose.

"I'll be back shortly," he said and left us.

As soon as he did, Raven spun on Crystal.

"Why don't you tell him what we found in the car? Why don't you tell him why we don't want to go back with Gordon Tooey?" she asked.

"Why would they believe us, Raven? And then what . . . Gordon changes his mind, presses charges and they split us up? Do you want to see that happen? Do you?"

"Of course not," Raven said, "but . . ."

"Then no buts. Just be patient, be prudent and wait for another opportunity," Crystal said softly.

"But you know what he's going to want and when he finds out what we did . . ."

"What's he going to do, turn us in for throwing away his cocaine?"

"I hate to think what he's going to do," Raven said. She looked to me for help.

"For the moment, Raven," I said, "we have no other choice."

"It's easy to say that now," Raven cried, "but in a while Gordon Tooey will be coming through that door."

No one spoke.

The thunder of our own hearts filled our ears. It was enough.

14

The Evil Men Do

*E*very time the door opened, our breath caught in anticipation of facing Gordon. After Mr. Glashalter left, the first person to come in, however, was the deputy who had brought us from the hospital. He carried bags of burgers and fries with some sodas under his arm. The delicious aromas made my stomach churn.

"I thought you girls might be a little hungry. Looks like you'll be here awhile," he said, putting the bags on the table. He stood back. "Go on, eat them while they're hot. Compliments of the county," he added with a big grin.

I looked at Crystal. She nodded and we passed the burgers and fries to each other. The deputy watched us a moment and I could see the wheels turning in Raven's head. I squirmed in my seat and glanced at Crystal, who looked just as anxious about her.

"Suppose you found drugs in someone's car but you didn't tell the police, is that a crime?" Raven blurted.

I think the mouthful of burger bun I swallowed turned to stone in my throat.

"It's always a crime to withhold evidence or not report a crime you know is in progress," he replied. "Why?"

"I just wondered," she said.

"Are there drugs in that station wagon?" he followed. He would have had to be dumber than a rock not to have asked her, I thought.

"No," Raven said.

"Were there?" He waited. "If there were, there might still be some residue."

191

"And if there isn't?" Crystal asked. "You can't prove there were any, right?"

"Absent of physical evidence or an eyewitness, no," he said.

Crystal glared at Raven.

"I'm talking about another car," she said. "A boyfriend of mine back home."

"Oh. Well, you better drop him like a hot potato," the deputy advised. "If he gets picked up with that stuff and you're with him, it won't go well for you." He looked at Butterfly. "I bet you'd like an ice cream cone. What's your favorite flavor?"

"I like strawberry," she said.

"Anybody else? Better get me while the getting is good," he said.

"I'll have a vanilla cone," Raven said. Crystal and I declined and he left to get them.

"That was really stupid, Raven. Can you imagine what would have happened if he ripped apart the wagon with Gordon watching and they found nothing?" Crystal asked. "Gordon would see his drugs were gone and he would have been furious. I'm sure he would press charges against us then."

"I just wondered if there was another way out of here," Raven moaned. "You know I don't want to do anything to break us up."

"I'm scared," Butterfly whimpered, her lips quivering ominously. "I was never arrested before."

"You're not being arrested now," Crystal assured her. She fixed her eyes on Raven. "No one's going to do anything or say anything more."

Everyone was quiet a moment.

"Well, I'm scared too," Raven admitted. "I'm sorry, but I am."

"We're going to be all right," I said. "Don't worry about it."

"Right. I won't worry. You'll call super mechanic and he'll come flying in his, what did you say he called it? His Betty Lou?"

I glared back at her, tears of rage burning my eyes. She looked down and folded her arms.

The sheriff's deputy returned with the cones and told us they had just gotten word that Gordon would be here in an hour. Then he left us again.

"How could he get here so fast?" Raven wondered. She looked at Crystal.

"He flew from someplace closer," she said and then added, "the credit card."

Raven snapped her head around at me.

"That's right. He's been tracking us because of it."

"It was a good idea in the beginning, Raven," I said defensively. "We all thought so. And what difference does it make now whether he's here in an hour or four? He's coming. There's nothing we can do about that."

"Brooke's right, Raven. Please," Crystal pleaded, "let's stop this bickering."

"I don't want to go back with him," Butterfly said, looking from Raven to me. "I don't, Crystal. I don't." She started to shake her head so vigorously, I thought she would snap her neck.

"Oh no," Raven said. "If she goes into one of those catatonic states now . . ."

"Let's join," Crystal cried quickly. She was like someone throwing a pail of water on a smoldering fire.

We all rose and circled Butterfly. Her eyes were already beginning to roll back. We put our arms around each other and lowered our heads to hers.

"We're sisters," Crystal said. "We'll be all right. We'll always be all right as long as we are together. We're strong."

"We're sisters," Raven and I chanted along. "We'll be all right."

Butterfly clutched our hands and the four of us held on to each other as if we thought the floor was soon going to fall out from under us as we continued our chant.

"What are you girls doing now?" Mr. Glashalter asked. We hadn't heard him enter. We stopped and parted. "What is this, some form of witchcraft?"

We all returned to our seats. Butterfly looked much better. Color had returned to her face and she wasn't breathing as hard.

"It's nothing," Crystal said. "We're just comforting each other. That's our way."

He stared at us for a moment and then took a seat across from Raven.

"Okay, I've worked out all the details. The authorities are in agreement. You will be signed over to your foster father, who will once again assume responsibility for you. The matter of driving without a license, bringing a stolen vehicle into the state will all be put aside here, but the details will be given to your agency back in New York. You're all very lucky to get off this easily," he added.

"Yeah, I feel like we won the lottery," Raven muttered just loud enough for everyone to hear.

"You better start appreciating favors when people do them for you, young lady," he snapped. "Nothing's coming to you in this world just because you're here," he added, his mouth twisting as if his face were made of putty.

Raven's shoulders hoisted as she leaned toward him.

"Raven!" Crystal warned. She could see Raven was about to explode and who knew what would come out of her mouth this time. Instead, she looked at Crystal, retreated, wrapped her arms around herself tightly and bit down on her lower lip.

Mr. Glashalter completed the paper work he was doing and then went out to wait for Gordon. A short while later, Lieutenant Mathews came for us.

"Your foster father has arrived," she announced. "Let's go, girls."

Crystal took Butterfly's hand quickly and we all rose and followed Lieutenant Mathews out. Gordon was leaning against the dispatcher's desk, a wide grin on his face. He wore a light brown leather jacket and dungarees. His hair was down over his forehead and he looked tired, unshaven, with shadows under his eyes. I imagined him driving night and day in hot pursuit.

"There they are, my girls," he cried. "Louise is so worried about you. I should be very mad, girls. I should be mad," he said. Then he turned to the dispatcher and shook his head. "I would be, but I keep thinking of all the pranks I pulled when I was their age."

The dispatcher laughed with him. He glanced at Lieutenant Mathews, who was eying him suspiciously, a look of disgust on her face.

"That's what makes me a good foster father," he told her. "I understand teenagers. I was one myself." He laughed again before turning back to the dispatcher. "Is there anything else for me to do?"

"No, you've signed everything. They're all yours, Mr. Tooey."

"Yes," he said nodding at us, "they're all mine. Lucky me. Come on, girls. We've got a long ride home and lots of explaining to do on the way."

He stepped forward and we started toward the front door. Butterfly had her head down and clutched Crystal's hand so tightly, I could see her fingers turn white.

I glanced back at Lieutenant Mathews. For a moment I thought she was going to say something or ask something and stop us from going with Gordon, but she hesitated and he stepped between us.

"Go on, Brooke," he said, his eyes fixed coldly on me. "You know the way."

I caught up with the others and we left the sheriff's office. Gordon's station wagon was parked right in front.

"You three in the back," he said to Raven, Crystal and Butterfly. "You ride up front with me," he ordered.

We all got in and Gordon quickly started the engine and pulled away. He said nothing until we were well on the road.

"Well now," he began, "I guess you all had quite a time of it, quite a time." He glanced at me. "I know you had to be the driver, right, Brooke?"

Instead of answering, I turned and looked out the window.

"You could have all ended up in jail, you know. I did you all a big favor and I expect a big favor in return," he said. He poked me in the shoulder with his long, right forefinger and I jumped. He looked back at the others. "You made up a phony map too, and sent me on a wild goose chase. Very smart, girls. I can see I have some real geniuses on my hands."

He drove in silence for a while before lighting a cigarette and leaning back.

"Okay, girls, we're pretty far away from that sheriff's office now. I had to go to the pound to claim my car. I signed it out and drove away. Then I stopped to look for something I had left in the car and guess what?" He turned to me and smiled. "Go on, guess, Brooke."

"You're not scaring me, Gordon," I said, filling my face with as much defiance as I could muster.

"I'm not scaring you? Oh. Okay," he said and then he slammed his hand down on the dashboard so hard, I thought he had cracked it. After that he hammered it with his fist, not once, but three quick times. The whole car shook. Something in the glove compartment rattled. I half expected the windows to shatter. It was an impressive display of physical violence. Everyone screamed, including me, only mine was inside. My heart was thumping and my throat felt like I had swallowed a lump of coal. Butterfly was crying and Raven, brave, defiant Raven had her head down. Only Crystal looked like she had regained her composure the moment Gordon stopped.

Gordon sat back again, calmly, looking so relaxed, it made me feel what had just happened was in my imagination. He was a madman, I thought, which made him even more dangerous.

"You want me to scare you?" Gordon asked me. "Is that what you want, Brooke?"

"No, Gordon," I said.

"Good. Because if I have to scare you, I'll get even angrier than I am now and I just don't know how I can be any angrier and not tear you all into little pieces," he said in a voice so controlled, his teeth were locked together as he spoke.

"What do you want from us?" Crystal asked in her composed demeanor.

"What do I want? I want what's mine, Crystal. I want what you found under that seat. Where is it?" he asked.

"We didn't find anything under the seat," Raven cried.

He pointed at her in the rearview mirror.

"Don't treat me like a fool, Raven, or I'll start on you first. Or," he said with a cold smile, "do you want me to stop the car and pull the little one out and ask her? I know she'll tell me everything, won't you, little one?"

Butterfly's face turned a shade redder than rose. Crystal put her arm around her quickly.

"We discovered it by accident," Crystal declared. "We were looking for loose change and we didn't even know what it was at first."

"Loose change?" He smiled and shook his head. "Okay. I'll buy that. Then what?"

"Once we realized what it was, we got scared and we stopped along the way and buried it," she said.

"You buried it?"

"We didn't want any children finding it and we didn't want to be stopped with it on us," she continued.

He looked thoughtful for a moment and then he slowed down and turned off the road onto the shoulder and stopped. After he took a puff on his cigarette, he spun around. "Where did you bury it?" he asked. "Or are you going to tell me you forgot?"

"No, I remember where," Crystal said firmly. She barely blinked.

I looked at her and raised my eyebrows. How could she say that? What would happen if we took Gordon to the actual place and he saw we had dumped the bag?

"Okay, okay. You'll show me then," he said.

"I won't be able to find it in the dark," she said. Night had begun to fall rapidly now. The cloud cover kept any moonlight from illuminating the highway.

Gordon stared at her, but Crystal still didn't wince. Good old Crystal, I thought, when it came to Gordon doing mind games with her, he was definitely outmatched. He sat back a moment and thought.

"Okay," he said. "Okay. We pull into the first motel for the night. Tomorrow, we find what's mine and then, I'll tell you what, girls. I'll let you run away again, only this time I won't report you. How's that? Raven? That make you happy?"

"Yes," Raven said, her eyes glowing with pain and rage. "It does."

"Fair enough. I get what I want and you get what you want," he said.

"What about Louise?" I asked. "I thought her heart was broken when we left."

He glared at me.

"She'll get over it. She always gets over it," he said.

He put the car in drive again and started away.

"I know you girls aren't fond of me. That's okay. I never asked to be a loving foster parent. That was all Louise's idea. It was never easy running that place when it was a rooming house. Her parents treated me like the hired help, never a son-in-law. When I got out of the navy, I had skills. I was worth something. It wasn't my fault the place fell apart. Customers stopped coming around and there wasn't any money. Then Louise came up with the foster home idea. Sure, I went along with it, but having you creatures around all the time hasn't been a ball, exactly. I don't apologize for taking advantage of an opportunity. That's always been my motto, girls, take advantage of an opportunity."

He laughed and glanced back at Raven and then at me.

"You girls have guts. I'll say that for you. I think we understand each other now. We're going to get along just fine. There," he said seeing a neon sign flashing an advertisement for a motel. "We'll rest up and tomorrow, we'll part friends. Okay?"

None of us said a word. He took the exit and headed for the motel. I gazed back at Crystal.

Now what? I wanted to ask, but that would have to wait until later.

Gordon acquired two rooms for us, but when we pulled up to the doors, he turned to us and said, "I know what you girls are like, so here's the deal: one of you stays the night with me."

"What?" Raven asked, a cold look of terror on her face. "Stay in a room with you?"

"Don't get me wrong. I just want one of you where I can see you. I know the rest of you won't run off on me that way. You girls stick together, right? All right," he continued looking at the three of them and then at me, "who's it gonna be?"

Crystal looked absolutely terrified, even more so than Butterfly. I was afraid for us all, afraid of what he might make us do.

"I should probably take the little one in with me," he said. I could almost hear Butterfly's terrified scream.

"I'll stay with you," I said quickly.

He smiled.

"Fine. Let's get a good night's rest, eh girls? We have a lot to do tomorrow, a lot to do." He got out and we followed.

He opened one room for Raven, Crystal and Butterfly and the other for himself and me.

"Can I stay with them for a while?" I asked him.

"No," he said. "I don't feel like having to worry about it. Just get in there and get to bed. The rest of you do the same and no monkey business, hear? Move!" he ordered and everyone jumped.

Raven took my hand.

"I could change places with you, Brooke. I can handle him better," she said, glaring at him.

"It's all right," I said. "I'll be fine, Raven. Thanks. Take care of Butterfly," I told her and then I went into the room.

Gordon took something out of the back of the wagon and followed right after me.

"Go on, use the washroom first," he commanded when he entered.

I went to the bathroom and when I came out, he had the television going and was lying on his bed. He was also sipping whiskey from a pint bottle.

"Didn't you bring your nightie along?" he asked when I pulled the blanket back on my bed.

"I don't sleep in a nightie," I said.

He smiled, his eyes fixed on me in a way that made me very nervous. I tried not to show it. With Gordon, it was always best to appear brave and undaunted. He was the sort who pounced on weakness and took advantage of kindness and innocence.

"Who's idea was this running off, huh? That Crystal come up with the plan?" he asked finally.

"No," I said. "It was my idea."

"No kidding? Where the hell did you think you would all go anyway? Who's waiting for you with open arms, huh? Who?" he demanded.

I turned sharply to face him.

"No one's waiting for us, Gordon. We just wanted to get away from you and Louise and that whole scene back there. You complain how it hasn't been a picnic for you. Well, it hasn't been one for us either. We know you and Louise are not going to make it easy for anyone to adopt us. That's a dead-end for us, so we decided it was better to leave.''

"And steal my car!" he screamed, making his face even uglier than it was. "Why my car?" He pounded his chest so hard, I heard the thump and actually thought I felt it myself. He's a time bomb, I thought. "I got people depending on me back there, people who are very angry at me because of you. Why didn't you all just get on a bus? No one would have cared then, believe me."

I lay down again, shivering. If I said the wrong word, did the wrong thing, there was no telling what he would do in response. Anyway, I thought, he was right. It was a mistake to take his car. He wouldn't have cared otherwise and we might have gone all the way. Then again, it would have been easier to catch us on public transportation.

"Crystal says you buried it. Is she telling me the truth? Huh?"

"Yes," I said.

"I better find that tomorrow or there will be hell to pay, Brooke. If you're all lying to me, you're going to be sorrier than you ever were living back at the Lakewood and even sorrier than you would be going to jail. Trust me on that," he threatened. "Did you hear me? Did you?"

"Yes," I said.

My heart began to pound again. I wished I could speak with Crystal and see if she had any plan for tomorrow. How far did she think we could lead him and what would happen when we finally stopped?

I heard him get up and then pause by my bed so I opened my eyes. He was staring down at me in the strangest way. It was as if he was trying to decide something and he was being pulled in different directions.

"So, you ever been with a boy?"

I closed my eyes.

"I guess that's a no," he said. "You're a virgin. I bet you wonder about it every night, huh? I bet you lay awake in that bed of yours and think about what it's like. Maybe you pretend, huh? Huh?"

"Leave me alone, Gordon. We're going to do what you want tomorrow, so leave me alone," I pleaded. His voice was softer, but darker and he was beginning to frighten me even more.

"You have a period like every other girl, don't you? You ever think about having babies?"

The tears were hot and heavy under my eyelids. I kept them closed and tried not to sob.

"I could show you," he said. "I could show you what it's like better than any teenage boy can show you. Just like that," he said snapping his fingers. "It's different with a real man. Experience is important when it comes to things like this."

I didn't move. I didn't open my eyes, but I sensed him drawing closer. I felt my body tighten up. I wished I could turn myself into a ball and roll away. When his fingers touched my hair, I jumped up and pulled the blanket around me with my knees against my chest.

"Stop!" I screamed.

He stood there, gaping at me, his eyes wide.

"If you touch me again," I said, "I'll scream so loud it will bring the manager or people from the other rooms. I swear I will. Then they'll call the police and we won't show you anything tomorrow."

He stood there, wavering a moment, his eyes opening and closing.

"Take it easy," he said. "I'm not that desperate. But you just passed up the best thing that could ever happen to you, girlie."

"That's not true! I have a boyfriend and someday I'll marry him."

He laughed. Anger replaced fear, rage rushing over me, making me feel like I was bathed in blood. If he came toward me again, I vowed, I would scratch out his eyes. He saw something in my face and backed down some more.

"Ahh," he groaned. He wavered, took another drink from his bottle and looked toward the bathroom. "I'll be right out. Don't you even think of going anywhere," he said, pointing that long finger at me as if it were a knife.

The heat receded from my face and I relaxed again. I knew I wouldn't fall asleep tonight. I would be up all night just in case he tried something. Crystal, Crystal, what are we going to do? We should have taken our chances with the police. How can we protect Butterfly? We can't protect ourselves.

He stumbled when he stepped out of the bathroom and then cursed. I didn't look directly at him. He went past my bed and I kept my back to him, but held my breath. The television droned on, the light flashing on the wall above me.

Suddenly, I felt him grab my right arm. I started to scream, but he put his hand over my face and brought his own smelly mouth close to me. My stomach did flip-flops and I almost threw up the burger I had eaten at the sheriff's office.

"I'm not touching you," he growled. "But I ain't taking no chances. I want to get some sleep tonight and I know how sly you girls are.

Don't you scream, Brooke," he warned, "or I'll pound this fist right through your face," he threatened, holding his mallet of a hand above me. He released his grip on my mouth and I held my breath. I felt him twist my wrist around and then I saw him tying a small rope around it.

"You ain't going to sneak out on me," he muttered. "This here," he said as he tied his knot, "is a sailor's knot, an eight," he bragged as he turned and wove it around my wrist.

After he was finished, he wrapped it around his own wrist a few times and returned to his bed. There was just enough slack for me to turn over if I wanted.

"What if I have to go to the bathroom?" I asked him.

"You went. You'll hold it in until morning now," he said. "I want some sleep, so shut up."

He took another long drink on his bottle, nearly emptying it, and then he lay back and closed his eyes. I gazed at the knot. It was tied so tightly, it was worse than handcuffs, I thought. Frustrated, I lay there with my eyes wide open. He never turned off the television set. Programs changed until it was one of those late talk shows. When I looked at him again, his eyes were shut tight, his arm dangling over the side of the bed.

He moaned in his sleep and tossed and turned a little before he started to snore. I wondered about the girls. Did Crystal and Raven have to join with Butterfly again in the next room? Were they all lying awake, just as terrified of what would come tomorrow? What plan could Crystal possibly have concocted?

I looked at Gordon again and then decided I had to try something. Slowly, moving almost an inch at a time, I slipped off the bed until I was on all fours on the floor. Then I moved as quietly as possible to Gordon's side. I studied the way he had tied the rope around his own wrist and then I started to untie it, moving so slowly, it took what seemed like hours just to unravel the first few turns. He grunted and turned on his side. I held my breath and waited. He didn't wake, but now I had to stand and lean over the bed to get to his arm. Any moment, I thought, his eyes would pop open and he would do something terrible to me.

Finally, I had the rope off his wrist. I gathered it up and wound it around my waist. There was no time to try to get it off my own wrist now. I tiptoed across the room to his jacket and took out the station wagon keys. He turned again, mumbled and then threw his arm over the side of the bed as it had been before. I waited and listened, holding my breath. His snoring was regular and deep.

Moving as though I were on a shelf of air, I crossed to the door and slowly turned the lock until it snapped open. I thought the tiny noise might wake him, so I watched his eyes. The pupils moved beneath his eyelids violently, but he didn't open them. He continued to snore. I opened the door only as much as I needed to slip out and then I did so, closing the door softly behind me. My heart was racing so fast, I had to catch my breath.

It was very late and quiet. Only one other room had lights on and the office was dimly lit. I went to the girls' door and knocked softly, hoping they would hear. I waited and then knocked again.

"Who's there?" I heard Raven whisper.

"It's me," I said.

She opened the door quickly and I slipped in. Crystal and Butterfly were in one bed. They had the blanket clutched to them and looked at me with wide, surprised eyes. I indicated complete silence.

"He had me tied to him," I whispered and showed them the rope, "but I got the rope off him when he fell asleep."

"Tied to him? Oh, Brooke," Crystal said. "We've been so worried about you."

"He's crazier than he was, Crystal. I don't know what he'll do tomorrow. I took the car keys," I said holding them up. "We can get away," I said.

"You want to steal his car again?" Crystal asked. "Oh, Brooke, no."

"Well, what did you have planned for tomorrow, Crystal, because if it's not a great idea, we're in a lot of danger," I told her. "He as much as told me so back there. What's your plan?"

"I don't know," she confessed. "I was hoping something would come to me tonight."

"Well, there isn't anything coming to you and we don't have much time to waste. This is what we have to do," I said holding up the keys.

"He'll have the police after us again," Raven said.

"I'm keeping this rope around me just the way he tied it. I'll show it to them and I'll tell them what else he wanted to do to me."

"What?" Raven asked.

"Don't ask," Crystal said, throwing a look at Butterfly. She thought a moment. "Okay, let's do it," she said. "Come on, Butterfly." She and Butterfly got out of the bed and put on their shoes.

I opened the door and listened. The three of them hovered behind me. It looked clear. Gordon was still asleep, I thought. Rather, I prayed. I nodded an all clear and then we moved with whisper steps to the wagon. I unlocked it and taking great care not to make too much noise, opened the doors. We all got in and I inserted the key. Raven put her hand on mine.

"Wait, Brooke. He's going to hear it start," she warned.

"Maybe not. He did a lot of drinking. I think he's dead to the world for now."

"I can't imagine his rage when he wakes up and discovers we've taken his car again," Crystal said.

"Imagine what it will be like when we reveal his drugs are gone," I said. I looked at Raven. She took a deep breath and nodded. All of our eyes went to the door of Gordon's room.

I turned the key. The engine started. Gordon's door remained shut. Without turning on the lights, I backed out of our spot and slowly accelerated through the lot, Raven keeping her eyes on that fearful door.

"He didn't hear us," she said in a heavy whisper.

When we reached the entrance, I turned on the headlights and then I shot out and down the road. It was a very dark secondary road with no streetlights and very few houses. There were no road signs either. For the moment I had lost all sense of direction.

"My heart is beating so fast, I think I'm going to faint," Raven said.

I don't think any of us let out a breath for at least ten minutes. Darkness seemed to be closing in around us. Images of Gordon's ugly face close to mine back in that motel room flashed before me. I drove faster, squealing around turns, riding on the shoulder of the road, fighting to maintain control.

"What are we going to do?" Raven asked. "We don't have any money or the credit card or anything."

"I don't care," I said. "We've got to get away from him."

"Well, where are we going?" she followed, turning to look back at the motel as if she expected to see him running after us. Butterfly clung tightly to Crystal.

"Away," I said. "As fast as we can."

All I could think of was putting as much distance as possible between us and Gordon. Whatever came after that had to be better. Didn't it?

15
ಐ

A Desert Oasis

Our fear kept us under a veil of silence. The station wagon's headlights sliced away some of the darkness, but without houses and lit windows, other traffic and activity, we felt alone in the night, far from any sign of civilization. Trees towered like sentinels guarding the clearing sky. I felt as if I was driving us through a tunnel from one world into another. Soon, the tree line disappeared and was replaced with long, barren fields. Any houses we did see were dark or only vaguely lit, their inhabitants surely snug in their beds. When I gazed into the rearview mirror, I saw that Butterfly had fallen asleep in Crystal's arms. Raven had her head against the window, her eyes closed. We had all sunk deeply into a pool of numbness.

The terrain changed again, this time looking more rocky. The sky became even clearer, now with only occasional, thin, wispy clouds drifting across the stars. I was no longer driving fast. The tires hummed until the road turned rougher and we began to bounce more.

"Where are we?" Raven asked after a particularly rough bump shook the vehicle.

"I don't know. I haven't seen a road sign for miles and miles," I said. "Crystal?"

"I don't have the map anymore. The last house was back about twenty or thirty minutes," she added.

"Something should come up soon," I offered as a straw of hope.

We rode on with nothing but the same monotonous scenery. In fact, it became even more primitive. I spotted cactuses and then saw a long, dark line of mountains silhouetted along the western horizon. Butterfly woke when we hit another rough piece of road, making the wagon shake and rattle.

"I'm thirsty, Crystal," were her first words.

"Me too," Raven said, "but I haven't seen any place where we could even beg for water. Where are we?" she asked again.

A new sort of fear began to unravel at the bottom of my stomach. In our crazed frenzy to escape from Gordon Tooey, I had not taken any notice of direction. Now, with no signs to give us any sort of hint as to where we were or where we were heading, we were truly lost. It seemed we could only go from bad to worse.

"We better stop at the next sign of life," Crystal said, "and find out where we are."

I nodded and drove on, the road beneath us now turning into something only a little better than dirt.

"Maybe we should turn back, Brooke," Raven suggested.

"We've come so far," I said. "And I didn't see any other turns to take."

"This looks like it goes to nowhere, though," Crystal said leaning forward. "Raven might be right, Brooke."

Our anxiety began to boil. We were all leaning forward now, watching the road, looking for anything hopeful. A pair of rabbits crossed the road on what looked like legs made of springs. The tires were crunching over small rocks and gravel now.

"I think we did it," Raven said. "I think we reached the moon. That's what it looks like out there."

"It's molten rock that has flowed out to the surface of the earth through cracks or fissures. Lava," Crystal explained. "Very much like the moon's surface."

"Thanks. I needed that explanation," Raven quipped.

"It does look like the moon," Butterfly said, "because no one lives here."

I couldn't drive anywhere near as fast as I had been driving. The road began to jostle us.

"This is crazy, Brooke. I think we should turn around and . . ." Raven began, but stopped when the engine sputtered. "Oh no, what's happening now?"

I checked the dashboard, something I should have done before we had gone too far. In our haste it never occurred to me that we would run out of gas.

"It's on empty," I moaned.

"Empty? We're out of gas!" Raven cried.

"That's what empty means," Crystal said dryly.

"Brooke?"

"I'm sorry. I didn't think to look. In all the excitement . . ."

"No one's blaming you, Brooke," Crystal said sharply.

"Yeah, well what are we supposed to do, get out and hitchhike?" Raven cried.

The wagon rolled to a stop. No one spoke.

"This is a road," I said finally. "It has to lead to somewhere."

"So?" Raven asked.

"So we get out and walk, Raven."

"Walk?"

"We haven't exactly got a whole lot of choice now, do we?" I shot back at her.

"I'm thirsty," Butterfly reminded us.

"Maybe we should just stay in the car," Raven said, "and wait for someone to come along."

"No one's coming along this late, Raven," Crystal said. "And there could be someplace just down the road. Brooke's right. Let's get out and walk."

"Fine," Raven said petulantly. She shoved open the door and got out. We did the same.

For a moment the four of us stood there in the darkness with only the stars above and pondered. There was enough light to outline the road before us like a long, winding dark blue ribbon snaking its way over the next hill.

"We're in some sort of desert," Crystal declared.

"Great. Maybe we'll all soon see a mirage," Raven said. "It's cold, too." She hugged herself.

"Let's take our stuff," Crystal said, referring to the pillowcases of clothing. "We can all put on something more and stay warm."

I opened the back and we sifted through our clothing, putting on extra shirts. Butterfly had her little pink jacket, so she would be the warmest of us all. Crystal suggested we leave everything else behind.

"I don't think we need to carry it with us," she said.

"Okay. Everyone ready?" I asked.

"Nature," Raven said, "my favorite place in which to get lost."

I started and they followed, Crystal and Butterfly right behind, Raven holding up the rear. The road was nothing more than gravel and dirt. Sagebrush and some small cactus were all we saw in the way of vegetation. The plateau seemed to go on forever, with the mountains very far in the distance. We went over one slope and then climbed another, plodding along. We spoke little. I realized it was very late, probably something like four in the morning. The only thing that warmed my heart was the sight of the sky. I never saw it so ablaze with stars— more stars than I'd ever seen before.

Crystal started to describe some of the constellations just to keep our minds occupied. Raven complained that she couldn't see them and thought that Crystal was making it up.

"You have to concentrate a little, Raven. They're not hard to distinguish," she told her.

"I see the Milky Way, too," Butterfly said, and that reminded her of a cold glass of milk and how thirsty she was.

We rounded a turn and discovered that the road went straight for what looked like miles and miles. There was a collection of boulders on our right just a few hundred yards away, but other than that, it looked like more desert, no homes, nothing.

"We could die out here," Raven said. "What a dumb move. We should have stayed in the car."

"I don't want to walk all the way back now," Butterfly said. "Do you, Crystal?"

"By the time we got there, it would probably be morning. We could rest here just as well," she said, indicating the rocks. I agreed.

Probably because they were under the hot sun all day, the rocks were actually warm to the touch. We found a small flat opening between two boulders and sat. Almost as soon as we settled in, something scurried across the top of the boulder on our right and Raven screamed.

"What was that?"

"It looked like a kangaroo rat," Crystal said calmly.

"A rat? Why are there rats here?" Raven moaned. "There are no slums or garbage."

Crystal laughed.

"It's a different sort of rodent, Raven. They're like a field mouse or something."

"Let them hang out someplace else," she said.

"This is their natural habitat, not ours. We're guests."

"Oh, we're guests. Thank you, but no thank you, Crystal. I'd rather be a guest in someone's house," she said.

"Me too," Butterfly said. "I wish we were back with Norman and Nana. When I lived with the Delorices, I had grandparents, but they didn't come around very much and I was never asked to stay at their home. I don't think they liked me."

"They probably didn't like the idea of an adopted grandchild," Crystal said. "It wasn't you. They wouldn't have liked anyone your foster parents brought home."

"I tried to get them to like me. I used to dance for them, but they never invited me to their home," she said sadly.

"It was their loss, not yours," I told her.

The four of us pulled closer together. Butterfly curled up and I told her to put her head on my lap if she wanted. She did. Raven sat with her knees up, her head down for a while. Then she sighed deeply.

"We'll always be alone," she said. "No matter what we do, what we try, we'll always end up like this, alone."

"Talk like that doesn't do us any good now, Raven," Crystal advised.

Raven turned on her.

"Just once, Crystal, just once I'd like to see you act like a human being and not some sort of computer shaped like a person. Don't tell me you're sitting here, lost somewhere in the desert with no money, no plan in your brilliant head and you're not feeling just a little sorry for yourself and a lot scared, too. Don't tell me that."

"I'm not," Crystal replied quickly. "I'm probably more frightened than you are. I'm probably more depressed, but I don't see any value in moaning and groaning."

"At least you get it out, Crystal," Raven said. "At least you let everyone know you have the same feelings. That's got some value, doesn't it?"

For the first time in a long time, I thought Raven was right. I think Crystal did too. She was quiet a long moment.

"All right," she said. "I'll admit I'm afraid. I've been afraid lots of times. I remember right after my foster parents died in that car crash and no one wanted anything to do with me, I was terrified. The state people came for me and there I was, off to another facility to live with strangers again. A part of me wanted to throw a tantrum, break down and cry a river, but I didn't."

"Maybe you should have," Raven said.

"Maybe I should have. Maybe people would have treated me more kindly. Maybe it's not so bad to need sympathy and compassion and ask for it," she said. "Maybe I'm not always right."

She stopped and leaned back, her hands behind her head and then quickly wiped a tear from her cheek.

"You don't have to bawl your head off now," Raven said. "I'm not asking for that."

I almost laughed aloud.

"I never told you," Crystal continued, looking up at the sky, "but I often wish I was more like you, Raven."

"You do?"

"Sure I do. I see how popular you are with the boys and I know you're very pretty and someday you'll get someone to fall so much in love with you, he'll give you everything you want. You'll get it all handed to you on a silver platter, Raven. Whereas I, I will have to earn it, to work for it. I don't mind that, but I'd be a liar if I didn't admit it would be easier your way."

Raven stared at her in the darkness.

"Don't you think I'd like to be a little more like you, Crystal? Don't you think I'd like people to see beyond my looks?"

"Maybe we can merge into one person and give each other what we think is positive about each other," Crystal said.

"We already do," Raven said.

Crystal stared at her and then she sat up and the two of them hugged.

"I'm going to puke," I said, "if we're all going to start being nice to each other now."

They laughed.

"I'm still thirsty," Butterfly complained. That made us laugh too.

I stroked her beautiful hair. Raven hummed a song she remembered her mother used to hum to her. Butterfly's eyes closed and then we all squeezed closer and closed our eyes.

"If we just get a little rest," Crystal said, "things will look more hopeful in the morning."

"Kangaroo rats," Raven muttered.

I smiled. I worked on getting the rope off my wrist now and finally did so. After that I closed my eyes, and moments later, I, too, was asleep.

The first time I opened my eyes, I thought Raven was right. We're going to start seeing mirages. I closed them again and then opened them, but no, he was still there, a man in his thirties, wearing a cowboy hat, his hair tied back in a ponytail. He sat on a beautiful black and white horse and wore a dark blue shirt, vest and dungarees, but he also wore a pistol and a badge on his vest. He was dark skinned with emerald green eyes. He sat calmly, staring at us, the horse munching on what surely was the only blades of grass for miles. It snorted and Raven woke, along with Crystal. Butterfly ground the sleep out of her eyes and sat up.

"Is that your station wagon broken down back there?" he asked.

"It's not broken down. It's out of gas," I said.

He shook his head and smiled.

"You know it's about fifty more miles before you're off the reservation and can find stores and gas stations," he said.

"Reservation?" Crystal asked.

He nodded.

"You didn't see the sign?"

"No sir," I said.

"Well you're on Navajo reservation land. I happen to be an Indian Peace Officer."

Butterfly moved closer to me. He saw her fear.

"Who are you girls?"

"It's a long story," I said.

He smiled. "This is the land of the long story. Can you all walk a ways?"

"Yes sir," I said.

"Good. Follow me," he ordered. He focused on Butterfly. "How would you like to ride with me, little one?" he asked her.

She started to shake her head.

"Go on, Butterfly," Crystal said. "You're very tired."

"Come on. Jake here is about as mild a horse as one can be without being stuffed," he said. He got off and brought the horse to Butterfly. "Pet him. Go ahead," he said. She did so meekly and then he reached into his pocket and produced a lump of sugar. "Give him this and he'll be your best friend," he said. He handed it to Butterfly and she started to offer it to the horse. "No, hold on," he said. "Hold your hand out flat like this and leave the sugar in your palm. He'll get it easier."

Butterfly did as he instructed and Jake took the sugar. Then he nuzzled her hand and she laughed.

"See? Best friends. Come on," he said and helped her up and onto the horse. She looked back at us with a mixture of glee and fear. He mounted behind her and looked at us. "Right this way, ladies," he said. He turned the horse and headed around the rocks.

"Arrested by an Indian?" Raven said. "What's left?"

"Scalping," Crystal said.

"That's not funny," Raven cried, hurrying after us. "Crystal. That's not funny."

Just over the hill, we saw a ranch house, a corral with horses, some chickens in a pen, a garage and a barn. It was an oasis in the desert, the lawn long and wide, some citrus trees in the rear and what looked like a brook running through it.

"We were so close and we didn't know it," Crystal remarked. The Indian policeman was talking to Butterfly and she was nodding. I saw him hand her the reins and show her how to tug and turn the horse. Her laughter was as refreshing as a cold glass of water would be.

When we reached the ranch house, he dismounted and helped Butterfly off.

"My name's Tommy," he said, "Tommy Edwards. It's just my wife and myself here. Her name's Anita. Right this way, girls," he said leading us up the steps and over the porch to the front door.

The aroma of something delicious hit us the moment we entered.

Tommy Edwards smiled at us.

"Bacon and eggs," he said. " 'Nita," he called. The four of us closed against each other. Crystal had a streak of dirt across her forehead. Raven's hair was wild. We were all still wearing three shirts. I was sure we were a sight to behold.

Anita Edwards came from the kitchen, wiping her hands on a dish-towel. She wore dungarees and a light blue cotton shirt. Her hair was as long as Raven's and just as dark. She had the same dark eyes, too. Her features were small and about as perfect as any woman's nose and mouth could be. She had high cheekbones and a lightly tanned complexion. Despite her looking not much more than thirty, there was something old in her eyes, something tired, painful. She gazed at us with interest and looked to Tommy.

"I found them by the rocks. Their car had broken down and they had walked a ways. They slept there last night," he explained. Before she could ask, he added, "I guess they must have gotten lost. They didn't realize they were on the reservation."

She stepped closer. Her lips were soft and full. There was a hint of a warm smile in them, but it was as if everything had to be kept tightly controlled, her looks, her words, her feelings.

"Come with me," she said, "and I'll show you all where to wash up."

"Great," Tommy said. He looked at us with a more official face. "Then we'll talk over breakfast."

"This way," Anita said, leading us through the house. The kitchen was in the rear, but the living room was on the left and the bedrooms on the right. We passed what looked like a den–office, too. The walls were covered with Western art, beautiful skins, woven blankets, ritual masks, guns, bows and arrows. On the floor were bowls and small statues. There was even Native American art in the bathroom.

"Go right in," she told us and then brought in some towels.

"Thank you," I said. She handed us the towels and told us to come to the dining room when we were finished.

"I'm going to jump into the shower," Raven said, eying the shower stall covetously.

"Be my guest," I said. I just washed my hands and face, as did Crystal and Butterfly, so we were out first, now wearing only one shirt each. Anita had already placed four more settings on the table.

"Sit here," she ordered, pointing to the chairs on the sides of the table. "Where's your friend?"

"She's taking a shower," I replied. She raised her eyebrows and came the closest to a real smile or laugh.

Tommy returned before Raven came out of the bathroom.

"I'm about as hungry as a bear," he said, winking at us.

Raven entered, looking fresh, her hair back. I pointed to her seat and she joined us just as Anita brought in the plate of eggs and bacon.

"You girls hungry?" Tommy asked.

"Hungrier than a bear," Raven said.

He laughed.

"All right, why don't you tell us your names?" he said. We went around the table. As we did, Anita poured water into our glasses.

"Don't wait for me," she said, and returned to the kitchen.

"You heard her, girls, dig in," Tommy said, and we did.

"Thank you," Crystal said. We all followed with thank you's as we took from the serving dish. Anita finally sat and ate. She seemed to do it mechanically and not with any real appetite.

"So," Tommy said when we were all close to finishing, "tell me how you girls ended up sleeping by the rocks. Where are you from?"

Raven looked at Crystal and Crystal looked at me. Butterfly had been watching Anita with interest and I had noticed her looking at Butterfly too, a small smile on her lips.

"You're going to find out anyway, Mr. Edwards," I said. "We ran away from a foster home in New York. We took our foster father's car and we were finally caught the day before yesterday."

Tommy sat back and looked at Anita, who shook her head.

"You were caught but you drove out here? I don't understand," he said.

"Our foster father came for us. He came for us mainly because he had a package of cocaine hidden under the back seat of the car. We found it quite by accident and threw it away," I continued. "We were afraid to tell him. We pretended we were taking him to where we had buried it and last night, after he had gotten us to a motel, I snuck out while he was asleep and we ran away again. And then we ran out of gas," I said.

"We were frightened and just drove off, not paying attention to where we were going," Crystal added.

"Now that's quite a story," Tommy Edwards said.

"Why did you go back with him?" Anita asked sharply.

"If we didn't agree to go back with our foster father, we were all going to jail for stealing his car and we were afraid of being split apart," Raven explained.

"We're sisters," I said. "We have to stay together."

"We don't have any money," Crystal said. "We're afraid of what he's going to do to us, especially now."

"I see," Tommy said and thought a moment. "Well, we have something of a situation here."

"Will he find us?" Butterfly asked.

"Not here he won't," Tommy said. He looked at Anita. "I'll go make a few calls."

She nodded.

"Can I help you with the dishes?" Butterfly asked Anita.

"Why thank you," Anita said, her face brightening with a genuine smile.

Butterfly started to clean the table. Tommy rose and left us.

"The rest of you can go into the living room if you like," Anita said.

"Thank you," Crystal said.

"I guess we're going to be going back to jail," Raven said when we sat in the living room.

"What else are we going to do?" Crystal said. "No one wants us and returning to Lakewood isn't what we want. I'm tired," she said, sinking further into the chair. "I'm tired of the struggle."

"Wonderful," Raven muttered. Her eyes went to the mantel and then she stood up and went to look at the pictures. I sat there feeling as if I could burst into tears at any moment. "Look," Raven said, "they have a baby girl."

She brought the picture of the three of them to show to Crystal and me.

"Please don't handle my pictures," Anita said from the doorway.

"Oh, I'm sorry. I was just admiring your baby," Raven said. "Where is she? Sleeping?"

Butterfly came in and looked at the picture.

"Yes, she's sleeping. In the ground," Anita said coldly.

All of us looked at her, no one able to utter a sound. She saw how hard the news hit us and softened.

"We lost her when she was a little more than three. She would have been five next month. She had a problem with a valve in her heart."

"We're very sorry, Mrs. Edwards," Crystal said.

Anita took the picture from Raven and looked at it a moment.

"Her name was Annie," she said, "named for my mother. Now they're together." She put the picture back on the mantel and turned to look at us, deep lines cutting across her forehead as the pain of her loss returned.

"One day," she said, "the light goes out of your life. It's like a candle flickering and flickering and suddenly, a wind comes and there is only darkness."

She sucked back her tears and pressed her lips together. Then she took a deep breath.

"My husband will help you. You can wait here or go outside if you like," she said and walked out of the room.

"How sad," Raven said.

"She looked at me and started to cry in the kitchen," Butterfly revealed. "Then she said, just leave the dishes. You can go back to your sisters."

"I feel bad for her," Raven said.

The air around us felt too heavy to breathe.

"I'm going out," I announced and rose from my seat.

When I stepped out, I looked around and saw a tractor parked next to the barn with its engine cover up. There were tools on the ground. Curious, I started for it. It looked like Tommy Edwards was replacing spark plugs. I saw that he had the manual out by his tools, so I sat on the ground and studied it, thinking of Todd and how much I missed him.

"There's always something to get after around a ranch," I heard Tommy say as he came out of the house and approached.

I dropped the manual and stood up quickly.

"I didn't mean to frighten you, Brooke," he said. "I had to contact the FBI office about your foster father's car and all you told me, Brooke. The FBI is involved in any crimes committed on or involving Indian reservations. We police ourselves, too, but I thought that was best. I don't want the other girls to get frightened about it."

"I'll explain it," I said.

"They'll go over that vehicle from top to bottom and see if there is any evidence left. Whether there is or not, he'll have some explaining to do. I've also contacted the Child Protection Services about you girls. They're sending someone up, but it will be a while. They have to come from Albuquerque and they are quite understaffed."

"I don't mind how long it takes. I don't think any of us do," I said.

Tommy started working on the tractor and I headed back to the house to break the news. I found Raven coming out the back door.

"What's wrong?" Raven cried when she saw the look on my face.

"Tommy told me he had to contact the FBI."

"The FBI?"

"They have to be contacted when there is a question of a crime on Indian reservations. It's not just because of us," I added quickly.

"You're not worried?" Raven asked.

"About what?"

"Maybe they'll arrest us for not turning in the cocaine. We could go to a federal prison!"

"I doubt it," I said. "Where are Crystal and Butterfly? We have to let them know."

"Butterfly went back into the kitchen to help Anita. Funny, how she's not shy with her. I think it's because she feels sorry for her. Crystal says Butterfly is drawn to other people's sadness like a moth to a flame."

I smiled.

"Yes," I said. "I guess she is."

We heard the barn door slide open and turned to see Tommy leading a palomino. The horse had a limp in its right rear leg.

"How's it going?" he called.

"Okay," I said. Crystal and I walked toward him. "What's wrong with your horse?"

"She stepped in a gopher hole. The vet says she'll be fine, but I've got to give her a good half-hour or so of exercise twice a day." He looked at Raven. "Think you can do this awhile?"

"Do what?" she asked.

"Just walk Pony Tail in a circle," he said.

"Me?" She looked at me and then at Tommy.

"Sure," he said. "She's a pussy cat," he added, handing her the reins.

Raven took them, looked at the horse and then at me again before starting forward, her face full of fear and excitement. The horse followed obediently.

"That's it, keep that pace," Tommy called to her. She nodded and walked on, looking as proud as I had ever seen her.

"I told Tommy I was going to explain to Butterfly about the FBI," I called to Raven, and headed back toward the house. As I passed the front of the house, Crystal came out with a book in her hand. She saw me, smiled with curiosity and then looked at Raven.

"Butterfly all right?"

"She's fine. Anita is showing her how to weave on her loom," she said.

"I've got bad news, Crystal," I began. "Tommy called the FBI. He had to."

Crystal nodded knowingly. "I figured he'd have to report us."

Before we could go inside to tell Butterfly we saw a car approaching in the distance. Probably the Child Protection Services, I thought. My optimism had a short life. It was a dark blue car and two men in suits emerged to talk to Tommy. He turned and beckoned to Crystal and me. Raven was walking the horse in circles and Butterfly was still inside with Anita.

"Brooke, Crystal, this is Special Agent Wilkins and Special Agent Milton of the FBI," Tommy said. "They want to question you about your foster father and what you girls found."

"Okay," I said. "But Raven should be in on this too."

Tommy took the horse from Raven and she joined the two of us on the porch. We told the FBI agents everything about our flight from the Lakewood House, how we found the cocaine, about where we dumped it, and what happened afterward. Tommy joined us after he had put Pony Tail back in her stall.

"Our forensic man found the residue," Agent Wilkins told Tommy. "They're telling us the truth about it. What are you doing about them?"

"We've contacted Child Protection and they're coming up later today."

"Okay. We just want to know where they are," Agent Wilkins said. We watched them leave.

"You did good, girls," Tommy said.

"There's Butterfly," Raven said, looking toward the chicken coop. She was walking toward us excitedly, Anita at her side carrying a basket.

"I picked the eggs!" she cried. "By myself. You have to nudge the hens a little, but they don't peck you," she explained.

Anita stepped up beside her. There was a different look in her face. It was as if she had woken from a dream. Her eyes looked brighter and her lips softer, more willing to form a smile.

"We're going to make a cake," she said.

"I'm helping," Butterfly declared. "Right, Anita?"

"Yes," she said. "We'll have lunch in about a half-hour," she added to Tommy. "You going to be around?"

"Sure," he said. "Maybe afterward, I'll take the girls for a short ride on the horses."

"If they like," Anita said.

"Ride a horse? I don't know about that," Crystal muttered.

"Oh come on, Crystal. If I can do it, you can do it," Raven teased.

"Since when can you do it?" Crystal asked.

"I can do it." She looked at Tommy. "Can't I?"

"Nothing to it," he said.

"Can I go too?" Butterfly asked. Tommy looked at Anita.

"Sure you can," she said. "Tommy will saddle up Princess," she added and started for the house. Butterfly followed quickly.

I saw by the expression on Tommy's face that something significant had been said.

"Which horse is Princess?" I asked, looking toward the corral.

"The pony," he said. "She was our little girl's horse, Annie's horse, and no one has ridden it since . . . since Annie died.

"Before this," he added with a look of wonder, "Anita wouldn't even consider it."

16
✂

Home at Last

"**W**e're going to have a picnic," Butterfly announced excitedly when we entered the house.

"It's not exactly a picnic," Anita said from the kitchen doorway. "We'll just have lunch in the back. We have picnic tables there."

"Can we help?" Raven asked.

"Everything we need is here on the counter in the kitchen," Anita explained. "Butterfly will show you."

Proud she was given a leadership role, Butterfly led us to the plates and silverware, the place mats, glasses, fresh lemonade, loaves of home-made bread and condiments. We each took something and Butterfly showed us the table.

The back of the house was a wonderful setting for eating outdoors. From here we could see the mountains and we noticed the very tops had snow on them. The brook ran close by, the water gurgling loud enough for us to hear it wind around the rocks. Anita came out with Tommy right behind her. She was carrying a large clay bowl and set it down on the table. We all sat. Tommy looked very pleased.

"Thanks to you girls, I've got my favorite soup for lunch," he declared.

"I make it often enough, Tommy Edwards," Anita said and began to ladle it out to each of our bowls.

"It smells wonderful. What is it?" Raven asked.

"Tortilla soup with chicken, avocado and lime," Anita said. She served herself and sat.

"As good as ever," Tommy said after his first spoonful.

"It's very good," I said. It was.

"I helped make it," Butterfly beamed. "Didn't I, Anita?"

She lifted her eyes to her and smiled.

"Janet cut the tortillas and fried them herself," she said.

"A tortilla is Indian food, isn't it?" Raven asked.

"Southwestern, Mexican, we all share in its origins," Tommy said.

"Are you both full-blood Navajo?" Crystal asked.

Anita shifted her eyes to Tommy, who smiled.

"There's a debate about that," he said.

"I was reading about the Navajo in that book you have," Crystal continued. "The tribe is divided into more than fifty clans. I thought it was interesting that descent is traced through the female line."

"Yes, we are the first true women's liberators," Tommy joked.

"You are also the second largest Indian tribe in the U.S.," Crystal said.

"Crystal's an A student," Raven cut in. "Give her a day and she'll tell you more about yourself than even you know."

"I just don't like wasting time," Crystal said defensively, "so I read."

"I'm flattered that you wanted to know more about us," Tommy said. "You probably will soon know more than I do."

"That's for sure," Anita said.

Tommy raised his eyes and then smiled. Anita seemed to realize that she had said something funny and immediately looked down. She was like a candle trying to flicker again. Every time there was a small spark of hope, she smothered it herself with guilt.

"This area may not be rich in gas or oil, but to me it's rich in other ways," Tommy said.

"I've always been interested in Native Americans," Crystal said. "Do you believe the wind is spiritual?"

"I believe there is something very spiritual about all of nature," Tommy said. "I believe the farther you go from nature, the farther you are from what is spiritual. That's why we live out here."

"I love it here!" Butterfly said. Actually, she just burst out with it as if it were something ready to explode in her heart. All of us were silent a moment. Then we heard the phone ringing.

"I'll get that," Tommy said and hurried into the house.

"Do you have any Indian costumes?" Raven asked Anita.

"Costumes? Yes, I suppose you would call it that. I have something you might want to see," she added. "After we eat, I'll show you. My mother made it for me a long time ago, and I think, it might just fit you.''

"Really?'' Raven's eyes filled with excitement. Anita actually smiled. It was as if her face was slowly unfreezing.

"That,'' Tommy said returning, "was the Child Protection Services.''

"Are they on their way?'' I asked sadly.

"No. They can't make it out here today. They asked me to bring you to the sheriff to have you shipped to Albuquerque.''

"Shipped? What are they, produce?'' Anita said before we could react.

"I told them it was all right for the girls to stay overnight,'' he said. He waited. "Is it?''

"Of course,'' Anita said. "You didn't have to ask,'' she added, and with tears in her eyes she got up to start bringing things back to the house.

Butterfly jumped up immediately and began picking up our bowls and dishes. When she had her arms full, she followed Anita. Tommy sat quietly.

"Anita,'' he began slowly, "has not been well since Annie's death. She has moments when she simply cannot stop crying and then there are times when she is so withdrawn, I feel she's not really there. Don't be upset with her.''

"Oh no,'' I said.

"Never,'' Raven added.

"We understand what it means to lose someone you love,'' Crystal added.

Tommy smiled.

"I know you do, girls. Well, let's go to the corral and saddle up some horses. I might as well show you some of this reservation before you have to leave,'' he said.

"Can't we just ride around in your Jeep?'' Crystal pleaded.

"It's not the same. You want to feel what it's like, experience authenticity. You're the one who's learning all about us,'' Tommy kidded.

Crystal's face fell.

"Stop worrying,'' Tommy said. "You'll do fine. I'll give you Horse With No Name.''

"No name? Why doesn't he have a name?'' Crystal asked.

"He never stands still long enough for us to get him to understand one,'' Tommy said.

"What?'' She cried.

Everyone laughed. Then we got up and helped carry the rest of the dishes back to the house. Afterward, Anita came out to watch Tommy saddle the horses and the pony for Butterfly. He began with a little lecture about riding.

"Your horses will all follow mine," he assured us. "They are trained to do that, so don't worry. The key is never panic, never transmit your fear to the animal. He will sense it and he will become nervous. You're in control."

He helped Butterfly mount the pony. She looked like she had been put on a throne. Never had we seen her look more radiant and happy. When I looked back at Anita, I saw her standing there, her arms folded, staring with a small smile on her lips.

Tommy shouted something to her in language we didn't understand and she shook her head.

"You just be careful with them, Tommy Edwards, policeman," she warned. He laughed.

"Okay, girls. Do what I told you to do," he said. We nudged our horses with the heels of our shoes and they started after Tommy. Everyone bounced a bit. Crystal was holding on for dear life.

"Tommy said not to hold the saddle," Raven reminded her.

"I know what he said," Crystal quipped. She held her breath, closed her eyes and continued to look terrified as we trailed along toward the mountains, the four of us, never expecting in our wildest imaginations to be on horses with a Navajo Native American showing us his world of natural wonders.

Despite her fears, Crystal enjoyed the ride as much as any of us. She and Tommy talked about rocks and animals, the desert and the Navajo people. Raven was a natural and Butterfly looked like she could ride forever on her pony. We really didn't go that far, but it seemed that way to us. At one point we stopped to rest and Tommy asked us more questions about our life back at Lakewood. Crystal explained why we felt trapped. That was when Tommy revealed he had been adopted, too.

"I was still with family," he said. "My uncle and aunt."

"What happened to your father and mother?" Raven asked.

"My mother had me out of wedlock. My father never acknowledged me and my mother's parents were very upset. You might have caught Anita smiling a little when you asked if I was a full-blooded Navajo. Some felt I wasn't. I think the most important thing is what's in your heart. That will tell people who you really are. All the rest is superficial. You know what that means."

"If we didn't, Crystal would jump to tell us," Raven inserted. Tommy laughed.

"You have a different sort of saddle sore, girls. It comes from traveling with each other," he added, laughing. "But," he added after a moment of looking at us, "I bet you would fight like a trapped mountain lion if someone tried to separate you all from each other now."

"Yes," I said. "We would."

He nodded, and a look of sadness crossed his face.

"The sun's descent tells me it's about three-thirty. We had better head back. I have some chores to do and a short patrol before dinner," he added.

We mounted and started back, watching the sun reach the top of the mountains. The shadows grew longer in some places, filling the crevices and valleys with a soft darkness. Above us a hawk cut a wide circle in the sky. Tommy said it could see a desert rat even from that height.

What a strange and wonderful world this place was, I thought. For a while it had made us forget our dreams. Raven hadn't talked about being a singing star. Crystal didn't mention school, and I had stopped fantasizing about finding my real mother.

Anita was waiting for us when we returned. We expected to get off the horses and that would be that, but Tommy explained that we had to walk them a little and he wanted us to help put away the livery.

"You must take good care of the things you love out here or you won't have them long," he told us.

"Sometimes, that doesn't help," Anita commented. Their eyes met for a moment and he looked away. Butterfly was excused to return to the house with her so she could wash up and help Anita prepare our supper. "I'll get the beds ready, too," Anita said.

"Wasn't there anything that could be done about Annie?" I asked Tommy.

"We tried, took her to the biggest hospital and they operated, but her heart was too small. Anita has been afraid of having another child. She thinks it will be born with the same or some similar defect. She's more superstitious than I am," he added sadly.

"There are ways to test the fetus as it develops," Crystal told him, "to see if there are any defects."

He smiled at her.

"There is a different drumbeat in Anita's heart now. Maybe someday soon it will change."

We worked on our horses and then we all went into the house to wash up. Anita had fixed the two guest bedrooms for us. On one of the beds was a beautiful deerskin dress decorated with turquoise beads. She told Raven to try it on and she did. I had to admit that she looked fantastic. Everyone thought so.

"Maybe you have Navajo blood, too," Tommy laughed.

Raven asked if she could wear it to dinner and Anita told her she could. Before dinner Butterfly asked Anita about the drums she and Tommy had in the living room–den area. To Tommy's surprise and our delight, Anita played and sang a Navajo corn-grinding song. Her voice was deep and rich and I could feel her heritage, proud and alive, still thumping in her injured heart. Tommy showed Butterfly some ceremonial dance steps and in seconds, she was doing it as well, if not better than he. Anita actually laughed, the sound of it cracking the layers of icy sadness that had fallen over the walls of this home.

For our dinner Anita, with Butterfly at her side in the kitchen, had prepared chicken fajitas with rice and beans. It was a Mexican feast and something none of us had experienced before.

"My stomach is grateful you girls got lost on the reservation," Tommy declared.

"Tommy Edwards, if you let these girls believe I don't cook for you otherwise, I'll scalp you," Anita snapped. He laughed and held up his hands.

"I'm just fooling, girls. She would do it."

The difference between the atmosphere at breakfast and now at dinner was remarkable. We were all more relaxed. It had been a wonderful day, a surprise of joy. The phone rang again before we had completed our clean-up and Tommy returned to tell us the FBI had located Gordon Tooey.

"He made it back to New York," he said, his eyes shifting to Anita.

"What's the rest?" she demanded.

"He got someone awfully mad at him. You don't have to worry about him coming after you anymore, girls," he added.

Despite our fear and dislike of Gordon, the news was shocking. We all looked at each other and felt our hearts skip beats.

"Louise will probably lose the foster home," Crystal remarked.

"Most likely," Tommy said. "They'll revoke her license. There is a big need for foster homes all over this country and it's growing," he added.

"Where will they send us now?" Raven wondered.

The light, happy mood we had created dissipated like smoke and was soon replaced with a heavy air, erasing smiles, weighing down our moves, turning us into something mechanical. Raven decided to take off the Indian dress. Afterward, she joined Crystal and me outside on the porch. Butterfly was still helping Anita put things away.

"Wherever we go," Crystal said, "it won't be long for us. As soon as we turn eighteen, we'll be on our own. I'll go full-time to college," she added. "Maybe you'll go back to live with Todd, Brooke."

"I don't know. I haven't spoken to him. He probably forgot me already," I said.

"Not if he really felt something for you," Raven told me. "I'm still going to try to be someone in show business. I don't care what I have to do. I'll work as a waitress, clean houses, anything, until I get my big break. And if that never happens, I'll come live with you and Todd."

"Stop rushing my life, you two. I have some things to do first, also," I said. "I still intend to go to California."

"How will you find her?" Crystal asked. I spun around.

"How do you know what I want to do?"

"You've let enough hints slip, Brooke. Actually, it's easier today to find someone than it used to be. Maybe you will," she said.

She reached out and I took her hand. I reached for Raven and the three of us sat there in the darkness with the stars twinkling in a clear desert sky above us. Somewhere in the distance there was a strange howl. Crystal said that was a coyote.

"She's right," Tommy said, coming out of the shadows. We didn't know how long he had been there. "How do you know the sound, Crystal?"

"There's this computer software program I used when I was doing a project for science class," she explained.

"School sure is different from when I went," he said.

"What time are we leaving tomorrow?" I asked him.

"Right after breakfast, I'm to take you girls to the sheriff's office in Gallup and the child welfare people from Albuquerque will take it from there," he said. "You're all great girls. I know you'll be fine," he said.

We were all silent.

"Well," he said, "I'm feeling tired. Around here, we're up with the sun. See you in the morning."

"Good night, Tommy," I said.

We sat quietly for a while and then decided we were pretty tired too. We partnered up the way we usually did. The beds were very comfortable, the rooms all paneled yellow oak with southwestern style furnishings. The night air was cool and it made for pleasant sleeping, except none of us was able to put off our anxiety easily. Before Raven and I even tried to sleep, Crystal came in to tell us Butterfly was acting strange.

"She won't talk. She's curled up in her bed," Crystal said.

"We're all just tired," Raven told her. "You were right. It's exhausting to run away and too much for a fragile girl like Butterfly, especially if it's too much for us."

"Anita gave her a real Indian necklace. She's wearing it to sleep," Crystal said.

"That's nice," I said. "Anita's a lot nicer than I first thought she would be."

"Everyone we meet seems wounded in some way or another," Crystal commented. It was one of those deeply philosophical statements she was capable of planting in my mind and then leaving to let it grow on its own.

She returned to her room. Raven and I were silent, not even saying good night to each other. She turned over and fell asleep before I did. I listened to the wind for a while, saw a small cloud touch the quarter moon and then I closed my eyes and finally drifted off, not waking until I felt my body being shaken vigorously. My eyes popped open. Crystal was standing there in a panic.

"She's catatonic, worse than I have ever seen her, Brooke! Hurry."

I jumped out of bed and we woke Raven. That was like waking the dead, but when she heard what was wrong, she moved faster and we gathered around Butterfly, who was, as Crystal had described, twisted tightly, her legs pulled up against her stomach, her arms turned in, the hands locked like claws, her eyes slammed shut and her lips glued together with just a line of drool trickling out of the right corner. She didn't even look like she was breathing. An electric surge of panic shot through my heart.

"Oh Crystal, I've never seen her this bad. Her face is so pale and her lips are turning blue."

Crystal nodded.

"It's very bad," she agreed.

We joined hands and brought our heads down to Butterfly's. Crystal started the chant.

"We're sisters. We'll always be sisters. Nothing can hurt us as long as we're together."

Raven and I joined. Our voices grew more and more desperate as we finished a chorus and saw no change.

"Crystal!"

"Keep trying," she cried.

We chanted louder, the desperation building in our voices.

"What's going on in here?" Anita asked from the doorway.

We stopped. Butterfly was still catatonic. Anita came charging in and looked down at her.

"What's happening?" she demanded.

"She gets this way sometimes," Crystal said. "It's an emotional thing. We've always been able to help her by joining and reciting our chant. It usually brings her out of it, but it's not working."

"Oh, my God!" Anita cried. "She's stopping her own heart, her own breathing. Tommy! TOMMY!"

He came rushing into the room. The moment he saw Butterfly and heard the explanation, he scooped his hands under her and lifted her into his arms.

"We'll take her to the hospital," he said.

"Hurry, Tommy," Anita ordered.

We all piled into his Jeep. Anita held Butterfly in her lap and the three of us squeezed in behind them. Tommy pulled away, bouncing over the dirt road. Still, Butterfly's eyes did not open. Anita rocked her and kissed her forehead. She stroked her hair and held her tightly. All of us looked at each other, each thinking the same thing. If Butterfly dies, it will be because we had decided to run away. It was our fault. Heads bowed, we prayed and held hands. The Jeep rocked as Tommy shifted down and made turns.

And then, miraculously to us, Butterfly moaned. Anita increased her consoling and kissing. She rocked her more and called to her and finally, Butterfly's eyelids fluttered. Color returned to her face.

"She's better, Tommy," Anita declared, laughing through her tears. "She's better."

"Good, great, but we still better take her to the hospital," he said.

By the time he pulled in, however, Butterfly was fully alert. She actually walked into the emergency room, holding Anita's hand. The three of us waited with Tommy in the lobby while Anita went into the examination room with Butterfly.

"That was the first time we failed to bring her out of it ourselves," Crystal reminded us. "It was Anita who did it."

Tommy's eyes widened and he nodded. Nearly an hour later, Anita came out to tell us Butterfly was doing fine.

"All her vital signs are good. The doctor feels it was caused by a psychological shock, which is not to say it isn't serious. She needs a great deal of care and nurturing," she said, telling Tommy more than us. He nodded. "She won't get it where she's going, Tommy."

He simply nodded.

Afterward, Tommy decided to take us to a small café nearby for breakfast. No one was really very hungry, however. We left more on our plates than we put in our stomachs. The ride back to the ranch was slower, quieter. When we got there, we organized ourselves, gathered what little we had, and waited for Tommy to take us to the sheriff's office.

"Anita gave me this dress," Raven said, showing us the beautiful deerskin garment. "She said it belongs to me because I wear it well. Tommy and Anita have been so nice to us. I'm glad you ran out of gas when you did, Brooke."

"Me too."

It was finally time to go. Anita decided to go along and sat with Butterfly in front again. The social worker from the child welfare agency was waiting for us at the sheriff's office. She was a pleasant lady of about forty with curly, dark brown hair. While we waited, she went into an office with Tommy and Anita and caught up on details. They were in there a long time, and I could see through the windows that the woman, Mrs. Wilson, was on the phone. She talked with Tommy and Anita some more and then Tommy came out by himself.

"It will be a little while longer," he said.

"Where are they taking us?" I asked quickly.

"That's not exactly been determined yet, but it looks like you'll return to New York. Don't worry—you won't be going back to the Lakewood House." He paused. "Mrs. Wilson would like to speak with Janet."

Butterfly, who had her head bowed most of the time, looked up with surprise.

"Is that okay?" Tommy asked. Butterfly looked at Crystal and Crystal nodded. Then she nodded. Tommy reached for her hand and took her into the office. He returned and asked us if we would all like an ice cream soda. "We have an old-fashioned soda fountain here," he said. "Come on."

We went out with him and down to a drugstore that had a fountain with booths in the rear.

"What's going on?" I whispered to Crystal. She shrugged.

"What's new about being caught up in bureaucratic delays, Brooke?" she said.

Tommy got us sodas and we sat in a red booth with chrome buttons.

"Every time I come here, I think I traveled back in a time machine," he said.

"It's nice," Raven admitted, gazing around and sipping her soda.

"You girls have been through a lot together. Years, huh?"

"Yes. There were times we thought, we hoped, we would be separated to go to nice homes, but as time went by, we realized it was getting less and less likely," Crystal said. She then told Tommy about the most recent chance Butterfly had had to be adopted and how Louise had sabotaged it.

He shook his head.

"It's very sad when people are cruel to children. I have something to ask you girls," he continued. "I know from the short time I've been with you that Butterfly would never do anything without your approval. We asked Mrs. Wilson if we could take her in with us, be her foster parents and eventually adopt her."

"You did?" Raven asked.

"What did she say?" Crystal followed.

"She's finding out what has to be done, but there is a good chance it could happen. How do you all feel about it?"

No one spoke for a moment.

"We would feel very happy for her," Crystal finally said. "We're not going to be together much longer anyway, Tommy. We're all reaching eighteen soon and then we'll be cut loose from the system. Butterfly deserves to find a loving home before that happens."

"That's very generous of you, girls. I wish we could take you all, but that would be much more difficult to make happen and I have a feeling you would all rather be where there is more action: a better chance for education for you Crystal, some place where there is more opportunity for you, Raven, and I've heard Brooke talk a lot about California and some guy she wants to call soon. Maybe you should check in with him now," he added, reaching into his pocket to produce a handful of change. "Let him know you're all right, huh?"

I looked at the money as if it were gold and then I looked toward the pay phone.

"Go for it," Raven said.

It didn't take a second offer. I was up in a split second. Todd answered the phone on the first ring.

"I just happened to be sitting in my office," he said. "Where are you?"

I told him as much as I could squeeze into two minutes and then promised him I would call him as soon as I knew where I was going.

"Wherever it is, Brooke, I'll be there," he swore. "I really miss you."

"Me too," I said.

Everyone had a big, silly grin on their face when I returned to the table.

"Well?" Raven asked.

"Betty Lou is just waiting for directions," I replied and Raven laughed. Crystal smiled and hugged me. "Thank you, Tommy," I said.

"Thank you, girls. You helped give me back my 'Nita. Make no mistake about it, we need Butterfly more than she needs us," he said with tears in his eyes.

We all had tears in our eyes.

Butterfly was waiting for us when we returned. Tommy went into the office with Anita and Mrs. Wilson and continued their discussions. Papers were being sent through fax machines. The process was under way.

"Anita wants me to stay with her," Butterfly told us.

"We know, Butterfly," Crystal said. "That's wonderful if you want it, too. Do you?"

"Yes," she said, "but I don't want to have to leave all of you."

"It's not like you won't see us again," Raven said comfortingly.

"As soon as we can, we'll come visit. Tommy's already invited us," Crystal added.

"Really?"

"Yes, really," I said.

She smiled.

"I'm going to take care of the pony myself," she said.

All of us laughed and hugged her.

Finally, Tommy, Anita and Mrs. Wilson emerged from the office. Arrangements had been made. Butterfly could stay while things were being formalized.

"What about us?" Crystal asked.

"I'm taking you to Albuquerque where you will be housed until we return you to New York. I'm sure you'll be in a nice facility back there,'' she said.

Crystal didn't laugh, but she gave her one of her "Don't be stupid" looks that made Raven and I smile.

We followed her out to the car. Raven decided to sit in the front and Crystal and I got into the back. First, we hugged and kissed Butterfly once more and then hugged and kissed Tommy and Anita.

"As soon as we can, we'll arrange for you to visit," Tommy promised.

"Good. Crystal just can't wait to get back on a horse," I said. He laughed.

Anita held Butterfly's hand and Butterfly clung to her fingers, the two of them looking as if they had found their reasons to be, to go on, to love and to cherish everything that was beautiful and good about the world.

We started away, none of us saying anything.

I was thinking about my real mother and what it would feel like to hold her hand. I wondered what Raven and Crystal were thinking. I wished it was something happy. We had come too far to have sad thoughts. The sky ahead of us was too blue. Butterfly's finding a home gave us all renewed hope.

Could we, should we be optimistic? Do we dare?

Without warning, Crystal suddenly reached out and took my hand. We looked at each other and smiled.

"Didn't she look so happy?" she asked.

"Yes," Raven said. She turned around, the tears streaming down her face, and she reached for us.

We held each other's hands.

"We're sisters," Crystal began.

"We'll always be sisters," Raven and I said.

"The Orphanteers!" we cried.

Our laughter rolled along with us toward our new promises.

Epilogue

Todd and I flew from our new home in Illinois to Albuquerque. Raven came in from Los Angeles, where she had just signed her first record deal and had gotten a small part in a movie. Crystal had been accepted at Harvard on an early admissions scholarship program. She worked in the library and earned a little income on the side. We arranged it so we could all meet at the airport and rent one car together. We had never stopped staying in touch. Crystal liked to write long letters. I saved every one of mine, telling Todd that someday they would be valuable. They were beautifully written, detailed letters that made me feel I was right there beside her, learning, experiencing college life. Raven jotted lines on postcards, but most of the time she called, and I did the same. We all called Butterfly, even Crystal, because the sound of her voice was so important to us, as was the sound of ours to her.

Butterfly was graduating from college. In a month she would become a social worker. She wanted to use her life experience to help other young people.

We had seen each other twice before, but it had been nearly a year and a half between the last visit and now. A little over a year after Butterfly began to live with Tommy and Anita, Anita became pregnant and gave birth to a boy they named Steven. That was quickly replaced with the nickname Popeye because he loved spinach and he had very strong little arms for an infant. He was everything Annie hadn't been able to be, healthy. The evil curse had been broken, and we knew Anita believed it was because of the good energy Butterfly had brought with her to their lives.

Todd and I were the first to arrive. We were there when Raven landed and sauntered through the gate. She was more histrionic than ever, flamboyant as could be, dressed in a buttercup-yellow sexy sundress, her beautiful hair down, her high heels clicking. Apparently, she had made a hit with the flight engineer. He was at her side, practically begging her to change her ticket so she could be on his flight when she returned to Los Angeles.

"Brooke!" she cried when she saw me. She rushed into my arms and we hugged and swung about like teenagers. "Hi, Todd." She gave him a rather intimate kiss that surprised him as well as me. "You guys look terrific," she said, holding my arms out. "I thought you might be fat and pregnant by now."

"No, Raven. We're not ready for that yet. I told you last time we spoke. We're expanding the garage, taking on wheel alignments."

"Oh, right. Wheel alignments. I had my teeth aligned," she joked. She scooped her arms through ours and turned us around. "It's so important to keep yourself looking the best you can. No matter what they say, the truth is they're always looking for the prettiest faces and best shapes. Talent is second, not that I don't work on my talent."

"Congratulations on the record contract," I said.

"I'm at it night and day. I had a gig at a small nightclub in Hollywood. That's how I got this movie role," she told us. "How long before Crystal arrives? I hate waiting. That's all I ever do anymore."

Todd checked his watch.

"Thirty minutes," he said, and we went for coffee.

"Can you believe our little Butterfly is graduating from college?" Raven asked when we sat at a table.

"Why not?" I said.

"Oh Brooke, you were always too . . . too realistic," she said with a laugh. She paused and looked at us for a moment. "I'm glad you're happy, Brooke. I hope I find someone who makes me as happy."

"You will, if you really want to, Raven," I said. She smiled and then laughed.

"Yes, if I really want to. I can't think of that right now. I'm in entertainment."

She rattles on with her Hollywood stories, speaking so quickly and so earnestly, I felt she was trying desperately to convince me she was happy with the decisions she had made. Finally, it was time to greet Crystal at her arrival gate. She was one of the first ten to get off, carrying her briefcase packed with her assignments. She really looked no different, still as unconcerned about her hair, wearing no makeup, not even lipstick, her glasses thick as goggles.

We all hugged and kissed and Todd went off to arrange for our car. A short while later, we were on our way to the ranch, as we had come to know it.

"I may specialize in psychiatry," Crystal told us.

"Why am I not surprised," Raven quipped. "You were always analyzing everyone. You might as well make money doing it."

Todd laughed, and once Raven saw she had an attentive audience, she continued with her jokes. Crystal and I looked at each other and smiled. Despite our ages and the passage of time, we were still acting like the Orphanteers, holding hands whenever we could.

Butterfly came bursting out the front door when we drove up. She was only another three inches taller, but her face had matured along with her now sweet little body. We held each other as if we were about to join and drive away the evil once again. Tommy and Anita came out, Anita holding the new baby, and we all went inside, Todd and Tommy bringing in our bags.

I thought we would never run out of things to say, things to tell each other. We were driven by a need to let each of us know every important or significant event that had occurred in our lives, no matter how small it might seem to someone else. Our chatter went right through lunch until it was time for Butterfly to prepare for graduation. We all dressed, Raven surprising everyone by stepping out wearing the Indian dress Anita's mother had made.

"You're really going to wear it?" I asked. Raven looked to Anita.

"I'd be very proud to wear it if Anita doesn't mind," she said.

"Of course not. You look even more beautiful in it, Raven," she said, which was all Raven had to hear, of course. The dress would have to be pried or burned off her after that. We piled into our car and followed Tommy, Anita, Butterfly and little Steven to the school, where an outdoor graduation ceremony had been prepared. I told Crystal I had butterflies in my stomach for Butterfly and she admitted to the same.

"You? Nervous?" Raven said. "I'll tell you what nervous is—preparing for an audition."

"This is the same as an audition," Crystal said with her eyes fixed and intent on Raven.

"Yes, it sure is," Raven agreed. She calmed down when the music began, the "Pomp and Circumstance" that brought the graduates down the aisle to the stage. Our little Butterfly's golden curls were dazzling under her cap. I looked at Anita and Tommy and saw them holding hands, their faces full of pride.

When Butterfly's name was called, we all cheered. Little Steven's eyes were full of amusement. Anita had him wave at the stage. Butterfly looked out to us, her smile full of sunshine and life.

She hadn't had a seizure since she'd moved in with Tommy and Anita. She was truly like a flower transplanted into rich soil—healthy and strong, climbing toward her potential.

I guess we all were now, even Raven, who I felt sure would find her way to some happiness. Everyone in the audience cheered for their own when the class was finally introduced as graduates. I looked around at the happy fathers and mothers, sisters and brothers, relatives and friends.

A long time ago, for various reasons, our fathers and mothers had surrendered us to an impersonal system and condemned us to an endless search for family. We tried. We hoped and prayed, but it didn't happen for a very long time to Butterfly and it never really happened to Raven, Crystal and me. What we discovered was that during the search itself we had found family; we had found each other.

For one precious moment on the grounds of a college in the Southwest, miles and miles from where we had all begun, we joined once more. We pressed our bodies against each other and clung to each other and drove away the darkness.

Once, when Crystal and I were alone at night, she looked out the window at the Lakewood House and said, "I used to dream about the mother I have never known. She had no face, of course, but in the dream I'm always holding her hand very tightly, and she's always trying to pull away. I fight as hard as I can to hold on, but finally I have to let go. I feel as if I am falling and then I wake up." She turned to me and smiled.

"I always felt that way, even with my foster parents, and then I was brought here and the four of us were drawn together and suddenly . . . suddenly I stopped falling, Brooke."

So did I, I thought.

I knew she was right, even then.

Our falling had come to an end.